I0575884

CALLS TO ADVENTURE

TALES OF SILVERTIDE: VOLUME I

MATTHEW O. THOMPSON

Copyright © 2024 by Matthew O. Thompson

All rights reserved.

No part of this publication may be reproduced, distributed, or transmitted in any form or by any means, including photocopying, recording, or other electronic or mechanical methods, without the prior written permission of the publisher, except as permitted by U.S. copyright law. For permission requests, contact the author.

The story, all names, characters, and incidents portrayed in this production are fictitious. No identification with actual persons (living or deceased), places, buildings, and products is intended or should be inferred.

Edited by Faith Okoro (@faithloveth on Fiverr)

Book Cover by Matthew O. Thompson

Illustrations by MOT and Inksxx

Second edition 2025

Contents

This work is specifically not dedicated to Mr. Ibigore Zbinski, as this fictional guy is probably the only person in the world that hasn't helped in its development. Specific credit goes to Hutch, as the core map, ideas, and several years of enjoyable gaming were created and inspired directly by him. In addition, the Sigma Tau Gamma fraternity from the University of Wisconsin at Superior need thanking – they introduced me to Dungeons and Dragons! Lastly, the groups with which I've played. This is YOUR work as much as mine. Payne, Groqx, Cade, Melathiel, Tuğrul (the 'G' is silent), Erend, Aerun, Ja'assa, Heimei, and many more are just some of the characters that have helped bring this world to life. Olhas Rogue has given much technical and immoral support (and may he forever rest in peace). Cyruin helped save my Starwalkers and tech devices. Wayne Ligon and Irma N. Knight are due special thanks, as their experience as published authors and their pointed questions helped make this project complete – and make sense. Johnny the Poopyhead gets some editing credit, though he didn't do much. Also, the River Region Writers Unite and the The Writers' Troupe groups on Facebook helped more than you will ever know.
Thank you all.

ALFAN ON THE WALL

His feet ached, and he was sure they were bleeding again, but Alfan wouldn't let them see him limp—or cry. The day's events had cut him to the core by a measure more than the events of the last three months. What unknown gods had he offended? What curses had been laid upon him? He stubbornly continued to march as he silently asked, *"WHY?"*

His future had been set early for Alfan Ellendar Rudda VII. Born of a moderately wealthy family in Stormhaven, he was fortunate enough to have been in the right place at the right time to pull a young girl from the path of a runaway horse and cart, a young girl who happened to be the daughter of His Grace, the Duke of Lyren.

For all his supposed bravery, the horse may have turned away or missed her at the last moment. But the Duke sponsored his admission to the prestigious Silverleaf Military Academy either way. Though he had no proof, Alfan also suspected that His Grace had his hand in his selection as Cadet Commander of his class.

What he was sure the Duke didn't meddle in was his skill at arms and his ability to lead his fellow cadets. The orders he gave were clear, his voice was strong, and his classmates fell into line whenever he barked an order. Alfan's skill at arms was above average—never poor enough to gain the baleful eyes of the Training cadre but rarely good enough to earn him recognition by the Commandant of the Academy.

While many of his fellow cadets left the Academy at graduation to pursue apprenticeships and to officially enter the Game of Crowns, Alfan decided to accept a commission in the military and was shocked to receive orders to the Golden Griffons, the renowned order led by his Ducal benefactor. Though Alfan was sure that this was no chance posting, he was proud of the assignment.

His first move was to join the Pathfinders Society, as it was a perfect opportunity to rub elbows and trade stories with the rich and powerful and enter the Game of Crowns himself. What he didn't count on was that girl, that girl with the piercing eyes, his loving Tina.

After drills and any daily training that his commanding officers wanted were completed, he stole time to be with her. Looking back, it seemed like a dream. He saved his salary for several months, secretly skimming off the bribes and gifts he gave his superiors to remain in their good favor, and was looking about to purchase a fine ring so he could propose marriage to her. But the night before the commissioned ring was to be ordered, guards burst through his door and arrested him.

Loudly proclaiming his innocence of any and all charges he could imagine, Alfan was hauled before his commander, who placed him in irons.

The interrogation was short and direct. "Do you know The Lady Clementina Walcott?"

"What? No!" Alfan was getting angrier with each passing second.

"Are you sure, Lieutenant Junior Rudda? You are not familiar with The Lady Clementina Walcott, daughter of His Grace the Duke of Lyren?"

The color drained out of Alfan's face at the mention of his benefactor's name. "No. No, Si…" and his voice faded, strangled within his own throat. *Clementina.* Tina. TINA! Oh, by the gods, no!

"A third time, Lieutenant Junior Rudda. Are you familiar with The Lady Clementina Walcott, only daughter of His Grace, the Duke of Lyren and Knight Commander of THIS VERY UNIT?!"

Alfan shut his eyes to try to regain his equilibrium. Quietly, he responded, "I know a proper young lady by the name of 'Tina,' of whose family pedigree I am unaware." He slowly opened his eyes to see if he could judge the reaction of his commanding officer and was stunned to see His Grace standing quietly in the corner of the room near the door from which he must have silently passed. The Duke's face was nearly purple with rage. Alfan could do nothing but swallow as he forced his eyes straight ahead once again.

"So, you admit the dalliance then." The Captain Major sounded almost resigned. With a sigh, he pulled a piece of parchment from beneath the stack on his desk and began to read. "It is the adjudication of this command that the commission of Lieutenant Junior Alfan Ellendar Rudda III be immediately revoked, and the convicted be sentenced to servitude for life in the mines of..."

The Duke cut him off. "I believe I can find a more suitable sentence for this... this... this... poseur... who would worm his way into social circles above which he should ever *dream* to aspire." Then, he handed the Captain Major a scroll with a thick wax seal.

Even through the blur of tears he was fighting to stifle, Alfan saw the wax was purple—from the desk of the Emperor himself. He felt his face flush, and his heart began trying to beat its way out of his chest.

Quickly breaking the seal and reading the scroll, the Captain Major quickly glanced at the Duke and swallowed. The look of sadistic gloating on the Duke's face made Alfan's heart drop to even lower depths.

"For service and dedication of the highest caliber," the Captain Major's voice was strong but forced, "The Emperor sees fit to bestow assignment to the 144th Battalion of the Golden Throne's own garrison." The commander's voice was both apologetic and final as he concluded. "Congratulations. You report tomorrow morning."

The one lasting memory of that evening forever burned in Alfan's mind was the sadistic glee in the Duke's eyes as he was dragged from the office. He had never known that Tina was the daughter of the Duke, and it was about a month into the journey North to Laupennin Perak that Alfan realized that this must have been that same girl he had supposedly "saved" so long ago. He tried his best to talk himself into that rescue and the sponsorship of the Duke as being mistakes and wrong, but he couldn't do it.

As he fell asleep in his quarters later that night, the gravity of his "sentence" dawned on him. The Golden Griffons and all of the other armies here in Stormhaven were local units; they were funded and commanded by the Dukes and other noble families as far as their funds would allow, and they never strayed from the city proper. They were used to quell uprisings or engage in squabbles between the nobles and their factions, but they never left the great metropolis of Stormhaven. Whereas there were accolades to be earned, riches to be gained, and opportunities to catch the eye of many benefactors that were well placed in the political Game of Crowns that may help elevate you into the nobility or at least help cement your place in the wealthy gentry.

The poorly named Imperial armies were the ones that ventured beyond the city walls. As far as anyone really knew, few returned, and none were seen participating in the Game of Crowns; they seemed to completely withdraw from society in general. The few he had heard rumors of had reputations as being lethal in combat but dirty and crude, without even having the decency of proper challenges to duel. Even their units lacked the normal custom of fanciful names, choosing instead numbers as if they were no more than entries in a merchant's ledger. The Imperial armies also had the reputation of losing nearly every new officer assigned to their ranks.

Alfan's first day with the 144th was eye-opening. The Captain Major, as well as three other Lieutenants Junior, were also newly assigned.

Looking them over quickly and accepting their introductory gifts to show their eagerness to impress and his willingness to consider their graciousness, their new Commander gave them each their assignments. Alfan was to lead Whip Company. Even the company names were without fanfare. Rather than robust and honorable names like Elite Eagle and Bounding Badger Companies, there were Anvil, Wave, Hammer, and Whip Companies. These cads had no couth and didn't even seem interested in finding any!

As the grizzled Sergeant Major grudgingly gave them a tour of the barracks, training yard, armory, and other extraneous amenities, the horrors of his new posting came crashing in. Every face needed a shave; boots hadn't been polished in months, and there was nary a shred of lace or velvet on any of the soldiers.

The group was reluctantly shepherded to the practice yard where a group of what must pass for soldiers lounged about.

The Sergeant Major said, "This is Wave Company."

The Captain Major smiled, "Troops!" he loudly announced as he gestured at another of the new junior officers. "This is Lieutenant Junior Carey, your new Company Leader."

There were a few grunts as a few more heads turned toward the voice. Only two soldiers slowly rose to their feet. Alfan noted that they seemed cleaner and more appropriately dressed than the others. He then noted a grinding noise from the Captain Major as Alfan noted his jaw clenching spasmodically.

"A-ten-SHUN!! GET ON YOUR FEET, YOU SCUM!" The Captain Major's face was contorted with rage as he screamed. On and on he went, using every curse word Alfan had ever heard and apparently making up several more as he bellowed at the men, who just continued to sit there, though a few more looked in their general direction.

"AT EASE!" The Sergeant Major's voice cut through the Commander's screaming like a hot knife through butter. The gaggle of troops snapped to positions of attention faster than Alfan thought possible. The Captain Major just stood there, mouth agape, as the Sergeant Major quietly continued. "We ain't used to your command style yet, Sir. Give the troops a day or two, eh?"

The dressing down the Captain Major gave them was epic, and it took a while for Alfan to notice that as the commander passed by each of the soldiers, the troops gave a sidewise glance at the Sergeant Major, who seemed to nod at each of them, almost conspiratorially.

Finally, the commander turned on the Sergeant Major and demanded, "Are all of the soldiers of this unit going to be this disrespectful, Sergeant Major?"

"Like I said, Sir, we just ain't used to the particulars of your command style yet. If you—"

The Captain Major cut him off, "If that's the case, I want a battalion assembly immediately. You have ten minutes to rally the battalion and NINE OF THEM ARE GONE! DO YOU UNDERSTAND?" He fairly spit on the senior non-comm as he finished.

"As you command, Sir." Responding laconically, the Sergeant Major seemed to have nerves of steel.

It took nearly the full ten minutes for the troops to form into ranks, and this just increased the rage of the Captain Major. He vented at the soldiers for nearly an hour until his voice sounded like it was going to give out, and somehow, only a few soldiers in the battalion seemed to be phased by his frenzy. Again, Alfan noticed that these seemed to be more well-kept troops than their comrades.

Finally, the Captain called out to identify four of the five assembled companies and introduced their new Company Leaders; Alfan assumed the empty position next to Whip Company, where their company flag should be posted. *Where was it?*

The Captain Major finished his tirade by calling out the Sergeant Major and dressing him down before the entire battalion. When thoroughly satisfied with his venting, the Captain Major announced that the Sergeant Major was being demoted to the rank of Private and he would personally appoint a new Sergeant Major. With no reaction, the former senior NCO saluted, spun on his heel, looked for an open spot in the formation, and assumed his new role. Alfan didn't know if he should be offended by or in awe of the man's self-control.

The next month met every definition of hell for Lieutenant Junior Rudda and his fellow new company leaders, and their stories were identical. The men and women of the 144th were rude, crude, undisciplined, uncaring, and were as willing as paving stones or cats to follow orders. The few areas where they excelled were keeping their kits in good repair, their weapons clean, and when practicing actual maneuvers. However, their reluctance to follow any other orders was maddening, and Alfan chafed at their recalcitrance.

Alfan ordered a full uniform inspection with a full kit and a complete weapon display, and when the allotted time came, seven of his entire company of 103 soldiers assembled in the quad. Again, he noted that these were those that were more well-kept, and after some digging, he found out they were the newest troops in the company. They were also the only ones who provided Alfan with the customary introductory gifts for new leaders and commanders, the more senior personnel ignoring that custom completely.

He was barely able to maintain his cool when he stormed into the company barracks to find the bulk of his unit lounging about, dicing and smoking, apparently unconcerned with the fact that they were both unprepared and late for his inspection. About to lose control completely, Alfan hissed for the Senior Sergeant and guided her out of earshot of the others before he asked why they weren't at the inspection.

The Sergeant seemed confused for a moment, then she responded, "Didn't think it was that important, Sir."

Alfan fought to keep his hands from shaking. "Not... not *important*, Senior Sergeant?"

"Nope. Not important at all." She seemed free of guile in her answer.

Through gritted teeth, Alfan hissed again, "Why would you think that, Senior Sergeant?"

"Well, Sir, you want me to do inventory? I will guarantee that we got 96 of us that have our full kits, and they're all in working order. 96 of us have serviceable weapons and armor, and nearly all of us are good on field commands and maneuvers." Then she conspiratorially said, "I got serious doubt about the other seven. They're *new* and all." Her emphasis on *new* told Alfan that she had little respect for her most recently arrived charges. She continued. "How important is it that we're pretty?"

Alfan was taken aback at the candor and the question. "Uh, I'm looking to see how well you will perform in drill and ceremony, you know, for parades and the like. I need to know that everything is spit and polished and will impress any visitors to Whip Company that might call."

"Sir, I been with the 144th for eight years, been to the Wall three times, we ain't never been visited by any nobles or visitors that needed impressing in that time, and I'll ask you straight up, Sir, what good will being pretty do us on the battlefield?"

"Well, Sergeant… uh… well…" Alfan glanced up at the Sergeant and recognized that 'You're caught' look in her eye. Straightening and adjusting his velveteen coat, Alfan leaned into the Senior Sergeant. "Would you arrange to have a kit inventory out in the quad tomorrow at noon? I believe you, but I wish to see it for myself." Hesitating for a second, he added, "And I want to see about those seven new troops as well."

"Well, Sir. Why didn't you ask?" Smiling, she finished, "I'll have the company assembled at noon tomorrow in the quad, SIR!" The salute was lazy and definitely not within regulation, but it was one of the first times he had been saluted. Alfan stood straight, returned the salute, and withdrew to lick his wounds.

All in all, the inventory went well. As promised, all of the veterans' kits were accounted for and serviceable, the only problem being in those seven newly assigned soldiers. Alfan also noted that the new soldiers' kits had exactly what was required, whereas the veterans' kits had extra socks and other sundry items to help in the field.

Satisfied, Alfan announced to the company that this would be the last inspection until they got orders that they were to deploy to the Wall. There were a few wan smiles, and the group was released for the day.

Three weeks later, the orders came down that they were to leave in a month for a year-long tour defending the Wall in Laupennin Perak.

Alfan had learned about the Wall and the Laupen in the Academy. They were supposedly in a constant state of war against unending waves of enemies. The more fanciful said, "Ooh, they fight orcs and giants," as if the horrid fables were true, but little more was known of the region outside of the brutal winters. Alfan made sure to pack extra socks and mittens in his kit.

The journey via troop ships up the Arazon River was monotonous, or at least it was for those not susceptible to getting sick from the constant rocking of the ship. This horrid trip, the realization of the true identity of his girlfriend, and the fact that Whip Company was even more recalcitrant than normal made the trip truly horrible.

The ships took them through Inondacare up to where the stench of the Great Ice Mire was noticeable. Then they headed west, skirting just south of Northcliff before reaching the limits of the navigable river. From there, it was marching.

For the first time since he took control of Whip Company, Alfan noticed that his troops seemed to be coming alive, with laughter and jokes being passed around, and most making eye contact and even smiling from time to time. Were he being honest, it was unnerving, and to make matters worse, they all seemed to be silently laughing at him as if they knew something that he wasn't privy to.

Two weeks later, the 144th reached the Southern Walls of Laupennin Perak, where the 79th Battalion manned the wall. As they got within the last 100 yards, the Captain Major gave the order to arrange into full battalion formation for inspection. Alfan was astonished to see the normally recalcitrant veterans march smartly to their appointed spots.

Atop the wall, the Captain Major of the 79th gave the loud command, "Prepare RANKS," an order that was unfamiliar to Alfan. As the veterans snapped to attention and loudly responded, "READY," he did his best to imitate their response.

Movement caught his eye as six soldiers moved rapidly up to the 144th's Captain Major, and as Alfan heard movement behind him, the Captain Major of the 79th ordered, "EXECUTE!" With lightning speed, he saw the six nearest the Captain Major move close and speak quietly to him. A light touch on his own back told him that he was likewise surrounded, and he heard his own Senior Sergeant quietly say, "Sir, you are relieved of duty and your rank. You now hold the rank of Private and will be in the front lines of Whip Company when we engage. Should you survive this tour of duty, your rank may be returned to you. Until then, fall in where we tell you."

With that, Alfan watched as the Captain Major was stripped of his epaulets as his own were removed, and he reeled with shock when he realized that the former

Sergeant Major put the command epaulets on his own shoulders. It was a mutiny! A coup!!

Alfan spun around to grab his epaulets from his Senior Sergeant, and the six soldiers behind him just smiled. That was when the beating began. The first blow landed before his sword could even clear its scabbard. It was a small comfort when he realized that they were using their fists and not their swords.

Three days of intense drills and maneuvers were held, lasting from sun-up until well after sundown, and Alfan—PRIVATE Alfan—did his best to learn his new role. He was too accustomed to his old rank and position, and after questioning orders or not performing up to standard, he was beaten again and again.

They formed up in ranks as the 79th was officially relieved of their tour of duty, and two members were pulled out to have command epaulets placed—or were they replaced?—on their shoulders.

The following morning, they received their first orders for a sweep of the northern hills.

Alfan noted that the veterans seemed almost eager to engage. When he hesitantly asked about enemy strength and what they might expect, the Senior Serg—Lieutenant Junior—announced to all that orcs had been spotted in the area and that the scouts were afraid that they might be digging trenches to prevent cavalry charges.

The barking laugh burst from his lips before he could stifle it, and all eyes turned to Alfan, who noted that a handful of others had joined in his laughter. Again, it was the new soldiers. "Orcs," he chided. "We are fighting against children's tales?" With a smile, he continued, "What's next, Ma'am? Ogres and dragons as well? Maybe monkeys on stilts, you know, juggling poisoned daggers?" The new troops joined his laughter again, but it faded as they realized nobody else joined in.

"Listen here, lace-boy," the Company Leader sounded angry. "You've grown up thinking these things were no more than myth and legend, while REAL soldiers have been up here for generations, dealing with these monstrosities and protecting your pampered ass. There are orcs up here. We may see an ogre or two, but they aren't expected today. Any dragons, and we're all doomed. As for your juggling monkeys," the entire company stifled a laugh, "just keep hoping you live long enough to see them once you return to your delicate home life in that cesspit you call home." Her stern gaze turned into an icy glare, and her command voice kicked in. "We march in one hour!"

A raised fist ahead, and the whole formation stopped cold. Two fingers left and right, and the twin columns split and began a wide sweep up a gentle rise with a light scrub and underbrush. His Sergeant swept his spear to the right, and Alfan and the other "lace boys," as they were now called, moved forward.

With a sudden roar and crashing of the brush, a large boar sprang into view, charging in their direction. Alfan faintly heard the Sergeant's order to brace for the charge. Dropping to one knee and straddling the spear haft with his trailing foot atop the butt of the spear to hold it in place, Alfan lowered the head of the spear to the direction of the boar. It seemed like slow motion as he saw the boar run through and gore the man to his left. Then, the beast pivoted and turned away from him.

With a huge sigh, Alfan realized that he had been holding his breath as he slowly rose to his feet again, but before he could stand upright, there was another roar, and more boars came crashing from the underbrush. The problem was that these were upright on two legs and wore armor, carrying dark, serrated scimitars in their hands with a malevolent yet intelligent look in their eyes. One focused on Alfan and charged directly at him.

Again, it seemed like slow motion. The creature charged, and Alfan numbly took mental notes. Massively muscled, the creature wore scale armor made from some sort of black iron. As its feet were raised, he saw black, hobnailed boots. The wicked-looking scimitar was made of the same dirty, black iron. It must not have seen Alfan's upraised spearhead because the beast impaled itself through the breastplate of its armor, and as it stopped, the creature looked down as if surprised by the sudden stop and the ensuing pain. The evil look in its eyes was replaced by one of shock as the scimitar fell to the cold ground.

Behind it, twenty more of the beasts burst from cover.

The battle should have been loud, but Alfan only heard his own breathing and the clang of the closest of weapons. Pulling his spear free from the corpse, he struggled to maintain his footing and keep the spear tip between him and the nearest creature. His focus shifted from beast to beast as they came close and then went out of his field of view until there were no more.

He faintly heard his Sergeant ordering the squad to reform, and he stumbled toward the sound, realizing as he got there that there were but five soldiers when there were ten earlier. His throat hurt for no good reason.

The Sergeant did his job well, checking each soldier in turn for injuries. He grabbed Alfan's forearm to survey a shallow cut through his vambrace and then asked how his throat was doing.

"What...?" he croaked, suddenly realizing that his words burned as he tried to speak.

With a smile, the Sergeant said, "You were screaming at them the whole battle. Unnerving as hell if you ask me, but you kept their attention, and we were able to flank around you. Good job!"

Alfan mumbled some reply and squatted down as he found being upright was difficult with the ground bucking and heaving the way it was. He watched his hands shaking as his squad mates all congratulated him on his bravery. Then, he dropped and vomited away everything he'd eaten for the last year.

That was the first of many battles Alfan fought.

For a time, he worried about what he would do with accumulated pay once he returned to Stormhaven and with which families he would attempt to curry favor. But those worries soon evaporated as he focused more on survival and how his fellow soldiers were doing.

The Senior Sergeant fell at a battle near the frozen river, and his Sergeant was promoted into the position. Alfan didn't bat an eye when he was chosen as the replacement Sergeant, and the men of his squad didn't challenge the appointment. One thing didn't change, though. The moment he engaged the first enemy, he would begin screaming, and it earned Alfan the nickname of "Wolf" because some claimed that he sounded like a lonely wolf on the battlefield, howling for his packmates.

Days were a blur, and the weeks melted into months. It felt like just a fortnight or two before a call came for a formation at the southern walls.

The Captain Major bore a few more scars than he had before, but he told them all how proud he was of them. He then called out a strange name, and a figure hobbled forward, leaning heavily on one crutch. With a hint of a smile, the Captain Major removed his epaulets and placed them on the limping figure, which Alfan suddenly realized was the former Captain Major!

The 'imposter' stepped aside and revealed his old Sergeant Major stripes on his sleeves, and together, they addressed what remained of the 144th Imperial Battalion.

Announcements were made, and awards were given from loot that had been stripped from their many kills. Of the 633 men, 471 remained. Of the 32 non-veteran "Lace-boys" that arrived, Alfan was the last remaining. He tried to feel pride when the rank of Captain was placed upon his shoulders, but all he could feel was a sense of responsibility for the 200 men now under his control. His former Senior Sergeant was formally awarded the Lieutenant Junior epaulets previously removed from his shoulders. As the shuffling came to an end, a low alarm was raised, and the whole battalion turned to see the approach of the 102nd.

In a ritual that was centuries old, the Captain Major of the 102nd ordered her battalion into a formal formation, and his own Captain Major sounded the once unfamiliar, "Prepare RANKS." Nobody approached the 102nd's commanding officer this time, but many junior officers and senior NCOs were surrounded.

Alfan remembered how he had thought that the men and women of the 79th looked old and haggard. He looked about and saw that what remained of the 144th now looked the same.

"EXECUTE!" the order came, and the non-veteran leaders were all stripped of their rank and sent into the formations. Alfan realized that this was how the Imperial Battalions stayed alive by only allowing seasoned leaders to take them into battle.

They would learn. Well, either that or they would die, he thought.

The trip back to Stormhaven seemed much shorter than it should have been. As they got closer, the entire battalion grew more and more quiet and taciturn. Upon their return, there were no parades, no fanfare, just a line of expectant and worried spouses and children.

The order was given to dismiss the battalion, and they scattered. Alfan saw a few of the dependents weeping quietly when they heard of the loss of their loved ones, but he felt no sympathy. The soldiers had died glorious deaths as they manned the Walls, keeping their loved ones safe from the invading hordes.

He visited home a couple of times, but all his parents could talk about was who he should be gifting and with whom he should seek to curry favor to improve his station in life, but it all seemed so hollow, so contrived.

On one of his visits, Alfan went to the local Pathfinder Lodge to have a drink and possibly trade stories with the wealthy members there. But he realized halfway through his goblet of wine that the men and women around him were posers who had never seen a real battle and were living vicariously through the valorous acts performed by others.

Alfan left in disgust.

Finally, his aimless walking led him back to the 144th's barracks to find nearly the entire unit lounging, tending to their kits, or staring off at nothing. As he made his way through the quad, junior troops nodded silently. As he passed, he smiled. Just a year before, he would have raged at their lack of formalities and refusal to salute. He smiled at their imperfect kits, knowing that each and every soldier's equipment was in perfect working order and kept in the quantities needed while in the field instead of some arbitrary amounts set by those who had never set foot outside the city.

Movement caught his eye, and Alfan saw the Sergeant Major crook his finger in his direction. Alfan made his way over to join the entire command cadre, who were walking toward the gate.

"It's time you became a REAL Pathfinder, Wolf," the Sergeant Major smiled and slapped his back.

They made their way just a block or two from the compound, and they entered a small pub. Going to an interior door, the Sergeant Major led each through one by one, Alfan being last. It was only a moment or two, but the wait was still uncomfortable.

Once they passed through the door, Alfan saw two doors before them. A disembodied voice asked for the token of the day, and Alfan panicked for a moment until the Sergeant Major held up a spoon.

"The token is a misdirection, Wolf. Face the doors and present anything you wish—a single coin, a diamond, a bloody rabbit's head—they don't care. Look here," he said, gesturing with his offhand, which was resting on his belt, one finger extended. "This here," he continued, wiggling the finger, "THIS is the real token. Just extend one finger around the hilt of your weapon or from your belt or your pocket. Imposters end up here." He pushed open the door to the right, which opened onto the alley. "True Pathfinders gain entrance."

With that, he pushed open the door to the left and led Alfan into a comfortable tavern with some two dozen soldiers from several battalions. Each of them had the same haggard expressions and distant look in their eyes, but all raised cups or nodded in the direction of Alfan. Brothers and Sisters all; he knew all had stood the Wall.

Joining the rest of the command at a table, Alfan took a long pull from ale and then returned the cup salute to the room.

He was comfortable. He was safe. He was home.

JAYCE FLYNN

Jayce Flynn was bored - not that today was any different than any other day. To be honest, his existence was a constant state of boredom and had been since his family had moved to the backwater nation of Sulon from the bustling city-life of Thalaria. And it wasn't that he had even lived in the capital - he hadn't. Again, honesty demanded that he admit that his hometown in Thalaria was out of the way and, truth be told, it had been a minor player in the thriving confederacy of city-states. Thinking back, Jayce was sure that those from the capital would have insisted that Springleaf was 'backwater' even though it had three very well respected universities and boasted the only Wizard's Tower in the entire nation. But compared to this, it was a gargantuan metropolis that was rivaled only by Stormhaven, itself.

Even the Flynn name meant something in Thalaria. His mother was a senior instructor at Silverleaf Academy, which gave the family a level of respect in the community that was totally missing in this misbegotten, tiny berg of an overgrown village. Here, she was the Headmistress and chief administrator of an entire school system... for the little it did for the family's reputation. Sure, the locals referred to his mother as 'Headmistress' and his stepfather as 'Master', but that was as far as any respect was extended. Even the live-in servant they had hired was less a servant than she was a boarding guest. Paula tidied up and cooked the evening meal each day, but wasn't... well, *subservient* enough for Jayce's liking.

Not that he had much experience with servants and such. When they had moved here two years ago, he had only been fourteen years old, and the first year had been a flurry of activity getting moved in and settled all while attending a newly constructed school. Well, that and dealing with his overbearing sister.

Andrea was scarcely more than a year older than he was, but she acted like she was about to be a senior instructor like their mother or a slave-driver, the way she bossed Jayce around. It was almost as if he had TWO mothers! She constantly picked at him for various infractions of whatever rules she could conveniently recall at any particular time. One of the problems was that Andrea had a much better memory when it came to things like rules and had a significantly different definition of 'well-behaved' than he did. All in all, she was an overbearing ogre who lost no opportunity to bully Jayce into obeying her every whim. Failure or refusal to comply led to sharp rebukes and well-aimed pinches to the insides of his upper arms, or a quick report to stepfather who had no time to waste on ill-mannered children. He had a sharp tongue and a skill at finding words that hurt, so Jayce was torn as to which was worse - sharp pinches from his sister or sharper words from his stepfather. The two bright spots in his life were the rare moment his mother could spare for him, or time spent with his grandfather.

Jayce's grandfather was his mother's father, and he had immigrated to Sulon with the rest of the family. He retired after a long career as an instructor at a Thalarian martial academy, then came to live with the family, and his company was nearly the only bright spot in Jayce's young life. Grandfather had taught swordplay when he was at the academy and had taken it upon himself to teach Jayce the ins and outs of the use of all types of blades, though he let Jayce choose which ones he preferred rather than pushing any particular style on him. As such, Jayce naturally gravitated toward the longsword and the seax, the latter being a heavy, hacking weapon used by the rivermen of Thalaria to cut lines and remove hands of those miscreants that might want to board your skiff unwelcomed.

Jayce took to the weapons naturally and he wielded them with a mature wisdom that was beyond his years — though he still got a thrill each time he drew either of them in practice, with their metallic *SCHWING* ringing out every time. It never failed to elicit a smile each time he heard that beautiful sound. Walking through this tiny, backwater village, each time he heard that sound, it reminded him of the long hours working through forms and practicing with his grandfather.

School was really the only other bright spot in his lackluster life. Now that he was about to be an official adult, he could take classes in whatever areas that appealed to him. Other boys were taking deep-dives into business and various trades so they could start their chosen careers with a leg up on others just starting out, but Jayce had no real aspirations. He didn't want to go into business, and the idea of becoming a teacher bored him even more than his normally boring life. No, he wanted to become an adventurer and become famous for daring deeds and wild exploits. The problem was that nothing exciting ever happened in this tiny town! In classes, he was learning magic and some alchemy, hoping that one day, if anything ever happened, it could help propel him to notoriety.

His arcana classes were going well; he had already learned the formulae for several minor cantrips, and was learning more advanced spell operations, though he hadn't fully mastered the procedures yet. In alchemy, he was learning of the alchemical properties of various substances and how they reacted and interacted with each other. There were very few students in his alchemy classes, as most considered the subject less than boring and useless, but with each experiment and each discovery he grew more and more enamored of the subject and how it helped explain the nature of things.

***

School finally let out for the summer and it looked like another sleepy season in this boring town. The locals were busy swimming and getting excited about a potential bumper harvest this autumn, but that was still months away. That left the entire summer to hack at the practice dummy and work on his sword forms as well as practice his meager magic. For some reason, his grandfather had been pushing him to practice his spells while being encumbered by holding a sword in one hand. Jayce saw no reason to hamper himself like that - but to humor his grandfather he did as he was told.

It was difficult work, as he had to relearn all of the requisite somatic components, as most of his cantrips used both hands to invoke the mystical sigils and now he was restricted to just using his offhand. Still, he persisted, and within a month or so, he was able to replicate the necessary somatic components for all of his cantrips with a minimum of effort.

***

At the height of summer, Jayce was delighted by his family to have a surprise birthday party, The local Sulouese didn't celebrate the date of each birthday, rather they threw parties during the summer for all, and his mother had decided to adopt the custom. So, some two months early, Jayce turned sixteen. It wasn't as special as it could have been, because Andrea's birthday was also celebrated, and things hadn't gotten any better between the two of them. Well, after consideration, perhaps it had; because he spent most of his days practicing his swordsmanship and magic, while his sister was giving more attention to the local boys, so they had fewer explosive encounters.

The highlight of the day was receiving his gifts. His mother and step-father gave him a maroon cloak, a brilliant-looking sword belt, and some fine, black, leather boots that came up nearly to his knees. Even his sister gave him a gift — four pastel-colored kerchiefs with a small coin sewn into one corner. She said it was to tuck into his belt so they didn't slip out and get lost, but Jayce doubted it. The gravy on the potatoes for today was his grandfather, who had purchased him a new, slender longsword, and handed down his own seax.

The small sword was heavy and had a hilt that was made up primarily of copper. The blade was mottled as if the steel had been folded many times, and there were strange glyphs etched onto it. As grandfather handed it to Jayce, he was admonished to always keep it well polished, and Jayce was quick to make the promise to do so.

Later that evening, grandfather approached Jayce with more information. He quietly informed the young man that the seax was very old, having been handed down to grandfather's great-grandfather. In addition, it was slightly magical. While the blade didn't flame or make the wielder invisible or anything like that, it acted like sort of a spell focus and would multiply the affect of any spells cast through the blade. Jayce didn't see any real benefit in it as he didn't use a focus for any of his minor spells, but he still thanked his grandfather profusely for the fine gift.

Sleep was difficult to find that night.

***

The following morning, Jayce got kitted up in all of his new finery — the new boots, cloak, and he attached both of his beautiful, new blades to his new sword belt. For no good reason, he even tucked his sister's kerchiefs into the belt. Grabbing some bread and cheese for lunch, Jayce took off for the day to explore with a new sense of purpose. No longer was he a kid out looking for fun. No, today he was an adult out seeking adventure. He didn't know where he would go, but today was the day!

Not having a destination in mind, Jayce let his feet guide him. It took less than an hour to travel through the entire town; By the hells, it had only about a thousand residents! At the central market, the locals were all talking about a group of adventurers that were in town. By all accounts they were; a Paladin, a Cleric, a Bard, and a Sorcerer. He wasn't interested in being an onlooker or a hanger-on with a group of experienced adventurers, so he continued on his walkabout. After completing his circuit — making sure that nearly all the locals in town saw his new setup, he headed south, not really paying attention to his route, just taking in the sights and sounds. Without realizing it, he headed toward one of the town's swimming holes.

Finally realizing where he had ended up when the shrieks and yells of frolicking kids broke through his reverie, Jayce snorted in derision. The *children* were busy *playing*! He, on the other hand, was an adventurer with, well, *adventure* on his mind!! As the kids in the wide pool called his name in an attempt to lure him into joining them, he turned on his heel and started walking downstream along the wide river banks without acknowledging their pleas.

The journey downstream wasn't as difficult as it could have been, especially with his new boots that allowed him to step into shallow water without worrying about getting his feet and socks wet. Scrambling over moss-covered rocks and dodging deeper water, he made his way for what seemed like a league or more, but was probably less than a quarter-mile or so, because he could still hear the occasional screech of the swimming kids. He didn't have time for such frivolous pursuits — he was *adventuring*!!

He eventually came to a small clearing in the trees and underbrush when he decided to practice some of his sword forms in total privacy. He grew to feel like he was being watched, though he couldn't see or hear anyone nearby, so he continued to practice with abandon. He ran through the sword forms that grandfather had taught him and included the stricture that he not announce each step of the forms as he proceeded. One movement flowed---or at least *tried* to flow — into the next, and as grandfather had recently begun to teach, Jayce began to mix up the forms; Cutting Swan was seventeen steps, but at step nine he shifted into Charging Bull. The challenge was to make each transition seem as seamless as possible. His imaginary battling of evil-doers morphed into fighting giants, then into combating mighty dragons.

He did rather well, in his opinion. Scythe in the Fields shifted into Ravaging Wolf which shifted into Wind through the Leaves which shifted into Picking the Cherries. Some of the transitions worked better than others, and Jayce made mental notes of how they fit together. He even attempted some combinations that grandfather hadn't prompted him to try. He was pleased with his progress and decided to take a break to cool off and eat his bread and cheese when the voice broke through his reverie.

"You are quite the swordmaster, young one." The voice was deep and guttural, with a strange accent. In a panic, Jayce drew his recently scabbarded sword and spun around to find the source of the voice, only to see nothing but the trees, brush, and river. He didn't recognize the voice.

"Wh-who is there?" Jayce's voice was almost panicked as he scanned about, looking for the source of the strange voice. Suddenly, slight movement at the river's edge caught his eye. Rising up from the surface of the water was a great, black, scaled head with leathery fringes where ears should have been.

"Be not afraid, human, for you are in the presence of true greatness." The beast's head rose up out of the water, higher and higher, stopping only when it was nearly three times Jayce's height. Jayce was awestruck. The reality of the situation hit him as he recognized the beast at the same time it spoke again. "Behold, human, a true dragon!" The creature stepped forward, mostly out of the river as Jayce unconsciously stepped back a couple of paces. Rearing up on its hind legs, the dragon flapped its wings like a bird in a birdbath, shaking the water from it's sinuous form.

The dragon was midnight black in color and looked slimy like an eel. On its hind legs, it was easily three times Jayce's height. As it dropped back to all fours again, he could see the dragon's body was nearly the size of a farmer's wagon and its head was nearly at twice Jayce's height. The massive head was nearly as long as he was tall, and Jayce concluded that it could easily eat him in just two bites. The claws were almost as long as Jayce's forearm. Half of the young man was terrified while the other half wanted to leap about in joyous rapture at the sight of a real dragon. This is what adventurers do, and this is what the bards tell tales about when they come to town!!

The dragon's voice almost seemed to echo in the small clearing. "You do not deserve to know my name in the draconic language, but in your crude common tongue, you may address me as *Venomfang*." As it spoke, a line of spittle fell from its maw to the wet ground beneath it and as it did, Jayce saw that it smoked and bubbled.

Ah, either a strong acid or alkali. Jayce was almost ashamed as his alchemical studies had come to him so easily. Then he thought, *Well, it came out of the water and I don't see smoke or evidence of heat, so this isn't a firebreathing dragon. I've never heard of an alkali breathing version, so this must be an acid spitting dragon.* Suddenly the name made sense.

"Venomf... *Mighty* Venomfang," Jayce corrected himself. "You are truly..." he paused, and then, for the first time in his life admitted, "... I am at a loss for words." The creature stood just a little taller, as if pleased by the admission. The dragon looked back and forth as its wings adjusted themselves. Jayce got the impression that the dragon was preening like a bird trying to show off for potential mates.

"What grand monsters were you battling here, little one?" Jayce got the impression that the dragon was being condescending. "Surely you were fighting giants or rogue warriors or something similar." The patronizing tone reminded Jayce of his stepfather's.

Jayce caught himself before he could admit that he was slaying dragons, "U h... I was battling, um... evil knights who were intent on preying on innocent townsfolk. I was the last hope in town to rescue them." The dragon laughed at the admission, taking it at face value, unaware of the falsehood.

"I seek nourishment, human. Is there something to eat nearby?" The dragon's shiny, black eyes seemed to bore into Jayce's very soul.

"Um... the sheep and cows are out in the fields, foraging. There are goats, pigs, and chickens at nearly every house in town..." Jayce offered as much information as he had on the subject.

The dragon snorted, a blob of bubbling mucous splashing onto the ground beneath it. "I am a water dragon, human. I seek something near or in the river or the lake I sense further upstream."

"Majestic Venomfang, this time of year the townsfolk keep very few animals near the river."

The dragon seemed to be getting disappointed. "What of the high-pitched yells and such I hear from upstream? The water carries the sounds very well."

Jayce didn't hesitate, "Oh, those aren't animals, those are children playing in a swimming hole."

"How many, human?"

"It looked like about twenty of them when I passed by." Jayce still hadn't deduced what the dragon was driving at until it was too late.

"Are there adults there to protect them? Adults with arrows or spears?" The dragon lowered its head as if planning something.

"No." Jayce was nothing, if not honest. "Why should they have guards? They're right there by town and there hasn't been a sighting of orcs or giants in years." As the dragon's mouth pulled back into a great smile and showed its dagger-like fangs, Jayce realized what he had done and what the dragon had planned. The dragon turned and reentered the river, submerging within seconds. "NO," Jayce screamed at the rippling water. "NO!!!"

In a panic, Jayce debated about what to do. Before he decided on a course of action, Jayce found himself sprinting upstream along the river's bank toward the unsuspecting children. Every few seconds he saw the wake created by the submerged dragon pulling away from him, moving faster than he could ever hope to run.

At a curve in the river there was a small peninsula of river rocks that Jayce had seen fishermen use to throw their nets into the river, Jayce paused and could see the frolicking children in the distance. Seeing the dragon's wake speeding ahead of him, Jayce knew he had to get the attention of the children — but *how*??

Throwing his left hand in the air, he performed the somatic ritual to produce flame, and as he recited the short incantation, a ball of fire appeared in his hand. Silently praying to the gods, Jayce threw the flaming ball as high into the air as he could, and it flew up, then arched down to splash into the shallows of the river with a brief sizzle. Looking at the 200 yards upstream, he saw his warning had been unseen by the children.

In another attempt, Jayce raised his hand and cast another incantation, producing a small spark of electricity in his hand. Repeating the gesture, he tossed it high aloft... to no avail. The children just couldn't see such feeble castings.

Now in full panic mode, Jayce knew he had to do something he had never attempted before. Using what he had studied in arcanum classes and what his grandfather had prompted, Jayce made slightly different somatic gestures, more grandiose than before, He spoke words he had practiced before but had never actually used, and raised his left hand high above his head. He was shocked when a sheet of flames erupted from his fingertips, flying up nearly fifteen feet above his upraised hand.

Looking again at the children, he saw them all looking in his direction. Struggling to be as loud as possible, Jayce screamed, "DRAGON! GET OUT OF THE WATER!!" He waved his hand as if to shoo them all onto the shore. He continued to scream and wave his arms, even as he noticed that his right hand held his new longsword. *How did that get there,* he wondered.

As if reading his mind, the children began shrieking and rushing for the shallows at the river bank, with the elder children helping the younger ones who were moving much slower. Within seconds, the swimming hole was empty, with the children running up the shallow slope and screaming in terror as the dragon erupted from the middle of the swimming hole, roaring its impotent rage at the retreating children. Jayce sighed in relief with the knowledge that the children had safely made it out of the water, then his heart stopped as he saw the dragon's massive head swivel in his direction. With another roar, the dragon dove under the water in Jayce's direction. In a flash, Jayce noted that the wake created by the submerged beast was much larger than it had been as it went upstream, and his analytical mind deduced that it was traveling much faster toward him than it had been heading toward its original prey.

Jayce didn't have time enough to run away before the dragon erupted out of the river with a great spray of water that doused the young man, making his new cloak and clothing stick to his slim form. "WHAT DID YOU DO, HUMAN?!" The dragon was enraged and seemingly incredulous. "You stole my meal from me!" The great beast lunged and swiped at Jayce with its razor sharp talons.

Throwing himself backwards, the deadly claws barely made contact with him, ripping through his cloak and shirt beneath, leaving three bright lines of red that quickly began welling up with blood. The mighty claw carried through and struck Jayce's new longsword, knocking it from his grasp. The sword clattered against the river rocks as it bounced away.

"You cost me my meal, so you will BE my next meal!" The dragon's rage was palpable, and Jayce noted that the beast's midsection had begun to spasm. With a start, he recognized that it looked like his sister's cat when it was throwing up a hairball. Thinking quickly, he grabbed the soaked hem of his new, maroon cloak and pulled it around him as he turned his back to the fell beast.

The sound of the dragon spitting up its horrific spray of acid nearly made Jayce sick up, himself, and he felt the slimy mucous spray all over his back. With one deft move, Jayce pulled the cloak from his shoulders and tossed the now ruined garment to the ground where it steamed and bubbled. Again, his alchemy instruction came back to him as he recognized that if his cloak and clothing hadn't been soaked with water, the acid would have been at full strength and he would likely be smoking on the rocks like his cloak. As he turned back, his hand naturally went to the hilt of his grandfather's seax and he drew it in what would probably be one of the last actions of his short life.

The dragon evidently didn't expect the young human to take the offensive and it backed up a half-step. Repeating the incantation and somatic components Jayce had used just a moment ago to warn the children, this time he extended his hand toward the dragon as the flames erupted from his fingertips. The dragon reared up as the flames lapped at its breast. Jayce knew that the slimy, wet scales of the dragon would protect it from the fire, but he wasn't intent on burning it, merely causing a distraction.

As the dragon reared up Jayce rushed in. Seeing the leg that had just ripped through his new cloak and clothing at eye-level, Jayce grabbed the hilt of his seax with both hands and swung it as hard as he could at the wrist of that deadly limb. The great beast roared in pain and came crashing down onto all fours — well, onto all threes — as the leg that Jayce had targeted was cut almost all the way through. The force of the dragon coming down had knocked Jayce on his bottom, and as he scrambled to get up, the fell beast again vomited up a gout of acid that splashed onto Jayce's new boots and formed puddles on the wet ground between them. He struggled to stand as the acid made the rocks and ground slippery and Jayce had a difficult time maintaining his footing.

As he fought to remain upright, Jayce's left hand got tangled in the kerchiefs from his sister that he had tucked into his belt. With another flash of insight, Jayce grabbed as many as he could, and as he pulled them free he flung them straight into the air over his head.

Not expecting another diversion, the dragon's gaze and head followed the kerchiefs up as they flew upward. Jayce had a sudden thought and began incanting another spell. This time, rather than flames or a tiny spark of electricity, he instinctively conjured up as much electricity as he could and willed himself to hold it within. In the distance he could hear thunder rumbling. As the dragon realized the kerchiefs were a ruse, the dragon began to tilt its head back down to bite at Jayce, but before it could fully react, Jayce charged the few feet that separated the two.

With as much force as he could muster, he plunged the seax blade deep into the breast of the dragon as he willed the electrical charge he held within him through the copper hilt and blade. As the blade bit deeply, Jayce could feel the shocking blast pass through his hand and into the seax, then into the dragon. What Jayce didn't expect was the backblast of electricity that knocked him back from the huge creature.

From the wound came a great gout of acidic blood that would have doused Jayce if he had remained where he was. As he scrambled to his feet again, he was amazed to see that he still had the seax in his hand. The dragon was hunched over, groaning and roaring in pain, veritably screaming at him. "What have you done, stupid human! You have no right!! Hhnnnnnn!" Knowing that it was still a serious threat, Jayce feinted left and dashed to his right, moving from the Rabbit in the Tall Grass form into The Whirlwind without thinking about the transition. The dragon's head moved to intercept his feint, and Jayce brought the seax down again as hard as he could, aiming at the base of the dragon's skull. As it roared in agony, Jayce swung again and again and again.

When his blade clanked against the rocks beneath the dragon, he finally stopped. Jayce realized that the rumbling thunder had gotten close and had suddenly stopped, and he looked to the skies for the reason why. When blue sky met his gaze, his confusion grew, but a voice from behind brought him spinning about, slipping on the acid-covered rocks.

"Yo, dragonslayer! What have you done here?" Jayce numbly looked at five mounted figures, his overworked mind absently concluding that their hoofbeats must have been the source of the 'thunder' he had heard, and that these must be the party of adventurers he had heard were in town. Not really understanding what was said, Jayce looked down to see the dragon at his feet, head separated from its neck amidst a growing puddle of acidic blood.

Stepping out of the disgusting wetness, Jayce could only offer, "It was going to eat the children. Someone had to do something and I was the only person around."

"We heard the children screaming about a terrible dragon and we came straightaway." The woman speaking was dressed in full plate armor and carried a kite shield with the telltale holy symbol, the blue cross of Talon.

A man behind her spoke up, "You did this alone? Where is your armor, young warrior."

"I'm no warrior, I'm an adventurer. My name is Jayce Flynn." Jayce took no notice of the smiles his response elicited. "I have no armor because I don't have any yet because I'm just starting out." The smiles grew wider.

A third member of the party spoke up, but the words he spoke were in a strange language, almost musical, sounding for all the world like bells and chimes. A sense of warmth spread through Jayce's body, mostly in his chest and his feet. "I have offered up a healing word to aid you, as you look as if you may need it."

Jayce tried to take it all in, and he absently turned back to look at the huge dragon lying dead behind him. As the enormity of what had happened washed over him, Jayce felt his knees grow weak. Before the excitement drained completely from him and he fell unconscious, the last thing he heard was, "Go back to town to alert the town guards. And let them know that Jayce Flynn is the true dragonslayer."

OMEGA ONE

This truly sucked.

No, it was worse than that. It broke the known laws of physics by both sucking and blowing at the same time.

Tiffany groaned in pain. Her shoulders hurt, her hands were both burned and blistered, her head throbbed to the point that it occasionally caused stars to dance across her vision, the soles of her feet were bruised, and her knees were scuffed up and bleeding slightly. These trifles were nothing compared to her right hip and thigh.

To say her hip was bruised was such an understatement that she couldn't even think of a metaphor. The bruise started just below her ribcage and extended to just short of her knee and spread around her leg to the point that there was just a thin line of clear, healthy, brown skin down the inside of her thigh—the rest was angry red and purple, and throbbed with every beat of her heart or movement she made.

She shot an angry glance at the suspected cause of her injuries, the damaged pulse rifle. The damnable thing had been the last item placed into the cryopod with her, and it had been nestled firmly against her right leg—well, had been until the pod crashed on re-entry. Now, it sat in three separate piles of scrap outside the twisted remains of the cryopod. At least one charge had been expended—possibly more—and this explained her burns and probably her headache. But it was her leg that caused her—literally—the most pain. The small explosion from the power cell was the probable cause, and that explosion was most probably caused by some feedback loop when the damned thing was damaged when the cryopod crashed, and that simply wasn't supposed to be possible.

Then, the pods were put into service; they all had GPS maps installed in their limited navigation system, which would put them down within a few hundred feet of the surface before their equally limited propulsion kicked in to land them safely with a few radar scans of what lay below. Even a new building erected that wasn't on the maps would be scanned, and the pod would move slightly out of the way or, at worst, would land the pod on the roof. Even if there was a huge landslide or earthquake, the computer and propulsion system would allow for upwards of several hundred meters of differences in elevation and provide similar lateral movement to allow the pod to avoid all manners of obstacles at the landing site. Hell's bells: even if the area was flooded, the radar would sound the depth to allow for a safe landing or set the pod down so it was in a position to act as a makeshift raft.

It wasn't water that caused her mishap, though. From the scattered rock and skid marks on the slope of the low mountain, it was obvious that her cryopod had impacted well before the self-contained navigation systems kicked in. From the looks of the marks, the pod had struck near the top of the peak and then rolled and bounced nearly half a kilometer—well, from the marks on the ground *AND* how she felt.

Taking stock of her condition, Tiffany was pleased to find that it didn't appear that she had any broken bones in her leg, hip, or pelvis, though it hurt like the Nine Hells when she moved her leg. *Wonderful,* she thought snidely, *all soft-tissue damage. No permanent damage, just agony until it heals.*

The rest of her injuries were superficial, well, except for her burned hands and a massive headache. *Probably a minor concussion,* she concluded after failing to find any injuries on her head outside of a split lip with a little swelling. Fortunately, *HAH!* she laughed. Fortunately, the burns and blisters were on the backs of her hands, so she could still grip without too many issues.

As stars swam before her eyes again from the migraine, now that she had put that name on her headache, it dawned on Tiffany that migraines were supposedly common for those coming out of cryo-sleep and should pass with time and the ingestion of water. Throwing caution to the stars, Tiffany took a long draught from her meager rations. *Better to be clear-headed and thirsty than to be unable to focus my eyes.*

It took less than half an hour for her migraine to clear up, though it took another full liter of water. At that time, Tiffany was able to tie the broken barrel of her pulse rifle to her side and leg to partially immobilize her hip and provide a modicum of support. In addition, she was able to gather up her rucksack and load it with whatever rations and supplies she could salvage from her damaged cryopod.

Once able to think clearly, Tiffany slowly pushed herself up to her feet and only yelped once while doing so. Resting heavily against the hull of her cryopod, she caught her breath before pushing herself completely upright. Fearing a fall, Tiffany kept her right hand on the cryopod for safety and checked her balance. With several grimaces and some choice words said under her breath, she was able to stand without wobbling too much. A couple of tentative steps later, Tiffany knew she was, at least, nominally mobile.

With a groan, she bent to pick up her pack and then gritted her teeth as she hoisted it in place, a low moan escaping her lips as she twisted her torso slightly. But, at last, she was erect and loaded for travel. Slowly, Tiffany began walking up the slope toward the peak of the low mountain. Maybe up there, she could get a radio signal.

The climb was less of a climb than it was a slow, torturous, limping walk. Her hip meant that she had to favor her left leg, letting it do most of the work. Step, lean, drag, balance. Step, lean, drag, balance. Over and over. As such, it took nearly an hour to make the 250 meters or so to the low peak above her. The last few meters were on all fours, both because she didn't want to be silhouetted against the skyline by any unwanted eyes and because she knew she was going to lie down at the crest and didn't trust her hip to be able to do it without giving out and falling. Besides, a fall up here could mean that she might roll all the way down the steep hill, and she wasn't sure she could survive such a mishap in her condition.

Finally able to see over the crest of the small mountain, Tiffany bent her left elbow to allow herself to collapse in a heap while protecting her right hip. Rolling quickly, she winced and let out a pained growl before giving in to the tears that she had been fighting since she had awakened. It didn't take long, as she just needed the time to take the edge off of her pain and frustration.

Finally, after several minutes, Tiffany pulled out her handy-talker and wiped away her tears. After a few too many abortive attempts, she finally had her voice under control. She selected the *Broadcast All Freqs* setting and keyed the vocal pickup.

"Hello, all stations. Hello, All Stations. This is Tiffany Williamson of Omega-One..." She hesitated. "Uh... formerly of Station Omega-One, now crash-landed on the surface. Mayday, Mayday, Mayday, all stations. Again, this is TIFFANY WILLIAMSON, formerly of Station Omega-One. Mayday, Mayday, Mayday, all stations. Do you read me? Come in, over." Releasing the controller, she waited.

Nothing. She repeated the call over and over again, all with the same result: silence from the other end. After what seemed like hours, Tiffany couldn't keep the tears of frustration from overwhelming her again. This time, she didn't try to shut them down until after they had run their full course.

It wasn't supposed to be like this! She had secured an internship in civil engineering with the government that was to start just after graduating with high honors. Tiffany had even been planning her university graduation party when the world went to the hells. The masscomm screens had broadcast the disasters as they cascaded. First were the volcanoes—exploding with no warning all over the globe. Then, the earthquakes began, leveling cities and even entire nations. Then came the meteor swarms that exploded in the atmosphere and then crashed into the ground, indiscriminately falling wherever they wished. So many millions of lives were lost in those first few days and weeks.

Then, the refugee disaster started. 'Gees from the countryside began pouring into what few cities remained, and then Gees from the cities began pouring out into the countryside. Then, the looting began. What wasn't nailed down was stolen in the first waves. What *was* nailed down was pried up and stolen on subsequent waves. The Gees left nothing. Livestock was slaughtered and eaten on the spot, and pets fared no better in the End Times.

If it weren't for her mother and her paranoia, the entire family would have died. Though they had lived far outside of the usual paths of tornadoes and were inland enough that hurricanes and typhoons weren't a danger, Mother had insisted—no, DEMANDED—that Father have a shelter installed in the backyard. It was finished the year she graduated from secondary school.

The shelter doubled as a safe room and was stocked with months, if not years' worth of food and supplies. She remembered her professors laughing at the folly when she inadvertently mentioned it in class one day. Tiffany was sure they stopped laughing when the End Times began.

Her family had remained holed up for nearly three months after the masscomm broadcasts had ended when they decided to venture out to see what their security cameras failed to reveal. They had seen a few well-armed guardsmen on the cameras, but they didn't stick around long enough to tell if they were imposing order on the masses or were part of the scavengers.

Per usual, just after nightfall, she had ventured forth to root through the slim pickings remaining. Their house had been ransacked, and fire had almost destroyed the entire home. And if it weren't for the buried shelter in the backyard, Tiffany was sure that they would either be part of the Gees or dead. It was three weeks later that she was captured. Sure, they claimed it was actually a 'rescue,' but she was more honest about it.

There were pockets of government that still operated, and it was decided that every satellite that could support them would be retrofit to be home to as many cryopods and workers that could be supported. Her name had been on the list of possible residents of the orbiting havens. Her professor had remembered the shelter, and because she was on the Administrator's List of high achievers, she had been selected. They watched all potential targets until it was proven that they were dead or they were picked up, then moved on to the next target.

She hated being referred to as a 'target'; it made her feel more and more like a victim rather than a potentially thankful rescuee. All of those rescued received two weeks of rushed quasi-military training and were then loaded like sardines into troop transports that held upwards of five hundred people but were rated at just 150. The conditions were horrific, and when one of them got sick, it started a mass vomiting event. Thankfully, the journey was over in about six hours.

The techs that greeted them all wore gas masks, so they knew what to expect when the hatches were opened. In the press, they had two fatalities and another few dozen injuries from the overcrowding. In mere hours, they were cleaned up, briefed, and headed for their individual cryopods. All the gear they were to have was already stowed for them, and there was precious little room for any additional items they wanted to take with them.

The things that really stuck with her were that the techs had told them that they were on Station Omega-One and that they'd be on ice for a couple of weeks, perhaps months, but nowhere near a full year. They weren't to worry, though, because most of the processes were automated, and if there were issues, the pods could be jettisoned to land back on the ground in a safe area.

Right! The tears came harder. *Some safe spot!* She was homesick and missed her parents horribly, and now she had crashed onto some hellscape with little food and water and a bum hip. *This sucked AND blew!!*

Once she was able to gather her wits, Tiffany needed to take stock of her surroundings. Wiping and blinking away the tears, she pulled her monocular from her vest and began to look down all of the slopes of the mountain. It wasn't long before her blood ran cold.

A group of people was in the valley down to the east. From the variable zoom scope, she was able to tell that they were refugees of some sort, as they were armed with clubs and blades. What alarmed her was that they were sneaking along the foot of the mountain in the direction of her ruined cryopod.

Before she could panic completely, Tiffany zoomed out to scan the rest of the valleys at the base of the hill she was presently trapped on. Her finding to the southwest made her breath catch. There were four other people! Zooming in, Tiffany grew confused because the range finder told her that they were over 300 meters away and that they were over three meters in height. *Great!* She thought, *Even my monocular is on the fritz.*

Pulling her radio out again, Tiffany broadcasts her mayday message again. Again, there was no response. Fiddling with the volume control, her heart stopped as she heard an audible *CLICK*. *Oh, by all that is holy, unholy, and secular! The damned thing wasn't even TURNED ON!!*

Breaking squelch a couple of times to ensure the volume was acceptable (and that the unit was even turned on!!), Tiffany repeated her mayday again, and with less time than it took to inhale afterward, she got the response she had been praying for.

"Tiffany Williamson, this is Tango-Two. We read your Mayday four-by-four. Our scanner says you are approximately three kilometers from our location. Are you able to travel at an azimuth of 050 from your location over?"

Gasping with excitement, Tiffany responded, "Yes, yes, thank you, Tango-Two." Then she thumbed the vocal pickup. "DAMMIT! Er... Yes, thank you, Tango. This is Tiffany. That's a no, uh, a negative." This military stuff was difficult, considering that all she had was two weeks of rushed training prior to being tossed on ice. "I can't go anywhere. I'm injured, and there are two sets of refugees heading south to intercept me and my cryopod. I don't have my pulse rifle and my monocular is haywire because it's telling me that one of the groups of Gees is over three meters tall." She released the controller before remembering to key it again. "Over." She hoped she wouldn't get yelled at for her breaches of radio protocol.

"Say again, Williamson. Over how many meters tall? And how tall is the other group of Gees, over?"

"That's over three meters, TANGO, HOSTEL, ROMEO, ECHO, ED-WARD, *three* meters tall." Looking through her monocular at the first group again, she keyed the communicator again. "The other group is under two meters tall—all between 150 and 170 centimeters, over." Quickly keying the vocal pick up again, she added, "The short group of Gees are armed with clubs, pipes, and long blades. Oh, and one has what looks like a pick-ax that you'd dig in a garden with. The big ones are armed with big clubs, though one has a long blade strapped to his back. Both groups are about 400 meters away from me and heading toward my cryopod, which is some 250 meters from me." In a panic, she keyed the button again. "Over! Over!"

"Roger that, Williamson. We will be at your location within fifteen minutes, within five to ten minutes for long-range support. This is Tango-Two, out."

"Oh, Tango-Two, thank you! Over!" It was difficult to speak without getting loud and alerting the refugees below her.

Dropping her radio back into her vest pocket, NAME kept her monoculars glued to her eye to view the progress of the groups below her. Looking about, she saw that the "tall" group was almost at the cryopod when she saw one of the four points in the direction of her pod. *Great, they've spotted it.* Moving quickly, the four covered the last couple hundred meters faster than she thought possible.

Scanning left, she saw that the larger group was approaching cautiously. Going back to her cryopod, Tiffany grew concerned. The four people towered over her pod-like... well, *giants,* and with no ceremony, they began to dismantle her cryopod with their bare hands, ripping great hunks of hull and electronics out with little problem at all, as if their strength matched their great height. She could hear the rending metal and crashing debris from her perch, some 250 meters away.

With the noise, the other group of refugees doubled their speed. Getting within about 100 meters from the giants—*well, what else should I call them?* Tiffany thought—they stopped, and then two of them began waving their hands before their faces as if shooing away biting bugs. From one came a tiny, glowing red mote of light that sped toward the giants. From the other, a huge arcing bolt of electricity shot forward in a jagged line, shocking three of the giants. That little mote of red light flew to a spot above the cryopod and exploded in a great ball of flame.

Tiffany's shriek of surprise was drowned out by the reverberating sound of the explosion and the accompanying screams of pain from the giants. One lay on the ground, kicking and thrashing about in agony, while the other three screamed in defiance and charged the group of men. Two of the giants stooped to grab large stones from the ground as they advanced, and as they ran, they threw the stones as hard as they could at the other group of refugees. Both rocks found their marks, and two of the Gees fell from the impacts. Tiffany didn't believe that either would rise again. Then, the two groups crashed together in a horrific melee.

The giants swung their mighty clubs to great effect, and men died with each swing, while the men's blows seemed ineffective on the giants. The two spellcasters, however, hurled motes of light and force at the giants that seemed to find their marks. Unfortunately for them, this got the attention of two of the giants, who charged at them. Their demise was quick and painful.

As the casters died, the third giant dropped to his knees and fell under a crowd of men. It dawned on Tiffany that her monocular wasn't malfunctioning—she could readily see the difference in height between the two groups—the one group really did tower over the other group like giants! What madness had she stumbled upon?

One of the men was obviously a leader of some sort. He barked an order, and the majority of the group swarmed one of the giants, leaving the other to try to smash just a few, dodging targets. By the time the beset giant went down, there were just over a handful of men remaining. As soon as it fell, the remaining men charged the last of the giants. There were only three men remaining, and Tiffany noted that the leader was one of them.

In an attempt to remain unseen, Tiffany tried to crab-walk up the rest of the slope, only to kick sand and rocks loose. In horror, she watched the detritus roll and bounce down the slope toward the men. Her heart stopped when she saw the three spot the falling stones and sand and follow their telltale trails back up the slope to her location. Pointing, the leader gave an order that needed no translation, and the three spread apart and began climbing toward her.

It took what felt like hours for them to cover half the distance, though it was only just over 100 meters. It was then that she remembered her radio. Grabbing it, Tiffany fairly screamed into it as she keyed the vocal pickup. "MAYDAY, MAYDAY! THEY'RE COMING, THEY SEE ME!!"

"Overwatch, this is Two. Are you set, over?"

"Two, this is Overwatch. Set and awaiting orders. Three bogies. Range 1438 meters, over." This was a different voice.

"Overwatch, Roger that. Break, break. Williamson, this is Tango-Two. I need you to yell at those three and throw a handful of sand and rocks into the air. Do you understand, over?"

"DO WHAT? WHY??"

"Williamson, you will point at them as you yell, then throw a handful of shit in the air, DO IT!! Do it in five, four, three, two, one!"

Not understanding, Tiffany did as he asked, pointing and screaming, "STOP, YOU LOUSY BASTARDS!" Then, with her other hand, she tossed a handful of sand and rocks as high as she could.

The men stopped dead as she yelled, then shared evil smiles between them. From nowhere, one of the men dropped like a bag of hammers. Within just a couple of meters of the other two, two small clouds of sand and dirt exploded near their feet. With looks of terror, they looked at Tiffany again, then turned on their tails and ran down the slope to their right—back in the direction from which they had come.

With relief, Tiffany scanned about in a near panic in case some other horrid threats were sneaking up on her. *Nothing nearby,* she concluded.

Next, she began searching to the south for her rescue party. When she finally spotted them jogging toward her in the distance, she let the tears of relief come.

CHALLA OF THE AL'HAM

The journey was uneventful. No, it was worse than that—it was boring—Another Al'Ham, as his people called themselves, another might
have welcomed the quiet—even relished it, but Challa didn't. If he had to leave
his homeland as an escort for some misguided diplomatic mission, he, at least,
wanted to experience some *excitement*!

Emissary Ralec mal'Kresh ban'Alta con'Nar was being sent to some distant
land called Barranae, where the local people spent much of their lives underground, living in caves and mining. Why they did this was a mystery to Challa,
but such were their ways. He knew from Ralec con'Nar that they seemed to
enjoy the idea of being away from the sun, they were short (he had been warned
against staring), and their names were strange, usually only a given name and then
one Williamson to identify them, and the names were in the wrong order. For
example, Esenda Tamucin (Esenda the Smith) would be called Tamucin Esenda,
yet he would still be addressed as Esenda.

Al'Ham names were so much easier! His own name, Challa mal'Timma
ban'Rondal, was simple. He was Challa, child of Timma, of the village of Rondal.
Ralec con'Nar's name was just as easy: Ralec mal'Kresh ban'Alta con'Nar; Ralec,
child of Kresh, of the village of Alta, and the con'Nar was his title as Emissary.
Important members of his people got titles like that—Emissary, Chief or Chief-

tain, Great One (for warriors of legend), and others. con'Mitta was the one he hoped to get one day—Challa the Great One.

They traveled light, with the four escorts taking turns carrying the heavy pack with gifts from the Al'Ham homeland for those they might meet. Each day, they carefully unwrapped and rewrapped each of the items. Perfumes in delicate glass bottles, jewelry of gold, silver, and brass, trinkets like small statues of monsters and insects of the desert, a small collection of daggers and knives, and a large, embossed golden wrist shield that was almost big enough to cover Challa's entire chest. Why someone might like a shield of that outlandish size was beyond Challa's grasp. His own shield was scarcely larger than his two hands laid flat, side by side. Why would someone want one larger—and how would it be used? Granted, this shield was ceremonial, but the question remained.

Their route was circuitous. To avoid too many questions and prying eyes, they were to head east around the foothills, thereby avoiding Thalaria. The Thalars weren't supposed to be a danger, but they were very inquisitive and would want to speak with the entire entourage at length, and Ralec con'Nar didn't want the four escorts to be made to feel like creatures on display to be ogled and prodded. Challa had heard that in the Shiavo lands, the *Wetlander* lands, they had entire compounds where they kept trapped animals in cages for others to walk by and just look at them. Utterly barbaric!

The route would take them between the mountains of the Iron Clawed Beast and the Elven forest of ban'Legar, or Legarotha as the Elves called it. Before reaching their destination, they would stop by the Dark Dwarves' homeland. After a stop in Mellaron at the far eastern point of Barranae, they would head inward to the capital of the nation to speak with their great Chieftain, Khagan Varian Aletus (*Khagan Aletus, don't forget their stupid naming conventions!*)

The greatest excitement thus far came when the small group went through the supposed 'Southern Pass' between the Iron Claw Mountains and a small mountain (*huge hill?*). Tachi's keen eyes spotted a half-dozen or more wyverns circling high above the small mountain. Fortunately for the dragon-cousins, they didn't come down to try to molest the party. Granted, there were only seven

Al'Ham strong, but all seven were experts in using their short composite bows, and all were used to battling the wyvern that came over the great wall from the Morgaloth swamps far below.

Of the seven, Challa and three other escorts were there with Ralec con'Nar, his understudy Balad, and the cook/servant, Capit. Though only one had a title, they were essentially equals, though Challa and the other escorts knew they were the lowest in the hierarchy. Even though all seven participated in meal preparation, camp set-up, and tear-down, Ralec con'Nar made sure to instruct Balad that no matter the title, many hands made for light work and that titles meant nothing in the face of hunger or to those who were overworked. Challa wondered if the lessons were for Balad or everyone to hear and learn.

Three days south of Mellaron, the group came around a corner where a group of orcs were attacking a powerfully built man and a huge wolf. The man seemed to be holding his own, and the orcs had just regrouped, with several grabbing bows and taking up positions to shoot the strange duo. Without permission or even a second thought, Challa and Balad both grabbed their own shortbows and engaged the orcs.

Each had fired two arrows apiece before the orcs realized they were even there, and the remaining archers only had a chance to lose one arrow apiece before they shifted their aim. As he reloaded another arrow, Challa saw out of his peripheral vision that the man almost looked like he was dancing as he dodged the arrows. Two more flights of arrows and all the orc archers were down.

The man dove in low beneath the spearpoint of one of the orcs harassing the giant wolf. Challa was shocked when he realized that the man seemed to be actually actively *defending* the wolf. Going in low as he did, the man was able to avoid the point of the orc's spear and gut him. Without hesitation, the man vaulted from his toes into the air, drawing everyone's attention with the move. Almost in slow-motion, he pirouetted as he flipped in mid-air, and this drew the spearpoints of the other three orcs that had been harrying the giant wolf. With this, the wolf launched an attack of its own, lunging at the spear of the orc farthest from the man, breaking it in its mighty jaws.

A sudden *TWANG* from next to him tore Challa from his reverie. Nocking again, his first choice of a target was already falling, so Challa picked another, sinking an arrow into the orc's thigh. The wolf snapped at the throat of the next nearest orc, and Challa noted a spray of dark blood coming from the now ripped neck. Four more arrows, combined with the actions of the man and wolf, finished whatever fight was left in the orcs as the last of them fell. Finally, the wolf made quick work of the one Challa had wounded in the thigh, and it was over.

The man tenderly touched the wolf's neck and pressed his forehead against the massive beast's skull, looking for all the world like one of the dusky Night Riders from Katima Mulalo with their beloved horses.

Challa was a bit put off when the man assumed a defensive posture next to the wolf as if guarding it against the group of emissaries.

"Put your weapons down and unstring your bows," Ralec con'Nar quietly commanded, "and follow me." With that, he stepped deliberately toward the man and wolf.

As Challa and Balad unstrung their bows, Challa noted that, outside of the Emissary, all had drawn their weapons.

The man looked very powerfully built, with a wild shock of light brown hair that was pulled back with a headband. He was dressed in soft leather boots with fur on the uppers, and a leather and fur loincloth covered his midsection. His weapons were a long, curved kukri-looking knife and a curved longsword that looked almost dainty, though Challa had witnessed its deadliness. Outside of several arm and wristbands and an open brown vest, the man was nearly naked.

"Well met, traveler. I am called Ralec con'Nar, of Calderon. We mean no harm to you and mean no disrespect in our actions," the Ambassador said with both palms exposed, gesturing vaguely at the rapidly gathering group at his rear. *"Some of my comrades are quick to act and less quick to think."*

With a start, Challa realized that Ralec con'Nar was speaking Elvish. Besides having to learn it before the trip, Challa had never actually heard it spoken.

Ah, this man must be one of the Rothar, Challa thought. *Those are the Humans that live in the great forest with the Elves.* He knew their tongue was closely related to Elvish, so perhaps the Emissary was being formal.

With a flourish, the man wiped the gore off of his blades and sheathed them with a practiced motion. Placing a calming hand against the growling wolf's neck, he responded. *"Well met, Ralec con'Nar of Calderon. I am called Timon."* With a pat on the wolf's neck again, he added, *"And this is Red Eye. What brings you out of the rocky wastes to the lands of the many waters?"*

"We are set to visit the Humans in Barranae to establish trade relations. What brings you out of your forests, wolf-brother?" the Emissary asked.

Challa was a bit shocked to hear Ralec con'Nar call the man that, as the only 'wolf-brothers' he knew of, were Human shapeshifters (both cursed and uncursed varieties) and the Wild Elves. With a lurch as he stopped, Challa saw the man's ears were quite pointed and stuck out from his head, along with his unkempt hair, which had blended in with the wild tresses.

An Elf! A real Elf! Challa was beside himself, though he suddenly began to take stock of his limited knowledge of their customs to see if he had possibly offered offense.

"We regularly patrol near the forest edge, and I saw this orc patrol and decided to engage them. There was scarcely a score of them, so the risk was minimal. I do appreciate the assist, though, Ralec con'Nar. Might I inquire as to who tossed the arrows in this direction?" The man—er… Elf—didn't seem overly upset if he was upset at all.

With another start, Challa realized the Elf had switched to the Common tongue to ask about him and Balad. The two stepped forward as Ralec con'Nar gestured at them in turn.

"This is Challa mal'Timma ban'Rondal and Balad mal'Selad ban'Alziz."

The Elf stepped forward with long, quick strides until both young men were within reach. He suddenly swept his right hand out toward Balad as if to strike him, and Balad instinctively attempted to block the blow. To everyone's amazement, Timon the Elf grabbed Balad's forearm and soundly slapped him on the shoulder in greeting with a huge smile. Turning quickly to Challa, he repeated the move, and Challa was disappointed to have half-reacted like Balad as if he were about to be struck.

"Challa, son of Timma of Rondal, and Balad, son of Selad of Alziz, it is an honor to have met you both." Looking over Challa's shoulder at the other four, Timon the Elf added, "It is my honor to have met all of you." Squeezing Challa's forearm with his left hand and grabbing Balad's arm again, he continued, "With marksmanship like that, I would not have been surprised to see pointed ears on the two of you."

Challa and Balad's eyes met in confusion as they instinctively looked at each other's ears. The Elf's pronunciation was strange, and his mother tongue gave the Common words an odd accent.

"Th-thank you, Master Timon," Challa and Balad croaked out in unison, even with the stutter.

Timon dropped his grip with a deep smile, and with another squeeze to their forearms, he turned back to Ralec con'Nar and said, "I have nothing to trade, but I would give these two, two arrows; one of mine, one from the orcs, to remember this day. Is this acceptable, Ralec con'Nar?"

Ralec nodded.

Quickly stepping to one of the orc corpses, Timon the Elf picked up a bow and a beautifully made quiver with green-fletched arrows in it. On the way back, he stopped long enough to pull two black-fletched arrows from the quiver of the orc. He must have dropped his bow in the melee, and Challa silently wondered why he hadn't just engaged the orcs from the safety and cover of the forest.

Almost as if he had heard the question, Timon the Elf spoke up as he brought the gifts to the pair. "Even Elves need sport from time to time." With another smile, he added, "There were only 22 of them. Between Red Eye and myself, it made for a good afternoon fight."

With the realization that their help wasn't required, Challa and Balad accepted the two arrows apiece, each as different as night and day. One was perfectly straight, with perfect green fletching and a razor-sharp hunting tip; the other was heavy and imperfect, with ratty, black fletchings that seemed almost haphazard with a nasty, barbed tip. One was meant for precision and deadly accuracy, while the other was built for damage and efficiency—night and day.

Ralec con'Nar extended his hand in farewell and handed Timon the Elf with a pair of golden earrings, "Timon and Red Eye of Legarotha, I bid you fare well in your travels, and if you visit the wastes, ask for me—or any of us—and you shall have a share of our water.

"Challa, son of Timma from Rondal, and Balad, son of Selad from Alziz, I thank you again. I wish you safe travels. If you ever enter the Legarotha, ask for me or my companion. You will always have a place by my hearth."

The rest of the trip was almost anticlimactic after that.

***

The stop in Ral Zanor to visit the Dark Dwarves was interesting. Their skin was even darker than the Mulalan horsemen, looking like glittering obsidian in the limited light of their underground home.

When the Qormit greeted them at the front doors to their mountain home, they wore strange conical hats of woven fiber to shield their eyes from the sun, even though the doorway was shrouded in shadow. Ralec con'Nar had told them it was because they were underground for so long that their eyes were sensitive in the even dim light of a shaded vale.

The Emissary gave their king a coffer of gold and brass filled with pearls from the freshwater clams they had traded for from the Yenishe traders that had visited the previous winter. In return, as a show of being open to trade, each got small buckler shields that were as hard as steel but weighed almost nothing. Each was indeed a masterpiece of art.

After a feast, the party departed en route to Mellaron, which they reached just before dusk the following day. The great walls were imposing, and the entire group felt diminished by their sheer mass. There were a number of small encampments outside the walls, and they were closely watched as they approached the wall and the massive gate at its center.

A small pedestrian door opened at the base of the gate, and a short man dressed in leather and furs stepped out. He was easily a hand shorter than all of the Al'Ham, and his clothing was all leather and fur, from his furry hat to his fur-trimmed boots. Challa didn't see a bit of woven fabric on the man's person at all. In his hands was a tablet covered in wax and a stylus in his other hand.

In the Common tongue, the fur-clothed man asked, "What is the point of origin, names, and purpose of the visit?" He was perfunctory to the point of being rude.

"We hail from the nation of Calderon. I am Emissary Ralec mal'Kresh ban'Alta con'Nar," The Emissary replied.

The man's eyes never left the tablet as his hand fairly flew across it as he made marks upon it.

Ralec con'Nar introduced the rest of the party and then added, "We come with gifts for your great Chieftain, Khagan Varian Aletus. We have no intention of formal trading within your fine nation."

The man sniffed almost dismissively. "Thank you, Ralec mal'Kresh ban'Alta con'Nar. We will check out the records and get back to you as soon as possible. Please establish a camp outside the wall anywhere there is space." Without another word or gesture, he turned on his heel, knocked twice upon the door, and went back within the massive wall.

"Our destiny is in his hands," Ralec con'Nar said. "Let us establish a camp, as we may be here for days or weeks."

Even Balad grew concerned. "Days or weeks? Surely not!!"

Ralec con'Nar was almost apologetic. "They must check our names against a great archive of names of merchants and visitors to ensure nobody in our ancestral lines cheated or offended them. If our names are clear, then we will be admitted." With a shrug, he added, "If not, then that person or people will be forbidden entry, if not the entire party."

"That is almost barbarically bureaucratic, Ralec con'Nar." Balad was less than impressed.

"It is their way," was all Ralec con'Nar could respond.

After camp had been established, merchants and guards from other encampments came over to greet the party and inquire about their purpose and willingness to trade. They were soon left alone when they stated their intentions and steadfastly refused to trade. Ralec con'Nar quietly announced that a guard would be posted that night—two men per shift. His sidewise glance let the entire party know he did not trust their neighbors.

Fortunately for any possible interlopers, the night passed quietly.

The following morning, the small door opened again, and a similarly dressed woman emerged, loudly announcing, "Master Eborian and the trading envoy from Legaroth, please advance."

With muted cheers, one of the groups began breaking down camp, and their leaders went up to speak with the fur-clad figure.

After a muted conversation, the person Challa took as Master Eborian turned and announced, "We're cleared to enter except for Mellian and Saral." A man and a woman from the rapidly packing camp howled loudly in protest. Master Eborian quietly spoke with them, and Challa saw coins exchange hands as the two were paid for their time and were dismissed.

With sagging shoulders, the two grabbed their gear and began walking away from the gate and wall. The others finished packing and quickly loaded their gear onto small carts drawn by single oxen. In single file, they approached the main gate, which was cracked open to admit them. Then the clerk reentered through the small door, and everything grew quiet again.

Shortly after noon, the small door opened again, and another clerk emerged, announcing, "Ralec mal'Kresh ban'Alta con'Nar and the emissaries from Calderon, please approach. When they had all gathered around the clerk, he quietly said that all had been granted admittance and that their actions would be recorded for future visits as well as for visits of their descendants.

Challa suddenly realized why it took so much time!

The trip through Mellaron to Barrannen was quiet, though beautiful. The Barranaean cities were almost all built into the walls of the steep mountains, with bright-colored paint on the walls and many-colored roof tiles. Great tubes of solid stone rose like giant earthworms along the steep slopes, and Ralec con'Nar explained that they served as chimneys for every home that they passed by, drawing the smoke up to the peaks of the ridgelines along the mountains, keeping it from choking out each level of the house above the last. Challa thought it was ingenious.

A wide, straight river traversed the entire valley, and Ralec con'Nar explained that it was man-made, a great canal. They made a detour to check it out.

When Challa reached in to get a sip of water, he was shocked at the temperature. "It's warm water!" he exclaimed.

"The river is fed by a lake that is, in turn, fed by heated springs that provide water for the entire nation. In the winter, they never freeze and produce a fog that can freeze unsuspecting animals and travelers to the ground as it settles as dew," the Emissary explained.

The very thought brought smiles to the entire group.

In addition to the strange communities built into the mountainsides and the strange canal, there were wide swathes of beautiful mountain blooms of every color of the rainbow throughout the valley. Ralec con'Nar warned the younger men that the Barranaeans spoke in the languages of flowers, and if they picked any blooms, locals may misinterpret the flowers chosen, so it was safer to leave them where they were. Everyone heeded the wise advice, though they appreciated the blooms from afar.

Once at Barrannen, it was only a few hours wait to be seen by the Chieftain, Khagan Aletus. Ralec con'Nar stepped aside and let Balad speak for the entourage. Challa was surprised by this, but it must have been set up beforehand, and it also explained why Balad had been so nervous as they approached the capital.

The meeting was short, and the Khagan seemed appreciative of the ornate ceremonial shield they had carried so carefully from their homeland. He inquired if the group had any trade goods they might wish to part with. With that, Ralec con'Nar withdrew a wrapped bundle from his pack that the party hadn't seen. Motioning for Challa and another escort, he quickly unwrapped a large silken cloth of the whitest white. They grabbed opposite ends and unfurled it to lay it down on the ground as a trading cloth. Once in place, they stepped back into place as Ralec con'Nar deftly unwrapped and arranged almost all of the packed trinkets they had hauled from Calderon. Ralec con'Nar then knelt at the long side of the crescent trading cloth and waited.

Over his shoulder, he quietly said, "Take three steps back."

Not understanding, the group did as he bid, and the Khagan waved his hand. The assembled guards in the throne room stepped forward to stand beside each of the assembled Al'Ham. Once in place, the Khagan personally approached, kneeling opposite Ralec con'Nar to view the wares. The trading was done within moments, with Khagan Aletus picking up some trinkets for his queen consort and son. In return, the Khagan deposited gold and silver trade ingots onto the cloth where each item had been placed, so it was clear that the ingots were in trade for those specific items.

Challa heard the guard next to him clear his throat several times before the guard eventually lightly touched his upper arm. Turning his gaze toward the guard, Challa saw him meaningfully touch an ornate golden dagger at his waist, looking down at it repeatedly as if conveying some secret message for only him. Challa nodded slightly to give his assent, and the guard gave him a small smile as he sighed in relief.

The Khagan finished up and thanked Ralec con'Nar for trading with him, and with a low bow as he knelt there, Ralec con'Nar began to very quickly pack up the items on the trading cloth as the Khagen returned to his seat upon his throne.

In no time at all, Ralec con'Nar finished, and Balad stepped forward to thank the Khagan for his hospitality and the opportunities to open limited trade between the two nations. Negotiations at an end, the party all bowed and backed out of the throne room.

At the other side of the door, Ralec con'Nar asked their guide where they were to set up, and Challa grew confused—trading had been conducted; why were they to set up again?

The dignitary motioned the group to follow him, and they quickly found an antechamber where Ralec con'Nar set up again. A new group of guards came in, followed closely by a regal-looking woman and a young boy about ten or twelve years of age, both wearing small coronets that denoted their position as Khagan's queen consort and their son.

This time, Challa noted that all of the items they had carried from Calderon were on the trading cloth, with a line of the ingots the Khagan had traded in a line between the previously viewed items and those that Ralec con'Nar hadn't displayed for the Khagan to see. The queen knelt at the opposite side of the cloth with her son standing at her side. With a few words between them, they chose their items and traded jewelry for the items, unlike the Khagan. The boy had chosen a pair of gold and silver filigreed knives that were close enough to match to be a set, while the queen consort chose several rings, one of which was obviously a man's ring, obviously to be given as a gift to her husband.

Without a word, the queen nodded at Ralec con'Nar, and the audience was done. After she departed, most of the guards followed her, and within seconds of their departure, the sounds of pounding boots on flagstones arose from beyond the door. Challa and the others were alarmed, but the remaining guards seemed nonplussed. Coming to an end at the other side of the door, there was a quiet knock that seemed out of place, considering the noise the moments before.

Opening the door, the guards revealed the noise had come from the previous guard detachment in the throne room. As they rushed in, all out of breath, the one that had nudged Challa's arm made eye contact and made a beeline to greet him. Not knowing each other's languages slowed things down for a bit, but it was obvious that the guard wanted to trade his golden dagger for something of Challa's. Not knowing what to trade, Challa knelt to arrange his possessions in a crude crescent shape, imitating the trading cloth. Confused, the guard also knelt and watched.

The man's eyes lit up when Challa came to his old buckler shield. When Challa allowed him to handle it, he, in turn, checked out the golden dagger. Truly a work of art, the dagger was clearly worth more than a plain, if masterfully crafted buckler. When the man grasped the shield as if claiming it and nodded his head at Challa to indicate his willingness to accept the trade, Challa shook his head in the negative because it wasn't an equal trade—the golden dagger was worth much more than his buckler. The man looked concerned and crestfallen at the thought that the deal may not go through.

Not seeing anything of appropriate value, Challa panicked. In desperation, he cast about for something that might equal the value of the exquisite dagger. Trying to calculate in his head, Challa's hand came to rest on the knife on his belt. Then, inspiration hit.

It wasn't beautiful, but it was of masterwork quality. It had been his father's until he had come of age, and his father's before him in like fashion. Outside of sentimental value, it was just a well-made knife. But, combined with the value of the buckler, the guard may well accept the difference in values.

Challa took the knife from its place on his belt and gestured for the buckler to be placed on the ground. The guard's shoulders slumped at the thought that he may not get the buckler, but he did as he was bid.

With an open palm, Challa placed his knife atop the buckler and indicated the two items. Then, turning his palm down, he touched the floor near the golden dagger to indicate his willingness to offer the trade. The guard's eyes opened wide, and his mouth dropped open. Almost plaintively, the guard voiced his doubt about the values, and Challa suddenly wondered if he had offended the man.

Grasping the knife almost reverently, the guard turned it over in his hand and partially drew the blade where he saw the telltale designs of the layered steel. It was more than obvious that the man truly desired the knife. With a hopeful look on his face, the guard gently pushed the golden dagger toward Challa.

Steadfast in his appraisal abilities, Challa shook his head in the negative again and motioned for the man to place the knife on the buckler again. Confusion and frustration crashed over the guard's face as he placed the knife back on the small shield, though the expression froze when Challa pushed the buckler and knife toward the man's knee and, with his palm down again, pulled the golden dagger toward his knee just a touch.

The guard looked at Challa and then back at the buckler and blades on the floor between them. Realization began to dawn across his face, and the guard tentatively reached down and pulled the knife and buckler toward himself. Then, he met Challa's gaze as he gingerly pushed the golden dagger closer to Challa's knee.

When Challa nodded, the look of sheer joy and relief that came over the man's face made Challa smile. Eagerly grabbing the buckler with the knife atop, the guard stood and exclaimed something that Challa took to be 'happiness' in the trade. Then, catching himself, he placed the buckler and knife beneath his arm and bowed low to Challa. In turn, mimicking the actions of Ralec con'Nar, Challa bowed where he was on the floor, touching his forehead to the pavers.

When he arose, the guard was still towering over him, with a look of sheer jubilation on his face. Saying something that Challa could only take as, "Thank you," the guard fairly ran away with his newly acquired bounty. Challa picked up the golden dagger and slid it into place beneath his waistbelt.

Overall, it was an amazing trip, and Challa had a beautiful golden dagger and the accompanying story to give his son one day, should he ever have one.

Yes. It was a good trip.

Valmar the Innkeeper

Another good night, thought Valmar, adding with a small chuckle, *things are looking up for once.*

While he wasn't that far in debt, things had been tight at the tavern for several months since most of the regulars had all been called up in the Jarl's militia. The latest war with the orcs was stretching into its second year, and while it wasn't usual, the Jarl had made the call to the local militia members to augment his standing army.

Absently wiping a freshly washed mug, Valmar considered the call-up.

A few of the more seriously wounded regulars had been brought back to Vestak: Oron with his missing arm—his days of raiding were over—Royo the Tall with those burn scars from some sort of 'hellfire' as Royo described it, and Abreka were the three that immediately sprang to his mind.

Abreka was the most worrisome. Sure, Oron was his cousin, and Royo was his late wife's cousin, and he considered them both brothers. Their injuries felt almost personal to him, but Abreka was different. All she did was stare. When she was slowly led outside to sit in the sun, her sightless eyes would find a darker shadow, and she would stare in that direction for as long as you let her. Even when her husband, Kyre, wandered away to get drunk, she was found on her customary perch, still staring into the darkness.

As sad as that was, the sudden bursts of maniacal screaming were much worse. Without warning, Abreka would start screaming at whatever she saw in the distance. On the few occasions she managed words, they were always "They come" or something similar. Every time she panicked like this, it would last for several minutes before she finally lost consciousness. Valmar worried that her mind had been broken by what she had seen on the battlefields, but he knew she had years of experience on raids to the South and battles with orcs and giants. She had been fearless before she left. Cousin Oron had mentioned that the orcs seemed to have assistance from some sort of dark powers but never discussed it further, even when prompted or when Valmar plied him with many ales. Valmar did note that when his cousin spoke of it, he always tapped his left breast with his right fist to ask Orond for his blessings.

Valmar was a simple man, having lived a good life by Giali's standards. He had served in the Jarl's army for fifteen years before finding that small coffer of gold. That windfall was enough to buy his retirement and even pay nearly all of what this small tavern had cost. He'd gone on raids a few times since then, but he found that although he still enjoyed the thrill of battle, he wasn't as young as he used to be.

In the twenty years since he left the Jarl's service, his life in town had made him take notice of his advancing years even more. He smiled ruefully, rubbing his expanding belly as he set down the over-cleaned mug next to its brethren on the rack behind the bar.

He had even found a woman who agreed to be his wife after seeming to avoid him for a couple of years. Gwenna had been pleasant-looking with a hearty laugh that brightened even the foulest of moods. She had even given him four children, three of whom still lived. Two had found service in the Jarl's army, while little Ronna had become a cooper.

Valmar absently patted a barrel of ale. She had made every barrel in his tavern and most of them in the rest of the town.

That left Gwenna—Valmar winced at his wife's memory—his eldest child. She had been named after her mother, and as she grew, it was obvious that she would grow up to be a twin of his beloved wife. It had been three years since the ogre had been found raiding local farms. Every available hand had grabbed sword and axe to hunt the thing down, and it had to have been Gwenna that found him.

She didn't even know of the danger. Tears began filling Valmar's eyes as he remembered. She'd just gone into the barn to check on afternoon eggs when the ogre erupted out of a mound of hay and struck her down. Valmar's wife heard the ruckus from inside their small home and went out to investigate. It was her screams that alerted the militia. Her last scream was what Valmar had heard—the scream that was cut short.

After the beast was dead, Gwen had lived long enough to tell the militia what she had found, and that was when Valmar arrived. She looked at her horrified husband, gently squeezed his hand, and said, "Remember me well, my sweet." The memory ripped his heart as much now as it had then, and Valmar hung his head as the sobs came. Though the tavern was now empty, it wouldn't have mattered if anyone witnessed his pain; the whole town knew of it.

Morning came, as it always did, but today, it came with a light mist and the threat of afternoon rains. It always seemed to be that way—a heavy dew followed by fog, then mist, until finally giving way to large, lazy raindrops that lasted through the day. Valmar silently prayed that today's rain ended before dusk before it could ruin today's business. Even old drinkers disliked going out in the rain for an ale or four.

From nowhere, a low rumble of thunder rolled across the hidden heavens. *Hmmm,* Valmar thought. *Early thunder means earlier storms, but earlier storms mean harder storms.* His prayers included asking for mercy from truly damaging storms.

Two of his regulars had found their way in early to beat the storm: Oren, the lumberjack, and Tomas, the retired cooper who had trained his little Ronna in her trade before he took leave of his career. Well, second career, as the vast majority of the Giali in this village were raiders first before settling into less dangerous careers when they realized their mortality—and before they met their end.

Their silent reverie (and Oren's pipe) was interrupted by a brilliant flash of light and an explosion of sound from outside. Valmar didn't hear his wooden mug fall on the floor from surprise, but he noticed the high arch of Oren's pipe as it sailed across the room and crashed on the rough cobbles of the stone floor. Oren's wail of despair was all Valmar could hear as the door slammed open, and a cloaked man rushed inside, only to turn and secure the door behind him.

"I swear by the gods that I had nothing to do with that! I was wondering which one I may have offended," the figure said.

Valmar could hear the smile in the voice as the figure turned and pushed his hood back. The man's dark brown skin and black hair surprised him, but not as much as it had Tomas.

"By the gods," Tomas exclaimed, "A horse demon!"

The black man's smile was as large as it was brilliant white. "No horse today, I'm afraid. I was in a hurry, and when I heard a storm was expected, I didn't want to have to ask Master Valmar here to let my mount inside to keep her dry and safe." The smile and tone were disarming until Valmar realized that the stranger seemed to know him.

"I-I-I meant no disrespect," Tomas stammered. "We just don't get many horse demons — erm... Mulalalan-ans around these parts, and it kind of shook me, along with that lightning strike."

"No offense taken, kind sir." The stranger's friendly tone didn't change. "Excuse me as I change out of my wet clothes." With a wave of his hand and an accompanying scent that Valmar swore smelled of cinnamon, the man's dripping cloak and breaches kind of smeared, and the coloring seemed to bleed out of them.

Before the men could fully grasp what was happening, the stranger stood before them, now dressed in long white robes with an ornate longsword strapped to his left hip.

"Master Wizard," Valmar squeaked out. "I was... we were... nobody expected... a visit from a Wizard in this sleepy town today. What have we done to earn such an honor on this wet day?"

Lightning struck again, but not as close as the rain truly picked up outside.

"First things first, before we get to the niceties." With another wave of his hand, the Wizard somehow picked up the pieces of Oren's pipe that had been scattered on the pavers all at the same time, and they swirled around in front of him. The pieces of the white clay bowl melded together and fit into the long stem as they came together. Catching the repaired pipe in his long-fingered hand, the ebony-skinned Wizard walked toward the bar and held it out to Oren, who gingerly took it from him, staring at it in amazement as he turned it back and forth to try to see the non-existent cracks or seams. "I did the best I could. I'm no artist, but I know a well-made—and well-loved—pipe." With a flourish, the Wizard pulled another white clay pipe from seemingly nowhere. The resemblance between the two was astounding. "Master Blaylock from Vestak?" the Wizard asked of Oren.

"Y... wha— Yes, it was—IS!" Oren was flustered, as were the other two locals. "My son bought it for me last spring when he traveled to the west to see the capital. Thank you, Mister, uh... Master... er... Lord Wizard," he said, as crimson spread over his bearded face.

The Wizard smiled even more broadly. "Please, you may call me Josef or Wizard Josef. There are no Masters or Misters or even Monsters involved."

It hadn't been until he approached that Valmar noticed just how slight this Wizard was, the top of his head barely reaching Valmar's broad shoulder, and he wasn't known for his height, even in this village.

"My Lor— sorry, Wizard Josef, what brings you to this small hamlet so far out of the way on such a horrid day?" The lightning strikes were nearly constant as the heavy rain pounded the cedar tiles on the roof. Valmar silently prayed they would hold as he added, "And how is it that you know of me when I have never laid an eye upon you in my life?"

"Ah, yes," the Wizard seemed to smile even broader. "That bit... well, it would appear that I am in the debt of a man whom I have never met before."

Valmar's brow knotted a bit before he could smooth it out to seem uncon-cerned.

The wizard continued. "I have been at the Great Tower at Vestak for a significant time now—studying until I thought myself ready to face the dangers in the great unknown. Unfortunately for me, I selected spells that were woefully inappropriate for what I was to face," the smile grew rueful as the Wizard added, "I found myself surrounded by orcs without the benefit of spell or sword." He tapped the hilt of the weapon on his side and added, "I had thought this ceremonial and more fit for decorating a mantle than defending one's life."

The three Giali nodded in understanding, silently pitying that dark-skinned man before them; skill at arms was greatly honored here in Gedarian, and the idea of a man carrying a weapon for show instead of accepting its deadly purpose was shameful to them.

"The foul beasts were about to turn me into kebab morsels when this young man and his friends leaped out of the surrounding underbrush and engaged them. I managed to paralyze two of the orcs." He tapped his hilt again. "And I stuck this pretty thing through one of them when one of the other beasts fell upon me like a whirlwind." The three men at the bar leaned in at the story, eagerness clearly written on their faces. "I was sliced up pretty nicely before those Giali warriors downed the last ones. Without so much as a by-your-leave, they stripped me down to my smallclothes and began bandaging up my wounds. Hells bells! They didn't even know my name or my purpose at the time!!"

The men merely nodded—this sounded like typical Giali, and they could all see themselves doing precisely the same.

"Well, when they were done," the wizard continued, "I asked their names, and we became acquainted. Nice people, those boys." The Wizard smiled warmly at the recollection. I conjured up a feast for us all to celebrate my survival and offered to reward them for saving me. Three of them readily agreed, but the fourth hesitated, unsure of what reward he might desire. After the dinner and drinks later (I told you that my selected spells for the day were inappropriate), I told them that to honor the memory of my rescue and to honor them, I would name each of my wounds after them." He lifted his leg, lightly touching his calf. "This scar is named for Mikel, son of Mikel from Gedar. My arrow scar is named after Mildred, daughter of Olive." He patted his thigh. Putting his other hand on his left side, he said, "I was nearly impaled by a spear, and in memory of one of the youths who rescued me, this one is called Rikard the Wrong-handed, from Vestak." The Wizard's rueful smile made him seem almost... normal and average, but his dark skin and white robes reminded the men that he was far from average. "Master Valmar, I am in need of some of your legendary ale, and I have it on high authority that you've got the best in the region," he finished.

Without hesitation, Valmar turned to fill a wooden mug with the strong, brown liquid. As he turned the tap to stop the flow, he quietly asked, "Again, Wizard Josef, how is it that you know my name?"

"Oh, I'll get to that in a few moments." The Wizard was smiling almost playfully as Valmar set the mug before him. Quickly grabbing the mug by the handle, the Wizard took a hard pull, and by the sour wince, as he set the mug down again, Valmar knew that he either didn't like his brew, didn't like ale in general, or just wasn't used to drinking the foamy beverage at all. The smile quickly returned to mask his distaste, and Valmar began to grow leery of the Wizard's intentions as the dusky man was obviously trying to convince him that he appreciated and liked his ale.

"How many barrels of ale do you have in this fine establishment?" the Wizard queried.

"Oh, I figure I've got some fifteen, with several of those fermenting, so they won't be ready for a moon or two."

"How much do you think they're worth, Master Valmar?" The Wizard's smile was almost beginning to irk him.

"Well, I guess the ale's worth some sixty silver florins." Valmar began to absently wipe another empty mug. "Add to that the cost of my daughter's barrels, and I figure it would be some eighty florins."

Without missing a beat, the Wizard cut in, "I'd like to buy the lot from you, Master Valmar!" Valmar's hands froze mid-wipe.

"Ex... excuse me?"

"You heard me." The Wizard's smile grew even larger as if he was in on some epic prank.

"I... I could never... you wouldn't... you don't even like..." Valmar stammered worse than the first time he had spoken to his Gwenna.

"I am very sorry, Master Valmar, but I'm sure these two fine gentlemen," the Wizard gestured at Oren and Tomas, "would agree that you offered the fair price of some five thousand and eighty florins."

"NO!" Valmar fairly shrieked, "I said nothing about no five thousand of any-thing."

"Ah, so you admit that you offered to sell your stock to me." The Wizard's face was in danger of splitting across the middle from the smile that had gotten even larger. "Fine, then, fifty-one hundred florins, and that's my final offer. Dammit, man, top off my ale," the Wizard demanded, pushing his still full mug across the bar with a scowl, though Valmar noted the same playful glint in the man's eyes.

"Sure, Wizard," Valmar replied woodenly as he grabbed the mug, "but I never said anything—"

The Wizard cut him off. "Gentlemen, you have heard my offer of fifty-one hundred florins, and Master Valmar has agreed by saying, 'Sure, Wizard.' In any gentleman's land, that is a binding contract, is it not?" Oren and Tomas were dumbstruck but nodded absently. "Well, let's get the business out of the way," the Wizard said, a smile returning to his face as he reached into his satchel hanging from his shoulder.

Valmar noted that his arm seemed to reach in deeper than the satchel should allow, but what made the three men gasp was when the Wizard pulled forth two pouches from within—one of them was larger than the satchel itself, and there was no way it would have fit inside.

Magic, Valmar thought. His revelation was interrupted by the Wizard drop-ping the heavier of the pouches atop the bar with a loud *TINK* and jingle of what could only be coins.

"There's the five thousand. I hope you don't mind that they're all golden sovereigns, but they're easier to transport than fifty-thousand silver florins." The Wizard chuckled at what seemed like an inside joke.

Moving like a cat, he opened the smaller pouch and counted out one hundred silver florins faster than the men could follow. Valmar quickly noted that there were ten equal stacks of ten coins—almost as if the Wizard had planned this all along. The Wizard's hand shot across the bar, and Valmar took it without a thought.

Shaking Valmar's hand heartily, the Wizard said, "It has been a pleasure doing business with you, Master Valmar!"

"I—" Valmar started.

The Wizard dropped his hand and spun on his heels, heading for the door.

"Oh, son of a wounded basilisk! I forgot it's raining outside! Oh, BOL-LOCKS!! I don't even have a wagon to haul all these barrels!" The Wizard's shoulders dropped like he was defeated. He slowly turned back to the men at the bar. "I'll have to unload all this cargo in town." The smile was back, and his eyes sparkled with merriment. "If only I knew of an alehouse that had little to no stock that would be willing to take this off my hands." Striding back toward the bar, he announced a bit too loud for the conditions, "Barkeep, how would you like to buy some fifteen barrels of fine ale? I have it on good authority that several are still fermenting and won't be ready for a couple of months." The Wizard winked at Valmar. "How about five hundred ten sovereigns?"

"I... but... wait."

"Oh, damnable hagglers," the Wizard complained, still playing some private game as he smiled. "How about four hundred sovereigns?"

Valmar was getting desperate to figure out what was happening. "No... I—"

"Two hundred, then, by the gods!!"

"Uh... but—"

"Oh, by the hairs on the chin of a blink dog, ONE HUNDRED!!"

"I don't underst—"

"FINE!! How about TEN damnable sovereigns?" The Wizard's tone was terse, but his smile belied his serious tone. As lightning crashed yet again outside, the Wizard asked in a quieter voice, "Is it still raining?"

"Uh, yes?" Valmar answered. "But I'm confused. What game are you about here, Wizard?" Valmar was getting angry.

"You heard Master Valmar, gentlemen. He's agreed, and it's still raining outside." As fast as a cat, the Wizard scooped up the ten stacks of silver coins and dumped them unceremoniously in the pouch that remained in his hand. In a mocking tone, he added, "And he doesn't have the decency to pay me in sovereigns like we agreed," and with that, he dropped the bulging pouch into his satchel.

In his confused state, Valmar still noted that there was no sound as the pouch fell. *Magic.*

"You know, I have one more scar," the Wizard stated as he took another pull from his tankard, this time not even trying to hide his distaste. Wiping the foam from his lip, his hand continued to pull the neck of his white robes to reveal a nasty scar across his shoulder to his neck. "I was nearly beheaded by the last of the orcs when this amazing young man tackled me out of the way as his compatriots engaged the beast. I tried to reward him, but after thinking about it, he refused to accept anything, insisting that I give the reward to his father. He warned me that his da was a proud man who wouldn't accept it and would have to be tricked into taking it. I call this scar Willem, son of Valmar."

Valmar's jaw dropped. "I have a son named Will—" Suddenly, the truth of what had just transpired dawned on him.

"That young man is honorable and swore his father was as well. Well, also in this pouch is his share of the reward he would have received. I am sure, Master Valmar, that you will see to it that he gets it when he returns from Vestak?" The smile was kinder now. "It will be too late for him to refuse it when he musters out of the Jarl's standing army." Oh, the Wizard was truly enjoying this game. "If you will excuse me, gentlemen, but I must be off to my homeland." Adjusting his robes, Wizard Josef stepped back, and with a flourish of his hands and some arcane words, a door appeared in the center of the room. "Master Valmar, it has been a distinct honor to have met the father of a true hero." Rubbing his shoulder with that rueful smile, he added, "I'll carry the memory with me forever." With that, he flipped the door latch and pulled it open.

On the other side was a rolling tableau of grassland with many horses and almost as many people, all just as dark-skinned as Wizard Graeme.

Stepping through the doorway, the Wizard offered, "May the gods—and your ancestors—always favor you." And with that, the door closed and winked out of existence in an instant.

Outside of the driving rain on the cedar shingles on the roof, only silence remained.

WAWI AND THE DRAGON

Mannavegr was hunting, hunger driving him out from the filthy hole he had claimed since he had been freed from the giants' bondage. His grayish-white claws clenched, easily ripping through the frozen soil beneath his feet. He shook his head and repositioned his wings to support his rough attempts at stealth as his nose picked up the scent of deer. Staying low, his sinuous form wound its way to a spot where he could spy on his intended prey. The hunt was over within minutes, and he allowed himself to enjoy his frozen repast in the chilly morning air.

How the little beast had approached without Mannavegr sensing or smelling it was nearly as shocking as the sight of the human standing just meters away from him. Rearing up, Mannavegr unfurled his wings and roared as loudly as possible, fixing the human with a baleful glare, fully intent on intimidating the creature into a terrified flight that would give him a chance to chase it—and eat a second time this day.

As the deafening roar faded, the tableau was one of total silence—even the birds had stopped their incessant chirping—and Mannavegr was stunned to see that the human had not run away. It was just staring at him, mouth agape.

The human bent slightly to the side, and Mannavegr saw the bow with a nocked arrow as it was absently dropped to the frosted grass at its feet. Mannavegr tightened the muscles in his cheeks, extending the frilled scales around his head to make him look even larger than he already was. Instead of running, the human spoke.

"*Oda... am talvi wyrm...*"

The language was strange, but Mannavegr did not miss the fact that the human recognized the glory of what stood before it. The voice was hushed, and the dragon caught the sense of awe in those foreign words. The small beast continued to speak quietly—almost as if it were talking to itself—as it stepped, no, stumbled, to one side.

Mannavegr did not turn his body as the human moved; he just swiveled his large head to keep the creature in sight. He spied the human's eyes, scanning him, almost like his former giant captors had looked at mammoths when they were hungry. Mannavegr noted the difference in their eyes, though; this human beast still looked at him with a sense of wonder and awe, whereas the giants had only looked upon him with contempt.

Unbidden, the dragon's scales rippled as the anger and hatred washed over him at the memory. The sudden movement of his white scales elicited an exclamation from the human as it continued its clumsy circuit around him. For some reason, the beast's tone and expressions soothed Mannavegr's barely contained-rage in a way that he had never experienced before.

As the creature viewed his spectacular form, the dragon examined the human in return. Its arms and legs were spindly, like the young orcs Mannavegr had seen when he was in bondage, and it struck him that this human was a youngling. The flesh he could see was darker in color, like that of dried soil, making a great contrast from the Northmen in the area, but what really stood out was the human's hair. Red. Much more vibrant than the few Northmen he had seen before, almost like the flames in the braziers used to heat the irons used to... Mannavegr growled and shook his head as he felt the rage nearly boil over again. Like others of his kind, his anger was always barely suppressed, but how he knew this fact, he couldn't say, as he was captured before he had clawed his way out of his egg.

The beast stopped its circuit where it had started, just staring at Mannavegr, apparently trying to take in all his glory at once. Before he knew what he was doing, the dragon reared back on his hind legs, shaking his head and letting his wings catch the morning sunlight. As he fell back onto all four feet, the human squealed and clapped its forepaws together in what looked like... pleasure? It spoke again, rapidly, and seemed to be mimicking his movements in what could only be described as joy.

Two things struck Mannavegr at once: the first was that this man-child was not afraid of him, and the second was that he had just purposely displayed before the human specifically to elicit this response. He was used to the way that the cruel giants that had enslaved and raised him were immune to his attempts to frighten them, but the orcs used to run in terror when he presented himself as he had just done. The thing that really bothered him, though, was his unexpected move to get this human to express his adoration. This was new. Mannavegr truly *wanted* this reaction.

The human was speaking again—had it ever actually stopped? It was motioning to the bones and blood smears of the deer carcass that had been this day's meal. It seemed somehow impressed by this. Why? There was no battle; there was only a blast of icy breath, and the deer had become food. How could this impress the human?

It moved again, and Mannavegr instantly crouched lower. The beast was pushing both of its forepaws at him like it was telling him to stay where he was. The temerity of this creature! Ordering a *dragon* to remain still like a half-domesticated ice wolf? As he drew breath to growl again, the man-child reached down to pick up its dropped bow and arrow. It kept speaking and patting its other forepaw at him like he was asking him to remain in place.

Eyes narrowed, Mannavegr quietly inhaled as deeply as he could in case the creature raised the bow in his direction, ready to freeze the stupid beast where it stood. He had eaten man's flesh before, and while it wasn't his favorite, it did stop the hunger pangs for at least a while.

The human took a step away in the direction where it had apparently approached. It kept speaking and motioning at him and slowly backed away until it was out of sight. The dragon was stunned into inaction. What in the nine hells was going on? Why wasn't this creature afraid of his truly awesome glory?

Suddenly focusing on the sounds in the area, Mannavegr clearly heard the quiet sounds of the human's furry boots stepping as it slowly moved away. *Slowly?* Hesitations in the steps and... wait, was it HUNTING? A sharp *TWANG,* and he heard the frantic rustling of a small animal's death struggles. The dragon heard the human rush toward the sound, and the thrashing stopped.

From farther away, he heard the bowstring snap three more times, with two of the shots finding their marks. Then Mannavegr heard the steps—the strong, steady steps of the man-child approaching, and his rage rose as he remembered the approaching steps of the giants when they had drunk from those barrels of strange-smelling liquid and wanted to vent their rage on their draconic slave.

Mannavegr was about to unleash his icy breath in a mighty roar when the human just casually strolled around the tree like it was nothing. Breath caught in his throat, Mannavegr unintentionally squeaked as the beast held up two rabbits and a ptarmigan and smiled at him. Smiled? What was this creature *doing*?

Setting its bow aside, the man-child grabbed one of the rabbits and began swinging it in Mannavegr's direction. He didn't even realize that each time the dead animal swung toward him, his great head rose and fell like one of the half-trained ice wolves the orcs kept in their pens. When the rabbit was finally released, the dragon deftly caught it in the air like a mighty prize before dropping it to the ground at his feet. While he loved rabbit, Mannavegr liked it best when it was frozen, and he began inhaling to let his icy breath freeze the treat. As he felt the morning air mix with the draconic mist from within him to produce the deadly ice breath, he was again shocked into immobility as a small, dark hand reached into his vision and snapped up the rabbit from beneath him.

Growling loudly, frosty breath escaping from his slavering jaws, Mannavegr faintly heard the human speaking to him as he carried the rabbit back to the tree from where his bow hung, tying it to the tree with tiny nooses. From the same branch, it tied the ptarmigan and the other rabbit. Its words were unfamiliar, but the tone seemed conciliatory, and the dragon waited, fully anticipating a meal of two rabbits, a ptarmigan, AND a human within mere moments.

The dragon didn't even react when the creature withdrew a sharp knife from its belt and began skillfully slicing at the first rabbit. When the human grabbed the morsel and pulled the skin from its body in one deft yank, the dragon's head shot up in confusion. Moving quickly, the second rabbit was similarly skinned within just a few seconds, and the ptarmigan's feathery jacket dropped to the ground soon after. The human kept speaking the entire time, sometimes making statements, sometimes clearly asking questions that it seemed to answer itself.

The dragon licked his scaled lips as the beast grabbed one rabbit with each hand and then froze as it stopped and asked yet another question. It seemed confused by something, and it slowly turned its attention back to one of the rabbits. With a quick slice, it opened the rabbit's belly, and with two more quick cuts, the guts spilled out onto the ground. With a smile, the beast grabbed the intact rabbit and pulled it from the noose that held it. With no fanfare, the creature tossed the rabbit to the dragon in a high arc, and, not wanting the meal to disappear again, Mannavegr exhaled sharply to flash freeze the snack, then deftly caught it.

Chewing loudly, the dragon heard the human offering words of encouragement. Finishing the mouthful, the dragon looked expectantly at the gangly creature before him. Releasing the gutted rabbit from the tree, the human boldly strolled toward Mannavegr, seemingly without care. The dragon crouched low, growling deeply, ready to pounce, but the beast stopped just a pace from his great fangs and gently set the rabbit on the frozen ground, slowly backing away several steps before it crouched down.

The human began asking questions, apparently about the rabbit, as the delicate scent of the rabbit assailed Mannavegr's nostrils. Mannavegr took stock of the situation: the human seemed off balance and unprepared to attack—or defend—and while it still had the quiver of arrows at his hip, its bow and knife were both at the tree. Keeping his gaze on the creature, the dragon took a breath and froze this new treat. Not even blinking, Mannavegr leaned forward and took the rabbit in his mouth. Somehow, it tasted even sweeter than the last one, and the human seemed to recognize the dragon's reaction, and the constant flow of words became a torrent.

Rising, the human retrieved the ptarmigan and retraced its steps to gently set the bird before the dragon like a sacrifice before an altar, and Mannavegr realized that he was enjoying this. When the human retreated, though not as far as before, the dragon bent to examine the offering. He had never eaten birds before as they were so small and fast that he had decided they weren't worth the effort. With a quick breath, he bit into the frozen bird. His eyes shot open and locked on the young human. Slowly, he chewed that mouthful of meat more thoroughly than he had ever chewed before, savoring every bite. The human looked quite pleased with itself as it resumed its seemingly never-ending monolog.

Mannavegr settled down on his belly, wondering what would happen next. With a start, the man-child seemed to have an epiphany and suddenly jumped to its feet. Pulling a piece of cloth from a pouch, it smiled ruefully as it walked to the gutting tree. Smoothing the cloth out on the ground, the human gathered up the entrails of the rabbit and ptarmigan and, after carefully picking up the lot, approached Mannavegr as he lay there. Deciding the human's actions were benign, the dragon remained motionless as the human clumsily sat down just inches from his snout. Despite Mannavegr's nonchalance, the aroma of the entrails got his attention.

The human poked about in the mess and smiled as he pulled out a bloody heart, which he set on the ground before Mannavegr's mouth. As the wyrm raised his head to freeze the offering, he was shocked to feel the human's hand pushing his head away. Not realizing the danger of being within the dragon's reach, the human continued to root around in the mess, finding a tiny ptarmigan heart after a bit, then setting it down next to the rabbit's heart already in place.

Forgetting what had already occurred, Mannavegr leaned forward again and again felt that hand push his snout away. Feeling his ever-present rage rising again, the dragon rose higher to flash-freeze the man-child. Ignorant of its pending doom, the human continued. Curiosity winning out, the dragon held his action.

Within just a few moments, the beast had separated all the innards according to type, then wiped its claws on the cloth before scooting a few inches back and waiting—apparently to witness what was chosen first. Leaning forward to within a few inches of the human, the dragon roared with all the pent-up frustration, rage, and confusion he could muster, and as his great maw closed, he looked to see what effect he had on the puny human.

The horrid beast was leaning back on its forepaws with a huge smile, huge globs of dragon spittle dripping down its face. Quite unexpectedly, the human leaned forward and roared back at the dragon. The effect was ruined, of course, by the man-child's peal of laughter at the end, but, for its size, the dragon concluded that the roar was respectable.

Deciding the thing meant no ill, Mannavegr leaned down to inspect the prizes arranged before it. Sniffing deeply and nudging each selection a bit, a quick breath froze the lot, which elicited a shriek of pain from the human. Startled, the dragon looked up to see the human scrambling to its feet, stumbling as it rubbed at its knee joint. Mannavegr realized that its icy breath had also frosted part of the man-child's leg.

The human hopped about, hollering loudly, and the dragon heard pain in its voice. The pain, however, soon gave over to anger as the man-child began yelling at the dragon and jabbing its extended claw at Mannavegr's snout. It railed, pointing at the bloody furs at the tree, then to him, then to its knee, then to the frozen treats on the ground, then back through them all. The dragon saw wet streaks on the human's cheeks and actually felt a pang of pity for this creature.

Head low, scale frills pulled tight against his cheeks, Mannavegr quietly said, "*I meant no harm, human.*"

The man-child froze, staring at the dragon. Favoring his good leg, the human just stared at Mannavegr, eyes unblinking, mouth working spasmodically. For all his size and majesty, the dragon started when the human screamed, "Voit puhua?!" His injury was nearly forgotten, and the creature started leaping and cavorting about, yelling, "Voit puhua!" almost accusingly yet with great joy.

Finally settling down, the human then pointed to the entrails before the dragon and seemingly asked, "Well, which do you like?" The dragon looked down and, after a last olfactory inspection, gently picked up the livers, and the man-child seemed pleased. Turning toward the tree, the beast seemed in better spirits.

Cleaning and putting away its knife and recovering its bow, the human mimed what the dragon took to mean that it would return the following day, adding some sort of admonishment about its frozen knee with a rueful smile. Waving and offering salutations over its shoulder, the man-child limped away.

Mannavegr wondered if he would see the human again. The sudden recollection of the taste of gutted rabbit and ptarmigan made him realize that he would be pleased if it returned.

*****

"Talvi wyrm? Taaaaaalviii Wyyyyyyyrm??" The voice was faint, but Mannavegr's keen hearing picked up the sound. It had been many days, and he had nearly decided that the human would never return, but he found he was very pleased to have been proven wrong.

Slinking out of his filthy cave, the dragon moved quickly, close to the ground in the afternoon sun, to stay unnoticed. As he approached the voice, he redoubled his efforts to be as quiet as possible, in fully hunting mode.

The boy was wearing different clothing on this day but had a vile, bitter scent. This didn't deter Mannavegr, as he avoided last year's brambles to remain as silent as possible. Closer and closer, he crept, which was impressive for a dragon larger than a wagon with a yoke of oxen. Finally, within range, he gathered his feet beneath him and pounced, slamming the unsuspecting youth to the ground with a roar. The dragon felt the rage rising up within him as he felt the human squirming and screaming beneath his clutching claws. Overwhelmed, his head dipped low to bite when it struck him... the noises the man-child was making were indeed screams, but they were interspersed with laughter, and Mannavegr caught himself mere inches from the human's unprotected neck.

Crawling off the squirming beast, the man-child leaped to its feet as soon as it was free and, with much laughter, mimicked the pounce and takedown. When the dragon sneezed, the beast was pulled from its sad imitations and pulled the large satchel from around its shoulder. With a flourish, it extended a wrapping toward the dragon, and Mannavegr was ashamed to realize that it had reached out to smell the proffered gift, only to violently sneeze again. The human seemed quite proud of itself as it appeared to chide the dragon before setting the wrap on the ground.

Quickly untying a knot, the wrap fell open, and the aroma of liver rose up from the gift. With a quiet warning and raised hand, the youth pulled the wrap away, dumping the mess on the open ground before stepping away. A quick blast and Mannavegr dove into the exquisite treat.

As he reopened his eyes after thoroughly chewing the gift and swallowing, the dragon saw the beast had lowered its leg coverings and was exposing its knee to him—a knee with a mass of scabs with blackened skin at the edges—and Mannavegr realized it was from his frost breath on their first encounter. He leaned in to smell the wound and vowed to be more careful in the future. Extending his neck a bit more, the dragon sniffed at the wrap the human had used and sneezed again. The beast spoke and seemed to explain that the red, powdery dust was some sort of poultice, and it even sniffed it itself—drawing forth a huge sneeze from the human. This elicited a bout of laughter that Mannavegr joined in before he realized what was happening.

The youth sat down before the dragon and began talking, apparently telling a story, and the dragon feigned interest until Mannavegr finally said the word, "*Human*." The man-child's head snapped up, confused, but with dawning realization, smoothened the furrows on its brow.

The man-child pointed at itself and repeated, "*Human?*"

Staring at the youngling, the dragon nodded almost imperceptibly. This got the beast speaking faster than a winter zephyr until it seemed to get control of itself again. With no warning, it reached down and pulled its knife and sheath and, presenting it to Mannavegr, asked what it was.

Mannavegr looked at the sheathed blade. "*Iron tooth*," he replied.

The creature seemed confused as it repeated the word as it tied it back to the leather strap at its waist. It slowly rose to its feet and seemed to be having an argument with nobody at all, asking accusatory questions, pointing at Mannavegr, and then venting angrily as if trying to teach a reluctant ice wolf. After several moments of this, the man-child jolted as if stung by an unseen insect, straightened its furs as if trying to gain control of its wild emotions, and turned to face the dragon. It repeated the words it had learned several years before.

"It is with the most greatest and bestest honor that I greet you, lord dragon of the winter ice. I am Wawi of Barranae. And I would ask that you do not eat me."

Though Mannavegr had never heard this tongue before, he suddenly realized he could understand it, and their meaning crushed him beneath their weight, driving him to the ground before the man-child.

Mannavegr's mind wandered as it often did in sleep. Half-remembered visions and scenes that refused him entry passed by until he returned to the one that he dreamt of most often. A large, black bubble of impervious stone floated before him in the void. He had broken fang and claw against that bubble in his dreams, and not even his icy breath could crack the stone's surface. This time, however, it seemed different, and when he extended a claw, the ebon skin gave way beneath it. The bubble seemed to extend, enveloping Mannavegr, who struggled until he realized that he had been totally engulfed and that he wasn't about to be slain... or, worse, defeated.

Far in the distance, he could see a single light, and as he wondered what it was, he had the sensation of movement and was speeding toward the flame faster than he had ever flown. As he slowed to a stop next to the flame, he saw the yellow light illuminating a bronzed face. A strangely familiar bronzed face: the face of a dragon of immense size. Her voice was powerful, yet he felt no fear in her presence.

"Mannavegr. The giants that pulled you from the egg before you knew what you were gave you that name. In their tongue, it means, 'Eater of Man.'" The voice softened as if sorrowful. *"You have never known your kind."* Her face turned to look at him. *"I am Saratha, Herald of Apsu, Father of All Wyrms. We are great. We are mighty. We could rule all, but remember that it was the words of a*

fearless human that brought you back to us. Return now. Return to your benefactor and remember. Remember everything." With that, Mannavegr felt the sense of movement again, the flame moving farther and farther away. Then, all went black.

He became aware of a sense of warmth and cold, both of which were comforting. He felt a mother's tongue caressing away his worries, softly stroking the frills of his head. He could hear her voice, though her words were strange. He sighed deeply, totally content. His mother's voice sounded almost alarmed, and he struggled to rouse himself. The stroking of his frills continued as he fought to open his eyes, and he could slowly make out that distant flame again.

Slowly focusing, he realized that what he saw was flickering sunlight through newly sprouted spring leaves. Looking about, he saw that his head was resting on the human's lap, and what he had believed was his mother's comforting tongue was no more than the man-child's hand gently stroking his head. As their eyes locked, the boy sounded both concerned and relieved. Mannavegr lifted his head from where it lay.

The memories came flooding back. Genetic memories, the memories of a proud species that had lived longer than any other in the multiverse, memories that had been hidden from him because of how he had been raised, enslaved by giants from the time he had emerged from his egg. He looked at the boy and began to speak before he caught himself.

"How..." That was the language of the giants; he would never again use that horrid tongue. He lightly shook as if ridding himself of a bad memory, then spoke again in the beautiful language of Dragons. *"How long was I asleep, human?"*

The boy looked concerned and responded with unfamiliar words. He shook himself and repeated, *"It is with the most greatest and bestest honor that I greet you, lord dragon of the winter ice. I am Wawi of Barranae. and I would ask that you do not eat me."* The boy's smile was one of hope and a bit of shame, and Mannavegr realized that those were the only words in Draconic that the boy knew, and he had repeated them without a full understanding of their meaning.

"Wawi of Barranae, you have performed a great service to me, and it shall not be forgotten." Mannavegr smiled down at the youth and saw the human's smile broaden.

"Wawi of Barranae, se olen mina! Olen Wawi, olen alkane Barranae!!" The boy leaped to his feet and began cheering and leaping about like wolf pups do when they play. He had put together that Mannavegr knew who he was.

Barely able to contain his joy, Wawi stopped and pointed. "Miksi sinua kutsu-taan?"

"Wawi of Barranae, I am Mannavegr."

"Mah-nah-vay-grrr? Mannavegr? Sinä olet Mannavegr? Mannavegr? Se kuu-lostaa..." confused, the boy hesitated, then mimed as if he was biting, "Vegr?" It repeated this several times until its eyebrows rose as it recalled the older men of his village using the word. It was a word from the giants. The human pretended to bite at its own arm, saying, "Vegr" over and over until it recalled the other word root. "Manna." It pointed to itself, repeated the words, and then put them together. "Manna... vegr..." For the first time, Wawi looked frightened as the translated words made sense.

Mannavegr extended a claw and began scratching in the spring soil. A small figure next to a much larger figure. Jabbing at the small figure, the dragon said, *"Wawi."* Pointing to the larger figure, Mannavegr rose up on his hind legs and mimicked the rolling walk of the frost giants that had so recently had him in bondage. *"Jätti."* The boy seemed confused, but the fear was gone.

More scratches and the dragon told the story of the giants enslaving him and how he had been freed during a great battle. He tried his best to express that it was the giants that had given him the name of *Eater of Men*. Mannavegr took a deep breath and swallowed his pride for a moment, silently praying that his weakness would remain a secret, and pointed to the healing wounds around his neck where the spiked collar had been affixed. The spikes had been turned inward, so any movement of the chains that bound him was sure to dig in painfully.

Mannavegr was shocked when arms quickly wrapped around his neck as the man-child did its best to envelope him in a hug. Unfamiliar with intimacy, the dragon hesitated until the sound of sobs reached his ears, and he felt the little body heaving with body-wracking sobs. Totally unexpected, the expression of emotion caught the dragon by the soul, and it wasn't long before his own moans of sadness joined the boy's sobs.

"Waaaaaaawiiiiiiiiii? Waaaaaaawiiiii!!!" The dragon's ears picked up the voices in the morning light. *Morning light?*

With a start, he pulled his wing up and found the sleeping boy nestled next to his belly. The movement roused the boy, and he stretched and rubbed at his eyes as he asked a question. Leaning in close, Mannavegr touched his ear with a claw and pointed in the direction of the voices. Leaping to its feet, the boy made a startled exclamation and seemed panicked. Bidding the dragon to remain in place, Wawi bolted off in the direction of the voices, hollering loudly.

Unable to quell his curiosity, Mannavegr slinked low to the ground to get downwind of the voices and then silently approached. The other voices were angry, and the dragon identified both a male and a female from their sound and scent. Wawi tried but was unable to get more than half a word out before being angrily cut off by the other voices. Pushing his snout into a small thicket of dead brambles, the dragon caught sight of Wawi and the others in the distance.

A female: Mannavegr noted that she wore no armor but was armed with a large metal ladle. The male, on the other hand, was clad in thick leather and held a thrusting spear with a wide, wicked-looking head. *This human could pose a problem*, the dragon concluded. The adults were side-by-side, confronting a visibly chastised Wawi, and were loudly scolding him. The words were foreign, but the tone was clear. The male was angry but maintained control of his rage; the female, however, was different. Finally losing control, she snatched Wawi by the wrist and knelt on one knee as she roughly jerked him over her leg. As she raised the ladle to beat the boy's backside, Mannavegr charged.

The dragon had covered half the distance separating them before the woman saw him, and she fell back onto her bottom. As she tried to scramble away, she dragged Wawi with her. But in her haste—and fear—her feet got tangled in her skirts. The male blanched but stepped between the Mannavegr and the evil female, assuming a defensive posture.

Stopping at the edge of pouncing range, the dragon pulled out all the stops and did his best to instill the fear of dragons into these puny humans. The whole time, he was wondering how he could use his icy breath without harming Wawi.

The female was in full panic mode, and in her struggles to get her feet untangled, her grip loosened on Wawi's wrist. In a flash, the boy was up, and before the male could react, he had raced past the spearman and stopped directly in front of Mannavegr. Both hands extended, and the boy pleaded to the dragon. By the gods, he seemed to be defending those who would attack him! Momentarily caught off guard, the dragon hesitated.

Some internal powers in the female enabled her to shake off the dragon fear, and she stood, face white as winter snows, crying and screaming in anger and pleading at Mannavegr to get away from the boy. The male, however, did not speak to the dragon; his words were commanding and quiet, and he was telling Wawi to step aside. The male no longer had a defensive stance; his spear was raised, and he slowly advanced toward the dragon. Wawi placed his hand on Mannavegr's snout, and this snapped the dragon out of his battle reverie, and he focused on Wawi. The boy was crying again and seemed to be pleading. Then, quite unexpectedly, the boy spun around, turned his back on the dragon, and seemed to be defending Mannavegr from the man. Again, the man quietly ordered Wawi to step away. Again, foreign words but clear intentions. The dragon's frills extended fully, and he could feel the rage rising, ready to boil over.

Wawi pleaded for the man to stop, and it took a few times for the meaning of the words to reach him before a wave of confusion washed over his face. Looking past Wawi, the man's grip on the spear tightened, and he took another step forward. The woman was frantic as she plucked at the man's sleeve, seeming to urge him to attack. She simultaneously pleaded for Wawi to come back to her.

Mannavegr drew a breath deep into his lungs; one move to the side, and his breath would pass by Wawi without risk of injury. Tensing, the dragon started to lean.

The screaming roar was as unexpected as it was loud, reverberating through the spring forest, freezing everything in place as if transfixed by magic. All eyes turned to the source, and the sight was truly one of laughable terror. Wawi's dark skin had turned nearly purple from rage. He began roaring words, spittle flying in every direction as he stepped back and forth, arms sweeping in wide circles as he struggled to speak. Mannavegr watched with awe until he saw the face of the woman beyond the boy's tirade; her expression was one of shock, and it looked as if she could barely focus on the youth. This made the dragon look at the man, and he saw that the man had stood up, locking his knees. He had even raised the head of the spear as he witnessed the raging child. As Mannavegr made his move to expel his icy breath, Wawi's rage turned and focused on him, catching the dragon totally unprepared for the onslaught. The frigid breath was swallowed, and it *hurt*.

The rage didn't last long, but as Wawi started to cry, he went to the woman and took her by the hand. As if in a trance, she stumbled along as Wawi pulled at her and retraced his steps back toward the stunned dragon.

Stopping just a pace away from the dragon's snout, Wawi repeated the only words in the draconic tongue that he knew, "*It is with the most greatest and bestest honor that I greet you, lord dragon of the winter ice. I am Gucci of Barranae. and I would ask that you do not eat me.*" As he said, "Gucci," Wawi patted the woman's arm, and with a start, the dragon saw the resemblance in their eyes. Stepping away from her—and before he could react—Wawi gently put his arm around the dragon's neck and said to the woman, "Setta er vinur minn, Mannavegr." The woman looked positively horrified. Again, strange words, but the meaning was clear, "This is my friend, Mannavegr."

Wawi stepped to the side, gently pulling the dragon's head along with him, and motioned to the man to approach. Like in a trance, the man stepped up, spear before him in a barely defensive posture. "Da? Setta er vinur minn, Mannavegr." Releasing his hold on the dragon's neck, Wawi stepped up between the two and grabbed hold of their available clothing. "Mannavegr? Setta er ma og da," and he gently tugged at their clothes as he said "ma" and "da," the meaning clear. The smile on the boy's face was overwhelming.

Reaching out, Mannavegr opened his mouth and slowly moved to bite the spear's haft between the man's hands gently. As his teeth made contact, the man's grip instinctively tightened, and Wawi made some sort of encouraging comment.

Glancing at the boy, the man reluctantly released his grip on the spear. Mannavegr pulled it away and gently dropped it on the ground between them all. Wawi made a gleeful exclamation and rushed in to wrap both arms around Mannavegr's neck in a mighty hug.

"*Y-you no eat us?*" The man's grasp of the beautiful draconic tongue was truly revolting.

"*No, human, not today. Perhaps one day, but not today.*"

DAME ANNALISE

Annalise finally settled down into her feather bed after the long day. The ceremony had started right at noon as promised but had lasted almost four full hours—about three hours longer than it felt like it should have. There had been SO many long-winded dignitaries! Even His Royal Highness, the Crown Prince Matthew of Dybal, had said what he had to say in under five minutes; why did everyone else feel it necessary to drone on and on?

Then came the celebratory parties afterward. First, the newest Knights and Dames were honored by their respective Lord Graces, the various Dukes and Duchesses of the kingdom. His Grace, Duke Wenton of Asbury had personally come up to congratulate Annalise on her accomplishment. He even went out of his way to say that he would pay more attention to her family, the delCourtals, after the service she had performed for one of his pages.

The delCourtals were prosperous merchants specializing in importing horses from Thalaria until more recently, when they had the great fortune to start importing raw Ioun stones.

The stones were arcane gems and, when cut down to appropriate sizes, would float around the owner's head like tiny satellites. After being rough cut to about the size of dice, they could be further cut to various gemstone shapes and then have various spells cast upon them that would affect the owner as they revolved around their head. The wealthy and powerful just loved the items and, once ensorcelled, would pay a premium for them. So, this meant that her family fortunes had taken a jump in the past six years since she had started her duties as a squire under Sir Knight Mikel.

When she was old enough, Annalise was accepted as a page under Lesser Bannerette Dannel of House Rudd. She had spent seven full years learning how to read and write, as well as receiving valuable experience in the seven liberal arts and sciences: rhetoric, grammar, logic, astronomy, arithmetic, geometry, and music. This was all while running messages and doing various tasks and favors for the Rudd family.

She had delivered messages throughout Stormhaven, sometimes traveling many miles to deliver the missives. Most of the time, they were written messages, but on a few occasions, Annalise got to deliver the messages verbally, and that was when the pressure was on. She had to deliver the dispatches verbatim to the appropriate person and with the desired tone and volume requested.

There were times when the tidings needed to be given to a specific individual in secret and other times when a loud announcement allowed witnesses to *accidentally* overhear and spread the news to others as gossip and rumors.

Twice, when she was delivering written messages, she had nearly been intercepted by interlopers who tried to entrap her to steal the message. However, in both cases, she was able to elude them, once by worming her way through crowds of people in the street, the second time by loudly addressing a city watch patrol that happened to be going by. In both incidents, the representatives of House Rudd didn't seem overly concerned about potentially losing the messages; rather, they were concerned about her well-being, so that was nice.

Not two weeks after her service as a page and her start as Sir Mikel's squire, she had witnessed one of the men who had been following her following another page. Without a thought, she took stock of the situation. The young page seemed almost panicked, so he knew he was being followed, and there were precious few people on the street. Not caring about the consequences, she sidled up to the young boy and began to loudly engage him in conversation. She talked about the weather, how the autumn's harvest looked, and her service to Sir Mikel, making sure to show off her sash displaying his crest and those Houses he supported and who supported him in turn.

She continued her loud monologue until they saw a watch patrol, at which time she told the boy that she was sure the watch could assist him in finding his way to his destination. She also volunteered to help escort him if necessary.

As she turned away to lean against a building in a—hopefully—nonchalant manner, the boy murmured his thanks and approached the patrol. She waited until she was sure the boy was safe, and his tailing ruffians melted away into the nearly empty street before she went on her way.

As she departed the area, the young page subtly nodded his thanks in her direction. Sir Mikel had grilled her over what house the page was from and who he supported, and Annalise had to admit that she had no idea—she had helped purely because he was young, and she remembered her terror when she had been in the same situation.

Sir Mikel scolded her soundly for not ascertaining the page's House before helping because assisting or appearing to assist a rival House could foment rumor and innuendo. He explained that offering support to the wrong Houses could offend the Houses that supported him and their allies. The Game of Crowns was difficult, you see, and supporting the wrong Houses could lead to a disaster from whence there was no recovery.

He went on to offer examples of those who acted imprudently. Entire families were bankrupted overnight when business contracts were canceled, and creditors came calling. He told of cases where noble Houses lost their titles and lands, and all knights in their service were stripped of their warrants and commendations as well.

This all put the fear of all the gods in Annalise, and she swore that she would be more circumspect in who she offered aid.

Squire training was a little different than that of being a page. In addition to her usual lessons, Sir Mikel grilled her and his three other squires on heraldry. The grilling and lessons were so intense and detailed that, in very little time, she was able to identify most Houses at a glance from across the street, all while appearing to be looking off into the distance at something else entirely.

She also received training in weapon care and use, as well as equine care and riding. The only part of squire training she didn't like—no, that wasn't honest—the only part she LOATHED was dancing and singing, and it was because she was treated like a girl. Whilst dancing, she had to play the subservient partner, letting her male dance-mate lead her around the floor. Singing was worse, as the songs that Annalise was given were specifically for female voices and focused only on love and longing for unavailable boys. She much preferred less formal affairs where the squires were occasionally allowed to attend and sing songs of battle and of drinking.

But all that was behind her now. She had received her commendation as a Dame Knight, and for the very first time, Sir Mikel had slapped her shoulder before nearly crushing her in a huge bear-hug and whispering into her ear with a smile, "Dame Annalise, in private, you are to address me as Mikel. If you show up with Elven wine, you can call me anything you want." Had he not embraced every squire of his that received their commendations the same way, she thought that she might be offended at his familiarity. But, at least, now she knew what he had whispered to the other neophyte knights over the past six years.

Before the night's festivities were concluded, Sir Mik... Mikel had approached her and quietly enquired about what Duke Wenton had told her just after the ceremony. When she told him, and he realized that the page she had helped elude his followers had been in His Grace's employ, he smiled sheepishly and apologized for chastising her.

Having grasped the Game of Crowns long ago, Annalise responded, "Oh, Sir Mikel, the scolding was warranted and quite necessary. An error in judgment could have led to ruin for all involved; I thank you for your kind words of wisdom at my lapse." Quieter, Annalise continued, "It stung for a while, but the message behind the words was well-intended and well-delivered. Thank you." With a conspiratorial smile that was partially hidden behind her wine goblet, she whispered, "How was that?"

Mikel subtly saluted her with his own goblet. "You always were a quick study and good student. I feel that you'll do well in your new role."

Before the night had wound up, a servant of Duke Wenton approached her and said, "Dame Annalise, I have been sent to offer the most sincere congratulations of His Grace." He offered his hand, and Annalise saw something small palmed therein. "He wishes you well in your service to the Crown."

As she gently took his proffered hand, the small item was pressed into her fingers.

"I thank you and wish to express my gratitude to His Grace for the most kind words," she returned. The handshake ended, and she surreptitiously slipped the small trinket into her lace-covered belt. "I am sure that His Grace's wisdom and guidance will be most welcome and appreciated in the future." Bowing to the servant, she added, "Please, I would ask that he might hear of words of thanks and gratitude and my offer to being open to being of service to him in the future."

The trinket burned a hole in her belly all night until she was able to retrieve and examine it. It was a simple silver pin. On the face was a rampant owlbear, surrounded by a field of forest-green enamel, while on the back was just a simple clasp. Rampant owlbear... the left support in the crest of His Grace. She smiled. She had a new patron and room to grow within the House. If she did well and was recognized, she may one day sport the griffon that was emblazoned on the right support of His Grace's coat of arms.

As she attached the pin to her sash with the others, she did a quick assessment. House Asbury was powerful in the kingdom. Quickly cross-checking the other pins on her sash, she only found one that was in conflict with House Asbury, and after a quick consideration, she chose to remove it, but only after considering how its removal would impact the Houses and factions represented by the remaining pins. Seeing no apparent issues, she placed the removed pin on her desk with the others that had fallen out of favor.

Then came the hour of agonizing over the placement of the remaining pins, which was to be elevated over another, and how the various factions and Houses might react if they saw their placement.

Putting the thoughts and assessments away, she placed her shiny armor over the armor tree and put her sword on her desk, then she stripped down to her smallclothes and hung up her dress.

As she nestled deep into her down-filled bed, she thought, *Oh, yes. It's been a wonderful day!*

GRAEME THE TOY

Graeme was terrified, and the sounds of voracious eating within just a few feet of the rough sack in which he was so unceremoniously stuffed just made it all worse. He shut his eyes as hard as he could to try to block out the sound, but in the deeper darkness, visions of the horrors of his capture were suddenly replayed in his mind.

It was his first official job after being hired as a guard in training for the Redgrove Merchants' Guild. Oh, the title was appealing enough, but Uncle Bennett had forewarned him about what his actual duties would be. His title may be "Guard," but outside of four hours each night and daily sessions of allegedly "training" with his blunted spear (he secretly believed it was just a poor excuse for Sergeant Adair to beat him for being "woefully ignorant of anything resembling skill at weapons"), Graeme's duties were far from guard-like. Uncle Bennett hadn't been clear enough about how backbreaking they really were.

He spent hours helping the camp cook prep for the next meals—*just how many pounds of beans could they possibly EAT each day?* Hour setting up and tearing down the nightly campsite—and never fast enough—and even more hours tending to the oxen—nasty beasts with even nastier attitudes.

Once the evening meal was done and he had scrubbed the ridiculous number of filthy pots, pans, and sundries, he was able to stagger to his bedroll for some much-needed sleep. In eight of the ten days of travel thus far, he didn't even have the strength to actually unroll his sleeping blanket before he collapsed into unconsciousness. Then, after what felt like mere minutes, he was kicked awake to take his turn at watch, which lasted half of the night, before being able to get back to his underused blanket for what felt like another few minutes of sleep. Then the cook's toe would nudge him awake to begin prepping for the morning meal, and the routine started all over again.

Ten days. Ten. Graeme's perception of time was gone, with the hours speeding by in a blur of exhaustion and sleep deprivation. It was the morning of the tenth day when it happened.

Graeme was on his second shift of sleep when he was unexpectedly awakened by a wet thump that seemed somehow wrong, though he couldn't comprehend just how. He sat up and saw Sergeant Adair lying on the ground next to him, but this just confused Graeme further. Why was Sergeant Adair lying down while he was on guard duty? Why was he lying there in full uniform and armor? And what confused Graeme the most was why Sergeant Adair didn't seem to have a head.

The actual attack was over within seconds, and still, Graeme was confused. Three huge figures swinging equally huge clubs made short work of everyone else in the caravan. It wasn't until one of the towering giants pulled a swath of rough fabric from its belt and reached for him that Graeme realized he was in danger, but it was too late to even scramble to his feet. The oversized hand closed around him, and the last thing he saw was that the fabric was actually an oversized burlap bag that could have easily held one of the oxen. Without fanfare or even a sound, Graeme was unceremoniously stuffed within.

On several occasions when he had tried to get out or just to get more comfortable, the huge thing carrying the sack made him regret his actions; slamming the bag on the ground repeatedly. The first couple of times had jarred him and had even knocked the breath from his lungs once. The last time he tried to spread the threads of the fabric apart so he could see what was happening, he was slammed so hard that he actually lost consciousness. When he came to, he wisely decided he wouldn't move again.

In addition to his nearly overwhelming feelings of fear and dread for what may happen next, he started to get more confused. He could hear the wheels of a wagon and angry oxen and couldn't fathom the reasons. With all of the people slain—*oh GODS, they were all dead!*—what would the oversized marauders want with the wagons and oxen? The giants were definitely going somewhere, but why would they want bales of wool and big bags of rice? Why would they want HIM?

It felt like forever, but when Graeme's itchy prison was finally dropped to the ground, the nightmare worsened. The giants began to eat, and the moist chomping and low grunts would be a sound that he could never forget. Graeme tried to figure out what kind of giants his captors were. He remembered seeing metallic breastplates on the three goliaths, and they looked similar, so they probably weren't ogres or hill giants. A flash of memory hit him, and he recalled Sergeant Adair mentioning hearing rumors about ice giants, but Graeme couldn't remember any other details.

Oh, gods! If they are ice giants, they may be heading back to their mountain homes farther to the north! Granted, the caravan's route was to Peace Valley, which was also to the north, but he didn't know the area at all, so if he *were* to free himself, he would be truly and totally lost. His heart sank even further.

When a mighty hand suddenly opened the sack, Graeme recoiled. The huge thing said something Graeme knew was supposed to be quiet and comforting, but the booming bass voice jarred him nonetheless. A glance at the huge trio showed them all with greasy faces, and the other two were chewing on something, with one chewing bones that were snapping like so many twigs in its hideous maw.

The one that spoke to him thrust something at Graeme's chest, and without thinking, he grabbed it before it fell. The giant said something else and pantomimed eating, so the boy looked at what he guessed was to be his meal, and his heart stopped. In his hands was the pudgy forearm and hand of the cook, and with this revelation, Graeme's stomach revolted, spewing bile all over his hands and the cook's arm as it fell onto the sack. He even saw that some had sprayed onto the beastly giant's barefoot. The two other giants began to laugh uproariously.

The unintended target of Graeme's spray got so angry that even through his tears, Graeme could see its gigantic face turn as red as a beet. It grabbed its oversized club and beat at the ground between its feet as it wiped the vomit from its foot, and as it slammed the club down, it raged at the ground as if arguing. Graeme knew his time was up as the giant suddenly turned to him, and faster than such a huge monster should have been able to move, he grabbed the boy and stood up, carrying Graeme as if he were a child's dolly.

With a few strides, the giant tossed Graeme into the back of one of the wagons, and the boy landed atop a gruesome pile of naked bodies of most of the rest of the men on the caravan. The giant barked a loud order and mimicked eating again, and Graeme's legs gave out—the horrid beast actually intended him to eat... *PEOPLE*!! As he collapsed, his stomach again emptied itself, though there was nothing left to lose.

With more raucous laughter, the giant began bellowing again as Graeme's world began to spin. As he finally started hitting the wooden boards in the bed of the wagon, he realized that the giant was angrily pulling the dead bodies from the wagon like so much garbage, tossing them all on the ground at its feet. Graeme cowered near the remaining sacks and bales as the giant again bellowed out an order and made chewing motions with its huge mouth. Graeme suddenly realized that the giant wanted him to eat, not necessarily his dead friends, just *something*!

Looking about, he realized that the cargo in the rear of the wagon was all bales of wool, so he took a chance and peeked in the direction of the other wagons. Of eight wagons in the caravan and two supply wagons, there were only four remaining, all overloaded with bales and sacks, and it was only by luck that he saw a box on another wagon that he recognized as being from the cook's stores. He tentatively pointed at it and looked at the giant hopefully.

With a scowl, the giant's hand shot out and grabbed Graeme before the boy could react, and without even a grunt, tossed him some fifteen feet to the other wagon. By sheer fortune, he managed to catch hold of the pile and save himself from falling onto the hard ground below. As quickly as he could, Graeme opened the box and reached within. He could hear the giant's footsteps closing the distance as he withdrew his hand, holding up a large hunk of jerky behind him so the giant could see.

Peering out of the corner of his eye, he saw the giant pull up short and stop the downward slap of its mighty hand. Still cowering, Graeme didn't move as he continued to watch. The giant slowly lowered its massive head and sniffed the offered meat, at least gingerly taking it before smelling it more. Tentatively, it stuck out its oversized tongue and licked the offering. Surprise washed across its face as the boy saw the monstrosity had found the jerky to be quite tasty. The boy was taken aback when the giant spun around, yelled at the other two, and pointed at Graeme and the wagon. With spittle flying from its mouth, the boy realized the giant was warning the other two away from the jerky box.

The giant turned its attention to the wagon and pulled at the end of one of the tie-down ropes. Grabbing a bale of wool, it set it at Graeme's feet and, with a word, mimed the chewing action again. Graeme shook his head in the negative and gently explained that the wool would go to make clothing and blankets, not knowing if the giant would understand. The giant reached close and felt the texture of the boy's sleeping tunic, eyes growing wide. The giant spoke as its massive finger jabbed Graeme in the chest, then the bale, then again fingered Graeme's tunic. Realizing the query for what it was, the boy shook his head in the negative and did his best to explain that such textile work was beyond him.

With a snort, the giant pulled the remaining bales from the wagon and then spoke again as it poked at a large bag of rice. This time, Graeme nodded but pantomimed the process of soaking and cooking the rice over a flame. The giant nodded in apparent understanding.

It didn't take long for the giant to unload all the bales and sacks from the wagons and segregate out all of the other bags and boxes of gear. In no time, the giant had taken stock of the cargo and reloaded it all, though not as neatly as Graeme would have had to do it, especially under the watchful eye of Sergeant Adair. *But now, he's dead,* lamented the boy. *They're all dead.* He couldn't fight the tears.

The trip back to the giants' lair was uneventful, outside of the unending terror of the circumstances and threat of being eaten. Graeme was relegated to cooking duties, which was dangerous to all concerned due to his lack of experience. Fortunately, his few days at mess cooking gave him enough skill to not kill the giants or himself.

Back at the giants' large cave, Graeme noted that there was a high palisade built around the opening to cover the giants inside and provide a barrier to keep those inside from escaping. The massive gate was pulled closed as the wagons were brought in. Graeme started to cry again.

Within an hour, it was obvious that he wasn't to be immediately killed and eaten or, worse, just eaten, and his newly acquired leash and collar had been given to a young giant girl who was taller than Graeme's father. Along with the end of the leash, the young giant was given a stern admonishment of some manner; Graeme recognized the tone and reaction from the giant girl—she seemed to be agreeing to some stricture or command of some sort.

He was led around the cave system like some sort of trophy, with adult giants laughing and pointing. When a few had tried to reach out and poke him, the young giantess yanked hard on the leash, nearly breaking his neck as she pulled him from apparent harm. It only took a couple of hard jerks for him to stay close to the giantess.

Hours turned into days, and a welcome pattern developed. The giantess, and by proxy, Graeme, was relegated to cooking duty twice each day, and as long as he stayed close, the danger was minimal outside of being stepped on. It was obvious that the giantess wanted him to address her as *Tahsh*. She continually addressed him as *Igrush*, so it didn't seem that he'd be eaten soon, so long as the giants followed the human custom of not naming animals that were to be eaten, only those who would be around for multiple years. He prayed the custom held.

The giants were all huge, including an infant that was easily as big as Graeme was; the adult men were almost three times as tall as Graeme's father, and the women were nearly as tall. Their skin was black and dark bronze, and they all had red hair that seemed the color of flames. Most of them had gold and silver earrings and bracelets and wore loose tunics held with a length of rope or leather around their massive waists. The men also had iron armor that obviously weighed hundreds of pounds. Even their weapons were outlandishly large, and Graeme, or *Igrush*, stood no chance of wielding one of them, even one of their knives that were easily as large as a longsword but made for grips much larger than his.

The first few days were rough, as Graeme stayed hungry—the giants cooked and ate the men from the small caravan. Tahsh was upset when he wouldn't eat, and she found scraps of non-meat food for him to stave off the hunger. By the time the men's bodies were consumed, he was hungry enough that he considered the alternative and was glad when the choice was no longer available.

Tahsh was a prolific talker, almost continually speaking to him in her guttural tongue, and always insisted that he should be called *Igrush*. Each time he protested or tried to correct her, she, in turn, corrected him by yanking on the leash. At night, there was no respite, as Tahsh placed the end of the leash under a huge stone so there was no chance he could escape his captor.

By begging, Tahsh talked her father into allowing Igrush to cook small amounts of the stores from the wagons. Again, she was admonished and vociferously acknowledged her willingness to do whatever she was charged with. Graeme got the impression that it involved him. He hoped it was something positive.

The days melted into the next, with little difference between one and the next: get up, help Tahsh cook a huge meal for the oversized family, then clean up. After that, he'd cook for himself and eat. Then it was time to play with Tahsh, and each day was the same—it appeared that guests were coming, and they would pretend to cook for them, serve them, and then engage all of the specters in conversation. It didn't take long before he could understand some of the words in the giantess's tongue. Once Igrush translated a few words, they came much easier, and Tahsh was ecstatic with his progress, so she started trying to teach him words: this was a shovel, that was a pot, that was a cauldron, this was an eating fork, and that was a pillow. The only time it got confusing was when the topics of fire, stones, and rocks came up, and Igrush found that they had many words for each, depending upon their purposes and qualities.

Igrush panicked when he saw that he was on the last bag of rice. When he brought it to Tahsh's attention, she, too, got concerned, so she engaged her father.

"Father, mine, Igrush is nearly out of food, and it would be horrible for him and me if he were to run out. Could you please find more for him?"

The massive giant just grunted as he looked at Igrush. "We will send out a raiding party next week to see what we can find."

"Thank you, father, mine." Tahsh seemed satisfied.

While the raiding party was gone, the weather turned, and the first frost of the year covered the palisade and all exposed rock in the compound. The day the party returned, they had their first snowfall of the year.

The raiders brought back four wagons that were overloaded with bags. Igrush launched himself at the wagons to inspect the contents. He didn't bat an eye at the bodies in one of the wagons. Another had a pile of seven oxen piled in the back, along with a small collection of bags.

With each bag, Igrush cheered—rice, corn, wheat, beans, dried jerky, dried apples, potatoes, flour, and even a couple of bags of onions. Dinner that night was made for Tahsh and himself, and he treated her to what seemed like a feast—boiled jerky in a stew of potatoes, beans, and onions thickened with flour. They ate themselves almost sick.

In addition to the food, there were also three bales of various animal hides. Igrush thought he recognized a beaver, fox, and rabbit. The winter was one of supreme boredom. The men kept themselves busy smelting quantities of iron and steel and then forging weapons and armor for themselves. If any ore or pig iron were left over, they would make a pot, cauldron, or utensils for the cooking fires, but those things were definitely an afterthought.

Tahsh left him to his own devices more and more, and Igrush made himself furred trousers and a shawl to keep himself warm. They were crude and ugly, but at least he was warm.

The food lasted until the first sprouts of spring began to poke through the snow-covered branches. Again, a raiding party went out and, this time, came back with one fewer giant, so Segrum, Tahsh's father, was in a foul mood. He told

Tahsh that next time, she would have to come with him to get her Igrush food because it was just too dangerous for the raiders to do just to keep him fed.

It was only four days later that the raiding giants were raided. Spells blew apart a portion of the palisade, and then great cones of icy wind came blasting in, freezing several giants in place. Darts of black and red light unerringly flew in to strike giants, causing massive damage to the huge figures. Then the men came pouring into the compound, yelling battle cries and engaging the surviving giants. Swords and axes flashed in the sunlight, and where they swung they left evidence of their passing with great swaths of brilliant red blood in their wakes. Deadly arrows seemed to sprout from the giants' huge forms, though the boy could hear the incessent thrumming of bowstrings. To avoid being slain, himself, Igrush ran into the massive cave and just hid under his sleeping pallet.

It was over within a minute, and Igrush heard men coming into the cave from their stealthy steps, armor clanking quietly, and hushed voices warning everyone to remain alert for an ambush. Not wanting to be skewered where he lay, Igrush kicked the pallet off him and announced himself.

The men immediately charged and surrounded him before he could even squeak out, "I'm human, I'm a human!"

The confusion was palpable.

The questions came all at once, and many were repeated: "Who are you? Why are you here? How long have you been here? Why are you here? Why are you dressed like that? Where are you from? Why are you here?"

The young man stood up tall until they finally quieted. "They called me Igrush. I've been here almost a year. I was a part of an ambushed merchant train. I was captured. I dressed like this to survive the winter. My name is Graeme, but they called me *Toy*."

KELDRICK THE NIGHTWING

"Thank you, Tracker. We've been looking for this piece of dung for several months now." The guard captain was appreciative and readily handed over the obligatory pouch of coins as a reward for Keldrick capturing the wanted criminal.

"I learned of him after he hit my parent's shop," Keldrick Magnafari sounded resigned. "I'm just sorry it took so long to get him," he said, putting the pouch away inside his studded leather armor jerkin. "He provided quite a bit of info on his fence, so you can expect another reward paid out within the next moon."

"The fence, eh." The captain was intrigued. "That would be worth two or three times as much."

"I'll come in to negotiate it when I'm ready to apprehend them," Keldrick offered as he turned to leave.

"We'll see you then, Tracker. Good hunting."

Keldrick casually walked home, sticking to the shadows not so much out of a sense of protection or concealment but out of sheer habit.

He hadn't been born on the streets, though he was as comfortable there as he was at his parents' home. With a snort, he thought to himself, *I guess it's sort of our home since I paid it off.* He wasn't bitter about it; it was the least that he could do since they were responsible for getting him into being a Tracker.

Finally getting home, he went to his room to take his leather jerkin off and carefully placed the reward pouch beneath the loose floorboard with the others. Then, as the bath was being prepared, he stripped down to his birthday suit and waited.

'Maggie's Jewelry and Gemstones,' or so the sign above the door said. It only said that because *Magnafari* was too much of a mouthful for most of the locals to bother to say. Along with the words, for those few (and the foreigners) that couldn't read, there was the painted outline of a ring and bracelet and several raw and cut gemstones. Father insisted on a new sign every couple of years, while Mother and Keldrick both thought it would be fine with new paint. But Father was adamant.

"Would you rather do business with someone that cares for their shop or someone that has a ratty, old, re-painted sign?" his father would ask. "Besides, after twenty-five years, the locals expect it, and we have a bit of a reputation."

So, like the changing of the seasons, the sign was changed out for a similar but new design.

His family had emigrated to Thalaria from Barranae almost thirty years ago, about twelve years before Keldrick was born. Back in those days, things weren't as... pleasant... as they were now. Robbers and burglars roamed the streets with near impunity. Keldrick had grown up working by day in the shop and playing on those streets in the evenings, even though his parents hated the very thought of him being out there with the miscreants.

Keldrick ran the streets until he was in his fifteenth year, when, on a particularly cold night, the city watch had brought him home after being nicked trying to break into another local shop. If the guard hadn't recognized him, he would have been tossed in the dungeons without so much as a 'By your leave.'

As it was, for a few weeks, he almost wished he *had* been. Oh, his father was SO angry with him—angry enough that for a few moments, Keldrick almost thought Father would strike him. But, always the proper type, Father had caught himself before swinging and just struck Keldrick to the core.

"Your actions have consequences," his father began. "Imagine what other jewelers and finesmiths would think and say if you were put in prison or executed for some crime! Our reputation would be damaged to the point that we would likely never recover—our business—*ours,* not *my. OUR* business would be gone, and we would have nowhere to go. Is that what you want for your family?"

Keldrick had thought long and hard about it for the rest of the night. Father never mentioned the incident again, and Keldrick didn't give him any excuses to do so.

Two months later, the burglars struck.

The hit was at night, just after midnight. Keldrick heard something strange and went downstairs, where he saw three figures prying up floorboards to get to the bulk gemstones and precious metal ingots. Not expecting the trio, he audibly gasped, and the three stopped what they were doing and all looked up at him. In the moonlight and light coming in from the open door, Keldrick recognized two of the young men as being part of the crew he had so recently run with.

As two of the three ran for the door, one of the boys he recognized put his fingers up to his lips and whispered, "Shhhhhhhh," before joining the other two by running out the open door.

Though Keldrick identified both young men to the city watch as having been in the shop and they were picked up within just a day or two, however, since they weren't caught with any of the loot, they spent just a few weeks in lock-up before being released. Fortunately for the family, only low-quality stones and copper ingots were kept beneath the floorboards, so their losses were small.

Keldrick was disappointed by the entire ordeal.

In the following year, Keldrick worked hard in his parents' shop, and his skill as a jeweler grew. They were also burgled twice more and then straight-up robbed by a desperate pair of hoodlums who were armed with wicked-looking knives and clubs.

Keldrick was afraid this group would be released because of a lack of evidence, just like the other burglars. If it weren't for the passing watch patrol as the pair of robbers were making their escape and the fact that they literally ran into each other, the odds are that they would have walked away after a short stint in jail as well.

Because of the lack of justice in Thalaria, Keldrick decided that if the watch couldn't or wouldn't do it, the job of catching the criminals with booty in hand would fall to him. He knew he couldn't clean up the entire city-state, but he certainly could make life safer for his family, maybe even for the other shops in the Finework district.

He talked his father into paying tuition for entry into one of the city's fighting academies and stopped working in the shop.

There, at Kofal's Academy, Keldrick learned how to use a wide variety of bladed weapons, from knives and daggers to hand-and-a-half and greatswords. But what he fell in love with were the bows. He was in classes every morning, then spent all afternoon—and many times into the evening—practicing with short and longbows. After he was confident he could hold his own if pressed, Keldrick began sleeping on a pallet on the shop floor.

During the day, he kept a shortsword strapped to his left hip. Even being peace-bonded, he felt safer by a good measure.

Then, he began making a habit of visiting rival jewelers' shops just to check-in and ask for any gossip. He stopped in Otto Birch's shop the morning after it was burgled and eavesdropped on the City Watch Inspector as he went through the motions of asking questions.

After a couple more incidents, he began asking his own questions, and it was during this time that he discovered the difference between a burglary and a robbery. Burglars entered a building to grab stuff and run while robbers interacted with people during their thefts.

When he announced his 'graduation' from Kofal's Academy, his father surprised him with a gift—a composite short bow that was custom-made just for him.

It wasn't, but two weeks after that, the next group of burglars came.

His years of running the streets and skirting the law had taught him the sounds of the streets—what was normal and what sounded off or odd. The creaking floorboard of the porch woke him up. By the time the door locks had been picked, Keldrick was up and armed with his bow, with arrows set up for quick firing. Melting in the deeper shadows between two empty racks on the back wall, he waited.

The door eased open, and two shadows ghosted inside. Keldrick waited until they were both well inside before he let loose his first arrow, then three more followed it as fast as he could fire them. It was over before either figure could get back to the door, and both fell where they stood, wondering where the arrows were coming from. Each was only able to grunt as they died.

Keldrick pulled a chair up to the open door and waited until he saw a watch patrol approaching. Then, he alerted them of what had transpired and let them take control of the situation. After an initial suspicion that it may have been an ambush and double murder, the watch called in an Inspector who found bags of looted goods from the shop next door in a bag between the buildings. It also turned out that both were known miscreants, and one of them was one of the boys that Keldrick had recognized the first time they were robbed.

He felt a pang of regret and sorrow for the loss of one of his former acquaintances, but if they hadn't been trying to steal from the shops, they wouldn't have come to an early end.

Just a couple of days later, the Watch Inspector stopped at the shop to present Keldrick with the reward for stopping the criminals in their crime spree. The reward was modest but still enough for him to buy a nice studded leather jerkin. Keldrick had never considered that there might be a reward for his actions, so it was a pleasant surprise.

Keldrick began spending his nights patrolling the fine smith quarter. From time to time, he would take up positions to keep an overwatch along a length of street or alley, sometimes atop a roof, sometimes beneath the floorboards of a porch, sometimes just stationary in a dark shadow.

Over the course of the next two years, he was able to stop several robberies, assaults, and more burglaries than he could remember. He was also made an unofficial member of the City Watch—and the watch wanted him on full-time, but he refused.

Keldrick's skill with the bow increased with each passing month, and he began pinning his targets' extremities to floors, walls, or even the ground rather than killing them outright. The fine smith quarter was the first section of the city to be declared 'cleaned up' by the watch, and Keldrick's stash of reward money was evidence of his hard work. With one less section of the city to spend so much time on, the watch was able to focus on getting control of other areas of the city.

He didn't do this alone; there were others who joined him in his nightly forays—Dra'lon, another reformed street kid; Rotra, a former member of the city watch who had taken a spear to the hip and couldn't run anymore (or even walk very well, if one were being honest), Kaitra, a newly-minted Sorcerer, and a revolving wheel of others that came and went. But it was these four that were the core group. The city watch took up calling them the Nightwings.

It was just after bringing in the latest attempted burglar that potential disaster struck, and Keldrick discovered how much of a reputation the Nightwings had developed.

The group had heard a rumor that Talya's Treasures was being staked out, and a few too many 'non-shoppers' were paying attention to the shop over the past few days. Setting up a rooftop overwatch of the shop's back doors and putting Rotra, Dra'lon, and another new would-be vigilante inside, the ambush was set. Tonight, looking to change things up a bit, Kaitra was separated from the group in another overwatch location under the porch across the street in front, so all sides of the small jewelry and trinket shop were covered.

Just after midnight, the burglary began.

From a nearby rooftop, a pigeon cooed, which was very out of place at night. *Kaitra's familiar!* It was SO easy to forget that she had a familiar now! *She must have sent it a message to let out a warning,* Kendrick thought.

Keldrick made a mental note to give her part of his share of the reward money. The problem was that this was in the front of the shop, and his vantage point gave him a full view over the alleyway. Fortunately for Keldrick, this allowed him to see the gathering shadows of several groups of people massing in the darker parts of the alleyway.

From Talya's shop, Keldrick heard a heavy crash and the breaking of glass. *Probably a display case,* he thought. *Wait! The alarm was just raised; why is there action already? And who are all these people gathering in the alley?* Keldrick was on full alert. *What was happening inside already?*

From the street side of the building, he heard Kaitra's voice casting a spell. The sound was like ropes dragging across a wooden floor, followed immediately by several voices hollering and yelling invectives, then a male voice yelling, "It's an ambush! They're on to us!! GET THEM!"

Keldrick nocked two arrows at once but held his action. Below, the alley was alive with activity in the distance, but that distance was rapidly shrinking. Before he could act, the rear door of Talya's shop was kicked open from within. A crossbow twanged as it fired, and the bolt made one of the advancing shadows grunt as it fell.

A spearhead appeared in the doorway from the shadows within, and Rotra's voice rang out, "This is a set-up!" Then louder, "COME ON, YOU MUGS; YOU'LL NEVER GET US IN HERE!!"

Just like Rotra to draw all attention to himself to keep them from noticing anyone else in the group! From his vantage point, Keldrick could hear grunts at the front door of the shop and what he thought was Kaitra's voice swearing. *Totally unlike her,* Keldrick surmised.

The unruly mob in the alley surged ahead toward the now-open door of the shop. Holding his aim, Keldrick waited.

Another bolt came out of the shop with a *TWANG. Ah, it must be Dra'lon,* Keldrick thought as another shadow fell.

The group gathered before the door, loudly denouncing the Nightwings, telling Rotra that this was the last night that the vigilante group would operate. Still, Keldrick held his aim.

From the street, he could hear Kaitra casting another spell, then three loud bangs. *She must have opened the front door with her spell. I wonder why.*

From inside, he could hear Rotra hurling invectives and threats, keeping the attention on him.

The mob held back as a number of men armed with crossbows stepped up to take shots. As they quickly set themselves, Keldrick could hear Kaitra's voice again, intoning a spell.

"FIRE!" the leader of the ruffians shouted, and nearly a dozen crossbow bolts blasted into the open doorway.

Fully expecting to see the spearhead drop as Rotra fell like an inverted porcupine, Keldrick was shocked when he heard the man's voice. "Your missiles can't touch me, arseholes! Come up and taste my spear if you have the guts!!"

With a hoarse roar, the mob rushed forward.

Because of the doorway, only one or two men could engage Rotra at any time, and with his spear, they couldn't get close enough to strike the brave man. Suddenly, from nowhere, a bright light erupted at the peak of a nearby roof, and Keldrick barely made out a small bird that was glowing like a tiny sun to take off and fly over the alley to the other side of the mob. The rear of the mob watched the light warily while a couple of the crossbowmen began to reload. Still holding his shot, Keldrick waited, watching the tableau develop below him in the alley.

For no reason, suddenly, the mob of men crowding around the rear porch began yelling, and a large number of them disappeared without warning.

Then, Kaitra screamed, "NOW, KELDRICK!"

Keldrick knelt on the tiny landing at which he had stationed himself and let loose the two arrows he had nocked. One found its mark, while the other pinned a man's tunic to the ground. Quickly grabbing another pair of arrows, he nocked them as fast as he could and let fly. This time, he heard the crossbow twang from inside again as he fired. Three of the men fell.

As the men milled about below him, Keldrick could see a gaping hole in the ground in their midst, with more men falling into it like lemmings into the sea. Men screamed from below as more men fell on top of them.

One of the crossbowmen saw the arrow slam into his compatriot and hollered an alert to his fellow archers. As one, they turned. Unfortunately for them, the last target of their attention was the illuminated pigeon, and they struggled to make out any potential targets in the darkness.

Keldrick began picking them off one by one, shooting each as they seemed to be about to be able to discern his position. Then Rotra charged out of the door. The several men in front of him scrambled to stay out of reach of his deadly spear, and most fell into the pit that had appeared behind them.

Dra'lon's crossbow was firing so quickly that the twanging sounded almost like a bard's performance, and the mob fell apart. Men began running in every direction, not caring for their companions. As they ran, two more were shouldered into the pit.

That was when Kaitra stepped out of the door with a scroll in her hand. She loudly read the magical words inscribed thereon, and from the back of the parchment scroll, a network of sticky webs erupted and flew out to nearly thirty paces, where it spread out to attach to buildings on both sides of the alley.

Not being able to see the webbing, everyone that had run that way entrapped themselves on the sticky strands.

Keldrick turned his attention to the other direction, and as he fired his bow, the light source on the pigeon began moving past his position to illuminate the fleeing ruffians. This allowed Keldrick to pick off nearly a half-dozen more targets before they were able to dodge around corners and flee for good.

Running down the stairs from his landing perch, Keldrick looked over the edge of the pit to see nearly twenty men cursing and nursing various injuries from the fall at the bottom, some thirty feet below.

"How long will this pit last?" Keldrick asked of Kaitra.

"Only a minute. We must make haste!" she replied.

"Then make ready," Keldrick commanded as he nocked two more arrows. On the other side of the pit, he saw Dra'lon loading three bolts on his crossbow. Quietly Keldrick said, "That'll never work."

With a smile, Dra'lon replied, "They don't know that." As he raised the crossbow to the ready, Keldrick saw that, if nothing else, the weapon at least *looked* savagely dangerous.

Kaitra warned, "The spell is ending!"

She readied another scroll. and held a wand in her free fingers. Rotra spun his spear around his head and assumed a defensive stance. Between the four of them, the pit was surrounded on all sides.

Quickly, the pile of men disgorged from the magical pit like so many potatoes from an upturned sack.

"Drop your weapons, and you won't be harmed," Keldrick ordered.

Of the twenty, only four were still able to even consider attacking or running. Seeing their situation, they wisely threw their weapons to the ground.

The pigeon flew high above their position, then spiraled down until it landed on the peak of Talya's shop's roof. Quickly, the four men got busy restraining their former compatriots with rope lengths provided by Rotra. A few moments later, the city watch patrol arrived.

"We saw the light. What is going on... here...?" The query trailed off in confusion. The explanation took place as members of the patrol gathered up the men stuck in the webbing.

The guard sergeant's eyes grew wider with each added detail.

***

The reward was pretty sizable this time, as an entire guild of thieves and ruffians had been taken down. The Watch Inspector requested that all four be present when it was paid out, as he had additional information regarding the incident.

"It would appear that the Nightwings have made a name for themselves, and it's not all good. This was an organized operation to take you all out," he informed them. All four looked at each other across the table as he continued. "The Rotter's Association took particular exception to your work in the finesmith's quarter to the point that they sent one of their own to infiltrate your group."

Dra'lon responded laconically, "We knew when he tried to gut Rotra when we were getting set."

"Damned near succeeded, too. I was lucky I was wearing heavier armor than usual." Rotra didn't seem overly concerned.

The inspector continued, "They had every intention of taking the four of you out and taking over the finesmith's quarter as part of their territory." The four nodded with understanding. "As best as our spies can tell, only a handful of the Rotters made it out of there; they are through as an organization." This elicited smiles all around. "The problem is that your reputations are getting around, and unless you want attention at all hours, you are possibly putting your families and loved ones in danger of retribution." The smiles faded. "Now, I know your names, as do a few of the City Watch. I have a simple solution if you are willing."

"So long as it isn't giving up the finesmith's quarter, name it." Keldrick was concerned for the safety of his family and their shop. It was one thing to be targeted because of a potential score, but to be targeted because of his nocturnal activities was another issue entirely."

"I had these made by the Wizards of the Green Tower," the inspector said, pulling out some gauzy scarves or kerchiefs. "They were made especially for the four of you," he continued as he tossed a scarf across the table to each of them in turns. As they sat there, looking at them with confusion clearly on their faces, the inspector addressed Dra'lon. "Go ahead, put it around your neck like some Havish fop.

Hesitatingly, Dra'lon did as he was bid. As he finished tying it around his neck, the scarf and his nondescript face faded away, and a masked visage took its place.

Kaitra leaped to her feet. "Scarves of disguise?!" Her voice was incredulous. With a flourish, she tied her scarf about her neck, and, just like Dra'lon, the scarf and her face morphed into a similarly masked countenance.

Together, Rotra and Keldrick donned their scarves, and the four looked at each other across the table with no discernable expressions on their masked faces. But their confusion and excitement were readily apparent by their poses and voices.

"This is *AMAZING!*" Kaitra exclaimed.

"If you don't mind, the cost of the scarves is coming out of your rewards for this venture." The Watch Inspector almost seemed sad at the mention.

"Oh, that doesn't matter at all, Inspector!" Keldrick was elated.

"Now you must come up with new names or nicknames for each other because names can be traced back down to your homes. Addressing each other as Tomas, Rikard, and Harold will only lead those that don't end up dead or locked up back to your front doors."

"I'm sure we can come up with something," Keldrick was emphatic. "Tonight, the Nightwings will truly fly!"

ROGUE RIK

Spider was hungry again, but that was nothing new. Hunger was like the Copper watch—always around the corner and waiting to ruin his day. This time, however, he knew that it was getting serious. It had been three days since he was able to grab anything more than that bloody half-rotten apple, and even when he saw the rot, he ate it anyway. Then the stomach ache started, and not long after, the squirts. It was so bad that he even had to drop his breeches in the street, unable to even get to an alley to do his business. And not only once! It was more times than he cared to count!

Then it got worse, driving him to the riverside to wash out his breeches. Over and over again. It was so bad that he just slung his breeches over his shoulder, thankful to whatever fates would hear him that his ratty t-tunic was long enough to cover his private parts.

It hadn't always been this way, of course. He remembered being a child, living with his parents in the lap of luxury. At the time, he didn't realize it, but compared to his present state, his family must have been outrageously wealthy. They had three servants who lived with them, and their estate was on the hill past Temple Row—a section of the city where he was no longer welcomed because of how he dressed and... other reasons. Gods! Why would he have to go over that story again? He HATED it!

Rik was eagerly anticipating his eleventh birthday party in just two weeks, and his parents were arguing over the guest lists. His mother, bless her soul, tried to shoo him out of the parlor, but his father had allowed him to remain, permitting the eavesdropping as it were, saying, "The boy—the *young man*—needs to learn about Crowns eventually. Why not now?" He dropped into the empty chair across from the ornate coffee table—after, of course, grabbing a tasty treat from the crystal serving bowl.

Crowns. That damnable game of Crowns. According to Father, everyone played it, and it was supposedly like the game of chess he had learned while boarded at the Dybal Academy for much of the past six years. The teachers gave classes on history, biology, rhetoric, and music, but nothing was ever said about this game of Crowns. Since this was the first time he had heard about it, Rik listened intently as he feigned indifference and boredom, fidgeting in his over-wrought chair.

Father went on about how if this child was invited, that other family would be insulted, but if the child *wasn't* invited, his family's entire faction would be angered. Mother scratched names from the list and added others elsewhere. It took several hours before the events were finalized, and essentially, there were four parties, each with its own list of guests and themes. This way, all of the important families and factions could be invited to participate, and hopefully, none would notice the other soirees being set up or torn down in the process. Rik was a bit mystified that a company of some seventy neutral attendees would be paid to attend the day's festivities and that nearly fifty servants were to be hired to tend to all the details.

Mother and father asked for drinks when they were done, and Rik noted that they both looked exhausted; mother's laced cuffs on her sleeve were dark from ink after repeated contact with the much-revised lists, and father's silken collar was even darkened by perspiration. Rik quietly excused himself and escaped to his suite to ponder what he had heard.

The party, or *parties*, rather, were a smashing success, and Rik had enjoyed himself all day. His parents had kept his helpings of sweets and treats to a minimum to allow him to enjoy every dining session as if it were his first of the day, which he both understood and appreciated, but this was the last party, and he was allowed free rein. The children played tag, monster-hunter, and wizards-and-bandits and were now sitting down for the obligatory cake-cutting. After a night of little sleep due to the excitement of the anticipation of today's festivities, combined with little food and much of it being sugary goodness, Rik was feeling a bit lightheaded as he sat down at the head of the table.

The servants brought the cakes and treats out, with the largest plate set down right in front of him. Blinking back double images, Rik dove in with both hands, not caring about his velvet and silk clothing or that syrup and sugars were oozing from between his fingers. Rik looked up at his hovering parents as if in a dream.

"Oh, thank you so much for the parties today, mother and father." The words were a bit hard to make out due to the half-mouthful of treats that Rik had yet to swallow. "I've never had so much fun in my life!" He failed to catch the sudden look of alarm on his mother's face as he turned toward his guests.

Riva Oakenshire, the youngest daughter of the Anedin Oakenshires, members of the Green-leaf Faction (Rik was so proud he remembered all of that!), raised an eyebrow at him and asked, "What do you mean, Rik? Parties?"

As his mother rushed to answer for him, Rik blurted out, "Oh, yes. I've had four wonderful parties today so I could invite all the people we wanted to impress. This is the last of them where the lowest ranking guests attend, so they don't insult the sensibilities of my guests at the previous parties. It's okay if you are all insulted because none of you are important enough to really impact our position in society!"

His smile was genuine as he answered the young girl, and Rik honestly did not intend the insults; he merely wanted to provide correct information. When he saw Riva's parents stand up from their position on the couches arranged around the walls of the ballroom and he heard his mother's gasp as she fainted, he realized he had spoken out of turn. He stood up in alarm, and his head grew as though it were a balloon, and though he didn't want to, he got sick.

The fallout from the faux pas had been swift and total. Lord Dunnam's business contracts were rescinded within a matter of weeks, and all of the merchants in Stormhaven acted as one and refused to do business with Rik's family or their estates. Creditors came knocking at all hours, demanding immediate repayment of loans and outstanding debts, which, unfortunately, the Dunnam Consortium didn't have. All of the Dunnam's extended family, upon whom they could always rely, also withdrew their support of Rik's family. Within two months of his disastrous birthday party, Rik's parents were crying in their nearly empty home, claiming to be destitute.

Rik didn't quite understand when the door nearly exploded off of its hinges the next night. As he heard loud shouts coming from the foyer, Rik cracked his door open enough to see his mother and father in their nightclothes. What shocked him was the foil in his father's hand, pointed at the group of men coming up the stairs.

As the men pulled nightsticks from their belts, Rik's father saw him silhouetted in the door, and he yelled commands at the boy. "Rik! Put your clothes in your pillowcase and climb out your window!"

The men lunged, and his father clumsily stepped out of the way and lashed out. A man cried out, grasped his chest, and fell backward down the stairs. Another man with a helmet that looked like a Copper from the city watch stepped up the stairs to where Rik could see him.

"Lord Dunnam. You are hereby under arrest for obstruction of the course of Crown business in the repossession of your land and holdings—and now the assault of an officer of the law. Lay down your weapon and submit to the Crown's authority!"

Rik saw his father blanch, and his mother sagged against the bare wall behind him like she was going to faint. His father's voice sounded frantic, "RIK! RU-UUUNNNN!!!"

That's just what the boy did, unaware that this was the last time he would ever see his parents. Ripping his pillow out of its case, Rik stuffed his clothes and shoes inside as he sniffed back tears. Opening his windows, he climbed out onto his balcony, only to see the two-story drop to the cobbles below. Suddenly feeling trapped, Rik ran from one side of the wide balcony to the other, looking for a way down, and that's when he finally saw the ivy and trellis at the side of the balcony. Looking over the rail, Rik saw the trellis go all the way to the alley below, and he threw caution to the wind.

Tossing the pillowcase over the edge, Rik clambered over the rail, grabbed the trellis, and began climbing down. He didn't realize how precarious his position was until his sixth or seventh rung down, when the lightweight wood broke in his hand, resulting in Rik swinging outward and nearly falling. Leaning as close to the trellis as possible, he pretended he was a spider and scuttled the rest of the way down to the cobbled alley below. Grabbing the soggy pillowcase from where it had landed in a puddle from a chamber pot, Rik ran toward the lighted street in front of his house.

Greeting him was the sight of about two dozen large men and a full contingent of watch Coppers. Ducking back before he was seen, Rik tried to catch his breath in the shadows, trembling from head to foot. Realizing his clothing was soaked in indescribable stench, he tried to squeeze the nasty liquid from the case, not caring that it ran down his nightgown and puddled between his feet.

With no warning, a form suddenly stepped around the corner, and just out of arm's reach was a Copper Sergeant.

"We've got the runt over here!" the Copper yelled over his shoulder, and he reached toward the terrified youth.

Rik squeaked and spun out of the man's grasp, sprinting back down the alley toward the now familiar trellis. The city watchman stepped after the boy, but his first step was into the newly deposited puddle which had made the cobbles slick, and with a shout and grunt, the Sergeant's feet flew out from under him, and he landed heavily on his behind. Rik's flight led him past his balcony and down the alley, so he never realized that the pursuit had ended before it had really started.

The following day, Rik went to his grandfather's manor house, and after being told by the butler that he needed to return to the sewers he smelled of, Rik realized he wouldn't be seen until he was cleaned up. By midday, he was hungry and outraged when the street vendor laughed at him when he asked for a sweet treat. As Rik began to berate the tubby man, he never saw the blow coming as the man's heavy wooden spoon made contact with the side of his head.

Bursting into tears, Rik ran back into the alleys. By the time night came, Rik was sure he was about to die from starvation, and the egg-shaped lump on his temple had grown to a remarkable size. He also realized that he was lost. Not used to traveling through the city outside of his coach, he didn't recognize landmarks, and everything seemed strange and foreboding to the young boy.

It was on that night he was jumped and beaten for the first time.

The boys had come from nowhere, surrounding him faster than he could figure out what was happening. One of them demanded his coin purse and didn't like it when Rik said that he didn't have one. They didn't ask again, jumping on him en masse, pummeling and kicking the boy until any feeble defenses he may have put up were no longer even afterthoughts. They searched for a purse and when none was found, the boy who had demanded it stood up and kicked Rik directly in the mouth. Rik still had a gap from where the tooth used to be.

The days melted into weeks, and his wounds healed, but his only real enemy was hunger. He stole occasional fruit or loaves when vendors were busy elsewhere, and he once ate what he could from some fishheads that were left behind from a day's catch. When he dared to look, he could see his ribs begin to show. Rik finally caught a bit of good luck when an older woman took pity on him.

Taking the boy back to a tiny room with a small closet and enough room for a filthy sleeping pallet, the woman offered him some questionable-looking bread that Rik gobbled up without sparing a thought. Giving him a swallow of stale beer, she told Rik that he could sleep in her closet and, no matter what, NOT to come out or make any noise until she opened the door. He sat down in the cramped place, squirmed once to get comfortable, and fell fast asleep.

Rik was alarmed when he awoke and found he couldn't see. His room had always had at least a single shielded candle burning on his chest of drawers, and the thought that it had gone out nearly drove him to panic. As he tried to jump up, he realized that he hurt all over, and his entire body was stiff from sleeping in such a cramped spot. His head and mouth throbbed from the—by the gods—the beating! Did it really happen, or was this all a horrible nightmare?

Standing, Rik got tangled in clothing hanging from above, and he yelped, believing that more ruffians were out to hurt him. With a half-strangled cry, he spun around, falling against the unseen door and knocking it open. He fell with a thud onto a sleeping pallet and onto the form of a sleeping woman who startled and scrambled out from under him, pulling a stiletto out from apparently nowhere and holding it before her to defend herself. Light poured through broken shutters, and as Rik struggled to get unwrapped from various articles of clothing, he tried to explain himself.

With a sudden look of recognition, the woman coughed out a laugh and lowered her weapon, slipping it beneath her pallet again. "Fate's own fortune, boy; I forgot you was even in derr," she laughed again. "You's doin' okay, den?" She stopped to take a critical look at the youth, and he had freed himself enough to look her over as well.

First off, she was naked as the day she was born, her flabby body showing her age and a lifetime of hardship. She had sores around her mouth and what looked like a rash near her... private parts and Rik was a bit taken aback that she made no effort to cover herself.

"Well, looks a like you got it good, boy," she commented as she reached toward his head. He shied back as she continued. "I sees you gone an' lost a toot. Dat's okay, ya don' need 'em any-a-ways." She laughed, letting Rik see that there was more blank space in her mouth than teeth. The laughter seemed genuine, though, which helped to put him at ease. "Well, I gots a little bread leff an' a hunk of cheese I nicked from Old Smiley down on da corner." Her strange way of speaking was hard for him to get used to. "An' yer welcome to haffa it; I gots ta eats too." She jacked a thumb in the direction of a small, wrapped bundle.

It took everything Rik had not to eat all of the offered feast. He was hungry enough to ignore the small black flecks that moved of their own volition on the filthy crust. He finished his share and licked his fingers as he thanked the woman.

"So," her voice had a strident tone to it, "I's Lissa. What's yer story, boy?"

Rik cocked his head at the woman—at Lissa—and wondered where to start. But, once he opened his mouth to speak, it all came out in a torrent of words that culminated and mostly drowned out much of his story in wracking sobs and a flood of tears. He not only didn't flinch as she pressed him to her naked bosom, but he also melted into her embrace, happy to find a friend.

They talked through much of the afternoon, and once they had a plan, Lissa told Rik to return to his "bedroom" and get some sleep, repeating her warning about keeping still and not opening the door unless she opened it for him. While he was confused, he agreed and was asleep within a few moments.

The darkness was stifling when he awoke. The sound that had roused him was repeated, and he concentrated on determining what caused it. Rhythmic slaps started again, and he heard Lissa's breathless voice begging someone to go faster. Confused, Rik just listened. Within a few moments, he heard a man's grunts and a loud groan, accompanied by soft cries by Lissa and then silence. A moment later, he heard shuffling and muffled conversation, the sound of heavy footsteps, followed by a door opening and closing. As sleep reached for him again, Rik heard Lissa wordlessly humming a tuneless ditty.

It was several days before the nature of Lissa's occupation dawned on the young lad, and when it did, his world came crashing in on itself.

He had heard offhand remarks about prostitutes and even about 'common street whores,' but never actually believed the stories; they fell in the same category as orcs and dragons and giants.

He stumbled and avoided Lissa's gaze after his epiphany, and without skipping a beat, she slapped him on the side of his head. "Boy, I's gots ta eats, an' layin' wid rich blokes puts a few coins in mah purse. It ain't the best life, but it's better dan a debtor prison or lyin' dead in da gutter!"

While his brain understood the logic of her philosophy, Rik's stomach turned, and he nearly vomited on her filthy pallet. He wondered how many men had been on that bedding... he jumped up, ran, and sicked up just outside the door.

Rik walked in a daze, trying to rationalize the dichotomy of Lissa's warm heart and her evil profession. Not paying attention to his surroundings, he wandered into an even seedier section of the Lower City of Dybal. It wasn't until he saw several sets of bare feet in front of him that he became aware of the danger. Looking up, he saw several older boys blocking his path and sensed the movement of other figures behind him, preventing his escape.

A broken clothesline dangled against the wall to his right, and without a thought, Rik leaped as high as he could and grabbed the line. Seeing the small rope tied to an eye near an unshuttered window on the third floor, he pulled himself up as fast as he could, walking his feet up the wall to aid his climb. The boys below hollered, and he could hear them trying to jump up to grab him, which only spurred him to climb faster.

As Rik's leg hooked inside the open window, he heard one of the boys exclaim, "He climbs like a bloody spider!"

The unsuspecting residents of the filthy room he had entered did nothing; their sleeping forms piled like heaps of dirty clothing while waiting for the washing woman. Rik found it easy to sneak his way to the door. Gingerly opening it and easing it closed, he sat in the hallway outside, waiting until he figured the boys had departed the area.

An open window at the far end of the hallway seemed to beckon him, and he crept down the hallway to sit in the window and watch the sunset and the activity in the street below.

It wasn't long before the coaches and liveries gave way to pedestrians and horses and, finally, to just pedestrians who seemed to congregate at the intersections and beneath the magically lit lanterns atop their tall poles. The feeble light allowed him to see the activity of his neighbors, and it wasn't long until he realized that many of the ladies in the street below were actually harlots (as Father would have called them). Men would walk by as if shopping, and each woman and girl they passed would advertise their specialties and assets, hoping to attract the passersby. Rik noted that when the men chose their companion, they would return to the street within just a few minutes and hastily walk away toward the more affluent areas of the city. He didn't know why, but this thought made him smile.

The residents of the building he was in began to rouse from their daytime slumber and headed outside to conduct whatever business in which they were employed, and none paid him any mind—not even when the men who lived in the room he had entered had departed. He did note that as each room emptied, all of the occupants would securely lock the doors before they left. He tarried at his vantage point until he heard the criers announce midnight and began his journey to Lissa's room.

The door was closed when he arrived, and it shocked him how quickly he had accepted the accommodations as his new "home." Leaning his ear against the door, he heard the familiar noises inside and stepped modestly away until the man emerged, pulling his pants up as if he were rushing to get away from the scene of his indiscretion.

Rik knocked and entered the room as Lissa was finishing wiping the filth away. She barked a short laugh of derision, "Oh, back once it gets dark, I see! Now it's okay fer old Lissa to earn her coin to put a roof over yer sorry arse?" She just shook her head.

Hanging his head in what she would hopefully take as an act of contrition, Rik apologized. "Mistress Lissa, I was wrong to judge you the way I did, but it is just so different from what I was taught by my parents and tutors at the Academy. I beg your forgiveness and humbly request to be allowed to stay here until I can figure out what to do. I'll help clean or…" Rik faltered—outside of picking up random bits of soiled clothing, he had no real skills or talents.

Lissa laughed again, this time more gently, "It's alright, boy, even the men dat pay me feels the same way you does. They just needs da release. Why don't ya git some sleep? I'm a feelin' lucky an' feel a busy night coming!" With a playful swat in the direction of his bottom, Lissa dismissed him, and Rik felt a sense of warmth he hadn't felt in several months.

Considering the other activities that took place in Rik's new "home," he decided it was best if he were to make himself scarce while Lissa was working, so he spent his nights walking the streets and alleys of Dybal. On occasion, he'd even travel further afield, staying away for several days at a time, eventually even walking all the way to Stormhaven proper. He was used to tall buildings, but the mass of stone and the height of the towers—combined with their sheer number—made him feel positively claustrophobic. He hadn't even felt this way when holed up in that tiny closet! He remembered seeing paintings of huge forests and wondered if those who lived there felt trapped when surrounded by nothing but trees with only tiny bits of light shining down from above.

It had taken him five days to get to the main city, but after nicking a new shirt from an unattended laundry basket and a small basket of ripe fruit, the ensuing chase made the trip home much shorter. That washer-woman screamed like he had goosed her, which had diverted the attention of the merchant and her customer, allowing him to snag the basket of assorted fruit. Fortune hadn't smiled at him, though, as they both immediately turned to see his escape.

Their yells alerted every merchant in the bizarre, and they mobilized as one with the first cry of "THIEF!" He had run until his lungs burned, and his legs felt like jelly. Unfortunately, the merchants' hue and cry had also caught the attention of the Havish Coppers, and they drew close before Rik could eat any of his booty. Had it been anything else, he would have tossed it into the closest sewage ditch, but he was loath to get rid of any food.

Rik's heart sank when he caught sight of the Coppers, their polished copper helms from which they had gotten their name, readily identifying their employer. *Bloody Imperial Coppers!* he cursed, unaware that the words seemed to have crept into his everyday use. Crown Coppers meant they would have a spellcaster and at least one investigator as well. Oh, this was going to be a BAD day! He got up and began running again, leaving the alleys and heading into the crowded streets to try to lose them in the crush of pedestrians.

Every time he slowed to rest, within a moment of catching his breath, he could hear the hob-nails of the Coppers' boots on the cobbles nearby. Eventually, he resorted to just walking as quickly as he could so he could eat the evidence as he tried to elude the watch.

He spotted a young girl in ragged clothing begging on a corner and gave her the now empty basket, knowing it would fetch a Copper or two. He stepped off, glanced over his shoulder, and froze. A rough-looking man in lace, carrying a buckler bearing the imperial crest, stood across the street, eyes locked on Rik's. Rik spun and ran as quickly as he could, not letting up until he grew light-headed and his lungs ached for air. He slowed his pace enough that he could catch his breath, and within just a moment or two, the familiar face appeared across the crowd of people walking in oblivion through the street. Rik dashed off again.

The chase lasted for almost three days until he got back to Dybal, and that damned face haunted him the entire way. Day and night, he had run, trotted, and walked, and by this time, his feet throbbed, his filthy clothes were soggy with sweat, and his hands trembled. And no matter what he did, every time he looked for it, that face was just half a block behind him. Rik did take the time to thank the Fates for sending the rest of the watch squad back, especially if they had a Sorcerer with them, but he also asked the Fates to let him slip away from this damnable man.

It was nearing midnight, and he passed a derelict on a corner of an alley when he ran into the gang of boys again. And it was literal—he was running, straining to see if he had given the investigator the slip, when he slammed into someone, falling back in a heap. Leaping up—expecting it to be that man again—he smiled when he saw that it was the same group of youths that had beaten him so badly.

Scrambling to his feet, their leader snarled, "Oh, Spider! Getting in a lick, and now you are smiling? Get him, boys!"

As he spun, Rik ducked under the reaching arms of the nearest boy, and he sprinted into the alley. As he entered, he saw the beggar at the corner getting up a bit faster than Rik expected. As he ran, the dim moonlight revealed Rik's fatal mistake—it was a blind alley, ending some fifty feet after it started. His heart was sinking as he spied a dangling line and a broken downspout just above that. Running as fast as he could, he gathered and leaped, pulling at the line to get him up to the height where he could grab the downspout. As he pulled on the broken clothesline, it gave way in his hand, and, with no other choice, he threw himself upward as best he could.

His fingers closed on the bottom of the downspout, his left hand slipping off as his right caught on a remaining bracket that secured it to the wall. Scrambling, he pulled himself up, grabbed with both hands, and began climbing hand over hand as quickly as he could. He could hear the boys yelling at him from below, and something crashed against the wall next to him, thrown from below.

A man's voice from below almost made him lose his grip, but he pulled on reserves he didn't know he had and scuttled up to the rooftops. He wanted nothing more than to stop and catch his breath, but Rik still heard shouting from below. His hands hurt, and as he pushed himself up in the feeble moonlight, he saw that he had left two dark red handprints on the slate roof tiles.

With no time to dawdle or try to bandage his bleeding hands, he raced across the rooftops, knowing he was just a few blocks from Lissa's room. Finally finding himself in familiar territory, he deftly jumped from roof to roof and then clambered down to a wrought-iron fire escape and made his way around the corner to Lissa's.

Squatting in the darkness across the street, Rik waited. His breathing had finally slowed by the time he saw the creeping shadow down the block. Straining and looking just to the left and right of the darker shadow, the form finally moved up to where its face was barely illuminated by a distant torch, and Rik's heart stopped. The Crown Copper was still following him! How had he gone all the way around to find this place?

Without moving a muscle, Rik watched as the man repeatedly looked down at something clenched in his hand, something that faintly reflected what little light was available. Or... maybe it glowed. *Oh, by the gods, not MAGIC!* The thought frightened him even more than the fact that the Copper had stopped in front of Lissa's door to check that device again. Apparently satisfied, the man straightened as he put the trinket in an out-of-sight pocket, and he boldly stepped to the middle of the street and nonchalantly strolled out of sight. Rik waited until after dawn before he came down from his perch to quickly disappear into Lissa's room.

*****

Time passed rather rapidly. Rik had little to do but learn how to survive on the street and scrounge for his next meal. The winter came and passed; summer did the same. The seasons changing was the only indication of the passage of time, and as far as he could tell, three or four years had passed since he had lost his home and family.

In the spring, Lissa grew ill from that barking sickness that left her coughing nearly all night and prevented her from working. Knowing that they may starve, Rik began filching more food and even began lifting pouches from wealthy patrons of the working girls or boys in the area.

He also became a people-watcher, observing everyone to see what they may be carrying or hiding if they were armed, what house or faction devices they wore, and how they acted in general. In just a few months, he was able to identify those wealthy men who came to the alleys to seek some companionship, those who were shopping for less legal items or services, and those who were intent on violence—the destitute were prime targets for rich nobs looking to inflict pain and humiliation upon the less fortunate. After witnessing several beatings and stabbings, as soon as he recognized a small roving band, Rik would rush out ahead of them to pass warnings to those in their path.

On one such mission, a group of men were gathered around a small fire as a band of thugs approached. Rik ran up between two of the crouching men and put a hand on their shoulders, quietly telling them of the ruffians just down the block. As he turned to run to the next potential victims, a hand grabbed his collar and pulled him up short. A familiar—but older—face peered into Rik's eyes, then looked down the block. Rik's heart sank as he realized that this had been the boy who kicked his tooth out that first night on the streets.

The boy—a young man—looked down the alley again, let go of Rik's collar, and quietly said, "Thanks."

The group melted into the night as Rik rushed to continue his warnings.

Not long after that, Rik saw a group of Coppers checking each other out like soldiers on parade. What made this scene stick out to him was that the guards were removing all of their identifying gear, and Rik realized that they were going to make a raid in the alleys. As soon as the Coppers moved out, Rik raced to get ahead of them to warn anyone he might see. When he dashed out from behind a corner, he saw a young man lifting a pouch from a drunken merchant.

The man flinched as Rik raced toward him but quickly looked past him as Rik hissed, "Coppers raiding the area, get lost!"

It was two days later, in the middle of the day (prime sleeping time!), when a light knock was made at Lissa's door. Bleary-eyed, Rik stumbled over the soiled bedding to open the door. As he flipped the catch, the door was rapidly pulled open from outside, and half a dozen men filled the door.

Jumping back to avoid the anticipated attack, one voice quietly said, "Relax, it's only us."

Rubbing the sleep from his eyes, Rik struggled to focus before realizing that it was the gang of men he had warned when the ruffians were on the prowl.

"Whatcha want wid me?" Rik had found that he could quickly switch from High Common to street slang. Another gift of living in the streets.

"You been helpin' us out—kinda keepin' watch an' stuff. Jus' wanted to say that we 'preciate it." The man stuck his hand out. "Name's Coops. We's da Coops Crew."

Not entirely trusting the man, Rik slowly reached out to shake his hand. "I'm... uh... Ri..."

"Spider," the man cut him off. "We ain't much into names here." The young men accompanying Coops smiled and nodded in agreement. "We seed you when you wuz jus' a wee thing an' thumped ya. Nex' time we seed ya, ya jus' climbed up dat wall like a spider, so we been callin' ya 'Spider' ever since." The handshake was firm and reassuring, and Rik's fear began to subside. "We jus' wanted ya to know dat if ya ever needs a hand, jus' holler." The group—the Crew—turned as one as Coops said over his shoulder, "We be seein' ya, Spider."

Life didn't get easier after that, but at least Rik had one less thing to worry about. Unfortunately, Lissa had been taken ill more often, with the barking cough coming and going, and it was beginning to tell. She lost weight and even some hair, and she wasn't able to work as much as she had previously. Rik actually became concerned about her health. Death was common here in the alleys, but Lissa was as close as he had to real family, at least outside of Coops' Crew.

Just a few months ago, Rik was coming back after a successful night of collecting supplies. His parents would have called it burglary, but he couldn't afford such moral judgments now. As he approached Lissa's door, he heard her scream and heard a loud crash. Knowing that she'd be enraged by his intrusion, Rik grabbed the handle of the door and swung it wide. The scene inside still gave him nightmares from time to time.

Blood was everywhere. Lissa was covered with it and was feebly waving one hand in the air as bloody bubbles frothed from several holes in her chest. She was naked with her legs splayed, and Rik could see that her private area was a mass of blood coming from dozens of cuts. A man turned to face him as he angrily buttoned his trousers. Blood was spattered across his blouse and pants, and he grabbed a cloak from the floor as he made to walk out past Rik.

Enraged, Rik leaped at him, screaming, demanding to know what the man had done to Lissa. Rik didn't see the dagger still in the man's hand, but he certainly felt the hilt of the thing as the man slammed it against his temple. His vision faded to a pinpoint as he fell in a heap to the bloody floor.

When he was able to gather his thoughts, confusion reigned. How much time had passed? Seconds? Hours? Rik scrambled over to Lissa's still form, and Rik let loose with a wordless howl. Leaping to his feet, Rik bolted a few steps toward the door, and as he passed through, he grabbed a sharpened nail that was kept there in case of robbers. He had sharpened the thing himself after Lissa had been beaten one night, and he assured her that he'd always be there to keep her safe. His failure hurt him more than her death.

Racing up the street, Rik saw nothing. Spinning, he caught sight of what he believed was the attacker's cloak as he ducked around a corner. Throwing all caution to the wind, Rik sprinted after him. Charging around the corner, Rik saw the man walking down the center of the side street, cloak flowing out behind him. Rik raced up behind him and, at the last minute, threw himself full at the man's back.

Not expecting an attack, the man stumbled and nearly fell as Rik bounced off of his back onto the cobbles.

The man hissed, "Little vermin," as he drew his dagger—the same bloody dagger that he had used to kill Lissa. Rik didn't care and charged toward the man again, stabbing his sorry excuse for a weapon at the man's belly. Quickly stepping back, the man swept the dagger in a wide arc, slicing across Rik's face and both shoulders.

The boy felt the nail bite into something as the pain of his own cut made him realize the danger of his situation. Anticipating another slice, Rik dropped and rolled away, mentally noting that though he was bleeding from both shoulders as well as his chin, the wounds weren't debilitating. The nail had been pulled from his hand as he dropped, and Rik looked around desperately for another weapon.

The man hissed again, "You bastard! You've cut me!" Rik's eye went to where the man grabbed the end of the nail, which protruded from his inner thigh. Growling, the man yanked it from his leg and threw it to the ground. He stepped toward Rik and looked like he was about to speak when his hand went again to his thigh. That was when Rik saw the bright spurt of blood come from between the man's fingers. The man started to speak several times but turned and began to hobble away, clutching at his bleeding wound. Rik walked behind, almost as if in a trance.

With every step, another gout of blood gushed from between the man's fingers and down his leg to the cobbles. Every few steps, he got a little slower and a little less steady on his feet. Every few steps, Rik grew more and more confused. He couldn't quite understand what was happening since he had just stuck the nail in the man's thigh, and the man's reaction didn't make sense for such a minor wound.

Finally, the man stumbled and lurched to his knees. He crawled a few more feet before falling to his side and rolling onto his backside to face Rik. Waving his dagger in the boy's direction, Rik saw that the man couldn't quite focus on him, so he remained where he was.

"Twenty-two years. Twenty-two YEARS, I've been hunting on these evil alleys, redeeming the souls of the lost for the glory of the gods, and now, a mere gutter snipe has taken me down. ME! A man doing the work of the gods..." his voice began getting weaker as he leaned further and further back. "A fatherless bastard... doing the work of demons and striking me down..." Rik stepped forward, closer to the man, as he slumped back and laid his head on the cobbles. The man's voice grew soft. "How does this happen? Is there no good left in this world?"

As the dagger fell from his numb fingers, Rik stepped in and snatched it up. Seeing an array of family and faction pins on a sash under the man's cape, Rik sliced the sash and pulled it away, tucking it in his belt. He did the same with a chain pendant and a couple of pouches. Rik stood up, and the light went out of the man's eyes. It wasn't until then that the boy realized what had happened.

The man was dead, and Rik had killed him. Turning, Rik sped away, tears filling his eyes and spilling down his cheeks.

Rik never saw the danger until it was too late. Blasting around a corner, he ran smack-dab into a man's chest. A man made of iron and stone because he didn't flinch as the boy slammed into him. Unexpectedly, the man's arms drew around Rik's shoulders in an almost comforting way, and the boy lost all composure, devolving into a sobbing mess. The man just held him as he wailed.

It was several minutes before Rik was able to gain a semblance of control, and he and the man sank onto a step of a doorway, sitting next to one another, the man's arm still draped over Rik's shoulders.

"Was it bad?" The man's voice was deep, like a wagon wheel rumbling across cobbles in the street.

Sniffling, Rik responded, "The worst. I never killed anybody before."

"Why'd you do it?"

"He... he..." the tears began again as he mouthed, "He killed my Lissa."

The man leaped to his feet. "Lissa?! When?"

"Just a few minutes ago. She's dead..." The sobs began again. The man took off, sprinting down the alley away from the boy. Somehow, knowing he was needed, he followed the man, trying to rein in his sobs with little success. As he rounded a corner, he saw the man disappear into Lissa's open room, and Rik ran up behind him.

As he got there, Rik saw the man place something in Lissa's mouth, and he pulled out what looked like a wand from some hidden spot. Mumbling some strange words, the man broke the stick with both hands, and sparkling powder-like sand poured out onto Lissa's blood-covered belly. A faint glow passed over her whole form, and her back suddenly arched as she drew a breath. Turning his hand, the man fumbled with a ring he wore, and Rik saw that he turned the top like some sort of combination lock. With a few more strange words, the man pressed his hand with the ring onto Lissa's belly, and her whole body began to tremble.

She suddenly sat up and stammered, "Wha…? Who…? You dirty ba…" then she swung a hard slap at the man who deftly blocked her arm.

"It's me. Are you okay?"

"I… You? Oh, you! Yeah, I's… that bastard! He raped me an' den starts stabbin' me like some butcher at da market."

"Well, you don't have to worry about the Hunter again." The man looked over his shoulder at Rik. "Spider here has killed him."

"Spider? My Rikki? Bah! He wouldn't hurt a flea! Da only fights he been in wuz when he wuz beat up!" Lissa seemed like her old self, though Rik noted that she was still covered in blood. He also saw that the holes in her chest seemed to have stopped their bubbling.

"Well, it's over now. You lay back, and I need to have a talk with Spider." The man pulled a natty blanket over Lissa's bloody form and plumped a wad of rags beneath her head. The way he did it looked almost tender.

As he stood and turned toward Rik, he quietly said, "We need to talk."

Rik's heart sank as the man's cloak spun wide enough for the boy to see an Imperial crest on a leather pouch on the man's belt. With a sudden realization, Rik recognized the man's face as the Copper that had been so successfully chasing him several years back. With that, Rik's knees gave out, and he collapsed in a heap.

The smell of eggs and bacon pulled Rik from his slumber. He snuggled deeper in the blankets and tried to pull the pillow over his head to block the sunlight streaming in from the open window. Then he froze. Eggs and bacon? Bed? Blankets and pillows? His eyes snapped open, and he slowly pulled his head from beneath the pillow to look around. He was in a small room—though it was twice the size of Lissa's—and there was just this bed, a stand with a washbowl and pitcher, and a small stool with clothes folded on it. As he quietly slipped from between the blankets, Rik was stunned to realize he was naked and then realized that his filth had soiled the clean, white sheets and pillow slip.

Standing up, he looked about again and saw the note on the washing stand. "Spider," it read, "Wash up and get dressed. Breakfast will be served when you get to the main room. Don't steal anything."

Snorting quietly, Rik dropped the note and reached for the pitcher to clean himself. Surprisingly, the pitcher and water within were quite warm. Using washing cloths next to the basin, Rik scrubbed himself cleaner than he had been in several years. When done, he reached for the clothes and was surprised to find the dead man's dagger, pouches, and pendant beneath them on the stool. Dressing quickly, he stuffed his booty away and quietly opened the door.

The hallway outside was empty, but he could hear noises from one end. Creeping down the hall, he made his way to a short stairway that opened to a room below. As slowly as possible, he peeked around the corner to see a large room that had long tables with benches on both sides. Several people, men and women, were moving about or eating, but what caught Rik's eye was a very large man just a few feet away. Considering the bench height, the man was exceedingly short, but he was so very broad! Rik quietly mused that he must have to turn sideways to get through the doors. His hair was graying, but he still looked robust, and his beard and mustaches were larger than any he had ever seen before!

Rik was noting that the man's entire body seemed hairy when a loud voice burst out from the massive form.

"Whatcha lookin' at, kid?"

"…" Rik wasn't able to form a response, his mouth opening and closing repeatedly.

"Well, if yer did gaping' about, how 'bout ya sit yourself down an' get some breakfast?" The man's loud voice got even louder and seemed angrier as he hollered over his shoulder, though the man's smile gave away the humor. "THAT IS IF WE CAN EVER GET FOOD OUT HERE!!" With that, he nodded at the bench across the table from him, and Rik stumbled over to accept the invitation.

As Rik sat, he just stared at the man, who pulled deeply from a steaming cup he had in his hand. An approving moan as he swallowed, accompanied by his eyes fluttering and a content smile, told Rik that whatever the cup contained was good. He continued to stare at the strange man and jumped suddenly as the man bellowed, "AND BRING TWO PLATES; THE KID'S UP AS WELL!"

Movement from a swinging door drew Rik's attention, and a young woman approached, carrying two heaping plates, steam and mouth-watering aromas rising from each. She set the man's plate down and smiled as he thanked her.

As she set the plate before Rik, she began to ask, "Would you like—"

"Yes, he would," the man interrupted. "Give him all the fixings and another plate as well. Looks like he ain't been fed right since I was a young 'un."

The woman smiled and mouthed, "I'll be right back," as she disappeared back into the kitchens. Rik's attention was pulled to the steaming plate before him, and he dove into the mound of eggs and fried turnips and bacon and biscuits.

As he finished, he saw that the server was back with another plate, and as she set it atop the empty plate, with a friendly smile, she pointed. "Would you like to use a spoon this time?"

It was then that Rik realized that he had used his fingers to eat the entire first plate of food. With that, he blushed and grabbed the cloth napkin to wipe his dripping fingers before he picked up the fork and knife to start on the second plate of food. He noticed a steaming cup of brown liquid that was a sister to the one that the man had been drinking and he reached for it.

As he pulled it toward his mouth, the man quietly warned, "Watch it, it's hot."

Even with the warning, the liquid burned his tongue and the roof of his mouth—and then the glorious taste registered.

"What *IS* this?" he asked, awed.

"That, laddie, is hot cocoa, brought all the way here from the jungles of Dresina Malfiorenta, the 'Dark Mountain,' as the locals call it." With a smile, he added, "If ya don't be wantin' it… I'll gladly finish it for ya."

Rik playfully glared at him as he took another pull at the cocoa. It was the most amazing taste he'd ever experienced. As the food on his plate disappeared, Rik's attention was again drawn to the massive man sitting across the table from him.

"What kind of man are you?"

"Man? I was hungry a few minutes ago. Now I'm full. Next, after this cuppa's gone, I'll be having to relieve myself. But I'll tell ya honest, kid, I ain't no man."

"But what *are* you?" Rik persisted as an opening door interrupted them. The Copper that must have brought him here walked briskly toward the two—after stopping to draw a cup of cocoa from a large urn by the kitchen door. Rik made a note of where that urn was for later use.

"Well, kid, since your benefactor is here, I'll be excusing myself. Nice to meet you. I'm called Vallen. Vallen Ironheart."

Struggling to swallow, Rik tried to respond but was cut off by the Copper. "He's called Spider, Vallen. He's a thief, a robber, and a killer."

With a rueful smile at Rik, Vallen chided, "Well, the poor sod must of tried to get some of the kid's food. Watch yourself, Edroy. If you get your fingers too close to Spider's mouth, you'll lose them." With a wink and a raised cup of cocoa salute, Vallen strode off the dining room. Rik was pleased to note that the man had to turn a bit to make it through the doorway. Then the Copper sat down in Vallen's spot at the table and pushed the empty plate away.

"You know who I am, Spider?" The man's voice carried an air of authority and power. Rik tried to play off being unimpressed.

"Well, Sir, you're a Copper… an Imperial Watchman," Rik winced at the unintentional use of the almost vulgar name watchmen had on the street. "You have experience and are used to giving orders, so you are probably a Watch Sergeant, but I'd probably pin you as a Watch Captain. You know what you are doing, and you use magic to do it. I've seen you use some sort of device when you were first chasing me—some sort of pointing device that was leading you to me. Then, when you lost me, you used it to find Lissa's room, where I was staying. You have other magic stuff that can heal you, but you're not a priest. You and Lissa know each other, and it didn't seem like you were a client, so I'm guessing that she's an informant of yours. Am I close?" Rik sat back and took another sip of his cocoa, trying to act confident without being smug.

The man was quiet for a bit, long enough for Rik to start getting nervous.

"Well, I'm called Edroy. Captain Commander Edroy." Rik tried to hide the wince of finding out he underestimated the man's rank. "I spent eight years as a scout in the Imperial Army, the Golden Knights, with four tours up on the Wall in Laupennin Perak. When I got back, I..." Edroy hesitated, and Rik watched him closely. "I had some problems getting back in with life here in Stormhaven. The game of Crowns was too much for me to deal with. Some connections got me a position in the Imperial Watch, the Blackhawks, and I became an Investigator. Because of my experience up north—as well as some items I either found or had made—I got promoted rather quickly. I spend most of my time either here, in the Pathfinder Lodge, or on the streets looking for hardened criminals or potential recruits." Both of them took several sips of their cocoa before Edroy continued.

"That day I first encountered you, you caught my attention. We should have caught you within just a few blocks, but you kept slipping away." Pulling what looked like a large snuff-box from his pocket, he continued. "Even with this to help point out which direction you were in, you still kept a few steps ahead. Then I managed to turn the corner just as you skittered up the wall away from those boys." Edroy laughed into his cup. "Never seen anything like it.

"Lissa's been a minor informant for a long time, and I knew you wouldn't get into too much trouble if she kept you under her wing, so I left you there." He took a long pull from his cup. "A while back, I got a tip on a killer, the 'Hunter.' He's been killing prostitutes and vagabonds for years, and I've never had the luck to see him, so I could get Old Dog," he patted the snuff box, "his scent so I could track him down. I finally got a tip and was on his tail when I saw him fall after you had stuck him. A witness said he bled out when you cut the artery in his leg when you stuck him. Then I ducked behind the corner and was trying to figure out what to do when I was nearly tackled by you." He took another pull at his cocoa. "And that pretty much ends this story for my part. What about you?"

Rik began haltingly, intending to spin a story to cover his tracks, but his confidence shattered, and tears streamed down his face as his entire story spilled out to the Captain-Commander. He included the shame of betraying his parents at his party and his escape from the Coppers—this time not avoiding the derogatory term. He described the beatings and the horrors of living on the streets. He told of his feelings for Lissa and how he hoped she was doing well. He also included the story of watching the Captain-Commander track him after being chased, and Rik barely noticed the wry grin as the man realized he'd been spotted. The story sputtered out as Rik confessed to every crime he could remember and how he expected to lose one or both hands or even face the gibbets for his crimes.

The Captain-Commander seemed to grow stern. "Do you know what kind of authority I have, Rik? Do you know what I can do? I can execute a sentence here. Without question, I can string you up on the corner or run you through where you sit. Do you understand that?" Rik nodded dumbly. L"Okay, you understand. I hereby sentence you to death. From this day forward, Rikard de St. Senz Wright-Smitt, son of Rikard Senior and Juliana de St. Senz Wright-Smitt of the now nonexistent Wright-Smitt family, formerly of the Tonial faction that lost more power the day of your birthday party than they have been able to recover in the years since I declare you dead and forgotten." Rik just sat there, not even trying to sip his cocoa. Even his tears had stopped. "From this day forward, you are officially 'Spider,' and you work for me. You will carry messages from person to person, and you will carry packages from one place to another. You will stay in one spot and watch people or places until you are told that you may stop. And, from time to time, you can come here to the Pathfinder Lodge to get sleep in a real bed, have some real food, and maybe—if the trade deals don't sour—get cocoa."

Rik's—*SPIDER'S*—head slowly rose until he was looking at the Captain-Commander's face, understanding slowly showing in his eyes.

"I think I can do that," he said slowly as though taking an oath.

"Good. Thank you, Spider. I think it will be mutually beneficial for us to work together." Edroy drained his cup. "Oh, by the way, Lissa's room is down the hall to the left."

The crash from the bench Spider knocked over as he leaped to his feet, still reverberated after he had dashed through the doorway.

****

Oh, by the GODS, I'm hungry! The pain in Spider's stomach became spasms. Looking at his hands, he noted that his fingers were starting to tremble. *Just my luck,* he thought. The door he was watching moved slightly, and Spider lifted his hand to wipe the hair away from his eyes. The clockwork pigeon on the wall near him cooed softly, signaling that it was active. Some 200 paces away, the unassuming door pushed open, and an equally unassuming figure stepped out, covered in a nondescript, brown cloak. Spider pressed the small gem on the ring he now wore, and his eyes fluttered open, looking down at his form on the rooftop.

Spreading his wings, Spider made the clockwork pigeon flutter to life, and his consciousness became fully awake in the small bird. Leaning forward and flapping, he took flight in the direction of the cloaked figure.

All I have to do is follow this dodger to the temple and raise the alarm. Then I can get back to the Lodge and get some food. If Lissa was right, a shipment of cocoa should have come in either yesterday or the day before. *Even though I get hungry now and again, it's a pretty good gig working for the Nighthawks and the Pathfinders at the same time. Just a few more hours...*

PRISONER OF INONDACARE

Juergen was bored—supremely bored. Every day was the same in prison. He'd been there for what seemed like decades but could have been anywhere between one and four years, considering his sentence had been for five long years. He had been one of the lucky ones.

He'd started his less than illustrious career as a world traveler as a guard on a merchant caravan from his home in White Bridge, Carinnia Vols, and his first job was on a twelve-wagon caravan to Barranae, hundreds of miles off to the East. The wagons were loaded down with more shovels, pickaxes, and sled hammers than he could count, and he was thankful that each wagon had a team of six oxen to haul them and that they didn't need to unload them each night.

The trip was uneventful if you count seeing several centaur raiding parties in the distance as a non-event. The guard captain rallied the guards each time, and emotions ran high until long after the all-clear was announced.

Though his training was limited and he hadn't been tested in battle, he knew that mounted opponents were supposed to be unhorsed as soon as possible, but how do you unmount a rider that is *part of the mount*?! Fortunately, he wasn't forced to find out the answer to this question.

His people, the Volar, weren't equestrians, so their experience with mounted combat was limited to occasional raids by criminals and bandits from Inondacare or the rare raids by the centaurs, and neither had happened anywhere near where

Juergen was, so he didn't know what it was like to face off against a charging horse—or horseman.

Their first official stop was going to be in Inondacare, with a week layover where the merchants were going to resupply and purchase possible new items to bring with them to trade in Barranae. There would be another stop there on the way back to White Bridge, this time for trinkets and memorabilia to take home to loved ones. There wasn't anyone but family waiting for Juergen, but there was one person he hoped to impress with a special gift.

The week was cut to five days when two of the guards had gotten into a fight with some local toughs and were arrested. With wine involved, there was no real way of defending the actions of the two, so the Train Master told the authorities that they would stop by to check their status on the way back.

Juergen was a bit upset because it was going to be a month or more, but the Train Master assured him—and the rest of the guards—that they were due for a month or more in chains for beating the two local men. She also told them that if they protested too much, their cargo was in jeopardy of being seized out of an attempt to recompense the two men—a bit out of spite—so it was better for all if the caravan continued on its intended route.

Reluctantly, Juergen and the others saw the light and agreed to continue.

Full cargo lists and itineraries had to be given to the Inoondan authorities so the tolls and tariffs could be paid, and the entire crew was warned about selling any cargo anywhere in the militaristic nation to avoid more taxes being levied. The Train Master had assured the authorities that no selling was to be done at any point within the nation.

At the last stop in Inondacare, the guards were given the night off with a small advance in their pay to blow off a little steam. As for Juergen, he received more money than he had ever seen in his hand at one time. Immediately, the vast majority of the guards ran off for what passed for taverns in Inondacare. Juergen and a few others, on the other hand, ran off to the merchant's quarter to check out the wares in the open-air market.

Shopping with one of his friends, he found a wonderful silver bracelet at one stand but didn't have enough money for it. Reluctantly, he continued window shopping, seeing amazing prizes that soon made him forget the bracelet.

As the day was winding down, the shops and carts began to close up and travel back to their homes or permanent shops, and Juergen and the other shoppers went to have a cup of wine before heading back.

The young man he had been with elbowed him conspiratorially and, in hushed tones, told him, "Give this to that special someone, and you're sure to get kisses." He then extended his closed fist to hand him something.

Confused, Juergen extended his hand, palm up, and the boy slapped something hard into his hand.

Looking down, Juergen saw the bracelet that had caught his eye earlier. "By the gods! Why? How??"

With a laugh, the fellow guard said, "Don't ask questions you don't want the answers to." Slapping Juergen on the shoulder, he continued, "I saw how you looked at it and the look of disappointment on your face when you realized that you didn't have the coin for it." With a smirk, he concluded, "I believe a little bird grabbed it after you left and dropped it into my hand."

"You can't... I can't... Why did..." Juergen couldn't process the information.

With a wink, the other young man said, "It's too late now. We're leaving just after dawn tomorrow, so it can't be returned. By the gods, that merchant may not even be there tomorrow." He added, putting an arm around Juergen's shoulders, "Just take the gift and don't look in the slag heap for answers if you don't want to be burned."

Unable to come up with an adequate counter to the guard's comment, Juergen just stopped where he was in the street, looking at the beautiful bracelet. Suddenly overcome with guilt and overwhelmed with paranoid thoughts of City Watch eyes upon him, he stuffed the bracelet into his boot and tried to nonchalantly walk back to the caravan.

It took a long while for sleep to find him that night.

In the morning, Juergen kept the bracelet in his boot purely because he didn't know what else to do with it. The majority of the guards were in foul moods because of the quantities of wine they had drunk the night before, with some of them even getting sick and relieving their sour stomachs.

The caravan was ready to move shortly after dawn, with no opportunity to dash off to the merchants' quarter to return the bracelet.

Disaster struck at that last stop in Inondacare. Juergen noticed that one of the wagons looked like it wasn't packed as high as it had been, and, fearing theft, he went to the Guard Captain to ask about it. It was then that the Tax Assessors and King's Watch descended upon the caravan like death flies onto a dead carcass.

The accusation was illegal mercantile transactions, and the Train Master immediately objected, saying that no illicit trading or sales had been made by any of her caravans. Juergen immediately looked at the trader on the light wagon, and his heart sank when he saw the man almost shrink from view. He visibly sagged on his seat next to the wagon driver.

Juergen's breath caught in his throat when the Inondan authorities immediately accused that exact trader of making illegal sales. Juergen was sure that if the man could have, he would have shrunk down to the size of a flea and hopped away.

That was when disaster turned into a calamity.

One of the hungover guards took particular offense at the accusation and the proximity of the watch members, so he drew his sword and attacked. In almost no time at all, almost all of the guards had drawn their weapons and joined in on the fray.

For his part, Juergen had just raised his hands in surprise and took several steps back. Before he could fully comprehend the enormity of the situation, even some of the drivers and traders joined in, armed with staves, whips, and tie-down pins.

Juergen stepped forward and cupped his hands around his mouth. "STOP IT!! LISTEN TO WHAT THEY HAVE TO SAY!!" he yelled.

Over the melee, he could hear the Train Master yelling similar commands, but to no avail. Unfortunately, their voices were lost in the fracas.

Swearing mightily, Juergen spun around in frustration over the actions of his compatriots. Halfway around, he froze. Directly behind him were three members of the King's Watch with spears leveled at his stomach. Not knowing what to do, Juergen raised his hands up to shoulder level. The spears looked horrifically sharp, and there was no way he could draw his weapon before he was spitted like an animal to be cooked.

It was all over within a minute, with two members of the King's Watch lying motionless in the street and several of the guards in similar positions.

A Watch Officer pointed to a number of the drivers and traders, then motioned toward Juergen. In a short time, there were two groups of prisoners: one group with Juergen and the other on the other side of the wagon. Absently, Juergen noted that all that had entered the melee were on the other side of the wagons, while those that stayed out of the abortive battle were with him.

With a spearman on each side of every member of the caravan, they were led through the city toward what Juergen could only imagine to be a horrid end.

One of the combatants tried to elbow his way out of the line and ended up on the end of three different spears. With that, the gravity of the situation was felt by all, and no more attempts to escape were made.

When the Train Master quietly inquired of everyone's status, she was nudged none-too-gently with the point of a spear, and she desisted.

The trial was as quick as it was brutal. All who had entered the melee were ordered to be put to death with the testimony of several Watch Officers who had witnessed the fracas.

Juergen was terrified.

The group of non-combatants was asked if they understood the crimes they had been accused of and if they had any knowledge of any other crimes for which they could be charged. When it came to Juergen's turn, he began to cry, and without a thought, he took off his boot and upended it. Out fell the bracelet with a silvery jingle. Between the sobs, he explained that he thought it was stolen and that it had been given to him.

The justice handed down much lighter sentences to this group. They were just being exiled from all Inondacare-held lands. Each was to depart immediately. Their cargo was forfeit because they broke the trade agreements the Train Master had signed upon entry. Then, the justice mentioned Juergen by name.

"Juergen of White Bridge, normally thieves or those with stolen objects are subject to losing one or both hands," Juergen blanched, but the judge continued. "In light of the situation, you are sentenced to five years in the mines, after which you are exiled like your compatriots."

That afternoon was the last time Juergen saw the sun or moon in a long, long time. Days melted into weeks, which melted into months, with no concept of the passage of time. Any attempts to count the sleep-wake-sleep cycles were foolish, as all who tried lost count within a few days. All Juergen could do was pay attention to which jailors were on duty and when. When Tristan and Rogerio were on duty, there was a lot of work left, but when Mercurio came on duty, within a period of time, it would be time to sleep again.

The prisoners were all shackled together by the left ankle at three-pace intervals. Over time, Juergen got to know his two nearest neighbors. Lametto had been a mercenary who got drunk and punched his King's Watch Supervisor, while Nicola had been a merchant who had defrauded her customers.

Within a couple of months or so of his arrival, Nicola had completed her sentence and was released. Lametto, on the other hand, had been handed a fifteen-year sentence and fully expected to die in the mines; Juergen found that the only times a prisoner was taken out of the manacles were for release or death.

This was all compounded by the fact that the jailors and other prisoners all spoke Inondan and not Volar. Nicola, in their short time together, taught him most of the tongue, or at least enough to get by. He was mocked for his horrible accent, but he was able to get by with Nicola's help. When it was time, it was hard to see her go, but he was glad she was being released.

With the passage of time, Juergen found out that the only things that gave any sense of the passage of time were anything out of the ordinary. Every so often, at what seemed like regular intervals, a Supervisor would come through on inspection tours to see progress in the digging and check on the condition of the prisoners. Once, he even talked to Juergen.

"Prisoner! What is your name and crime?"

"Juergen of White Bridge. I was convicted of possession of stolen items and being partially involved with an assault on some members of the King's Watch."

With an obvious look of disgust, the Supervisor looked him up and down and asked, "What is your sentence?"

"My sentence was for five years."

The Supervisor sneered again and then asked Lametto the same questions. With another sneer, he just went on about his way. Juergen didn't give the meeting another thought.

Months later—or was it years—he and Lametto were pulled out of their manacles for no reason. The guards had another prisoner already with them.

Joking with the guards, Juergen asked them if he had died and hadn't realized it yet or if five years had elapsed already. True to form, they didn't respond. With a minimum of shoving and raps from their truncheons, Juergen and the other two were escorted to a large room.

Inside were a small group of people, including the Supervisor, and a large collection of what looked like junk. Apart from the Supervisor, the others were dressed in long robes like scholars, but they were speaking a language that sounded like Thalar, with long oes and oohs. What Thalarians would be doing here was beyond Juergen, especially in the mines.

They were weighed and then sat on short, strange-looking stools with cushions that also had long bars extending in all four directions like some sort of palanquin seat for nobles, save for the height. Manacles were placed at their feet but not put on the three prisoners, and Juergen thought, *I wonder why.*

After a scribe had done some calculations, an apothecary mixed some powder into two goblets of liquid and stirred. With no ceremony, one of the Thalar, with a silky voice, asked the two prisoners to drink the concoctions with an assurance that it was *not* poison and no harm would come to them. To show the truth behind his words, the man took a sip from each goblet.

Looking at Lametto and the other with fear and doubt in his eyes, Juergen took the offered goblet and tentatively sniffed at the contents. The immediate aroma was that of wine, though he could tell there were some other scents involved that were more elusive, so whatever the powder was, it was mixed with sweet, red wine.

Seeing no alternative, Juergen took a nervous sip. The taste was that of wine, blood, and cinnamon; not entirely bad, but off enough that the differences could be noticed. Setting his goblet aside on the ground next to his short stool, Juergen noted that Lametto was taking a long pull from his goblet before setting it down.

The man who presented them with the goblets said, "Excellent. Shall we get started?" Who he was asking was unknown, but the Supervisor let loose with an audible snort of derision.

Handed a similar short stool, the man squatted and sat opposite the three and began to speak slowly and quietly. He explained that the three of them had been selected to be part of an experiment that had already proven successful in Thalaria. The Governor General of Orienfuego had agreed to let it be done with several prisoners in his mine, and the three of them had been selected.

"It is rather simple: you are interviewed for a time, then put back on the line. Should the interview go well, you will be released early." He said, steepling his fingers before his face. "And if you do not do so well, you will serve out the rest of your sentence."

Starting in on the interview, the man's throat closed up. "I am call..." He suddenly stopped. With an exasperated look to the table and the apothecary, and said, "I am very parched. Water, please."

With what looked like a flourish, the apothecary dipped a ladle into a bucket and poured it into another goblet, which was brought over to the man.

With an almost exaggerated gasp, he took a long drink from the goblet. "I am called Roderick, a Wizard from Thalaria and associate head jailer in the Thalarian mines." With another pull from the Wizard's goblet, Juergen realized he was similarly parched. He absently picked up his wine concoction from the floor and took another small sip. It didn't taste quite so strong this time.

Wizard Roderick asked Lametto what his crimes were and what his sentence was, and as Lametto spoke, he took several more sips of his water, which prompted the three to do the same. *Why was he so thirsty?*

As Lametto finished speaking, he also finished his goblet. Juergen noted that Lametto had added some choice wording at the end of his response about the conditions and the Supervisor in particular. When Juergen turned his gaze to look at the Supervisor, he absently noted that it was hard to focus on the man's face.

Then it was his turn. When he responded, the words came easily, and he added that he had thought he was a victim of circumstances and shouldn't have been convicted in the first place because of how the situation had played out. As he finished, he noted that his goblet was similarly empty.

Roderick smiled and requested that all three be refilled with water, to which Lametto asked for wine, but Roderick insisted that the three share in water. It was amazing how thirsty the three of them were!

From there, Roderick asked about conditions, their workload, and how much time they had remaining in their sentences, and as he did so, his voice became more sing-songy and quieter.

Lametto admitted that he thought that he had completed nearly ten years of his sentence and only had five to go. He even admitted that he was getting hopeful that he would survive the mines to once again be a free man.

Roderick looked down and asked the three of them if they were aware of just how much time had elapsed, and both shook their heads in the negative.

"You each only have one year remaining of your sentences."

With that, all three men looked slackly at each other and offered up subdued cheers. Juergen felt like he was quite drunk, but after only one glass of wine he shouldn't be in this condition even after four years of being dry. He couldn't put enough into the words to properly question his condition, though.

After just a few hours—or a few minutes; it was hard to judge—Roderick thanked the three of them and said, "You will be escorted back to the line and told of the decision in due time. Thank you very much, gentlemen."

With that, the manacles at their feet were attached, and rough burlap hoods were pulled over their faces. Though curious, Juergen didn't ask why.

They were helped to their feet and escorted from the room. Juergen heard the sound of the bolt being released before they passed through and then sliding home after they departed. They were led around corners and through narrow and low spots where they had to squeeze. The guards were almost gentle on the journey back, which seemed like it took hours, whereas the trip to the room only took a few minutes.

As they sat down to be transferred to the line chains, it almost sounded like a voice was narrating what was happening.

When they were done, Juergen reached up to remove the hood, and the narrator reached out to gently stop his hand. The voice continued. "The lights are bright in the room, and the hood helps protect your vision. Leave it on for a short while as you sleep." The suggestion seemed logical, though something in the back of Juergen's mind told him that it hadn't been all that bright in the room; he did not question it and dropped his hand.

The night passed quickly, and both Juergen and Lametto awoke refreshed and alert. They took off the hoods and realized that it was difficult to focus, but the sensation soon passed. The day passed as so many others had passed, just melting into the next with scarcely a notice. More days passed, and Lametto laughed low that it probably was just a ruse to confuse them and that there was no early release headed for either of them.

That was when the first tremor hit.

Juergen noted the shaking of the ground as he sat. *Why am I sitting?* Prisoners only got to sit during mealtimes and at the end of shifts. He was confused, then realized as he thought, *oh, it must have been a mealtime. I wonder what it will be—gruel with bugs or without?* Either option didn't matter to him so long as he got a full share of the tasteless paste.

The shaking got more violent. But it was the screams and yells from up and down the line that really drew their attention. Panicked voices screamed in pain and fear as portions of the mine began to collapse. Waves of dust clouds rolled in and cut visibility to nothing, and rocks fell near Juergen, for he felt their impact on the walkway near him, and their splintered shrapnel struck his skin.

The ground began fairly throwing him around, and it almost felt like there were hands on him to hold him in place on the ground. Finally, he felt free. A great rock must have fallen directly between his feet and broke the chain that held him in place.

Hands gripped him and hauled him to his feet, and he was pulled along by other survivors. They ran around turns and corners, running into sheer rock walls from time to time in the darkness until after what seemed like hours of scrambling.

Juergen saw a large light from up ahead. "This way," he shouted, grabbing at the hands that had so recently been leading him, pulling them to the relative safety of outside the mine entrance.

The sun was hot against his skin, and it was too bright to properly look around without shading his eyes, but in a rush, it seemed like a hood had been removed from his head as he was able to focus a bit. Amid the running prisoners, he was face-down on the ground outside the entrance, within arm's reach of Lametto.

"You made it out!" Juergen was ecstatic that his only other real friend had survived.

"You did too, short timer!" Lametto's eyes had problems focusing, and it almost looked like he was drunk.

With a start, Juergen realized that he moved like he was, too.

"Sit back against the wall next to the opening so we don't get trampled," Juergen pulled Lametto with him until they were safe.

One of the surviving prisoners stopped near them, and when she saw them, she said, "We're FREE! Nobody's going to be looking for us for a while; let's get going!" Without another word, she dashed through the door to freedom.

Juergen and Lametto sat there for a moment, trying to process what was happening. Lametto suddenly stood up.

"Come on, kid, it's time we join them before we're caught," he said.

Juergen balked, "But we're so close to the end of our sentences. We scarcely have a year left."

Another escaping prisoner stopped long enough to address them. "Juergen, Lametto has just a tiny bit of his sentence left, while you have almost a quarter of your sentence remaining. You have more reason than him to run," the prisoner said and, with that, dashed out of the open door to freedom.

"Yeah, kid. I'm not spending another day in the mines. You've only done four of your five years. It makes sense for you to leave now; I should be the one to stay, but I ain't spending another day here. Come on, and join me!" Lametto almost seemed *happy!*

"If we leave now, we'll have a price on our heads," Juergen rationalized. "If we leave, we'll have to look over our shoulder for the rest of our lives."

"Lookin' over our shoulders is a small price to pay for freedom," Lametto argued.

"Lametto, you've done fourteen of your fifteen years. How can you risk getting caught?" Juergen was distraught. "You'll never see the sun again if you get caught!" Tears started to come.

"I don't care, kid. If we both don't leave now, neither of us may see the sun again. I say it's worth it—worth it for both of us."

"I can't, Lametto." Juergen was actively weeping now. "I may not have been convicted fairly, but I can't risk getting caught, and I surely can't look over my shoulder for the rest of my life. Even if I go back to Carinnia Vols, I feel like I'll always have to watch for a bounty hunter. I can't live my life like that. Let me just sit here until they come, and I'll go back to finish my sentence." Juergen pulled his knees up to his chest and wept.

"I hope to see you again one day, kid."

Juergen heard the sound of Lametto's feet on the flagstones as he loped away.

It wasn't long until guards came and took Juergen into custody again. With a minimum of prodding, he was handed a goblet of water that tasted faintly of mint and escorted back through the open door to the mine.

After just a few paces, Juergen was led through a doorway to a room with a bustle of people in long robes and the Supervisor with an amazed look on his face. Roderick was telling him, "...And it's easy as that, my Lord. Some drugs to soften their wills, then suggestions and hypnotic patterns in the voices, and they believe anything they're told." Roderick seemed a bit smug as he added, "And their reactions are genuine. Had they run, they'd be back in irons." The Supervisor shook his head, and as his own began to ache, Juergen couldn't tell if it was in disbelief or unwillingness to accept what he had witnessed.

There was activity at the door, and Lametto was unceremoniously pushed in, falling into a heap at Juergen's feet.

"Oh, Lametto, they caught you!" Juergen's headache was getting worse.

"Me?! They caught you, kid! Why didn't you run faster?" Lametto seemed confused as he held his head in his hands.

Juergen was confused. "Faster? I didn't run at all; you did." His head fairly pounded, and the young man thought he would get sick.

"I did no such thing. Even though they told me that they had bad info and that I still had five years left, I can do that standing on my head." Lametto groaned. "Oh, this head is killing me!"

Wizard Roderick stepped up and, without so much as a 'by your leave,' jabbed both of them with a wand he pulled from his sleeve. With just a single word, Juergen's head was clear and free of the crippling pain.

"That is a side effect of the drugs we used to make you susceptible to suggestions. The pain should be manageable now." Pulling his stool up and squatting upon it, Wizard Roderick explained. "You were drugged to be free with your thoughts and comments and to make you more open to our suggestions. After you were hooded, you were led around this room for a bit, then to adjacent rooms where you were separated. The cave-in was faked to see how you would react to being rushed about as if saving your lives; then we put you through the same scenario—the other wanted to leave, and it was up to you to make up your mind as to what you wished to do." Roderick seemed satisfied, and Juergen noted that he seemed tired.

"You both succeeded in the interview, gentlemen. As of now, your sentences have been commuted by the order of the Governor General of Orienfuego, and you have been remanded into my care." Roderick rose and helped each man to his feet.

Juergen asked, "What of the other prisoner?"

With a sigh, Roderick replied, "They did not succeed in the interview and attempted to escape." He genuinely seemed sad. "They're already back in irons on the line."

Juergen and Lametto both fell into each other's arms, weeping openly with confusion and relief. They had never been close, but their shared trials made them comrades in their struggle.

Roderick placed a hand on each of their shoulders. "What is your wish? I am headed back to Thalaria, but you are free to go where you wish. An escort can be arranged to Carinnia Vols if you would wish, Juergen."

They looked at each other, hope swelling in their breasts. Just what would the future hold?

They were FREE!

WERETIGRESS

The hunters are well trained, Thalia thought. She had used every trick in her modest book of tricks to elude them, all to no avail. She had doubled back—even quadrupled back—in an attempt to lose them. She had crossed so many streams and small rivers that her boots may never dry out. Still, they came after her.

What if they've got a Woodsman with them? Or dogs?! Oh, WHY hadn't I listened to Mother when she suggested that Father take this load of mushrooms into town? She lamented.

In the past three days, the hunters remained just out of view, though on occasion, she could hear the telltale sound of cracking twigs or jingling coins in loose pouches, and these drove her to redouble her speed.

It was time, yet again. She dropped a scarf, took an abrupt right turn, and jogged about 100 paces to a small stream, then turned on her soft-heeled shoes to carefully walk back in her own tracks—what few she could make out.

When she got back to her apparently discarded scarf, she picked it up and went off in the opposite direction, repeating her doubled journey. When returning this time, she stopped at a low-hanging branch. She leapt up to grab it, traveling several four or five paces of length along the slimy bark before carefully dropping to the moss-covered ground again, before carefully picking her way in her original direction of travel. After being as unobtrusive and leaving as little sign of her passage as possible, she again took off at a jog.

The day had started on such an up note—well, outside of Mother's constant suggestions that Father takes the cart into town. *GAH!!* She had been overprotective to the point of being smothering for the past season. The formerly tiring attention had grown truly unbearable until she fairly yelled at her mother to let her take the cart to town. Father had taken the last four monthly trips to town, and Thalia's argument was that he deserved the break, not that hauling the mushrooms was difficult. Sure, the trail was overgrown with moss and lichens, and there were the silver spiders to watch out for, but it was only a few hours to town to sell the mushrooms, then a good meal at Uncle Ri'ikard and Aunt Bet's house and a good night's sleep before heading back again.

Aunt Bettany's ham stew was the envy of the family, and Thalia had hoped she could talk Aunt Bet into sharing the recipe.

With the thought, Thalia's stomach growled in discomfort. Slowing her pace a bit, she sought out wild leeks to slake her hunger again. *Next time in town, I'd ask Uncle Ri'ikard what other kinds of plants were edible when raw.* Sure, we all know what ones are good when cooked, but even her favorite snack, the leeks, were getting old. They held off the worst of the hunger pangs, but their strong taste just grew tiresome after three days!

The glint of something just off to her right made her stop. *Spiderstrand*, she said to herself, and a horrible plan sprang to mind. Veering right, she slowed to a crawl. Spotting more strands dangling from high above in the dark canopy, she stopped to assess the situation.

Dozens of the silvery web filaments hung down to varying heights above the ground, just waiting to snag an unwary interloper. As the unfortunate creature snagged a strand, they would be dropped by the silver spider lurking far overhead, to fall down either on the prey or to the moss-covered ground nearby. This signaled the other spiders in the canopy to lower their trapping strands to the ground, and unless the poor animal was very fast or very lucky, they would be held in place as the huge spiders slowly lowered themselves down to wrap their dinner in a tight cocoon. Then, the spiders will slowly pull them back up to be devoured at their leisure.

The spiders were scary enough. She recalled when she was young, being out with her father, who showed her where a young fawn had found itself entrapped. Dozens of 'small' spiders came first, being large enough to span Thalia's entire hand without touching flesh. After them came the bigger ones, some larger than a dog that could walk the outer walls of a cart without touching the inside! She shuddered at the thought.

What was worse was their sheer beauty—furry bodies of white and silver that sparkled with the ever-present dew of her home forests of Legaroth. They bit the fawn repeatedly until it stopped moving—Father said it was their poison that immobilized their prey—before quickly wrapping it in its funerary cocoon and quickly hoisting it aloft. Father had told her that they would eat their meal and then cut their snag lines before they moved to another area to set another snare trap.

If this plan worked, she might be able to either lose her trackers or maybe even lure one or more to their... *Oh, gods, don't even say it!* She was horrified that she even had the idea, let alone what the consequences could possibly be. *Why does it matter,* she thought. *They're hunting me to kill me!*

As the justification fell upon her, she became emotional, and she felt her hands begin to swell and hurt. *NOT AGAIN!!* She struggled to push down her tears as she looked down at her hands... well.... paws. Her fingers had curled up, and great claws had erupted from her fingertips as yellowish fur marred with black splotches grew up the backs of her hands and threatened to cover her forearms before she regained control of her emotions.

I don't know if I can control myself for much longer, she thought as her skin quickly absorbed the hair and claws, and her fingers straightened out again. As the claws flattened out and disappeared, Thalia made two fists and clawed her own palms in frustration. Anger didn't seem to cause the change, only despair.

The first time it had happened was right after she had arrived in town. Thalia had pulled into a stall in the small market where she intended to set up shop and had begun unhitching the large goat from her cart. To the left and right were other merchants who were likewise setting up their wares for sale. Quick glances told her that they were selling wood carvings and pottery, so she had no immediate competition nearby.

Leaving her goat half hitched, she clambered back to drop the cart's tailgate, and that was when disaster struck.

A wayward cat startled the vendor's dog to her left, and the chase was on. The dog erupted in snarls and barking, and the cat went airborne, leaping onto the rear of her poor goat before it leapt over to the back of the goat to the right. With a lurch, the pain in its backside caused her goat to immediately lurch forward, dumping Thalia unceremoniously into the dirt as the entire load of mushrooms was dumped onto the muck-covered ground around her.

As her cart sped away, dumping what few mushrooms remained, the goats to the left and right reared in alarm and turned toward the empty space where her cart had been. Their jumping and pawing at the muck turned her mushrooms into an unsavory paste within seconds, and she was fortunate enough to scramble to her feet before she joined the unholy stew.

As the merchants to the left and right struggled to regain control of their goats, Thalia glanced at the ground beneath her feet. One large, intact mushroom was all that remained of the bushels-full that she had brought and that was quickly smushed under the heels of the merchants as they sought to keep their beasts from likewise bolting.

Looking up, she saw her goat and cart racing around a corner of a building and was soon lost in the distance. Her entire day—the trip—was ruined. Unable to do anything to save her beloved mushrooms—*Oh, how many coins were now lost in this debacle,* she thought—Thalia did the only thing she could do; she began to cry.

As the turmoil near her wound down, sobs wracked her small frame. That was when she noticed her hands hurting. Thinking she had fallen onto something when she broke her fall, she looked down.

Her fingers curled unnaturally into what looked like claws, and, horror of horrors, actual CLAWS began to erupt from her fingertips! As her wrists began to curl back and her palms grew puffy—like those of a cat or dog—Thalia saw the yellowish fur begin to erupt from the backs of her hands and grow up her forearms.

Looking up in horror, she recognized Uncle Ri'ikard as he helped calm the animals as only a Huntsman can. Meeting her gaze, Thalia saw his eyes fall to her hands and back up to her eyes as his gaze grew alarmed.

"RUN!" he commanded, and without a thought, she did just that.

The town's protective palisade had a gate that was just a few dozen paces away, and Thalia sprinted to and through it. Stopping suddenly, she thought, *Oh, gods, I'm a werewolf! I can't possibly go home. What if I eat Mother and Father or any of my brothers or sisters??* Turning to her left, she dashed up the wagon ruts away from town and away from her family. In the distance, she could hear Uncle Ri'ikard yelling something about Aunt Bet, the cart, and his sister.

It wasn't until many hours before she discovered that tears brought on the transformation. Each time she stopped to catch her breath and the crying overtook her, her hands began to transform again… and again. Fortunately for her, her rage at her condition quickly overruled the tears and repressed the change. Time and again, it happened, each time hurting just a little less. She never let it progress past her forearms before she pushed her tears away and let the anger take over.

Her life was over! Everyone knew that werewolves were rampant in the dark forest of Legaroth; even her father had been on several hunting expeditions to eradicate the damnable things. Mother told stories of were-creatures of all types that used to be hunted by an evil temple of clerics who used terror and torture to elicit admissions of being cursed so the creatures could be put to death in some of the most horrific ways imaginable.

Mother had told Thalia and her siblings that many innocent people had been subjected to the brazen bull and died in their attempted purge of werewolves. This temple had long since been destroyed, and its clerics were revealed as were-serpents, who were hunted and slain as ruthlessly as they had hunted the were-creatures until they were but a nightmare-inducing story to scare children. *It had worked,* Thalia thought ruefully.

The hunters behind her drove her to desperation—she would have to brave the dangers of a web-fall to possibly save her own life by slowing or stopping those that followed.

Steeling herself, Thalia quickly plotted a course through the web-fall to the other side, about 25 paces away, and then took to her heels. Just a few paces in, she discovered something that Father had not told her, or she had forgotten: that in addition to the sparkly silver strands suspended from so far above were invisible strands that were lightly anchored to the moss at her feet.

As she encountered the first invisible strand, she could feel slight resistance above it, and it suddenly broke loose from whatever anchor held it in place so far aloft. Like lightning, it snapped down at her and covered her back with its sticky length.

With a shriek, she fairly dove for the other side as she saw the shiny strands start to dribble toward the mossy ground at her feet in the spiders' attempt to cut off her escape. Four more invisible strands caught her before she got close enough to the other side, where she dove through the few sparkly strands between her and freedom.

Rolling, the sticky strands did their best to hold her down in the damp moss. So, quickly shrugging off her vest, Thalia bolted upright and looked up. In horror, she saw hundreds of silver spiders floating down on slender webs toward where she had just so recently been lying. Some were the size of her hands, and most of the others were larger than Lizbet, her cat back home, with a few gargantuan specimens whose legs nearly spanned her entire height. With another shriek, she darted off as quickly as her feet could carry her.

She continued to run through most of the night, only moving when the full moon above was able to drive its gentle beams through the heavy forest canopy. It wasn't until a rare breeze made a web-fall sparkle just ahead that she stopped. The idea of unwittingly tripping her way into a web-fall overrode her fear of being caught by the hunters that followed.

***

A wolf's lonely howl in the far distance woke her just as dawn was breaking, and she continued ahead again.

Not long after dawn, her heart dropped. Ahead was a large body of water, impossibly large. She must have run all the way to Linae Lokia, Lake Lokia.

Far off in the distance, Thalia could just barely make out the far shore in the distance, miles away. Too far away. While she was a good swimmer, Thalia knew that it was folly to even attempt to swim that distance.

Stepping into the water in an attempt to draw any hunters off her trail, she began to double back again, and it was then that she saw the hunter in the distance. Some hundred paces off, Thalia could see him coming around the bole of a tree. She saw the crossbow in his hand at the same time she recognized him. Da'anel Gresham. HUNTSMAN Da'anel Gresham.

Oh, by all of the gods! A Huntsman*!!* Thalia's heart quailed. *Why did they send a Huntsman?* Then her heart fell even more. *Uncle Ri'ikard must have told them; he knows I'm a werewolf. He's going to kill me if I can't get away.*

She looked at the lake behind her again as Huntsman Da'anel let loose with a loud, low whistle. *Wonderful, he's signaling the other Huntsmen.*

"Don't get any closer, Huntsman!" Thalia did her best to sound threatening. "Don't get closer, or... I'll swim out and drown myself." The stress of the situation was mounting, and she could feel the helplessness crash upon her.

"Don't try to be clever, girl," Huntsman Da'anel said. "There are people who have risked life and limb to find you." The Huntsman smiled and ruefully shook his head. "That was a pretty good trick with that limb stunt and then running through the web-fall. I almost lost a fellow Huntsman trying to verify that you weren't spider-lunch."

Even better, Thalia thought sadly. *More than one Huntsman.* She could feel the tears welling in her eyes, and she could feel her hands start to change again. This time, she couldn't muster the rage to stop it, and she didn't try.

Uncle Ri'ikard stepped out from behind another tree off to the right. "I know you're scared, Thalia. Please understand that we love you."

"Love me enough to see me DEAD!" Thalia yelled back accusingly, the last word coming as a snarl. Waves of agony spread across her entire body as she fell to her hands and knees in pain.

Looking down, she saw large, soft paws, and in confusion, she looked at her legs, seeing a tawny hip and a long, thin, striped tail. *I am the most stupidly colored werewolf in the world,* Thalia thought amusingly. With a start, she suddenly realized that she hadn't assumed the form of a wolf but rather that of a hunting cat—a tiger. She snarled out her confusion.

"There are things you need to know, Thalia," Uncle Ri'ikard sounded almost conciliatory. In the span of a few heartbeats, he knelt down and transformed into a huge tiger. Before she could even process this, another tiger broke into the area off to the left. Thalia recoiled as the tigress—*how did she know this?*—skidded to a stop just a few paces away.

As she tried not to fall over backward, this tigress transformed back into a human... not just any human, but her own MOTHER!

Trying to process this, Thalia heard a voice in her head. "Our family has been ailuranthropes—were-tigers—for many generations. It's not a curse; it's just a family trait, like out blonde hair, which you have inherited. All the light-haired people in our family share this trait."

Thalia fairly reeled at this revelation. *Not a werewolf?*

Her mother was openly weeping. Reaching for Thalia, she begged, "Come here, my baby girl. Come here and let mommy help you." Thalia growled, her confusion in response. "I know it hurts the first few times, but you get used to it. Let me show you how to turn back."

Thalia growled again, not understanding.

She was also surprised to see that Uncle Ri'ikard and Huntsman Da'anel had approached. Her Uncle was beseeching her. "Thalia, we have so much to tell you, especially about the Huntsmen."

With that, Huntsman Da'anel dropped to all fours and took on the appearance of a large wolf. Thalia roared her disapproval.

Just as quickly, the Huntsman transformed back into a man and fell back on his bottom as he laughed. "She's got some fight in her, Rik. I'd best stay back a bit."

Nodding his agreement, Uncle Ri'ikard squatted down on his haunches and began to explain. "Most of the Huntsmen are therianthropes—were-creatures—and have been since before the ice came so many thousands of years ago. For a long time, we were locked in a constant war against the Temple of Savinth, all while trying to slay the cursed werewolves and corralling up those of us who were born with the trait before they could be found by the Temple and killed."

Thalia's mother slowly approached and laid a gentle hand on Thalia's head. "Let's go, darling daughter. You've led us on quite a journey, very far from home. Let's go back and start answering your questions. I'm sure you have many, MANY questions. I know I did."

KOINET THE LION RUNNER

The trek had been arduous, but Koinet didn't let himself complain. By and large, the *Mulala*—his people—weren't complainers, but if there was something to talk about, they were sure to mention it. Still, he refrained. He was one of four youths chosen for this honor, and he didn't want to give the Elders a reason to second-guess their choice. Sure, he was the Chieftain's son, but that was no guarantee that he would be either chosen for the *Pundakisi* or even successfully complete it, especially since he was destined to become a *Mkimbai* or *Lion Runner* rather than a *Sujaa* or someone else that was blessed to spend the rest of their days in the saddle.

Lion Runners grew up lean and lanky, almost always towering over the rest of the members of the villages, and they were the only ones who maintained a shaved head after their Rites of Passage into adulthood. The rest grew their hair out, maintaining shorter styles when they were youthful and inexperienced, then finally letting their kinky hair grow out into long, glorious *Sukiyanda*, or *Long Hair,* that rose far above and behind their proud heads. They could also leave their hair in braids or locs that could eventually trail down to the saddles in which they spent so much time. His own father sported a *Daymuntu* or *Cloud Hair* that rose up and behind his head, nearly reaching the length of his arm when he was galloping on his beloved horse.

Horses played a very special part in Mulalan culture—they were horse people, after all—and this was even displayed in their name and the name of their land: Katima Mulalo in their tongue or Plains of the People of the Horse in the guttural Common tongue used by traders and travelers—the non-Mulalans.

They non-Mulalans, the *Tembea* or *non-riders,* always stood out in crowds when they visited, by their non-bow-legged gait, their straight hair, and almost always by their pale skin. They were even more pale than the skin on Koinet's palms, with some nearly as pale as the whites of his eyes. The Tembea also didn't have the same relationships with their horses.

Well, those reasons, and the fact that they didn't travel with their Ancestors. When a Mulalan passed to the next life, they rose again after a couple of days to continue their work with their families even after their deaths. Over a couple of years, since the Ancestor's hearts no longer sent blood through their limbs, the flesh would dry and slough off, leaving only ambulatory skeletons tending to gardens or children. After another generation or more, the skeletons of the Ancestors would crumble to dust. Then, it was the Ancestors' choice whether their spirit was to travel to the Beyond or remain nearby to offer counsel and comfort to the family. Koinet's own grandparents still walked with the tribe while his great-grandparents, great-uncles, and aunties shuffled about as skeletons. Several times, Koinet saw his father speaking to the spirit of a great-great-someone. Perhaps after the *Pundakisi,* he would be likewise blessed.

When the march was called for the day, the real activity began, and tonight would be particularly strenuous as Lebuu's beloved mount had just stepped in a gopher hole and broken its leg. There was no Shaman traveling with them to heal the injury, so she would have to be put down. That meant digging out a large pit to cook the carcass. This was done both to feed the travelers and to honor the mount, who had been part of Lebuu's family for nearly 20 years.

A large pit to be dug, and then hunting about for large stones for the cooking pit. The horse would bake all night long, and then the morning feast would be glorious, with huge servings of succulent and tender meat accompanied by stories of how Mupepe had served Lebuu over the years.

Koinet's stomach growled with hunger in anticipation, and a quick glance at his fellow future Lion Runners let him know that they were feeling much the same.

Only Lion Runners participated in *Pundakisi*, well, *future* Lion Runners. It was their Rite of Passage into the adult world, and Koinet had been dreaming of this day for the past six winters since he had passed ten summers in age. At 16, he was the eldest of the others chosen—in Naeku's case, by two years. Naeku was the youngest, with the twins, Surum and Sironka, being one year between the other two.

All of them were lean and lanky, whereas all of the other children their age had begun to thicken up in the middle and were invariably shorter than the four. Some of the other children tried to chide them for not being blessed, like the Mulala or *Riders*, but adults quickly put a stop to it. Collectively, their hearts filled to near-bursting as the adults explained the special place the Lion Runners held in society and how they contributed.

Lion Runners were scouts and trackers and raised the young horses, choosing which ones were suitable for riding and which were meant for breeding or milking, or for draft work hauling the tribe's wagons and skids, or ultimately for the cooking pits. After a Lion Runner had proven themself, they also undertook a dangerous journey where they sought out a lioness to be their companion for life.

After that explanation, the teasing stopped, and the others even treated them with more respect than before.

Mkimbai Simel ordered Tonkei to begin setting up camp while the twins were told to begin digging the cooking pit. Koinet was happy to hear that he was commanded to go find large, flat rocks, and he quickly dashed off to a nearby hilltop to see if he could spot likely locations. Gaining the high ground, he looked about and saw a thin ribbon of a river running about a kilometer away. Without hesitation, Koinet broke into a distance-eating lope to check out if there were any river rocks that would suit the purpose.

Several minutes later, upon arrival, Koinet trotted up to the highest hilltop nearby to survey possible eddies that would hold the cooking stones he sought.

Just down to his left, in a perfect little wadi, was an old Mulalan campsite that had a used cooking pit already dug out and lined with perfect stones. Turning on his heel, Koinet sprinted back to their campsite to tell Mkimbai Simel of his discovery. Arriving just a couple of moments later, Koinet breathlessly explained what he had found.

"Pack it up; we're moving another kilometer!" Mkimbai Simel's voice was commanding. The twins grumbled at the news that their few minutes of hard digging were for naught, and Koinet even heard Naeku mutter under her breath. In a quieter tone, Mkimbai Simel grilled Koinet to find out how he had ended up there, how he spotted it, why he chose that location, and even why he had made his decisions and why he had chosen to sprint back to the present site.

Koinet answered truthfully, explaining vantage points for viewing, looking for a turn in the river, and that he had come back as quickly as he could to save the group from having to set up a site and dig a cooking pit when there was one nearby. He also included that there was still daylight, so another kilometer would be easy to cover.

Mkimbai Simel then asked about the mortally injured horse, "Wouldn't that be cruel to make the mount continue to walk that far?"

"Well, Mkimbai Simel, I figured we could slaughter her here and just take the meat with us," came Koinet's quick reply.

Mkimbai Simel smiled, "It is good to first work with your head before you work with your back. You've saved the others from needlessly digging a pit and unloading the gear. You even saved yourself from carrying all the cooking stones back here." When Koinet raised an eyebrow in question, the answer came quickly. "After you were all done, I was going to remind the entire train of that other campsite and make you pack up everything and go over there, so all your work would have been in vain. Remember that site because we've been using it for generations. All the adults already know about the plan." Looking about, Koinet saw that the only saddle that had been removed was from Lebuu's mount, and all the riders had begun slaughtering the noble horse, having already bled it out and now were gutting it in anticipation of being quartered and put on a sled.

"Head back to the site with a shovel, tidy up the cooking pit, and set up the stones so we can get the fires started quickly," Mkimbai Simel said. Then his voice barked out, "Let's get moving as the sun waits for no one. Honor goes to Koinet for saving you all a load of work this evening. Remember when you talk with him later that it is best to work with your head before you work with your back!"

As Koinet grabbed a shovel and trotted off, he held his head a bit higher. The trip back seemed to take only seconds.

The old—er—new cooking pit was ready just moments before the others arrived, and Koinet was returning from the river after washing off the shovel and himself when they got there.

The other three arrived, and the four of them shared the task of setting up camp. As they worked, the three inquired of Koinet what he had done so they might be wiser the next time they were tasked with scouting the area. He shared his actions freely, and when they were done, they all watched the pit master, Lembui, prep the pit, then scatter the coals, add more wood, lay more stones, and season the meat thoroughly before finally putting the meat in place. He then covered the entire pit with more stones and sod cut from around the campsite.

Lebuu was quite sad through all of this, and the other adults spent their time comforting him, placing the palms of their hands on his upper chest and back in support. Even the youths would find a reason to pass close to him to place their hands on his forearms or shoulders to show their similar sympathies. From past experience, Koinet knew that the mourning would last for longer than when a fellow Mulalan passed, as horses were of this world and were not immortal like the Ancestors and did not rise again.

Well, except through powerful magicks, and then they were just mindless shadows of what they used to be. Plus, they rotted when they were animated. Their only use was as draft animals, and that was only for a few days until the stench got so bad that even the Ancestors complained.

The night passed quickly, and the youths were famished by morning as the amazing aromas escaped through the stones and sod to tease them all night. As far as they were concerned, breakfast was a feast that would be talked about for years by the *Shaha*—the *Tale Tellers*. Afterward, the cooked meat was divided up and placed in several magical bags that would keep it cool and prevent spoilage.

The camp was struck in record time, and they continued their journey.

Nearly two weeks later, the entourage arrived at their destination: a flat hilltop in the foothills of the Maji Mabaya Mountains, or Evil Water Mountains. The mountains rose like angry spearpoints in the near distance, lifting suddenly from the vast plains that the Mulalans called home. There was also very little land in the foothills that buffered the plains as they rose suddenly as if pushed high aloft by some angry god trapped far beneath the surface of the ground.

The *Mchawi*, or *Magic Wielder*, made a large smudge fire to produce smoke and began chanting the ritual to call the *Pepebampunda*, the great Flying Horses, or hippogriffs in the common tongue. The glorious beasts were like horses from the ribcage back to their midnight black hooves, but their front legs and head resembled raptors—mighty eagles—with huge taloned claws on their forefeet and great, vicious beaks on their feathered heads.

The other thing that set them apart from horses were the huge wings that sprouted from their shoulders, wings that were strong enough to lift a person. The one Koinet had seen several years back had left a lasting impression on him. Even after so many years, he was still in awe of the memory. And he was to see a whole HERD of them today! Koinet could barely contain the excitement.

Watching *Mchawi Nampazo* perform the ritual, Koinet waited. It was interesting as *Mchawi Nampazo* repeated the summons in all four directions of the compass, tossing colored powder into the smudge fire, which made the smoke change color. Then she repeated shorter summons in all four half-compass directions, adding different powders to the fire, which made the smoke almost pulse with different colors: red, green, blue, and many more. This ritual was slowly repeated over and over for hours before Mkimbai Simel announced that he saw the herd approaching.

Following his gaze to the southwest, Koinet saw nothing for quite some time before a small flutter of movement in the farthest reaches of his vision caught his eye. How Mkimbai Simel saw anything farther made Koinet wonder if he would *ever* become a Lion Runner like him.

It was nearly a quarter-hour before the hazy movement grew close enough to actually see kind of clearly, and Koinet's jaw dropped open—an entire herd of *Pepebampunda*, and it looked like there were several dozen of the glorious beasts!

It took over an hour—the longest hour of Koinet's life—for the *Pepebampunda* to arrive, and by the look on the faces of the other three youths and Tonkei was even crying in anticipation, it seemed to be the longest for them, too.

The *Pepebampunda* landed a short distance off, and Koinet was shocked at their screaming neighs, a perfect mix between the shriek of a hunting bird and the neigh of a horse. It was perfect for them, but the sound still stunned at the beauty—and the sheer VOLUME! The din was earsplitting as it seemed like each of the *Pepebampunda* had to scream as they landed, as if announcing their arrival or as if the land burned their hooves... claws... feet. Koinet wondered silently what you would call the collection of things at the ends of their legs because they were different. That would be something to ask Mkimbai Simel later.

Mkimbai Simel approached them, and a large stallion left the herd as if to greet him. Koinet heard the Lion Runner speaking to the herd leader in low tones, almost like they knew each other. He strained to hear what was being said to no avail.

The large stallion looked pointedly at the four youths, however, and Koinet guessed that they were the topic of conversation. The four were directed to haul out the half-dozen large sacks brought with them on the wagons. When they did, Mkimbai Simel cut them open to reveal that they had been full of dried corn, which came as a surprise as corn was a bit of a delicacy in Katima Mulalo, where smaller grains dominated. Nonetheless, the bags were cut and dumped into a large pile on the hilltop; then, the youths were directed to stand nearby as the adults stepped back to watch. The large stallion gave a great shriek, and the entire herd charged en masse to the great feast laid out before them.

Most of the *Pepebampunda* simply stepped around them, but the smaller, younger *Pepebampunda* stopped to skittishly sniff at them as they passed by. The proximity of these glorious beasts thrilled Koinet to no end, and judging from the smiles on the others' faces, they were likewise enraptured. Truly the best day of their young lives!

In but a minute, the corn was all gone, and the adult Pepebampunda left the area to return to where they had landed, leaving only the youngest colts—fledglings?—and the large stallion. Then, one at a time, the leader of the herd came to each of the four to sniff at them as if weighing them like so much meat or judging them for some unknown reason.

When it was done, it turned and pawed at the dirt and screeched at the young *Pepebampunda*, then spun and trotted out of the area with a small flap of its massive wings. The resulting gust of wind nearly toppled Tonkei and one of the twins, with Tonkei stepping back several paces while the twin just dropped to his knees to avoid the mini tempest. That just left the four youths and nearly a dozen young *Pepebampunda*.

Three or four *Pepebampunda* stepped up to each youth and made a production of sniffing and poking about at all of them as if inspecting newly purchased equipment. After several minutes of checking them out, the *Pepebampunda* rotated to inspect a new youth, a pattern that repeated four times. It wasn't until the last rotation that anything really changed.

As the last three inspected one of the twins, they stopped as if losing interest and began trotting back toward Koinet. One of the four inspecting Koinet seemed agitated and began clawing at the dirt with its impressive talons and screeching at him as if it had taken offense to something Koinet had said or done. With the loudest shriek so far, it suddenly darted at Koinet and buried its beak in Koinet's upper chest. The impact drove him to the dirt as the other young *Pepebampunda* began to likewise screech and shriek.

Numb and unwilling to look at his wound, Koinet scrambled to his feet to meet his attackers—not that he could do anything against a herd of *Pepebampunda*, even if they *were* young. What greeted his eyes surprised him into inaction.

The smaller herd of young *Pepebampunda* had dispersed save for the one that had bitten him. The large stallion had charged up and had taken a bite out of the left flank of the angry, young *Pepebampunda* and was slamming its head against it in a manner that left Koinet thinking that it was trying to beat some sense into it. Finally, the stallion spun around and kicked with both rear hooves, which slammed into the forequarter of the angry one. This tossed the colt's head over hooves, and it was very slow to get up. The stallion then repeatedly screeched at the colt as if reprimanding it.

This caused the colt to shake its head as if trying to get rid of a bad smell. When it stopped, it looked at Koinet, then at the stallion, then back to Koinet. It hung its head and slowly walked in the direction of the herd, blood streaming down its left hip, and it was favoring that leg. Seeing the blood on the colt reminded Koinet of his own wound, so he looked down to inspect it.

Blood covered his entire torso and was oozing quickly out of a gaping wound in his left upper chest area, right above his heart. All Koinet could hear was the continued screeching of the stallion, and he felt many strong hands as he sank to his knees in shock.

As the world shrank to a pinpoint of light, he could hear the adults telling each other what to do to stop the bleeding and how best to tend the wound. Then came blackness.

The journey back to the village was one of pain and sheer boredom. Koinet was relegated to sitting in a wagon with his arms strapped tightly to his chest to prevent it from moving and opening the injury. Mkimbai Simel told him that he, Tonkeierina, and Surum had been Chosen to be Mkimbai. Sironka was despondent about not being so Chosen, and it was with a start that Koinet realized that Sironka was the one the *Pepebampunda* colts had turned away from.

When he asked Mkimbai Simel about it, he confirmed that the *Pepebampunda* had made the choices for his people and that all of Mkimbai had been so selected. Koinet then quietly asked about Sironka's status, and Mkimbai Simel responded just as quietly that his path as an adult was that of a Tembea, a career in support of the Mulala that rode. Presently, he was being pushed toward becoming a pitmaster, but his decision would be made at a later time.

***

Five years had passed since Koinet was selected to become a Mkimbai, and he was out on his solo mission to entreat a long-toothed lioness to become his lifelong companion. As fortune would have it, he was far to the southwest, near where the *Pundakisi* had taken place.

Koinet was following a spoor that he knew belonged to a female lion that had two cubs with her when a movement in a neighboring valley caught his eye. It was a *Pepempunda*, and though he was nearly a kilometer away, Koinet knew it was either sorely injured or ill as its head was hanging low and its wings were dragging behind it.

Loath to lose track of the lioness, Koinet split his attention between the trail and the *Pepempunda*. Within just meters, the trail veered off to the left, and Koinet knew that the lioness was hunting something other than the wounded *Pepebampunda*. Giving up the track, he broke into a sprint, heading into the small valley.

Getting closer, Koinet could see that it was a young stallion and that, for whatever reason, it was starving to death. Many of the pin feathers on its wings had fallen out, and it was gaunt; his eyes were bulging, and you could clearly see his ribs and pelvis beneath dull-colored hair.

"Are you ill, mighty *Pepempunda?*" Koinet asked quietly.

Wheezing, the *Pepempunda* responded in a low tone, "Kill me, Rider. I am alone and will die soon and would rather I end quickly than starving for another tenday or more." The voice was raspy and low, barely above a whisper.

Shocked at both the request as well as actually hearing a *Pepempunda* speak, Koinet responded, "Mighty *Pepempunda*, there is a hungry lioness with two cubs in tow just over the rise right now. You won't have a tenday to suffer." Curiosity got the better of him, so he added, "Why are you alone, Mighty *Pepempunda*? Did your herd meet their end?"

"Human, I am not 'mighty'; I am exiled for breaking taboos and not finding the fault in my actions."

"Well, then, not 'mighty,' what is your name so I might address you properly?"

"Not that I deserve being called anything, but I was called *Tembemosi*." The *Pepempunda* sounded despondent.

Koinet thought about the name 'Lightning Mane' and wondered how he had earned such a noble name.

"I do not know your ways, mighty *Tembemosi*, but my people are named after portents when they are born. How did you earn this name?"

"Once, I had a bad feeling about a young human and tried to slay him. I have been an outcast since then. Then, I was finally driven from my herd several moons ago. I tried to make it, but *Pepebampunda* are pack hunters, and I cannot make a kill alone, so I starve. Stop talking, human, and end my suffering."

Koinet's curiosity was piqued. "What bad feelings did you have about this human?" Koinet nonchalantly moved to the *Pepempunda's* left side and saw a jagged scar on its left withers.

"I felt like we would be linked somehow, but I was young and didn't want to be associated with any two legs. I felt that that was beneath me." The *Pepempunda* still hadn't raised his head.

"And now?" Koinet asked as he approached the *Pepempunda*.

"Now, I have seen what happens when one is alone. Perhaps it would be better if I had learned this years ago. Now, I die because I am alone."

Koinet knelt down before the *Pepempunda* and pulled aside his bone armor to reveal his vivid scar. "Would you accept this human's help, mighty *Tembemosi*? If you can hold on for a few more hours, I can return with enough food that you will at least be able to sleep comfortably while I hunt for more food. Will you do that, Great One?"

The *Pepempunda's* rheumy eyes struggled to focus. Then they opened wide with recognition. "It is YOU! Why would you do this?"

"I learned the strength of family long ago. My people hold community highest in our hearts, so we all know that life is easier with others. I am not here to dominate and put you in bondage."

THE BIRTH OF MAGIC

The gang had all morning to play and explore; Thelar, the village soothsayer, said that the storms wouldn't be coming in until after the sun had reached the top of the heavens. This meant that, with the crops planted and the morning chores done, the morning was theirs to do as they wished, and they ran like wild toward the ruins west of town. Abrea thought it was a good idea as well because the ruins were on the crest of a small hill that gave a good view of the dark clouds approaching from further west. She thought she could even smell the rain on the warm air but shook her head at the crazy thought as she ducked to avoid a branch that was released by Marco ahead of her. He laughed at the near miss, and they continued their mad dash toward their goal. Who built the site was unknown, but in a child's mind, they must have been amazing.

The kids scrambled over toppled pillars and atop archways that must have once stood taller than a giant, holding magnificent marble-tiled roofs aloft to sparkle in the sun. They imagined grand processionals traveling along spectacular paths, festooned with magical lamps to provide a hedge against the dark and great throngs of people waving at the parade participants as they passed by. There were only seven of them here today, but the children reenacted their fantasy scenes with choruses of laughter and cheers as their peers bowed and curtsied as they passed by the onlookers.

Abrea was the eldest here today, and it was one of her last chances to relax and play before her life would be irrevocably changed by the midsummer Choosing. This was when the eldest boys of the village would be selected as apprentices by the Masters, who would teach them their life's trade, and the eldest girls would parade through the square to announce their availability for marriage, and men would express their interest. *How unfair,* she thought.

Abrea's sense of inevitability in the Choosing this summer began to gnaw at her this past winter when her mother told her that Old Man Ronna's wife had passed. He was as old as Grandfather Emm! Being married off to that fat old man would be a fate worse than death! Her mother looked crestfallen when Abrea told her that she would jump off the Widow's Cliff if he expressed his intent to marry her. Abrea knew that she had broken her mother's heart.

She shook her head to clear her thoughts and realized that the others had run off from their parade to investigate other parts of the well-investigated ruins. She thought she could smell sweet, pungent zing on the air and realized that the wind had shifted from the south to the northwest. With a glance, she saw the black storm clouds were closer, and with regret, she inhaled to call the other kids to start the journey back home. That was when the light appeared.

It began like a straight line, vertical before her, then grew wider like when Mother opened the curtains in the morning. However, this light was whiter than any she had seen before, whiter than the beautiful bolt of fabric that the traveling merchants brought through a few years ago—brilliant white and unblemished. The light grew so wide that when Abrea looked to the left and right, she felt like she was in a huge, white chamber.

That sweet, pungent zing was so strong that she felt like she was in the middle of a storm, though she didn't hear the wind or rain. She moved toward the wall... wait! She looked down and saw that her feet weren't on any sort of ground or flooring—she was FLOATING! She also noticed that her sandals were off, her left leg had a huge, red welt running all the way from mid-thigh to her ankle, and her left foot looked like it was burned. Abrea absently noted that it didn't hurt, nor was it bleeding, so she continued toward the wall. As she touched it, the whiteness rippled like the lightest of silken curtains, and it brushed aside like a breeze.

The storm smell was stronger, but she knew there was no threat about which she should worry. *Wait, how did I know that?* she mused. Blue sky surrounded her with light, puffy clouds as far as the eye could see, save for immediately behind her. She was shocked at the inky blackness of the clouds from which she had just emerged, and she felt herself floating away from the roiling storm clouds with breathtaking speed. Somehow, she knew that she caused her own flight.

Within seconds, she was more than a mile away from the threatened storm, and she felt safe enough to slow down and look around again. Still, there were blue skies and puffy clouds on the horizon, except there was no horizon.

"By the gods, there is no ground at ALL!" Suddenly aware of her height, Abrea realized that to prevent herself from falling, she was flying straight up. With a start, she halted her panicked flight and decided that, without ground, there WAS no *up* or *down* and that she couldn't *fall* in any direction!

"Why are you here, little one?"

Abrea shrieked at the sudden voice from behind her, and she realized that she was moving at break-neck speeds again in an attempt to get away. Unfortunately, the creature, no, *creatures,* no, *men,* no, *creature-men,* were easily keeping pace with her, just out of the reach of those wicked-looking spear thingies they carried so nonchalantly. When she realized they didn't seem angry or actually threatening, she willed herself to slow down and stop, and then she looked over these three *things* with a more critical eye.

They were taller than Rollof, the tallest man in her village, but only by a hand or two. All three men were well-built and heavily muscled, and with a shock, she realized that one of them was a woman! They had no legs; their bodies just seemed to fade out from flesh to a cottony-cloud that trailed away to nothing about where their feet should have been. They all wore short, white vests trimmed with polished silver and baggy, white... well, Abrea guessed that would have been breeches, but with their lower halves dissolving out to wisps of cloud-stuff, they looked almost like diapers, and these diapers were held in place by braided, silver ropes. All three had the sides of their heads shaved. *Maybe they are naturally bald there,* Abrea thought to herself. Their hair was of the whitest white.

The two men had their hair tied up in topknots like those wandering pilgrims that stop in the village from time to time, while the woman wore hers loose, her snowy curls wreathing her face and extending down past her shoulders.

What was most shocking about the three figures was their skin color —it was of the most exquisite turquoise-blue Abrea had ever seen. The color seemed painted on, but Abrea couldn't see any smudging.

"Are you going to eat us, little one?" the man in front asked with a smile.

Abrea realized her mouth was agape and shut it so fast that her teeth clacked together. Then it hit her. When he spoke to her, his smile didn't waver or move; he didn't actually *speak* to her, but she still heard his rich, baritone voice.

"Uh... er... how...?" Her mind was spinning so fast that she couldn't form a sentence.

The blue man on the left looked at the speaker with a look that Abrea could only take for one of concern, and she distinctly heard a faint noise, or at least *felt* a noise in her mind as he looked.

"Don't mask your voice, Khala. Let the little one hear your concerns." The blue man in front continued his smile, and Abrea silently decided that it was genuine. The blue woman's face suddenly split in a wide, toothy smile.

Oh, gods! Can they hear what I'm thinking? Abrea was aghast.

"Yes, child," the blue woman said from behind her smile. "I am Leda." Gesturing at the blue man in the middle, she continued, "This is Taramond, and you've already heard Khala."

The blue man on the left nodded at Abrea as if he were a noble, acknowledging the existence of a peasant as he passed. Abrea decided that she did not like him, and as the thought struck her, Taramond and Khala erupted into laughter, legitimate laughter, with mouths wide open and sounds that her ears clearly heard. Abrea was silently pleased with the apparent approval and then was suddenly mortified that she had offended the scowling Khala with her conclusion.

Very deliberately, Abrea formed her thoughts as if she were read-ing them from a wax tablet like the boys used when they went to school. "I—am—sorry—that—I—may—have—offended—you—Khala…" she faltered. "Lord—Khala… Master—Khala… " she trailed off, hoping her cheeks wouldn't be revealing the depths of her embarrassment.

With a deeper nod of his head, his gaze locked on her eyes; Abrea heard his words in her mind. "I will accept your apology, mortal, but I ask that you do not shout at us… you fairly screamed your apology, and everything within sight must have heard you. Please. Form your thoughts normally, and do not repeat them. Just think your…"

"It is easy to work around this," Taramond cut him off, still smiling, his deep, rich voice pleasing to Abrea's ears. "Until you return to your home, we will use sound-speech like you are used to using, girl." The other two just nodded their approval. "Now, the questions at hand," he continued, "is just how you got here and what we should do with you."

Nothing in his gestures indicated anything ominous, so Abrea told her brief story: a morning off, the ruins, the taste of the storm. "That storm over there," she concluded, pointing.

That familiar buzzing sound in her head and the sharp looks of disapproval from Taramond and Leda made Khala momentarily hang his head in shame. His voice wasn't as rich as Taramond's but was much deeper. "The elementals are battling again."

All three of them looked back at the storm raging in the distance.

Leda turned suddenly to face Abrea, her face open as if she were in shock. "Wait, you said the 'smell' of the storm? Have you smelled storms before?"

"Oh, yes, Mistress Leda," Abrea was somehow proud of admitting this, though she would never have done so to her friends and family. The words came out in a rush as if she had been holding them back all of her life. "I smell them all the time. I love to be outside and smell what the winds bring me. I've smelled the tanneries from Waringtown nearly five leagues away, and I can smell the storms approaching even when Thelar, our soothsayer, says it won't rain that day. When it's storming too bad to be in the fields, I'll sit under our eaves and watch the storm. Sometimes, I can even close my eyes and tell which direction the next bolt of lightning will come from! And, sometimes, I even hear sounds in the storm like when..." Abrea's eyes locked with Khala's, and all three of them nodded in full understanding.

Taramond's voice was gentle as he faced Abrea, but he spoke to his companions, "She is Stormborn, which is why she can smell the storms and hear the thoughts of the *Jinn*." The other two nodded in agreement, and even Khala's face seemed to soften a bit as he still looked deeply into Abrea's eyes with an understanding and grudging feeling of resigned acceptance.

Abrea didn't care if her cheeks reddened as she amended her opinion of Khala to one of respect, like how she respected Bonnick, head of the Elders' Council, but how she still feared his fiery temper and harsh tones. Khala's mouth tipped up in the corner as Abrea realized that not only her conclusion but the reasoning behind it was broadcast to him.

Leda's spear thingy suddenly winked out of existence, and Abrea was unable to react as the blue woman closed the few feet separating them and began picking at her hair and clothes and skin like her Grandmother did. As Leda circled around her, making comments while picking and prodding at her, Abrea turned around in a futile attempt to keep facing the blue woman; no, that was wrong, the *Jinn*. Now, the question of the day was, just what was a *Jinn*? Abrea decided that she'd ask the soothsayer when she returned to her village.

Just then, Taramond spoke up. "Leda, leave go. Let the little one be. You see, a Jinn is—"

Leda cut him off, "But I've never seen a mortal before! She is a human, isn't she? Aren't you? Why do you wear this scratchy fabric against your skin? Why is your skin so washed out? Why does it vary in hue from place to place? Does this fabric leech the coloring out of your skin when it makes contact? What is this on your leg? Does it hurt? Is that blood? Real, red blood?" The questions were rapid-fire, and Abrea wasn't able to answer any of them before the next was asked.

"LEDA!!" Taramond's command was loud and overwhelmed Abrea. She suddenly was horrified that her first attempt to think at the *Jinn* was this loud.

She quickly mulled a question about the word *Jinn: what do you call more than one? Jinns? Jann? Jeenie,* **Genie**?! Her mind suddenly reeled from the possibilities of where her thoughts had taken her. Was there some relation? Genies live in lamps and are all smoky, like the *Jinns,* like the blue-peoples' legs-tail-things.

Abrea was suddenly crushed in a hug as Leda's arms surrounded her. "Oh, she's smart," she announced to the other two. Then she spoke to Abrea as she released her from her powerful hug. "Yes, dear, we are related to the Genies. There are many more of us than them, and their magic is much stronger, but our numbers more than makeup for that." Leda's smile was overwhelming to the young girl. Leda turned to Taramond and tipped her head down in respect, "*Akhoond*, this one is Stormborn—she is of our blood—and she is hurt. I would heal her myself, but I lack the strength. I would ask that you heal her bottom arm—leg?" she said as she plucked the thought from Abrea's mind, "before we send her back."

The thought that the red, jagged wound on her leg and foot was real, combined with the realization that she would have to leave, made Abrea sad.

Taramond approached and sank down so his face was even with Abrea's knee. "You are right, Leda. She is Stormborn." He reached his huge, blue-skinned hand out for the gaping slash down Abrea's leg. "I will do as you request, Leda, but in a different way. I will help her heal it herself, but I will also impart two extra gifts to her." Taramond's eyes sparkled as he looked into her eyes and gently touched Abrea's injured leg. "*It is my wish that Abrea Stormborn's wound heal with no residual, debilitating effects. It is also my wish that her bond with air continues to strengthen and that she should learn to harness her abilities. So mote it be.*"

The power of his words washed over Abrea, and they seemed much more powerful than they ought to have been. A sudden feeling washed over her, an absolute cold that penetrated her very soul, and she felt her breath get sucked out of her lungs. She closed her eyes tight as she felt the cold run through her, and Abrea felt her whole body convulsing in agony.

Suddenly, she opened her eyes to silence. Total, absolute silence. She was on her pallet in her small cabin, and she saw her mother and Grandfather Emm silently preparing a meal. Wait, Grandfather Emm stirring a pot? A *man* cooking?

Then, the pain hit her. Her entire world was in pain. Pain and silence. Her family quickly came when they realized Abrea was awake and tended to her as best they could. It was three days before her hearing returned, and there had been many visits from Mother Aolin, the village healer and wise woman. Her mother filled her in on what had happened.

On the day of the storm, two of the children witnessed Abrea climb atop a fallen arch at the ruins. It looked like she was about to say something, and without warning, a great bolt of lightning struck. When the other children recovered from the explosive noise, they found Abrea and the other two kids on their backs, unconscious. The swiftest of them ran back to the village to get help, and the rest just stood there, guarding their fallen friends. Abrea was the worst of the three, with a jagged burn down her leg with the bones in her foot exposed, while all three were deafened from the thunder.

Nobody had seen or heard anything of the Jinn and never heard Abrea say a word. Her family waved off her story as a fever dream, but Abrea was sure it had happened. Her leg healed quickly, and within two weeks, the last of the scabs had fallen off, leaving a barely noticeable silver tracing down her leg to her foot. Her ears still rang from unheard noises from time to time, but she was healing nicely. Even Mother Aolin was concerned that Abrea was healing too fast to be natural.

*****

A small band of men stopped in the village late one day, hoping to get a bed in an inn that didn't exist in their little village. What the travelers got was a chance to sleep in a hayloft, but since it was dry and they were tired, they accepted the villagers' offer. In return for the hospitality, one of the men took out a fiddle to entertain the gathering throng of villagers, hoping for a glimpse of the strangers and maybe to hear a tale about their exploits or from other towns.

One of the men hung back, sitting on a cut stump of wood at the side of the barn, seemingly more interested in some huge book that he had taken from an impossibly small backpack. But it was probably the ferret that rode on the man's shoulder that drew the children, and Abrea found herself among them.

The man realized that the babbling children wouldn't leave him alone, so he shut the big tome with a loud bang that made the gathered children jump. With a twinkle in his eye, the man leaned forward toward the gathered children, and they erupted into cheers as the ferret jumped onto a child's head before making a huge leap and landing back on his Master's shoulder.

"Would you like to see some magic?" the man asked, the twinkle in his eye never disappearing.

The children howled their approval, and Abrea moved closer.

The man wasn't much of a showman, and his skills in prestidigitation and card tricks were mediocre at best. His tricks were entertaining to the younger kids, but even the older children wanted to see real magic.

"Okay," he said, exasperated. "Watch this." Standing up, he spread his fingers wide, thumbs touching, and raised his hands to the sky. As he did so, he spoke words that Abrea could hear but not remember, and suddenly, a great sheet of flame erupted from his fingertips into the sky, going as high as the roof peak of the barn!

Abrea felt something inside of her lurch when he cast his spell, and he looked at the assembled children while seeming to wait for applause. What he obviously didn't expect were the sudden screams of terror from the youngest children. Several adults came running in alarm from around the corner, not knowing what had happened. The man, the *wizard,* seemed taken aback and repeatedly apologized to the very cross villagers.

The Wizard sat back down in a heap, dejected, muttering to himself as the children were led away. Abrea was sure she caught several of the swears she had heard from the men who worked in the fields.

Quietly, Abrea approached the Wizard, who was now quite alone outside of his pet ferret. Abrea thought that the furry snake seemed like it was actually trying to cheer him up. The wizard opened his tome again with a disgusted gesture, and

Abrea's belly lurched again as she felt the power. He hadn't touched the book; he just used his magic to open it up.

"Oh, looks like I didn't terrorize all of you, eh?" The Wizard's sarcasm was thick as he gave a rueful smile. "Are you looking to be turned inside out or turned into a newt?"

"No, Sir," Abrea replied. "I was hoping to see some more magic."

"Yeah. About that..." the wizard continued speaking as he dropped his head in disgust and maybe in shame. "Well, for spectacular magic, I'm a bit limited. I can shoot out bolts of magical energy, but only at living things," he told her, gesturing to emphasize his meaning. "So unless you want to see that pig over there turned inside out, you're a bit out of luck." Her face must have displayed her disappointment because he quickly added, "Wait. Come on, sweetie, don't feel bad. Hells, it ain't showy, but I have a couple of tricks up my sleeve." The fatherly tone of his voice drew her closer.

With some grandiose gestures that Abrea somehow knew were just for show, the wizard spoke a few words that made the flutter come back to her belly, and she got the feeling of ants crawling all over her body, and just as fast as she jumped to wipe them away, the feeling subsided. She looked for the pesky vermin and suddenly stared at her hands. Her normally dirty nails were clean and not jagged from her biting them short; they were smooth and looked like a real Lady's nails should look. Then she saw the dirt was gone from her arms. She spun around and noted that even her dress looked and *smelled* clean, and that bit of torn hem was fixed. By the gods, even her sandals and *feet* were clean!

As she looked down in amazement, she realized that her stringy hair was, well, not *stringy*! It was curly and *clean*! It was like she had just had a bath with real soap and had put on a brand-new dress and sandals and *everything*! As she looked up at the wizard's face, his smile touched her.

With a low chuckle, he said, "There. That was the reaction I was hoping to get before." He repeated the spread fingers from that flame spell and gave Abrea a crooked smile.

She clapped her hands with delight and said, "Again. Again!"

The wizard sat back down and said, "Well, that's about it, kiddo. I figured I'd prettify you so you could see what it looked like, and that's all I got that would be visible." His sad face touched Abrea's heartstrings. Suddenly, his head snapped up, and the glum expression became a smile that grew to expose the wizard's entire mouthful of teeth. "Oh, it ain't much, but I can do this one all day!"

As he sat back and cracked his knuckles with a genuine bit of flair, Abrea saw her mother's form come around the side of the barn as if to check on her. Abrea was sure Mother saw her wide-eyed expression, but she didn't care.

Well, it certainly didn't start as much, to be honest, and Abrea's heart sank almost immediately. The wizard held up his hand and spoke another word that was erased from her mind the moment he said it. He began to touch his thumb and forefinger together repeatedly. It looked, for all the world, like he was trying to imitate the jaw movements of a tiny mouse, and Abrea's smile faded. Then she felt that thrill run through her belly again. It was happening!

It started small, just the tiniest pinprick of light that flashed between the pads of his thumb and forefinger as he made the biting movements. It grew, and she realized that it wasn't just light—and it wasn't even flame—it was a spark! Each time the wizard separated his thumb and finger, the spark would appear, and she realized with delight that each time he was spreading his fingers wider and wider, and with each movement, the spark got larger and larger.

Abrea giggled excitedly as she clapped her hands in front of her, totally in awe of this amazing display of power. And the wizard called this "*minor*"? Abrea could barely contain herself!

Finally, after nearly a minute of making the spark wink in and out of existence, he spread his thumb and forefinger as far apart as they could go, and the spark arced from the finger to his thumb and back again. The wizard spread all of these fingers apart like when he did the flame spell, and the spark began to arc from finger to finger and then back again. The sun was setting, so the spark made the wizard's face seem to glow in the gathering gloom, and Abrea's eyes could see his smile and the satisfaction in his eyes as he made the spark dance.

Raising his other hand, he slowly brought them together, and the spark began to arc between the outstretched fingers of BOTH hands! Abrea couldn't contain her laughter as she clapped in unadulterated joy.

As the spark danced, Abrea could almost imagine that it was a living thing, that there was a life within the tiny mote of light.

The spark-play must have gone on for several minutes when the Wizard quietly said, "I'm sorry, sweetie, but it's getting a bit late, and I'm a man that needs his sleep. If you'd like a quick shock, I'll let you put the spark out." He held his hand out, two fingers outstretched toward her, the spark doing its magical dance between them.

Though Abrea's attention was on the spark, she saw Mother start toward the two of them before catching herself. Abrea reached out, eager to touch the spark yet terrified that it would somehow hurt her.

As her finger got close, she was thrilled to see that a tiny arc of electricity reached out and touched her fingertip. The man's smile faltered a bit as she reached closer. The spark began dancing between their three fingers, never wavering in intensity, until she uncurled a second finger toward the dancing mote.

The spark jumped from the man's fingers to her own, and began to dance. Abrea could feel the joyful tears running down her face as the spark leaped from fingertip to fingertip, and she spread all of her fingers wide. Apparently, the spirit in the spark was happy with its new home, and Abrea could see the light intensify and grow as it played between her fingers.

Cupping her left hand, she gently placed the spark in her open palm as she did with bugs for two reasons: keeping the tiny things there for close inspection and so they would also know they were safe. Lifting her left hand, she gently poured the spark into her right hand, again cupping the tiny light.

Spreading the fingers on her left-hand side, the spark began to send arcs of electricity to each finger while it gently rested in her palm. Suddenly, awareness of the smell hit her—*LIGHTNING*! The smell of storms was lightning! That slightly bitter tang came from the smell of lightning!

Abrea raised her right hand up and spread her fingers, letting the spark dance between them like the man's ferret had played between the formerly assembled children's audience. That familiar feeling was back in her belly, but it wasn't a sense of wild jumping; she felt a controlled heat from deep within her.

Somehow sensing what to do, Abrea spread her arms farther apart, the spark growing in size and power as she did so. As they separated, the one spark became two, then four, then more than she could count. When her arms were well out to her sides, she became aware of what the sparks' bright light illuminated. Her mother was arguing with the man right in front of her.

"What are you doing to her? She's just a girl!"

"Doing? Nothing!! She's doing this! The spark should have winked out when she touched it!"

"You're killing her!"

"Damn it, I'm not doing ANYTHING, woman!!"

From deep within her head, Abrea heard a familiar voice. Leda spoke softly, "It is time, Stormchild. You know what to do."

Abrea took that funny feeling in her belly and fed it into the sparks, feeling them grow. Her imagined thought that the spark was alive became a proven conclusion because she could feel the life pulse within the tiny lights. The man just stared at her while Mother drew back in what looked like horror. Speaking words that just poured from her soul, Abrea clapped her hands together and suddenly felt like she had been kicked in the chest by a mule.

Abrea heard Mother screaming for Father to come help. She sat up and saw the Wizard leaning back against the wall of the barn as if asleep, the ferret on his chest looking, for all the world, as if it was standing guard. Nearly the entire population of the village came running to see what the commotion was, and their cries of confusion and concern were deafening. Not knowing what had happened or what to do, Abrea ran home as fast as she could.

Morning brought the angry voices. Abrea could hear Mother and Father trying to quietly argue with several strange voices—*the visitors,* Abrea thought—and she got up to see what the commotion was. Quietly kneeling under the window sash, Abrea eavesdropped intently.

"... and I don't care what you think. You ain't talkin' with my daughter!" Father was angry.

"You don't understand, good Sir. She used magic to knock me out last night..." The Wizard didn't seem too upset about it.

"My little Abrea doesn't know any magic! You're spelling just went wrong!" Mother was angry as well.

"I could commune with..." This was a new voice.

"Oh, shut up, Priest. This is magic, not gods or demons." The Wizard seemed to be getting a bit testy.

"Listen," a third voice interjected. "I'll give you twenty gold coins just for you to give the Wizard a few minutes to speak to the girl and you can be right there to watch the whole time."

"Gold will never change our minds, you goat-licking, son-of-a-whore!" MOTHER was using those curses! Just the thought made Abrea's head spin! That was Man-talk!

"... Wait a minute, Anna. Twenty pieces of gold would set us up with several new head of cattle, a new chicken coop, and seed for next season, as well as new clothes for the whole family." Father's logic rattled Abrea to the point that she forgot her plan to remain hidden. She stood up in the open window; arms crossed sternly at her breast.

When her father saw what the visitors were looking at, he turned and reddened when he saw her.

"I was only thinking of the family, and a little talking won't hurt anything, would it, Bree?"

Abrea just glared before she realized that he couldn't see her tapping her toe behind the wall. So she stepped to the door, opened it, and stepped outside.

"Talk, Wizard." Where she got the courage to address a man in this tone was a mystery. "I'm not sure what you want to know because I don't know what happened either. I just felt life inside the spark and knew what it needed. I didn't know you were gonna be hurt by it, and I don't even know if I hurt you. All I know is that it knocked me on my bottom parts, too." Abrea's face reddened at the blue words she used. Saying 'bottom parts' in front of men, and *strange* men, no less! Scandalous!

As she stood there, feigning confidence, she felt a familiar tickle in her mind, but it was a strange mind that was touching her own. She felt a tiny puff of breeze whiz past her face and knew the tickle came from that spirit.

As the Wizard began asking questions, Abrea answered them as best she could, waiting for the tiny breeze to zoom past her again. When Father suggested it had something to do with the lightning strike, the Wizards became even more interested. Abrea answered bits and pieces but didn't volunteer any of the Jinn's story.

The breeze whipped around her again, this time around her ankles, tickling her, making her choke back a giggle at the light touch.

When it became apparent that there was no additional information forthcoming, the three visitors drew back to converse amongst themselves.

"What else do you need to know? What could she know? Why do you care?" Her parents questioned the visitors.

Abrea's parents came to her and softly spoke, expressing their concern for her wellbeing, wondering what had happened, and offering to run the men off using pitchforks if necessary.

Abrea felt the breeze rush through her hair, and she grew bold. "Wizard!" The man's head snapped up. "Make it one hundred gold coins, and you'll get your story. Fifty for my parents and fifty for me." She held her hand out, palm up, and waited. She felt the tiny air spirit rest in her palm for a brief second.

The Wizard held out his hand to his companions, then started slapping at the larger of the three to hurry; that man evidently carried all the money for the group.

A small pouch was set in the Wizard's hand, and the man approached with a sardonic grin on his face. As he set it in Abrea's outstretched hand, he smiled and said, "I knew you were special when I saw your eyes in the window a moment ago. It looked like an angry storm cloud was passing over your face." His smile faltered as Abrea carefully opened the pouch and dumped the coins into her open palm. This was more gold than she had ever seen in her life! She couldn't resist biting her lip as she carefully dumped them back in the pouch, pretending to count them. Being a girl, she had never been taught to count to more than ten, and the number of coins seemed like a lot—and all of them looked like gold—so she feigned satisfaction.

Slowly thinking the words, *Spirit of the air, I need you. Come dance with me*, Abrea absently tossed the pouch over her shoulder, her father evidently catching it behind her. She then stepped away from the Wizard as she began her story. She tried to make her voice sound as sultry as Leda's, and she hoped she was being dramatic as she began the tale of the storm.

"I am Abrea of Riverbend, daughter of Len and Anna of Riverbend, and, until a month ago, I was happy with this life and resigned in the knowledge that I would soon be married whether I wanted to be or not." She saw the visitors frown as one, not knowing of the customs of her village. "But I have known I was special since I was a little girl. I would hear Thelar, the soothsayer, speak of approaching storms and would know if he was right or not. I could smell the rain and lightning approaching. Until a month ago, these were just the secrets of a little girl.

"A month ago, I was struck by lightning from a storm that was miles away. A storm brought by the spirits of air—the elementals. In that brief flash, I saw my destiny; I realized the truth. I *was* Abrea of Riverbend, but I now know that I am Abrea Stormchild." She smiled as she thought to herself, *now, my friend.* "And I am the daughter of the storm." She felt the tickle of the breeze on her leg, and she raised her hands to the sky. "I am a sister to the wind and the cousin of the spirits of the air who come to speak to me when I have need." She felt the tiny breeze fly up beneath the hem of her dress and was shocked to feel another tiny breeze whipping around her ankle and yet another around her wrist.

"You wanted a story, Wizard, you've got one. I hope you got what you paid for." She dropped her gaze to look him in the eye as she felt the breezes whip under her dress, making it billow in ways that weren't explained by the light breeze in the air, and her hair began to flutter in their gentle caresses.

Abrea's attention was on the Wizard and his friends, but she caught Mother's horrified expression in the corner of her eye, and her heart broke. Father put a protective arm around Mother's shoulder as she buried her face in his chest. It was everything Abrea could do not to burst into tears as well.

The Wizard just gazed at her, and Abrea grew concerned that she may have well-overstepped her bounds. She saw the big man's hair flip up, and he jumped as if stung by a bee, slapping at his unseen assailant. "Well, bull's balls! That's good enough for me, Alric. Come on, let's get out of here and get to a town with a REAL inn!"

Abrea's cheeks reddened deeper at his curse.

The ferret suddenly snapped at something unseen, and the Wizard smiled. "Welcome to the fold, Abrea Stormchild." He extended his clenched fist in her direction, and after a moment's confusion, she did the same. When he lightly touched his knuckles to hers, he tipped his head at her in some sort of salute and turned on his heel. The third man seemed genuinely confused, and as they all turned to leave, Abrea could hear him asking his compatriots what had occurred.

With dread growing in her heart, Abrea slowly turned to face her parents. Behind them, standing at the corner of their tiny cottage, stood Grandfather Emm, smiling sadly at her, nodding his approval.

Before she could speak, Grandfather said, "Child, here's some coin. Can you run into town to get me some tobacco? I seem to have run out. It'll give the adults a chance to talk while you're gone. That's a dear." He pressed two silver coins in her palm and squeezed her hand with his free hand to show she had his support. He quietly added, "You might want to take the longer path; this may take a while."

The months sped by, and Abrea grew to hear even the slightest whispers in the wind. She was visited from time to time by the tiny air spirits, and each time, she seemed to learn something new. All spring, the villagers came to her to ask about the weather instead of Thelar, and even HE came to her to try to learn how she knew what the winds would bring to this tiny village. The only people that seemed to avoid her were the ones she loved the most.

Father talked about everything outside of the weather and what had happened, and Mother just avoided her. When the two of them would come face to face at the door or around a corner, her mother would drop her gaze as if ashamed and scurry away. The silence was slowly driving Abrea mad, and she hated it. To escape, she spent even more time outside to listen to the wind.

Then, at the spring equinox, Mother Aolin stopped her to ask if she was prepared for the Parade of Brides at the Choosing on May Day, and Abrea's heart crumbled. All that had happened had driven the thought of her inevitable marriage from her brain. Then Mother Aolin drove the dagger through her soul by also telling her that Old Man Ronna had been asking about Abrea's availability. With scarcely a month away, Abrea felt trapped, and her feeling of dread rose as each dawn broke.

The day before the Choosing, Abrea found a brand-new dress on her sleeping pallet and, beneath that, a new pair of sandals. She had never had a new dress AND sandals at the same time, but even this thought brought no joy to her dead heart. She ate a silent dinner alone and slept under the tree next to her family's cottage. As the moon crested, Abrea swore she heard the sounds of Mother crying from inside the cottage.

As the five girls stood in line for the last of the boys to be Chosen, Abrea hated each of her fellow maidens more with each passing second. All they did was prattle on about who they hoped would stake a claim for their hands in marriage, while all she could do was smell the faint smell of ozone in the air from a slowly building storm, but she knew that it was hours away and would offer no respite from the inevitable fate that awaited her. The black clouds on the horizon matched her mood.

The boys' names were announced first. "Ewan, son of Sigrid and Jana," to be answered by the potential Master, "Master Oddar, baker of Riverbend, would have Ewan!" Things got a bit more interesting when Kris was spoken for by Masters Jon and Dale, the barrel wright and Cooper, respectively, but Kris was allowed to choose for himself and walked away with a beaming Master Dale. Then, the final announcement was made, "It is time for the Parade of Brides."

Mother Aolin shooed the small gaggle into a semblance of a line, and they began slowly walking down the main pathway through the town center.

The other four still nattered and giggled as they walked, smiling like fools as Abrea plodded along behind them. Each time she made eye contact with someone, they would suddenly look alarmed and quickly look away. It suited her mood perfectly.

As the Parade finished its short course, the girls were brought to the raised dais and lined up like so many sheep for auction.

"Ellie, daughter of—"

"I offer my hearth and heart," a strong voice cut the Elder off in mid-announcement, earning the speaker a stern look of disapproval. The four girls screamed in delight—it was Jimma, apprentice to the Foresters who helped protect the town.

Ellie shrieked, "I accept! I accept!" as she fluttered down from the raised platform to run into Jimma's arms.

Abrea's stomach knotted tighter.

The other three were also spoken for, and Abrea noted that Old Man Ronna had worn a new, only slightly stained shirt and had his hair greased back. He had also remained silent as the other girls received their pledges. Her stomach did a flip, and she choked back the taste of vomit.

Finally, the Elder came to Abrea and seemed a bit hesitant. "And, finally, we have Abrea, daughter of Len and Anna. She would have been at last year's Parade, but her injuries prevented her participation. Her leg has healed up quite nicely if you notice." Abrea felt more like a piece of meat than ever before, and all the Elder was doing was hawking livestock for anyone who would pay. "Are there any potential suitors who would pledge hearth and heart to this beautiful young woman?"

Blinking back tears, Abrea broke tradition and took a step forward, glaring out into the crowd. She quietly noted that many of the single men in the crowd were actively looking either away from her or glancing at Old Man Ronna. She saw Grandfather Emm in the back of the crowd, and she saw him mouth, "I am so sorry."

Her stomach knotted even tighter, and the tears came freely. She couldn't even wipe them away for fear that the movement would make her vomit or release her pent-up rage. Then her heart stopped as Old Man Ronna stepped forward.

Her world began to spin as she heard him say, "I offer my hearth and heart for Abrea, daughter of Len and Anna."

As her vision clouded, she saw the crowd spin around her as her knees gave out.

The sense of calm was almost overwhelming. She was lying down, and someone was cradling her in their arms. She peacefully opened her eyes to see those of Old Man Ronna just inches from her face.

He gave her a greasy smile and leaned into her ear. "I've been dreaming of this day for quite some time, Abrea. It will be weeks before you will wear a dress again, and probably a month or more before you'll be able to walk right. I love young women." He pulled back, and the smile became lecherous. She truly felt the depths of despair.

It was in that unending abyss that she rediscovered her rage.

That funny feeling in her belly when the Sorcerer did his magic came to her unbidden. She reached up and, with a single movement, grabbed both sides of Old Man Ronna's head in her hands. She pulled on that feeling in her gut and reached up toward the gathering storm.

With a scream, Old Man Ronna tried to drop her, but the death grip on his face prevented her from falling, and she stood up before the kneeling man. She poured all of her hate and revulsion into him, and she felt the sparks dance between her fingertips, dancing through the old pervert's head. She watched as his eyes rolled back into his head, and the foam started to gather on his lips. She watched as blood began to drip from his ears against her palms. She watched as fiery light started to appear in the old man's gaping mouth as his brain burned within his own skull. Finally, with a scream of pain and rage that would make her throat hurt for days, Abrea released him, throwing Old Man Ronna to the ground like so much trash. He didn't move when he fell.

"I am Abrea Stormchild, daughter of Len and Anna, and I offer MYSELF my own hearth and heart." Through her rage, she saw Grandfather Emm push his way through the crowd of stunned onlookers. She continued, "I am the daughter of the Storm and cousin to the spirits of the air, and I claim my *own* birthright!" Grandfather had made it through the crowd, and he was carrying two walking sticks. "I seek the storm, and I will ride the lightning! One day, you will all hear the name of Abrea Stormchild, and you will remember this day."

Abrea watched as Grandfather Emm calmly took off a small backpack that had been slung over a shoulder and set it on the ground before her. He took his own walking stick, kissed it like Father would sometimes kiss Mother, and set it down atop the backpack. Then he reached into his tunic and pulled out a small pouch, a small pouch filled with fifty golden coins, and winked as he set it on top of the backpack.

He quietly said, "I'll always love you, Abrea," as he turned and hobbled back into the frozen crowd.

A solitary form blocked his way. Grandfather Emm went to push the man out of his way, but the large man didn't budge. Grandfather looked up, realized that it was he who needed to move, and he stepped aside. As he passed the large man, Grandfather Emm gently reached up and patted the man's arm as if to say, "I understand."

The man walked up to Abrea, and it wasn't until he was a few paces away that she recognized his stern face. The coloring was all off from the way she remembered him. Abrea bent and quickly slung the backpack over both shoulders, tucked the pouch away inside her dress, and took up Grandfather Emm's walking stick.

Looking at Khala, she boldly said, "I am ready."

For the first time, she saw Khala smile. He offered her his arm and waived his hand, growing in stature, and the illusion of human form faded away to beautiful turquoise blue. A ball of arcing electricity formed around them, and suddenly, they were gone.

The villagers spoke of that day in hushed tones, the way they used to tell the story of when the wolves came to town. The Elders also decided to do away with the Parade of Brides the very next year.

SPELL-LESS SORCERER

College was such a bore! Granted, Lane was at school to become a learned Sorcerer, which was interesting, but when you don't have the spark of magic and can't sense it to save your life, it becomes tedious. Everything was theoretical with no practical application of anything. He should have been at college for two years or so, and this was his fifth year. So many of his friends had graduated and had gone on to start careers for themselves already. Yet, here he was.

He had been here so long that he was even used as an interim instructor for various magical theory classes, as some of the younger students could relate better to him than a stodgy, old professor. Sure, he enjoyed it, but without being able to actually control magic, it was an empty joy, much like a chef who could only cook and never dine.

He gently threw a heavy tome onto his bed and sighed; he could be angry and frustrated, but he still respected the learning. Tomorrow was an extraplanar field trip; he and Professor Jayden were leading a gaggle of second-year students through the ethereal plane to an island oasis on the elemental plane of water.

Lane Bodicam had been granted admission to the Silverleaf Academy at just seven years old. Primary school had been simple for him—just rote memorization and regurgitation of facts, dates, and names. He had done well enough in the ten years at the Academy that he got a full-ride scholarship to Silverleaf College, and that had run out three years in. He was grilled by the instructor cadre to ensure that he actually understood the lessons. When they discovered his "handicap," they allowed him to stay so long as he caused no trouble, got good grades, and stood in for theoretical professors as needed.

Still, life was boring and tedious.

He didn't need to worry about family, though, as his mother had died when he was in year three of primary school. His father had remarried within just a couple of years, and his new wife treated Lane's siblings well. Lane's father was on the City Watch and made a good living for himself and the family. Three of Lane's younger siblings had also attended Silverleaf Academy. But, only one sister went on to college, being granted admission to Namekogan University, where she had been trained as a herald.

Since graduating, Lane's sister had earned a prestigious position as a field attaché for the Thalarian College of Heraldry. She had traveled all over the Known World, where she helped her sponsors design and record coats of arms, banners, and pennants for newly titled nobles, knights, and dames.

Sure, he got to occasionally visit other planes of existence, but he was still jealous of his sister's travels. At least she got to DO what she was trained to do instead of… "GAAAAHHHH!!!!" Lane's scream was only partially muffled by his pillow. He cried as he packed his travel bag, and his tears of frustration wet his pillow when he finally found sleep.

***

Feeling better in the morning, Lane quickly washed up and got dressed before grabbing his bag and running down to the cafeteria to grab a bite before heading out. Breakfast was simple: a bowl of oatmeal with some clotted cream and molasses and a cup of diluted wine. He was such a fixture; all the cooks and servers knew him by name and greeted him as he raced ahead of the line of other students waiting their turns.

He was first to get to the conjuration field and began to trace out the sigils on the grassy ground for the spells needed to summon the gate for traveling. Though he couldn't cast the spells, he knew all the proper runes and glyphs required. Hells, he knew the incantation and somatic components as well. He swallowed his frustration as he saw others arriving from the corner of his eye.

"Hey, DonLane." The honorific hurt. The other students knew his plight, but they still gave him the same respect as other junior instructors.

One looked at the sigils drawn with chalk containing bits of silver powder on the short grass. "Why are you using Albeth here instead of Goreth?"

"Well, do you want to end up in the adjacent ethereal plane, or do you want to end up near an ethereal storm?" When the student shot him a quizzical look, Lane continued. "Gareth, in that position would place us within sight or within a permanent ethereal storm, and if that happened, the odds are that we'd lose our way and most probably lose any number of students, and I don't want to try to explain that to the Dean or to your parents." Lane smiled crookedly, and the student's eyes opened wide as he nodded with understanding. Sometimes, his depth of knowledge was a good thing.

Not too long afterward, Professor Jayden arrived, quickly surveyed the glyphs and symbols on the ground, and with a few questions to ascertain that Lane had taken the moon phase and season into account, he gathered the students together so he could begin the conjuration of the gate.

Three times, Lane counted the students—eleven plus Professor Jayden and himself, eleven plus two, and eleven plus two. This would make getting back that much easier. The anticipation and excitement in the air were palpable, and though he had made this trip nine times before, even Lane felt the thrill of something new go through him.

The magic built, and the entire area was bathed in bright light that settled into a foggy tan or beige color. As far as spells were concerned, a gate to the ethereal plane was anticlimactic; a bright light, and then that horrible fog spread in. It wasn't cold, but it seemed to pull the heat out of the air and any exposed skin.

Lane could see several students exhale deeply in a vain attempt to see their breath, only to be disappointed. Lane smiled because he had done the same thing the first few times he had gone.

Professor Jayden's voice sounded muffled in the fog. "Everybody, place your hand on the shoulder of the person next to you and get a good grip. We don't want anyone getting lost here. Lane, you bring up the rear, please."

Knowing the routine, Lane had already positioned himself at the rear of the line. Almost immediately, the gaggle straightened itself out into a line, and they were traveling.

Lane loudly announced, "Though it feels like we are walking, there's no reason to actually walk here. As the texts say, we're moving by the power of the mind—in this case, the power of Professor Jayden—so we're just along for the ride." He gently squeezed the shoulder of the student ahead of him. "Just be thankful that we don't have to spend a long time here."

The journey lasted just long enough for Lane to get a bit bored by the featureless landscape when the ground beneath his feet changed from firm grassland to soft sand. With a jolt, the travel stopped as the fog dissipated unnaturally fast.

Lane and Professor Jayden both took a step as the journey ended, but the other eleven weren't as fortunate, and they tripped over their own feet as the movement stopped. Lane smiled; the first time he had come here, he had stumbled and fallen on his face. His smile deepened as he recalled spitting sand out of his mouth and blowing sand from his sinuses for several days afterward.

Two Sorcerers were here to greet them, and after quick introductions, the students were bundled off for various field trips to different parts of the island. Before leaving, the group was sternly warned to stay away from the sloping beach off to the left, as there were unspeakable dangers, including quicksand and huge elemental crabs that lurked beneath the surface of the sand and were just waiting to snap up unsuspecting prey.

The students all looked worried, though Lane noticed that this time, a couple of the students looked at each other and then down at the sand... almost conspiratorially. Lane looked at Professor Jayden and saw that he had likewise seen the looks.

The students erupted into excited conversations as they were led off. When they were out of earshot, Lane couldn't keep himself from asking.

"Professor, why is that section of beach off-limits? This is my tenth time here, and I have never seen anything dangerous there."

With a snort of derision, Professor Jayden responded, "That's because that's the safest part of the entire island, DonLane. When told to avoid an area at all costs, those brave or foolhardy enough will immediately head there. If we warn them, they will go—and where better to drive those interested in breaking the rules but the safest area around?" He finished with a hoarse laugh and slapped Lane on the arm in a friendly manner.

"Come, let's get some wine and make some bets as to how many of the fools will be caught down there," Lane offered.

"Thank you, DonLane," Professor Jayden accepted the proffered goblet enthusiastically. "There is a matter I've been asked to offer to you."

"Yes, Professor?"

"The instructor cadre and administration want to offer you a permanent position here at the Silverleaf College as an adjunct Professor. You have mastered every theoretical class and subject we offer, and you've been invaluable in stepping in to cover for instructors as they fall ill or get called away. It is time you get paid for what you do." Professor Jayden took a deep sip of wine. "Personally, I believe you are the finest theoretical sorcerer I've ever seen, and you could teach any subject we offer." He leaned toward Lane's chair. "What say you, DonLane?"

"It is a fine offer, Professor," Lane replied thoughtfully. "If you don't mind, I'll have to think it over for a while."

"I hope you consider the offer favorably, DonLane." Professor Jayden sounded genuine in his recommendation. Lane would have to really think about it.

After several hours of light conversation, Lane asked, "Professor, the students all know of the most dangerous part of the island," they shared a wry smile, "Where is the safest, most boring part of the island?"

With a grin, Jayden replied, "Probably the low mountain in the center of the island. There's nothing there but rocks and sand... and maybe a cave or two." He quickly added, "Oh, did you hear about the potential cheating scandal at

Apalache University? It involves most of the students in their divination program! Go figure," he finished with a chuckle.

Lane let the change of topics go and continued with small talk for the rest of the day. If it weren't for the regular bells of the water clock in the main lodge room, the passage of time would be imperceptible, as there was no sun to rise or sail across the horizon here—it was just as light all day and night.

Just before dinnertime, the first group of students came back, complaining mightily about sore feet and calves and sand being everywhere—and they meant EVERYWHERE. The remaining students arrived just before dinner was served, and the class got to hear the same complaints and bellyaches about sore calves and sand.

During dinner, two of the students drifted off to sleep, and it wasn't long after that that the rest expressed their desire to find their beds for the night. As they were settled in, Lane feigned being similarly tired and bid Professor Jayden a good night. *Was that a smile that the Professor hid behind his goblet?*

It wasn't difficult to climb out his window and escape into the distance, and Lane was on his way toward the low mountain just a mile or so from the hostel.

Jogging to put as much distance as quickly as possible between himself and the hostel (and prying eyes), Lane found the journey was easier than he had expected. In just about fifteen minutes, Lane began walking up the gentle slope of the 'mountain.' All told, it only rose about 300 paces above the surrounding area, but it seemingly towered over the landscape.

Lane found several indentations in the rocky slope, but nothing that he would call a 'cave' like the Professor had alluded to. Frustration mounting, Lane was about to turn around and go back when he neared the crest. There, surrounded by a low wall of rock and sand, was a rocky staircase leading down into the mountain.

It was dark in the tunnel, but Lane's partial Elven heritage had given him superior night vision compared to others. It was the only Elvish trait he had, and the only way others might have an idea about it was that his eyes flashed in bright light, like a cat's.

He quickly walked down the stairs without incident, and when he reached the bottom, he could detect light coming from far ahead. As quietly as possible, he inched forward, unsure of what he might see. Finally, he emerged from the tunnel into what could only be a shallow caldera of the mountain he had so recently walked up.

A bamboo contraption filled with water from an unseen spring then loudly thunked down to empty its contents onto a rock and then into a small pool. A few palm trees provided shade, but it was the flowers and the skeletons that caught Lane's eyes. The flowers were deep indigo, almost black in color, and the blooms fairly covered the entire caldera. The skeletons were the disturbing part, and Lane was sure he could count at least two dozen of them in varying stages of being covered by sand and flowers.

With a start, Lane realized that there were three people there. All three were in varying stages of undress and looked like they hadn't had a meal between them in weeks. One man was lying down near the pool, apparently watching the bamboo contraption. Another, a halfling man, was walking about with a dagger in his hand, and Lane was horrified to see great gashes on the man's arms, legs, and torso. The last was a Dark Elf woman who was sitting beside a skeleton and seemed to be in deep conversation with it.

Lane stole up toward the pool as quietly as possible, but as he approached, he abruptly sneezed. As he recovered, it was then that he saw the prone man watching him intently, his rheumy eyes bloodshot and sunken well into his skull. The beard gave away the man's identity, as Lane had seen that long, split beard many times.

"Professor Antes? Is that you?" Lane scrambled toward the gaunt visage, stopping a few paces away as the eyes blankly inspected him like a piece of meat. There was a flicker of recognition on the man's face, which quickly faded as the eyes trailed away. With a loud sigh, all signs of life faded from those red, watery eyes.

Professor Antes had gone on a sabbatical last year after several field trips to this island. As a matter of fact, Professor Jayden had taken over for him when he was gone. A few students had inquired about his whereabouts, but the faculty had been tight-lipped, just saying he was on sabbatical and may or may not return.

Another sneeze and Lane caught movement out of the corner of his eye. The halfling man with the horrific injuries was approaching; dagger held out in front of him like a magic wand. "Oh, you need to see this! The colors that come out are amazing!" He shuffled forward faster and, for all the world, looked like he wanted to cut Lane with his dagger. With a start, Lane realized that the man's wounds must be all self-inflicted.

"Colors? What do you mean?" Lane was concerned. "Stay back. Stay back, I say!!"

The man did not slow down and seemed intent on cutting Lane. Rearing back, Lane pushed the short man with his foot, driving him backward. The push was intended to stop his forward movement and keep him at a distance, but in the man's addled state, he lost his balance and fell hard against a rock at the side of the pool.

Sitting up quickly, the Halfling raised his hand to a wound on the back of his head and looked at the small bloodstain on the rock. "Oh, the colors! Look at all the colors!!"

With a shriek, Lane spun and made to dash back to the tunnel and stairs. Unfortunately, after just a few paces, he stepped on a half-buried skeleton and his foot broke through the ribcage, making him fall face-first into a patch of dark flowers. His open mouth caught a bloom as he crashed into the earth.

Sitting up as quickly as possible, he spat out the flower and scrambled to his feet. In just a few paces, however, he fell again, dizzy. Disoriented, he began to crawl in the direction of the only exit he knew about.

He made it only a handful of paces before he collapsed in a heap in an open area of sand.

When Lane opened his eyes, he knew something was wrong. As he moved his head from side to side, his vision smeared like a watercolor painting that was splashed with a bucket of water.

Screwing his eyes shut, Lane carefully sat up, hopefully facing the small oasis in the center of the caldera. Tentatively opening one eye, he focused hard on the Halfling man sitting next to the pool. With every movement, the colors smeared, and Lane was sure that he saw rainbow sprays coming out of the Halfling's wounds.

He opened both eyes and as long as he maintained his vision focused on a single point, the only smearing of the colors was from natural movement caused by the gentle breeze. Closing his eyes to prevent a disaster, Lane slowly got on his hands and knees, then stood up. Frightened at what he might see, he again opened his eyes in the direction of the Halfling. Much to his consternation, the Halfling man was looking at him.

"Do you see them? Do you see the colors?!" As he asked this, he cut his own forearm with the dagger, creating a huge gash that gushed blood and rainbows.

The Halfling looked up at him hopefully, and Lane could do nothing but reply, "Yes. I see them." Then, his curiosity got the better of him. "What are they?"

"What is it?" The Halfling seemed incredulous. "It's magic, you tall ninny, it's MAGIC!! It's all around us—and INSIDE us! It's just up to us to let it out to see it!" Every statement was growing more emphatic.

Magic? Lane asked himself. *Is this what it looks like? Is this what I've been missing?* He grew hopeful. Movement off in the distance caught his attention as the Drow woman stumbled into view. Keeping his eyes locked on her, Lane strode quickly in her direction.

"What is it you want, living Human?" Her question was curious.

"Living Human?"

"Yes. Living Human." Gesturing to a nearby skeleton and then to Professor Antes' body, she continued, "They are dead Humans. One day, you'll be dead like these Humans and dead like that Elf." She made another gesture. "And that Orc over there, and that Merman, and that Catfolk." She made more gestures with each mention. "I talk with them all as I talk with you. You approached me; what do you want, living Human?"

"I want..." Lane hesitated. "What are the colors?"

"Colors?" She seemed almost confused. "I see no colors. I see the weave of magic. I see how this tree is structured, how it sucks the water in through its roots, and how it leaks out water vapor from its fronds. I see the weave of magic that holds that fool of a Halfling together, and I see how it escapes from him every time he cuts himself. I see how the weave permeates through you, and I see how the weave of the lotus is worming its way through you." Her eyes became clear for a second. "You came here seeking insight and knowledge. Obviously, you knew about the effects of the black lotus flower."

With a start, Lane looked about at the massive swath of blooms. *Black lotus flowers,* he thought. Deadly poison if ingested in quantity. Even the spoors can be highly addictive if breathed for extended periods. Unfortunately, it also opened magical pathways in the brain, and some Wizards and Sorcerers sought out the blooms to hopefully enhance their abilities.

With a start, Lane panicked. *When I fell, I got at least one blossom in my mouth... and how long have I been breathing in the pollen?* He spat again and saw the smear of color fly from his mouth onto the ground and then explode into a puff of rainbow hues. *Oh, it would be so easy to stay and watch these amazing colors!*

Looking about, the smearing effect no longer bothered him. Peering upward, he saw a great streak of silver color spanning the entire expanse of the sky. "Oh, a ley line."

"Yes, dead Orc, he sees the ley line, now." The Dark-Elf woman's voice floated to his ears.

Looking for the Dark-Elf woman, Lane found that she was sitting on the ground again, talking to another skeleton, this one obviously an Orc.

"If he doesn't leave soon, he'll be here like all of you, and I will be able to talk with him for years—both before and after he dies." Lane looked toward the exit again.

It truly would be so easy to stay. But what of the students and Professor Jayden? He simply *had* to make his way back to the hostel.

Stepping carefully so as not to disturb the multitude of blooms, Lane walked slowly back toward the tunnel entrance. As he passed the Halfling, he saw rainbows and blood gushing out of a deep gash in his thigh.

"I fear I've gone too deep this time. But look at the colors! The colors are so beautiful!!" Halfling said.

It had taken just a quarter hour or so to get to the mount, but in his addled state, it took Lane several hours to get back. As time passed, he found that most of the side effects of the lotus wore off, though when he concentrated, he could still see the colors of magic all around.

When he was within a few hundred paces of the hostel, he heard the light tinkling of a bell, and Lane swore he had seen the tinkling of it as well. *It must be magical for me to see it like that,* he thought. He'd ask later because he realized that he was quite hungry.

Stepping into the hostel, the entire class was assembled, and every eye turned toward him. As they all looked, all chewing stopped; nobody even blinked.

"I hope I'm not late for breakfast," Lane tried to be funny to break the palpable tension in the room.

One of the students blurted out, "Breakfast? It's dinner time, and you've been gone for three days!"

The rest of the class immediately shushed him, and those close enough slapped him for breaking some unknown taboo.

Professor Jayden quietly rose and gestured at a servant who quickly disappeared to get another place setting and food for Lane.

"The class had been instructed to NOT speak a word of this to you until after you had eaten." Professor Jayden cast a meaningful glare and cowed the loudmouth. "I was beginning to lose hope. You were gone for so long that I feared the worst. Was Professor Antes still there?"

"He was. I watched him die."

"That is a shame. I'll be sure his next of kin are notified." Professor Jayden was subdued. "Are you alright?"

"I am well enough, Professor." The servant brought the dinner, and Lane began wolfing it down. "I've seen the ley line that crosses this island, Professor. I can see sounds, though I suspect only if they are from magical sources. I've also seen the beautiful colors of pain and death."

"I understand," the Professor responded. "Have you tried to cast any spells yet, DonLane?"

Numbly, Lane stopped shoveling food into his mouth. *I didn't even know what I was eating.* Holding his hand up, he let his vision fade out until he could see the threads of magic coming from his fingers and from the magical torch across the room that provided light.

With a twist of his hand and a few arcane words that he had known for years, a small ball of flame ignited in his palm. "Not until just now, Professor. It appears that I may take the position at the College." With a wave of his hand, the flames extinguished.

That's what had been missing—he needed to be able to see the magic in the world to be able to affect it. Now that he could see it at will, his great storehouse of spells that he had theoretically memorized could be cast successfully.

"One thing, Professor. If I take this position at the college, I will NOT be involved in bringing students here again. The draw is too great, and I have too many other things I wish to see and do."

THE SWIMMING HOLE

Clinton Cooper was feeling his oats—he felt like an honest-to-goodness *real* man today. His initial training for the local militia was complete as of today, and his spirits couldn't be higher. Well, that's not quite true. After the ceremony, where he had traded in his training staff and received his tabard and spear, Kaytelin Gresham congratulated him on his achievement and suggested that they spend a little more time together. As she spun around to giggle with her girlfriends, Clinton had seen a flash of the ankle from beneath her skirts. ANKLE! Positively scandalous! If any of the adults—the *other* adults of Meldorf—had seen it, there would have been several levels of Hell to pay for the brazen display. And he was SURE she had done it on purpose.

Oh, today was the best day of his seventeen years!!

To celebrate this spectacular day, he decided to head down to Fall's Pool to soak and work some of the stiffness out of his shoulders. *Who would have thought that something as light as a staff or spear could end up feeling so heavy after a day of just jabbing it into a bale of hay or a hay-stuffed dummy?* He thought as he tried to shrug some of the tightness away with no success.

He clutched his small bag of clean clothes under his arm and shouldered his staff—his new spear—to make it easier to carry (and for others to notice that he was officially a man) and headed down the trail for the two-mile walk to Fall's Pool.

He had chosen Fall's Pool over the usual swimming hole because of the beauty of the day and, if he were honest, because the hole was where the majority of the kids in town swam, and the Fall's was where adults spent most of their leisure time—whenever they had any. He secretly hoped there would be lots of adu... *other* adults there today so they could see that he was no longer a child.

The walk was quiet, and he only met a few other adults returning from the Fall's Pool. His step grew lighter each time they congratulated him on completing his training. As he approached the last quarter mile, he listened intently for any squeals of laughter or... he caught himself. Do adults still whoop and carry on like kids do, or are they always quiet or angry like they were in town? Well, he would find out today, he concluded, but he continued to listen for any sign of revelers.

Finally, he heard the sounds of the falls themselves. He knew that calling them "falls" was generous, because they were only all of the size of a man in height and man-made at that. Long ago, someone had made a makeshift dam of large rocks to create a large pool for swimming. Because of frequent use, there were no weeds or river grass, and even the bottom of the pool was covered in clean sand. He noticed suddenly that it was in much better condition than the swimming hole the kids used, as that location was natural and had a soft bottom, and there was a swath of muddy ground where the revelers entered and exited the small pond.

Clinton quietly wondered if that was on purpose or not.

As he approached the Pool itself, his heart sank to see no great assembly of adults, and not only that, the entire place seemed deserted. All he saw were some forgotten clothes that looked like they had been draped over nearby limbs and bushes to dry after being washed in the pool. *Wait a moment,* Clinton suddenly thought; *if I were to pay close attention to approaching adults, I could strip down and give the clothes I am wearing a good washing.* That would mean he would leave with clean clothes and bathe. *Well, I guess that's a good thing for Fall's Pool to be empty,* he concluded.

Propping his spear up against a tree near the abandoned clothes, he felt a thrill of exhilaration with the realization that he no longer had to keep his spear in his grip at all times now that he had completed training. With a rueful smile, he also felt a pang of guilt at the thought, having never let the weapon more than arm's reach from him for almost six months. He hadn't been officially training the entire time, but the Battlemaster had issued an edict that all trainees had to keep their staff within arm's reach and woe betide the trainee that allowed a member of the town guard or militia to steal it.

Fortunately, he never lost his staff or forgot it for the entire duration of the training. Those that did have paid hell to get it back—mucking out the militia stables and reorganizing thousands of hay bales from the winter stores for the militia's horses. Two of the trainees had actually quit training because of the additional work.

As he dropped his bag of clean clothes beneath his newly awarded spear, he smiled broadly at the recent memory and quickly peeled off his similarly new tabard and hung it from the spear's crossbar. The tabard had a large, embroidered design of a cave bear sewn onto the front and back—the prominent emblem of the Baron's crest. He proudly rubbed his fingertips against it and sighed sadly as he thought there were no adu... *other* adults here to see the spoils of his recognition. With that, he grabbed the hem of his long tunic and pulled it up to take it off.

The "Ahem" made him freeze, then quickly poke his head out of the tunic to see who had cleared their throat. It sounded uncomfortably close.

He couldn't tell what shocked him more, the fact that this person was barely three paces away or that it was a woman. A NEARLY NAKED WOMAN!!

She was dressed in nothing more than what looked like a woman's small-clothes—shortpants and a bandeau top to cover her. *Oh, by the gods!!* Clinton realized that he not only saw her naked ankles but her entire legs, all the way up to her shortpants—and her shoulders—AND HER BELLY! With a yelp, he pulled his T-tunic back into position and spun around to help protect what remained of her modesty.

Quickly facing the Pool, he locked eyes with two sets of eyes of women who were nearly submerged in the clear waters. With a look of sheer horror on his face, he realized that the clear water revealed that they were wearing even less than the woman behind him.

Spinning about, he realized that this brought him eye to eye again with the nearly naked woman so close to him. In a rising panic, he spun around again, only to be met with the sight of the two naked women in the Pool as they approached the shallows near him. Before they could climb out and expose themselves, he squeaked and turned around again to see the nearly naked woman next to him break into a broad smile.

"Are you going to keep spinning until you get dizzy and fall down?" Her voice sounded like she was chiding him instead of the anger he expected. "Maybe if you face off in that direction, you could stop turning like a manic top." She pointed to where she was referring to.

Without a second thought, he turned back in that direction and screwed his eyes shut at the embarrassing horror of what he had witnessed.

He could hear the bathing women emerge from the Pool, water dripping onto the sand and grasses that surrounded the Fall's Pool. As they approached the abando— *oh, by the gods, those clothes weren't abandoned; they are theirs!*

One chuckled and said something in a language he didn't understand, to which the other two responded with light laughs of their own. He could hear the sounds of the women thankfully getting dressed as they talked amongst themselves. The language was beautiful, and it made him feel dirty as if he was overhearing what they had to say.

In what seemed like hours, he heard, "It's safe; you can turn around now."

As he slowly turned about, he jumped with a start, "I am so sorry to have interrupted your bathing time and having seen..." he stopped in a panic. The women were ALL dressed in their smallclothes! The audacity!! And they had the temerity to tell him that it was *safe*!

They all roared with laughter as he spun around again to not destroy what tiny shreds were left of their modesty. As he struggled to stop his rotation, he could feel his cheeks burning red with shame.

"Young man, if you ever leave this backwater village, you're going to have to get used to seeing such things without spinning like a top." The three laughed again at his discomfort. "Turn back around and get it done with."

Clinton did as he was bid, slowly turning, keeping his eyes glued to the ground between them. As the women saw his gaze, they laughed again.

The one whom he had first encountered sternly said, "Look up, damn you, man!"

As quickly as he could—and covered by a prolonged blink—Clinton looked up toward the trees beyond the women.

The two former bathers laughed as the other (the leader?) said, "Dammit, boy! We aren't effigies of the Destroyer! Look us in the eyes if you can manage to control yourself. Treat us like sentient beings instead of the damned sun itself!"

Clinton closed his eyes and steeled himself, then opened them to lock eyes with the leader. In quick succession, he then locked eyes with the other two before returning his gaze to the leader's eyes.

The three gave a sad laugh as one of the bathers lamented, "Thank the gods that his eyes aren't holding that spear, or we would all three be run through!"

This comment got a laugh of approval and agreement from the other two. *Oh, by the gods!* This was difficult for Clinton because, in the periphery of his vision, he could see their naked limbs and more.

"Wh-what, what are you doing here? You're not from around here," Clinton's curiosity was piqued.

The leader smiled as she motioned to the drying clothing and then the Fall's Pool. "Bathing and cleaning up a bit. We've been on the road for several days and just wanted to freshen up in the safety of a community pool. I've been here before and knew of it. We had some good conversation with some of the local folks a bit ago before they had to leave." She smiled broader and added, "We didn't realize we'd end up in the presence of a wild-eyed, whirling dervish who would try to turn us all to stone with his eyebeams!"

His cheeks reddened even more. Unbidden, he couldn't resist sneaking a glance at the acres of skin before him. When one of the bathers put her hand on her hip, Clinton realized with horror that his glance had turned into a stare.

Tearing his eyes from the vista, he looked into the distance, where a moving branch swayed with the wind.

"What language was that you were speaking? Where are you from? Why did you come to our village?" After getting caught staring, Clinton continued to look off in the distance.

"Well, let's see... we were speaking Elvish if you must know. Not many know that tongue around here, and we wanted to talk about you without being overly rude."

Clinton's eyes flashed to meet her gaze, and she saw another broad smile. In a fraction of an instant, he tore his gaze away to watch that swaying branch. Absently, he noticed another moving in the same eddy current of wind. It was safer to watch the moving underbrush than risk looking at their eyes again—and seeing more than he could stomach.

"We're from Allencarna," the leader said. Clinton's eyebrows rose as he couldn't resist looking at her eyes again in surprise. "We're Scouts in the King's Brigade, and we're down south here just to make sure everything is quiet in the King's realm. I've been through here several times, but these two have never been to your fair village, and I wanted to introduce them to Battlemaster Marlon Wayans."

"You're *Scouts*?!" Clinton was gobsmacked. They were *WOMEN*!! Being a Scout was a *man's* job!

His curiosity got the better of him, and he quickly looked at all three again. Nope, they were definitely women. The leader had some scars on her forearms and a long, red crease along her left thigh, but even women get injured from time to time. *Scouts*? It suddenly dawned on Clinton that they must be toying with him, trying to pull a joke on him to pile on the embarrassment he already felt.

"Wait, you know Battlemaster Wayans? I'm in traini—" he caught himself, "I'm in Bear Company of Lord Rothmann's militia. I *know* him!"

The Leader's smile pulled up on one side. "I could tell you were a trained warrior from the way you gave us the once-over." One of the bathers snorted before she covered her smile with her hand. "Oh, and that brand-new, beautiful tabard and unused spear."

Suddenly, Clinton wasn't quite as proud of his new kit as he had been earlier. Just a glance at his kit, they knew he had just left training. Maybe he wasn't quite as 'adult' as he had thought.

Another waving branch caught his attention.

"I could introduce you to Battlemaster Wayans if you like, though..." how could Clinton say this judiciously without being demeaning? "Except for the fact that you're women and claim to be Scouts." *Yes,* he thought, *that should be good enough not to offend them.*

To a man... er... to a *woman,* they all lowered their gaze and looked at the ground, shaking their heads, almost in unison.

Another branch started waving a bit too violently, and Clinton noticed that it was closer this time. The way it was moving seemed out of place, not quite swaying in the same manner as the other foliage.

"Well, if you wait until we get dressed and kitted up, we can be on our way unless you are insistent upon not looking at us some more." With a quick glance at her eyes, Clinton noticed that her smile was gone. *Perhaps she didn't like being called out for pretending like that.*

A small twig snapping pulled his eyes back to the underbrush. All he could focus on was a big, ugly face from 30 paces away. Red eyes... greenish-gray skin... tusks protruding from his lips. If Clinton was right, it looked just like the drawing of an Orc that Battlemaster Wayans had made all the trainees study.

Except that Orcs were rare in these parts and supposedly hadn't been seen since before Clinton even needed smallclothes. Yet, there was one... truly amazing. When another face appeared, and then more limbs began swaying behind them, he was snapped out of his reverie.

"ORCS!!" The volume of his voice startled even him. "Get behind me, and I'll protect you as you escape."

With that, Clinton grabbed his spear and stepped through them to engage the Orcs. As he did—and they realized their ambush had failed—the Orcs began roaring battle cries and charged.

It wasn't that Clinton was overly confident; he was just doing what every man in his village would do—protect the women. He was untested in battle; hell's bells, he was scarcely three hours out of his initial training! Nonetheless, he stepped forward and readied his spear.

In a panic, he realized that his tabard was still hanging from the crossbar of the spear, and without thinking, he grabbed it and spun it around his head to don it like he had done so many times when the militia training cadre called a surprise inspection. He lightly tossed the spear in the air as he let the fabric settle over his head and jabbed his arms into place, then deftly caught the spear before it could fall to the ground.

As one Orc screamed and charged directly toward him, Clinton saw nearly a dozen more fanning out wide to avoid his spear and get to the women. The laughable memory of his squadmates practicing that tabard move vaporized in a flash as the Orc sprinted toward him. Holding a disgustingly filthy scimitar over its head with both hands, the Orc had murderous intent in its eyes.

Unbidden, the thought entered his mind that Battlemaster Wayans would have lost his mind if one of the trainee's weapons was in that condition. Without actually shifting his gaze, Clinton noted that every weapon the Orcs held that he could see was in the same horrid condition.

Crouching low, he gripped his spear tightly and waited to meet the Orc's charge, anticipating a mighty overhead chop that, should it land, would split his skull like an overripe pumpkin.

Just two paces from him, the Orc's toe slipped off a tree root, and its charge turned into an attempt to catch its footing. He let one hand drop from the scimitar's hilt to barely maintain balance. Clinton took the opportunity, taking one small step to his right and thrusting toward the center of the Orc's stomach.

The look of murder in the Orc's eyes wavered to one of fear and rage, and it dove at Clinton as it broke the charge to dive at him in an attempt to go over the deadly spearpoint. In a panic, Clinton dropped the butt of the spear into the dirt and just tried to make contact with the Orc to keep it from landing atop him.

The spearpoint touched the metallic chest plate of the Orc's armor. Clinton pulled hard on the haft to keep the Orc as far away as possible, but as the Orc sailed overhead, it swung the scimitar. The creature was just far enough away to keep the weapon from separating his hand from his arm, but the tip still cut into his left forearm with what seemed like the fire of a thousand cooking pits. His hand never lost its grip as the Orc continued to sail overhead, landing behind Clinton with an odd cracking sound.

Using his spear as a crutch to pull against, Clinton scrambled to his feet to face the Orc, which he found crumpled against the tree that had so recently been used to prop up his spear. Without a second thought, Clinton spun his spear around and buried it in the back of the horrid beast. As he yanked it out, the blood from the deep cut on his forearm let loose, and blood gushed forth. Just as he was about to spin around to face the rest of the maddening horde, Clinton let himself glance up to ensure that the three women were running to safety, only to see the empty trail, and that was when he heard the laughter behind him.

Wheeling about, Clinton was stunned to see the three women engaging in battle with other Orcs. All three held short seax swords, and two of them also wielded long, wicked daggers. Besides the fact that those silly women were ARMED, they were holding the weapons all wrong. Swords may not have been Clinton's strong suit, but he knew enough that you had to maintain a tight, strong grip on the hilt, and all three women seemed almost like they were loosely gripping them with two fingers, and they weren't hacking at the Orcs like he had seen the trainee swordsmen do, they were spinning them in elaborate arcs, only to suddenly stop them dead and spin them in the opposite direction without warning.

Besides, their stances were all wrong! They didn't stand their ground and let the Orcs come to them. The way they were shifting about looked almost like... like they were *dancing*!! Clinton couldn't explain it, however, when he saw several Orc bodies on the ground around the women.

He stepped forward to tell them to stop this silliness at once when *it* appeared from the distant trees—an Ogre. *By the gods, it was an Ogre!* The beast was looking directly at Clinton as it strode quickly in his direction!

Still a way off, Clinton let himself take in the entire tableau as he again commanded, "Get behind me; I'll protect you!" Their laughter tinkled in the air like wind chimes as he again focused on the approaching Ogre. It had almost sounded like those damned, fool women were ENJOYING being in battle!

The Ogre started to lumber faster toward him, and Clinton knew he was doomed. It took what seemed like hours for the beast to reach him, and as it raised its huge club to end him, the dancing women leaped in to engage it.

With its attention so focused on Clinton, all three women were able to dispatch the last of the Orcs and prep their own charges. The Leader dove in to slice at the beast's heel tendons as one of the bathers leaped in to jab her seax in the Ogre's shoulder. The other bather jumped in from the other side to get under the Ogre's raised weapon arm and completely embed her seax in the creature's ribs before deftly falling away to the relative safety of the ground.

The beast roared in pain and slammed its upraised arm down to protect its side, only to push the hilt of the seax into the wound, making it completely disappear inside its ribcage. Its eyes looked at all four of them as it roared in agony and fell to its knees. The roar slowly turned into a gurgle as the three women stood back to watch the Ogre die.

A quick comment from the Leader in that Elvish language again, and all three of the women turned their attention to Clinton.

The Ogre fell face-first to the ground directly in front of Clinton, and the Leader looked him in the eye and quietly said, "They're all dead. We're safe now."

Clinton snapped out of his reverie to quickly look around, and all he saw were Orc bodies surrounding him. His mouth working only spasmodically, he croaked out his agreement, "We're safe; they're gone."

A count of two or three after the words were out of his mouth, the two bathers began to laugh at him and cover their mouths to not appear rude. Bewildered, Clinton looked at the Leader, who had softened her gaze.

"We all do it the first time. It's nothing to be ashamed of," she reassured him.

Not understanding, he looked about as if to see that he had sprouted a third arm or something when his eyes caught a widening wetness on the front of his t-tunic. Confused, he looked down, trying to figure out if he had been injured or what was going on, when it dawned on him that he was pissing himself.

Shrieking in embarrassed horror, Clinton spun and took several steps to leap into Fall's Pool. "Don't look at me!" he yelped hoarsely, trying not to die of embarrassment as he continued to pee uncontrollably.

"Oh, young one. I said that we *all* do it the first time we see battle—so long as we survive. Hells, after fifteen years of being a Scout, I still piss myself from time to time." The Leader seemed conciliatory. Flipping her dagger to the bather that had lost her seax, she ordered, "Get your blade back and come clean it off. Breana, do a quick patrol to make sure there are no more of these bastards." The second bather, Breana, nodded curtly and disappeared in the underbrush like a shadow. The Leader turned and walked back into Fall's Pool. "Now, I've seen lots of blood on you, young one...," she caught herself, "young *man*, and cuts from Orc blades can fester and result in a fatal case of blood fever. Let's get that slice properly cleaned."

Clinton had forgotten that he had even been wounded and looked down to see blood flowing freely from his forearm and a pool of red around him. In a panic, he suddenly realized that his tabard was being dyed by his own blood. He shrieked again and started to wade out of the pool.

"Dammit, bo... *man*! Stand still so I can dress this wound—unless, of course, you would rather die sometime next week!" the Leader yelled.

With that, Clinton froze and faced her.

A gentle healer she was not, and he yelped several times as she fished out several small bits of black material from the wound. The whole time, she spoke to him about how fortunate he was that the wound was freely bleeding, as that could help wash out the wound. She also told him that the worst wounds were those that only bled a little or not at all, as the unclean bits stayed in those wounds and almost always caused a painful death after several days of raging fever. Orcs, she explained, made sure their weapons were all smeared with dirt and feces, so if they didn't kill their opponents outright, they'd still die several days on.

Through all of this, they managed to introduce themselves. The leader's name was Gwendol, while the second bather's name was Anna of Tarth.

"Anna of Tarth?" Clinton asked. "That almost sounds like a noble name."

Gwendol answered, "It is, Clint. Her mother is Baroness Livey Tarth."

With that, Clinton jumped to his feet and stammered, "I-I am so sorry, m'Lady! I had no idea!! Please forgive me if I offended you; I meant no offense." Then, he added almost to himself, "By the gods, I've seen your legs! And your... your..." The look of embarrassment made the two women laugh good-naturedly.

"Clinton, I may be the daughter of a Baroness, but out here, I am but a Scout. And to be honest, a *junior* Scout." She sounded subdued.

Gwendol cut in, "Junior, no more, Anna. Today, you've earned your badges." The two shared proud smiles. "Now, while on the subject of awards and decorations, Clint, how do you want to deal with this wound? If I just wrap it, you'll end up with an impressive scar that you will carry for the rest of your life. I can sew it up, and you'll have a much smaller scar..." They both looked at the wound. The blood had almost stopped flowing. "I'll tell you from experience that a bigger scar won't hurt you, and it makes for a good conversation starter."

"Girly girls like them," Anna interjected. She stood and displayed her clean blade as if inspecting it.

Inspecting it like a real *soldier,* Clinton thought.

Breana returned as if on cue, and the three began getting dressed, and it dawned on Clinton—*hmmm, maybe I should start going by "Clint,"* he thought—that the nearly naked women didn't concern him as much as it had earlier.

When the three were dressed in clothing, including light leather armor, the four started the trek back to the village. The conversation ran from life elsewhere in the kingdom to pissing oneself after—or during—battle.

Four compatriots.

When they returned, it was obvious that Battlemaster Wayans knew Gwendol, and he warmly met Breana and Anna. Four friends. Battlemaster Wayans wasn't even upset about the blood-stained tabard.

Four equals.

MERRICK'S EXECUTION

Merrick was sore. No, he was tired and sore. No, he ached as he had never ached before, and he felt as if he hadn't slept in weeks.

He quietly sniffed as he realized how strange this was because, as a farm boy, he was used to muscle aches when forking great mounds of hay into stacks each autumn, and in planting and harvest seasons, sleep was at a premium. *How long has it been since I've slept?* He mused. Keeping track of his fingers, he counted the days since he was able to sneak more than an hour at a time but was soon lost as the days had melted together into a haze of constant marching and fighting.

Weeks, he silently concluded with a disappointed sigh as he set to check the condition of his feet.

Footcare was one of the first things he had learned from his first Bull. The same age as Merrick, the Bull—*What was his name again?*—was his immediate supervisor and had a large part in changing him from a farm hand into a usable foot soldier. Well, he was instrumental until that arrow took him in the throat.

Merrick had stared at the arrow and the bright blood spurting out of the tiny wound until several more of the viciously barbed orc arrows thunked into the Bull's chest, sending Merrick and the other four members of the squad scurrying for cover.

As he gingerly peeled his boots and what remained of his stockings off, the young man mulled over the long succession of Bulls that had replaced his first leader. The next one had stepped into that staked trap within just a few days of taking over. Then there was the Bastard; cruel and cowardly, he had run the squad ragged with barely considered orders and communicated his orders poorly, driving Merrick and his squaddies to distraction with confusing and conflicting commands. It was a relief when he triggered an ambush and was killed as he tried to run away from the small skirmish.

The knight's son, Preacher, Toad-face, Bard... the list of Bulls kept growing as Merrick counted them down. Twelve, thus far. Or was it thirteen? How long had he been in this blasted war—six weeks? Eight? With a derisive snort, Merrick stopped trying to calculate the time and gave his feet all of his attention, praying silently that their new Bull would at least not be a total catastrophe like so many of the others had been.

His feet looked good today. With the tattered remains of his stockings, Merrick rubbed away the lingering dirt from between his toes and pulled out the new pair from his pocket.

New socks. While it was a pleasant surprise to get them when he was on the farm—how long ago was that?—it was a banner day now because clean socks meant less of a chance for foot rot. He had seen countless soldiers have to have one or both feet cut off to keep from dying because of foot rot. Just a few days ago, he had detected the unmistakable stench of it from one of his Squaddies and told him to wash his feet. As far as he could tell, the boy had barely avoided catching it.

Boy? Merrick snorted again. He was the same age as Merrick but had just come off the farm a few weeks ago; but seemed so much younger than Merrick felt. Because of this, Merrick did his best to keep the boy alive, feeling a sort of protective urge. He also didn't give the kid a hard time when Merrick had repeatedly found him weeping when on guard duty.

"PLOW SQUAD! Rally!" The Squire's voice was high in pitch but cut through the general noise of the camp like a hot knife through butter.

Moving quickly, Merrick slipped his boots back on, grabbed his pike and bag from the ground next to him, and approached. Noticing the boy approaching with hands-free, Merrick shook his own pike and looked back to where the kid had been sitting, reminding him to keep his pike with him. Embarrassed and mouthing a silent "Thanks," the kid quickly grabbed his weapon and joined Merrick as they assembled before the Squire. A figure in shiny, new leather stood next to the Squire, and Merrick's heart slowly dropped.

"Plow Squad, this is Ametta, the new Bull for your Squad. Treat her as you would, Sir Ligon." The Bull began to speak, but Merrick's attention was on her armor. Her new, unused armor.

Without realizing it, his eyes went to her hands—no callouses from using her pike, which he noted was also new and unused. His head dropped as he slowly shook it in disappointment.

Untested and unblooded. We got a Bull that has never seen a battle. He silently clenched his eyes tightly closed and tried to find a shred of hope in the situation. *Well, maybe she won't get any of us killed before she gets gutted.*

The kid's elbow startled him from his sad revelry. Everybody's eyes were on him.

"The Squad has relayed that you are the veteran amongst them. Is this factual?" Bull Ametta's eyes were piercing, but Merrick was confused by her words. *Oh, GODS! She's an aristocrat!* The realization suddenly made total sense—her perfect hair, clean hands that had never seen hard work, her expensive, new armor. His heart exploded in shards of disappointment. "HEY!" Her voice made his head snap up again. "You're the old man here, right? You've been here the longest?"

Merrick looked around the Squad and realized that he could remember when each of them had arrived. Quickly looking past them, his eyes scanned the Fork Squad that made up the other half of their Line. Then his eyes raced across the faces of his Platoon, the entire Wheat Platoon, and then on to the entire Company. With shock, he realized that he had seen the vast majority of the members of Ligon's Company arrive as replacements filled the holes in the ranks left by those who had fallen to the orcs.

"Uh, yeah," he mumbled. "Er, YES, BULL," he quickly corrected, giving her the respect due to her title. He distantly noted that he sounded tired.

"Thank you. Merrick, is it?"

He nodded. "Yes, Bull."

"Good. We have completed our introductory meeting. I want you to remain so that we might discuss leadership issues." Her speech was so flowery that it took a moment for Merrick to untangle them.

"Yes, Bull."

The Squad dispersed. Merrick noted that the Kid gave him a sad look as he went back to where he had been sitting.

"Merrick," Bull Ametta's voice was pleasant enough, and it didn't sound like she was angry, so he decided to withhold any further judgment. "Merrick, I must admit that I have a confession to make."

By the gods, her language was going to drive him to distraction. He concentrated on her face to make deciphering her speech easier.

"I am unused to conditions such as these, and I am out of my element," Merrick noted; a slight flush appeared on her cheeks as she confessed. "My family is relatively well-to-do, and while I have studied the matters of warfare and leadership thoroughly extensively—though father had strictly forbidden such dalliances—actual practical application has been non-existent. I possess the theoretical understanding of the matters of which I am expected to deal, but..." her voice trailed off. "Why are you staring at me?" When no answer was forthcoming, she grew impatient. "MERRICK!"

Shaking himself out of his reverie, Merrick responded with a reflexive, "Yes, Bull." He blinked vacantly at Bull Ametta a few times before he had finally worked out her flowery comments. "Sorry, Bull. I wasn't staring. I mean, I was, but..." He could feel the flush of embarrassment rising to his cheeks. "Your words are too rich and mighty for low folk like farmers, and it takes a bit to figure out what you mean. I was just concentrating."

A bit taken aback by his honesty, Ametta's voice grew soft. "Thank you for that, Merrick. What I am attempting to convey... what I'm trying to say is that I have..." she paused, searching for the proper words. "I have the book-learning to be a Bull, but I've never done it. I realize the continued survival and success of the company—I know that lives are on the line, and I don't want to die or get any of you killed—depends on me. I'd like to ask you to help me prevent any of these possibilities... please help me from getting anyone killed. Please?"

He stood slack-jawed, her candor giving him pause, before squawking out, "Yeah, sure... I mean, yes, Bull."

Like usual, the new Bull put the Squad through their paces for the rest of the day. It felt good to do weapon drills at low speed without having to worry about an orc avoiding your blow and gutting you, and the knots in his muscles slowly faded out. Her orders were crisp and clean, and she knew all the standard drills and even taught the Squad two new maneuvers. When she tried to explain their origin from some long-dead nation of warriors, Bull Ametta looked at Merrick, blushed, and quickly concluded with, "Great soldiers used this a long time ago, and it was very effective." The comment was accepted at face value by his Squaddies, and Merrick felt a spark of hope in her leadership.

A quick skirmish the following day led to a running battle that lasted through the night. With a preparatory warning, Bull Ametta ordered the Squad to use one of those new maneuvers, and they took out two hands of orcs in quick succession. Lord Ligon came riding up as the last orc fell, a Full Line of troops running after him, and pulled up short, pulling his helm off in obvious surprise.

As the Line came to a stop in confusion, as there were no orcs left standing, Lord Ligon loudly announced, "Fine work, Bull Ametta." He slapped a hand on the Kid's shoulder as she surveyed farther afield.

She responded with, "It was the Plow Squad that did it, m'Lord. All I do is yell at them." Merrick thought that her voice was a bit too loud when it dawned on him that Lord Ligon had likewise been louder than the situation warranted. A knowing smile spread across Merrick's face as he realized that his leaders' words weren't meant for each other; they were meant for the soldiers that surrounded them.

Quickly scanning the Line, he saw nods of respect in the direction of his new Bull, and when he looked at his Squaddies, he saw big smiles that reflected his own. His appreciation for her grasp of leadership fanned his small spark of hope into a small flame.

Marches, battles, more marches, ambushes, more marches, charges, pitched battles, and more marches highlighted the next few weeks. Since his realization that he was one of the more experienced troops in Ligon's Company, he noted that several of the soldiers that were more senior to him had fallen and had been replaced with fresh recruits. Everyone that arrived to back-fill the ranks looked younger than the last.

It was with a jolt that he realized that three in ten of the troops in the Company had fallen, but none in the Plow Squad had died or been seriously wounded. Merrick began to wonder how much longer this war was going to last.

Though he would have never admitted it at the time, life had been easy on the farm. Rise early, do all the assigned chores, eat a hearty breakfast of bread and cheese, then work in the fields all day, have a full dinner, and finish the day by tending to the animals and following the sun to bed. The only variations to this were for two days each month drilling with the militia and when the changes of the seasons came.

Seasonal changes were easy and were punctuated by flurries of activity. The drills were simple and an opportunity to meet with and talk to other people in the barony. There had been stories of battles and war that were brought in by traveling merchants and minstrels, but they were merely topics of idle conversation as they were obviously so far away.

Merrick remembered how he and the boys of the village would play *Soldier* and battle imaginary foes between the haystacks and around the sheep paddocks. Those days were long gone, and he now knew that being a soldier was nothing like he had imagined it.

Bull Ametta was now Wolf Ametta, the old line leader having fallen in battle just two days prior. When a new Bull wasn't immediately named, Merrick realized that they had no new replacements. Not only that, the 175-troop Company was now down to just over 80 soldiers, and many of the junior officers were gone. They had gone from four 30-pike platoons to only three 25-pike platoons. And now Ametta was in charge of a Line. Merrick silently prayed to the gods that she wouldn't be the next casualty.

He had noted that he hadn't had to offer her much in the way of advice after she became Bull. His only real act after the first week was to comment that he had seen her packing four pairs of stockings and that she still had the same four pairs in her pack. When she raised an eyebrow in question, he explained that feet were the heart and soul of soldiers (she later explained her smile at his unintentional pun) and that foot-rot would take her out of battle or kill her just as sure as an orc spear. She immediately changed her socks and made it a personal mission to check the Squad's feet daily.

Her leadership had been inspirational in the days—no, it had actually been several WEEKS since she had become Bull of the Plow Squad. Weeks, and not one of the Plow Squaddies had fallen. Actually, they had done remarkably well, with Bull Ametta's new tactics proving viciously effective against the never-ending waves of orcs.

Now, as Wolf, her new line of ten pikes, was learning more advanced drills. Merrick found himself quietly offering words of support for Ametta's efforts when the Linesmen inevitably complained about the changes in their long-memorized and familiar tactics. Somehow, the Linesmen actually listened to his comments, and the complaints subsided.

Lord Ligon assembled the Company late in the day and announced that a new offensive was underway. They had to force-march for two full days before they got to the planned attack location, but Lord Ligon assured them that they had the strength to get there and that they would help carry the day once on scene. When one of the newer replacements asked—out of turn—about the dwindling numbers of the Company, the Lord hung his head for a moment. When he lifted it again to address the man directly, Merrick was stirred by the speech. Thinking about it now just made him stand up taller as he marched along. The cheers from the Company still rang in Merrick's ears. He realized that he was actually looking *forward* to this battle!

Mile after mile disappeared behind them. Merrick noted that only a few of the newest replacements fell out and were left behind. Of course, their pikes, boots, socks, and other gear were collected, leaving the stragglers with assurances that the Company would return to collect them as soon as the battle was won. Merrick noted that none of them seemed to believe those promises.

For his part, Merrick made the rounds of Wolf Ametta's Line, asking about the condition of the Linesmen's' feet when they had last had water and how they were feeling. He earned several approving smiles from the Wolf as the hours dragged on. After realizing that the Wolf of the other Line that made up the shrunken Wheat Platoon wasn't making similar rounds, he took a little extra effort, and he began to ask about the status of all the members of the Platoon. He noted that the pikemen seemed to walk a little lighter after his short visits. Once, he thought he even saw Lord Ligon watching him make his rounds.

The ambush was textbook and devastating. Evidently, the orcs had been expecting their arrival and had set up a surprise introduction to the main lines. Rye Platoon was in the lead and was cut down almost to a man in the first seconds, with spears and arrows appearing like so many porcupine needles in their bodies and the steady tattoo of sling stones thudding wetly into bodies and ground throughout the formation.

Knowing their deaths were assured if they remained in the small meadow, Merrick began to scream for the members of his line to follow him to the woodline. Running and dodging incoming missiles, Merrick spun around as he got to the first trees. He took a knee and realized that he was with the Rye Platoon at the time of the ambush.

On the far side of the meadow, he saw Wolf Ametta leading his linesmen into the opposite woodline. Unable to rejoin, he looked about for the Rye Wolf. As the Rye Platoon joined him, one blurted out that both their Platoon Lion and line Wolves had fallen in the ambush. Aware that he wanted to live through this day, Merrick quickly looked about to take stock of the situation.

The closest orcs were dug in, hiding in shallow trenches dug into the gentle slope of the hill. Merrick saw lines of arrows stuck into the mounded dirt that gave them cover from any incoming missiles, arrows arranged to provide easy access for rapid-fire of their deadly bows. Behind the trenches were lines of spears for similar access for the orcs to throw as quickly as needed. In the chaos of the ambush, the orcs hadn't seen their rapid exit from the killing fields.

A quick look at the center of the meadow revealed that the Rye Platoon was gone, the Barley Platoon was trying to find shelter, and pikes were falling by the second in a hail of arrows, spears, and stones.

Knowing that he had no other choice, Merrick ordered the Scythe Line to run five paces up the hill, then take a hard left and charge the line of orc spearmen.

Looking at the Hoe line, Merrick said, "We're going to charge in and hack up the trench with the archers. This should get the attention of the spearmen," he said, adding a wry smile at the Scythe Linesmen, "which will let you cut them down like sheaves of barley." The terrified faces facing him looked shocked for a moment, then broke into wide smiles at his use of their Lines' namesakes. "Ligon's Company needs us to take them out. Ready?"

A score of heads nodded in eager approval as the Lines arranged themselves. With a loud whisper of "Charge," the Scythes raced low up the hill. The Hoe Linesmen followed Merrick as he ran hunched over, building speed as he approached the preoccupied archers.

With a mighty war cry, Merrick leaped high in the air, bringing his pike down on the unprotected head of the fourth orc in the trench, then shifted his grip as he raced past the first three orcs. Surprised grunts erupted as he heard familiar cries behind him as the Hoe Line engaged the first three orcs.

Holding his pike crossways at chest level, Merrick barreled forward, knocking down each archer in turn. He only prayed that the Hoe Line would dispatch them before they regained their feet.

Reaching the end of the trench, Merrick turned up the hill to see the entire line of orc spearmen staring at him, the looks of amazement quickly forming into a rage as they realized what had happened. As one, they all turned toward him as he began to charge up the few paces up the hill to their shallow trench, the nearest orcs holding their spears to impale him while those farther back drew back to throw their spears and end his charge.

It was at that moment that the Scythe Line crashed into their flank.

The Scythes plowed into the line of orcs, with the pikes of the first two crashing down onto the heads of the third and fourth orcs in line. Merrick smiled as he realized that they had emulated his own maneuver. The attention of the entire line of spearmen was drawn to the Scythes, which allowed Merrick to skewer the nearest orc in the chest.

With a cry of, "Take the hill," Merrick yanked his pike out of the orcs as he passed. Directly before him was a line of over a dozen orc slingers, their jaws agape.

As he crested the berm before their trench and swung his pike in a wide arc, the entire line of orcs erupted in chaos as the slingers began ducking and scrambling for melee weapons. With his pike spinning like a mad top, Merrick raced back and forth across the berm, blood spraying and orcs falling in every direction.

Looking about for a target, Merrick saw an orc racing up the hill to escape his deadly maelstrom. A spear whizzed past Merrick's ear to impale the orc. He turned as the orc fell and saw one of the Scythe Linesmen recovering from the throw, sheepishly explaining, "I learned how to throw 'em working the herd. Had to keep the coyotes away."

Merrick turned to continue in the original direction the Company was headed and quietly said, "We need to keep going to reach the other Platoon or link up with Lord Ligon."

When a response was not forthcoming, he shot a glance in the Platoon's direction and saw looks of admiration and awe. Quickly looking behind him for Lord Ligon or some other hero, the realization hit him so hard that they were looking at *him* that his foot caught an exposed root, and he fell full on his face on the berm.

The orc roars erupted as he looked up, and Merrick saw a large party of orcs charging in. Absently, he noted that one looked like he was recovering from throwing a spear. He quickly leaped to his feet and commanded, "Hoe Line, arc left, Scythe Line, arc right!" and assumed a fighting stance. The orcs threw any pretense of caution to the wind and blindly charged.

Seeing the incoming charge and wanting to stop the charge as quickly as possible, Merrick shouted, "Three closest to me, prep to brace for the charge. Outliers fold in as they hit. Wait for it..."

As the orcs got within just a few paces, Merrick roared, "NOW!" He saw several of the pikemen on each side of his drop, planting their pikes in the ground, bracing it with a knee. The orcs slammed into the pikes without knowing what hit them.

Trying to wrench his pike from the orc's stomach, Merrick realized that it was hopelessly caught up in the corpse. Releasing the pike, Merrick saw an orc had slipped past his improvised pike-wall. As those around him struggled to free their pikes, he took a step and launched himself at the green-skinned beast.

He was hopelessly outmatched. The orc was easily a foot taller than Merrick and outweighed him by almost half his own weight. As he desperately clung to the monster's shoulder, Merrick saw the wide-eyed face of the pikeman the orc had intended to kill. Merrick redoubled his efforts to hang on, knowing that he couldn't stop the attack, but perhaps he could deflect it a bit or distract the orc.

The next few seconds reminded Merrick of the time he had tried to ride one of Farmer Alow's boars. He dimly noted that at least the orc was wearing armor and clothing to which Merrick could cling. All of his efforts went into keeping his grip and buying a second or two for the boy as the orc spun around and around.

A heavy blow on Merrick's back drove the breath from his lungs, and, seeing stars, his grip failed. Landing hard on his back, Merrick looked up to see the orc supported by many horizontal bars like the spokes of a wheel. As they were cruelly yanked out, he realized that they weren't bars but many pikes.

Merrick was able to draw his first ragged breath as the orc fell. Trying to scramble to his feet, several pairs of hands offered assistance. Standing, he spun around to see how many of the orcs were still standing. His head grew light as he realized there were none, and he fell back to his knees as he continued to fight for breath.

By the time Merrick had collected his wits, he noted that the Barley Platoon had formed a perimeter around him, pikes in near-perfect formation, ready for attack from any direction. The boy that had thrown the spear a few moments earlier hovered over him like his mother when he was ill as a child.

Pushing him away, Merrick's first thought was of the boy the orc was looking to cut down, and he was relieved to see the boy's smiling face in the perimeter line. Asking if they had taken any casualties, the spear thrower informed Merrick that one of the Hoe Linesmen had received a cut, but it wasn't enough to put him down.

On the perimeter, Merrick saw the kid, his arm covered in blood-soaked bandages. Going off what he had seen from past injuries, the wound would be painful and would leave a nasty scar, but so long as it didn't get rotten, the kid would survive.

"We need to move out." Though few looked back at him, every head Merrick saw nodded in agreement. "I can't control all of you myself," he added, looking at the spear thrower. Calmly, Merrick asked him, "You're in the Scythe Line, right? What's your name?"

"Megar..." Merrick noted that he seemed to want to say something else.

"Something you need to say, Megar?"

"Yes, sir," he cut off the honorific. "Sorry about hitting you like that, but you wouldn't let go, and we knew we could take that orc out."

"Well, Megar, until we can get a Lion and some Wolves to take command, I'll need you to take charge of the Scythes. Got it?" Megar nodded, a look of panic on his face. Louder, Merrick announced, "Megar is in charge of the Scythe Line until we get some leaders. Scythes, follow what he says." Taking a cue from Lord Ligon and then Bull Ametta and lowering his voice just a bit—but ensuring that it would carry to the entire Platoon—Merrick told Megar, "I need you because you thought quickly and didn't hesitate to take action when that orc was running away. You also didn't hesitate to knock the goose-crap out of me so you could get the job done." Merrick's smile elicited an embarrassed smile. "So long as I can keep you from getting foot-rot, you may well make it out of this war alive." Merrick's wry smile was infectious, and Megar reflected it back to him. "Now it's up to me AND you to make sure that all of Barley Platoon makes it out alive as well. Don't let them down." Megar's smile faded as the weight of his new responsibilities rested on his shoulders. "Let's move out!"

Sounds of battle could be heard across the meadow as they steered their way forward stealthily. The entire Barley Platoon now had orc shortswords belted to their hips, planning for the eventuality of more orcs breaking through their defenses. The blades were dirty but well made, and Merrick knew that their uneven edges would leave deep gashes on any soft tissue they hit. None of the pikemen knew how to properly use them, but they all felt a bit better at having them available.

Two of the Hoe Linesmen had collected orc bows and quivers full of arrows, and Megar also carried three orc spears. Merrick nodded approvingly at each of them, giving tacit approval of their new acquisitions.

Nearing a small clearing that the original formation would have crossed had they not been ambushed, noises ahead alerted Merrick to pending danger. Leaving the platoon undercover, he sneaked forward to scout, his silent prayers his only real protection because he left his pike behind. Slipping from tree to tree and staying as low as he could, Merrick finally reached a vantage point that offered a clear view.

In the small clearing was a group of orcs with a huge ogre looming over them all. Flags in each hand helped identify two signalmen, allowing messages to be passed across long distances. One of the larger orcs barked something, and one of the signalmen began waving his flags. Merrick smiled. That meant that the orc that spoke was the Battle Master. The thing that bothered him was the ogre. *Why would a Battle Master have an ogre with them?* He had no answers for now.

The attention of the group was on the far side of the glen, and Merrick thought he saw flags moving in the trees on the far side. The only one paying attention to anything else was the second signalman, and it seemed to be searching for something in the trees on this side. Merrick crouched even lower and sneaked back to the Barley Platoon.

"Did any of the orcs that attacked us have any flags on them?" Merrick asked the group.

Megar answered, "Yeah, one had two flag things in his belt. We used them for bandages."

That answered Merrick described what he had seen. At the mention of the ogre, faces fell, and many of the soldiers began shaking their heads.

Merrick began to lay out his plan. "This will be kind of a repeat of the last battle." Pointing at the two carrying the bows, he continued, "As long as the two of you can use those, I want you two to take out the signalman on this side of the field." They nodded as he continued. "Then, it's a simple matter. We charge in a long rank, Hoe Line to my left, Scythes to my right. Start yelling as soon as we start running. When the first of them attacks, we'll wait until the last second and plant our pikes while the wings will fold in and surround them. Hopefully, it will be the ogre..." Startled faces snapped to look at Merrick. But he finished his plan. "And we can take it out first. Once it's dropped, it should be an easy task to clear the rest of them." The shocked faces began to nod as the pikemen looked at each other. "Are we ready?"

It took longer than Merrick had anticipated for everyone to get into position, but at long last, everything was set. Positioned between the two archers, Merrick had them nock their arrows together so they could fire at the same time.

Merrick gave them the order in a quiet whisper. "Get in position. Five. Four, Draw. Three. Two. Aim. One. Loose."

Though there were two distinct *twangs*, Merrick was happy—until he watched the arrows arc toward the target. One arrow caught the signalman in the shoulder and spun him around like a top. The other arrow was wide, right, and very high, thudding into the grass near the Battle Master.

As he heard the responsible archer whisper a quiet "Bloody damnation," Merrick roared out the command to charge.

The Barley Platoon rose as one and screamed as they began their charge. Merrick suddenly grew concerned as a commotion broke through the tree line on the far side of the glen. Lord Ligon was alive! His horse was bloody, as was the

Lord's armor and sword, and Merrick noted that the Lord's helm was nowhere to be seen.

The horse reared as spurs dug into her flanks, and the knight charged toward the assembled orcs. Merrick witnessed the true chaos of the battlefield as the Platoon raced in to meet with their commander in battle against the Battle Master.

The huge orc began snapping orders, and the ogre lumbered in the direction of Lord Ligon. Merrick's blood ran cold as he saw two of the smaller orcs step toward the charging Platoon. One waved its arms before it and spoke, and suddenly, the entire Scythe Line was caught up in great vines and grasses that grew from the ground and ensnared them.

Their cries broke Merrick's heart as he shouted, "They have a shaman! Continue the charge!"

Over the sound of the battle cries, the screams for help from the entangled pikemen, and his own heavy breathing, Merrick thought he heard the sound of a bowstring. A single arrow arced overhead from behind him and stuck into the dirt near the shaman. A glance at the Hoe Line revealed that one of the bowmen hadn't charged with the line, and with a sinking feeling, Merrick realized that it was the archer who had missed so badly.

The charge continued.

The Platoon only had about 200 paces to cover, and it seemed like miles. The remaining Hoe Line and Merrick continued and saw the ogre meet Lord Ligon's charge. The point of the knight's lance broke through the ogre's chest with a shower of blood as it shattered, and the ogre's two fists slammed down onto the man. The resulting cacophony was distracting, but Merrick saw the horse go down and screaming as it writhed in pain, rear legs limp and unusable. Lord Ligon flew from the saddle like a sheaf of hay tossed by a strong farmer's fork. Merrick couldn't see how hard he landed but mentally offered prayer to any god, listening that he would rise again.

The majority of attention was drawn to the shaman—the dancing shaman. Arrows rained down from above, never hitting the orc spellcaster as he deftly dodged them, but always close. Avoiding the arrows took so much effort that it was unable to cast any more spells. Merrick decided that the shaman was the greatest danger, so he headed in that direction.

The arrows stopped falling as he grew close, and with a start, he realized that he hadn't considered being slain by an allied archer. Unfortunately, this allowed the shaman to collect its wits, and as Merrick got close, it—no, *she*—held her hands before her in a wide arc and made sounds that sounded like gibberish to Merrick. It was then that the gods had their way with him.

Merrick kicked one of the arrows the shaman had avoided, breaking it off. The embedded shaft caught his foot as he swung his pike before him to impale the shaman. Ripping through the soft leather uppers of his boot, his foot remained in place as the rest of him continued his charge.

As a sheet of flames erupted from the shaman's fingertips, he fell face-first onto the ground, losing his grip on his pike. His momentum broke what remained of the arrow shaft, and he put a shoulder down to try to reduce the pain of slamming into the ground. Even years later, he couldn't tell you how it happened, but his shoulder hit the ground, and he rolled, head just inches below the magical flames conjured by the shaman.

As he struggled to draw his new shortsword, the flames suddenly stopped, and Merrick looked up to see the surprised face of the orc shaman looking down at Merrick's pike embedded in her belly.

Standing, he yanked his pike free of her falling body and realized that he was alone among the orcs. A quick glance back showed the entire Hoe Line some twenty paces behind him, tangled up by magical vines and such.

Looking forward, Merrick saw another shaman conjure up several bolts of magical force that slammed into Lord Ligon—HE LIVED! An arrow dropped from the heavens and spitted the second shaman like a pig, and she dropped immediately. His archer had finally hit a target!

Unfortunately, he was underwhelmed. Several orcs raced with drawn swords, charging the wobbling figure of Lord Ligon. Only one remained, and Merrick froze. Before him was the orc Battle Master. Grasping his great wavy-bladed sword with both hands, he stepped toward Merrick.

Dimly, Merrick saw activity in the far woodline and something going on off in the Company's original direction of travel, but his full attention was on the Battle Master. Holding his pike before him, he did his best not to look too terrified, but inside, all he wanted to do was run.

The great orc swung his sword in a lazy arc, and Merrick just moved his pike out of the way to let the blade continue on its deadly path. Again and again, the orc swung, and Merrick just moved barely out of the path of the huge sword. A passing thought of Ametta saying that the wavy swords were called ambergeez or flamerjee or something, and a pang of sadness went through him as he realized that she was probably dead and that he would probably be joining her within moments.

Again, the sword came whizzing toward him, and Merrick deftly moved out of the way. It almost seemed like this was actually *easy*. With no warning, the orc's sword reversed its course and came back to hit the haft of Merrick's pike, snapping it like a tiny twig. As the orc smiled, Merrick realized that the orc had just been sizing him up and seeing if there was a pattern in how he moved the pike. His repetitive actions had given the orc an easy means to disarm him. The orc stepped in and swung again.

A deadly dance ensued. The Battle Master would swing his sword or jab, and Merrick would use any trick he could think of to avoid being killed. He dodged left and right and then left, then down, doing his best not to die and not be predictable... again. The blade came at him from his left at chest level, and Merrick feinted to the right and went low to the left to avoid the blow, and as the sword made its way past him, it suddenly changed course. With apparently no effort, the great orc reversed the course of the blade, and it came at Merrick from the right and at a downward angle.

Seeing it coming in at an impossible speed, Merrick kicked up with his feet while trying to pull his head and chest downward to avoid the blade. The huge sword caught his leather armor at mid-chest, and the force drove the breath from Merrick for the second time today. Fortunately, because of his momentum and the steep angle, the blade merely sliced deeply into his armor without cutting him in half, though he felt the burn of the steel as it cut his chest.

With the impact and his feet rising upward, Merrick's body flipped completely over, and he ended up flat on his back. The blade swooshed in at where he should have fallen, missing him by inches, and the orc pulled back for a great overhand strike. With eyes wide in terror, Merrick went right—no, he went right last time—and rolled hard to his left. The blade slammed into the ground where his right-hand roll would have taken him. As his roll stopped, Merrick was looking at the head of his pike, still attached to that sad foot-long remnant of the haft.

Still, on his knees, Merrick looked at the Battle Master and just waited for his pending death. Knowing Merrick was finished, the orc smiled as he stepped in to deliver the blow. It aimed the blow at Merrick's neck but fully expected the youth to try to duck under it, so the orc purposely swung low.

At the last second, the puny human did as expected and ducked so the arc angled down a bit more.

Merrick didn't consciously try to dodge the orc's blade; he just fell forward. Forward. Onto the head of his pike that was just lying in the grass before him. Grasping the cut-off haft in both hands, he quickly rolled and managed to deflect the sword upward. The glancing blow knocked the pike-head downward, and it solidly hit Merrick's jaw.

Expecting the huge sword's trajectory to be stopped by impact with the human's neck or at least the skull, the orc was unprepared to counter the continued follow-through of the blade. As the orc spun around, it prepared to bring the blade down on the human with full force. With this much effort, it would easily sever the damned human's body in half.

Merrick continued his roll and, after a full revolution, bumped against the orc's huge, spiked boot. Pulling back with both hands, Merrick struck, aiming a slicing blow to the back of the orc's knee. At normal pike stand-off range, Merrick would have never seen the small area between layers of the Battle Master's armor, but he wasn't at that distance. The blade of his pike sliced through the thin fabric of the trousers the orc wore beneath its armor.

The orc's roar was epic and deafened Merrick. Tendons severed, and the orc crashed to the ground directly atop Merrick. As it writhed and screamed, Merrick struggled to get away from the enraged creature, finally rolling away. The beast was screaming something at Merrick and futilely swinging its sword at him. Merrick concluded that the words must be horrible curses and descriptions of what the Battle Master would do if and when the pikeman got within reach.

Merrick struggled to his feet and, as he gasped for breath, stumbled back several steps.

As his air-starved lungs slowly reinflated, Merrick's attention was drawn to the left, and he saw the entire Barley Platoon slowly approaching, with universal looks of awe painted across their faces.

Movement to his right made Merrick turn. Lord Ligon was staggering up to him, and behind him, he could see remnants of the Wheat Platoon. Wolf Ametta was nowhere to be seen, and his heart sank again with the knowledge that she was dead.

Merrick grew confused when Lord Ligon took a knee and bowed. Behind him, the Wheat Platoon did the same. Looking left, the Barley Platoon was taking knees, and it dawned on him that they were bowing in the direction of something behind him.

On wobbly knees, Merrick turned, swaying gently as the sight before him slowly registered. A large contingent of soldiers was arranged before him, and Merrick noted that the horses were breathing hard, and their flanks were flecked with foam, obviously having been ridden long and hard.

One man was closer than the rest, and Merrick tried to process what he had seen. Horse. Spurs. Armor. Tabard. Full helm. Coronet atop the helm. *Oh, by the gods!* Merrick thought, *a Baron! I wonder what he is doing around here.*

A baron. Merrick's mind finally did the math, and he moved to drop to a knee in the presence of nobility. Unfortunately, when he unlocked his knee, he lost his balance and collapsed to the ground. He was dimly aware of hands touching him and voices around him. A kind voice leaned in close to his ear and said a prayer to the goddess of healing, and it felt like ice-cold water was dumped all over him.

Merrick slept.

When he awoke, he saw that he was in a roomy tent and that Lord Ligon was with him. Knowing he was badly injured, Merrick gingerly tried to sit up and was shocked to find that, while he was quite sore, he seemed unharmed. Pulling the blankets down, he looked with amazement at a wide, red scar across his chest.

Lord Ligon smiled as he handed Merrick a small mirror, "That's a nice scar you've got, but this one will be the one that gets you noticed." Turning the mirror, Merrick looked at the wide red wound that ran from his lower lip to the tip of his chin. "I don't think I'd mention that it was your own weapon that caused that one," Lord Ligon chided.

In a rush, the battle came back to him, and he was just thankful to be alive.

The tent flap pulled aside, and an older man stepped inside, his face haggard and drawn. With a start, Merrick realized that Lord Ligon looked the same way, and even his own reflection in the mirror had that same haunted look.

"I've heard that you have problems bowing before nobles, so why don't you remain in bed." The voice was friendly, and the man had a kind smile on his face.

Absently, Merrick looked at Lord Ligon and realized that he was on a knee and was bowing deeply toward the old man. Merrick's heart sank. *Oh, by the gods, another baron.* While he was happy to be alive, this was not going to be his day.

The man ordered Lord Ligon to retake a seat on the edge of the bed while a servant pulled up a short stool for him to sit on. Using direct questions, he gently probed Merrick about his background and the campaign thus far. Being tired and resigned to the fact that his day was already ruined, Merrick answered clearly and was not afraid to tell the man he did not know the answers to some of his questions. Each of these responses drew a small smile.

Finally, the man came to the events of the day. As clearly as he could, Merrick related what he had seen and done.

After what seemed like an eternity, the man sat back on his short stool. Sleep was calling strongly to Merrick, and he felt himself fading out.

"You realize that commoners are not allowed to wield or carry weapons of chivalry, right?" the man quietly stated.

Struggling against the grip of sleep, Merrick responded, "Yes, m'Lord."

"And you know the penalty of illegally bearing chivalric weapons, right?"

"Yes, m'Lord. Death. Usually by drawing and quartering."

As sleep claimed him, Merrick heard the old man say, "You caught how he described what happened, didn't you?" There was a grunt of assent. Lord Ligon? "He always said, 'we' and 'us,' and only used 'I' when it was unavoidable." Another grunt. "He also confirmed what I thought about you, Ligon." And Merrick slept.

It was so difficult to sleep! People and things kept jostling him and throwing him about—and then he was back in battle with the Battle Master, rolling from side to side and being beaten by the sword in blows that he couldn't recall from the fight. Finally, he had enough and gave up the fight to remain asleep.

Sitting up, he drew a great breath to bring down the fires of all the hells upon whoever was disturbing him and held his breath when he realized that he was in a richly appointed wagon. A covered wagon that was trundling along—a snort told him it was pulled by oxen. There were boxes and finery in the wagon bed that bore a crest which he could not identify. It didn't matter because lord and noble stuff wasn't part of his life.

Kicking off the blanket, he found himself dressed in new trousers, and he noted that he still bore the scar from the orc sword. *Flamberge*—that was it! His joyous recollection was dashed with the memory that Wolf Ametta was gone. He quietly lamented. *It's a shame she was an aristocrat. She would have been a good friend.*

Wrapping the blanket around his shoulders, he pulled the flap aside to look outside. Dust. Oh, gods, the dust! Dust and horses. And soldiers. Merrick noted that the sun was riding low and logically concluded that the group would be setting up camp soon. Sitting back in the small space he had been in, his attempts to get comfortable were interrupted by shouts announcing that camp had been reached.

"Reached?" How do you reach camp? You set UP camp, but you don't 'reach' it. Curiosity got the better of him. Donning what he could find in his kit—the only item he recognized was his old leather weapon belt. Even the fighting knife sheathed on it was new—it seemed to match his well-worn boots at the foot of his sleeping pallet. Even the socks, trousers, and tunic were new.

The only emotion he could summon up was confusion. His last memories were of his admission that he had been wearing a sword and that commoners bearing chivalric weapons were put to death... and here he was with new clothes. Well, at least he'd be pretty when Lord Ligon put him to death.

With an effort, Merrick pushed himself to his feet and pulled the heavy canvas curtains back to look outside.

The camp was huge, with hundreds of tents in perfect rows. Merrick barely suppressed a smile at the competency of the leadership that had accomplished this seemingly simple task that proved to be so difficult in practice. A makeshift paddock was set up with repurposed orc spears and rope, with several dozen horses and a small group of their obligatory squires.

With a start, Merrick realized that his wagon was in the center of the encampment—with the BIG tents. *Oh, gods,* he thought; he had never been this close to nobility, and with the number of large tents, there was at least a half-dozen of the flighty bastards. He quickly began formulating a plan and route to sneak out and get back to his line.

As he stepped over the hind gate of the wagon, he was reminded of having stepped on the arrow as a sharp pain shot through his foot as he put his weight on it on the steps that led to the ground. As he stumbled down the steps, he cursed, "Oh, by all the bloody gods!" It was then that the previously unseen guards stepped forward.

Hastily, Merrick stood up and adjusted his tunic, trying, for all the world, to look like he had intended to stumble down those steps. Knowing he was caught, he raised his hands up to head height and turned slightly so his blade was clearly visible to one, if not both guards.

"I only have this one blade on me," in an attempt to keep from being gutted at once. *Why should I delay the inevitable? I'm due to be killed for arming myself like a Lord,* Merrick thought ruefully. *Maybe I'll be hung or beheaded and die quickly instead of being drawn and quartered.*

"Understood," the guard to his right replied, making no move to disarm him. Out of an abundance of caution, Merrick kept his hands elevated. "Adair, I've got this. Go alert Lord Ligon that he is up and about. We'll remain here."

Merrick's eyebrow shot up in surprise as he realized that the guards set to keep him in custody were splitting up, but he remained quiet.

The second guard grunted her understanding and took off at a run. Merrick's second eyebrow rose as he saw the woman run off in the direction of the big tents instead of toward the rows of tents below the hilltop. *Ah,* Merrick thought, *He must be in the audience with the Lord Baron.* A shiver traveled down his spine at the thought of having to spend time with a noble.

After a few very uncomfortable minutes, the main tents fairly erupted with activity, and seconds after that, the bugles began calling the entire body to muster.

Oh, by all that is holy and unholy, Merrick thought. *They're mustering the entire camp to witness my execution.* He quickly looked around for sturdy trees as he silently prayed, *No trees! Let's hope for beheading rather than having my guts pulled out and being ripped apart by horses. Oh, why did they have to do this in front of the entirety of Ligon's Company and not just Plow Squad?* Even the thought of being executed in front of his former squaddies made him squirm uncomfortably.

The entire encampment mustered quickly, and even in his panic, Merrick took note of how fast Ligon's Company assembled. As he spotted his squaddies, it dawned on him that there were several companies in attendance. *Oh, great!* Executed not only in front of his squaddies and Lord Ligon's entire company but there would be guests in attendance! *Oh, this day was getting better and better!*

The second guard came running back, fairly gasping for breath, and Merrick's dour mood grew even deeper. *That nasty beast almost seems HAPPY to be on duty today. Imagine how low morale has to be to be HAPPY to be guarding a dead man on his way to his execution.* His head bowed slightly as he shook it in sad shame.

On the heels of the guard was a trio of Clerics, seemingly donning their vestments as they approached. When they arrived, the High Priest of Apsu, the dragon god, spoke.

"Are you injured? How do you fare?"

Merrick stuttered, "I-I am well, Prelate. Well enough for what is to come."

As the Priest shot an eye to the guards, the guard that had remained with Merrick offered, "He favors his left foot."

"You are injured?"

"Not enough to delay the festivities, Prelate." Merrick was feeling his oats.

"Damnation, child, just answer the questions." The Cleric was angry. "What god or gods do you follow, Merrick?"

The use of his name caught Merrick by surprise. "Talon, the All-Father, Prelate. How... how do you know my na—"

The Priest cut him off, "I'm asking the questions today, Merrick." Softening a bit, the Cleric continued, "You are able to raise dissent, unlike last time." Merrick saw one of the other Clerics lower her face as her cheeks flushed. *She must have been the one to heal me on the battlefield.* "Would you accept healing from a Messenger of Apsu?" The Priest seemed almost conciliatory. *Why?*

"I do my best to follow the teachings of Talon, but any god may offer healing and blessings."

The Priestess stepped forward and quickly launched into a litany extolling the virtues of the dragon god, ending in a request that he allow his humble servant to heal this 'noble man.' The choice of words made his head snap erect, but his query was cut short by the sudden, icy wave of healing magic that left Merrick both gasping for breath and flustered.

As his eyes regained their focus, he realized that the two lesser Clerics were supporting his arms and that his knees must have buckled as his body rocked from the curative spell.

He locked his knees as he gingerly put weight on his formerly injured foot and was relieved to feel no pain as he stood tall.

"I didn't fully heal you out of fear of removing all of your existing scars," the Priestess whispered. "I have heard the tale that the orcish general gave you that wound on your chin." Merrick's hand flew to his face as his fingers found the raised line and knocked a loose scab from the former wound. "It has been said that a lesser man would have lost his head from that blow," she concluded.

As he opened his mouth to ask about the oddity of this whole debacle, the High Priest cut off all conversation with, "They are ready; we must make haste."

Merrick's arms were lightly held by the two Clerics, and as he was wondering why they hadn't put him in irons, they rounded the last pavilion tent, and he saw the entire assembly before him. As his mind swirled, it was with mixed emotions that while there were a couple of trees near the assembled nobles and knights, none of them were massive enough to support a hanging rope, nor did he see any empty nooses dangling.

So... beheading it was to be, he thought ruefully. Scanning the scene, Merrick looked for the headsman, but the only people he saw at the head of the assembled were a loose formation of a half-dozen nobles, including the man who had questioned him as he lay injured, and behind them, about six times that number of knights (he thought he saw Lord Ligon there, but the Clerics were hustling him to the assembly too quickly).

With a start, Merrick saw one more person who certainly looked like he was in charge of the entire formation—a younger man in resplendent golden armor and sporting a small crown that was markedly larger than Lord Ligon's modest coronet. *OH, BY ALL THE GODS!* The embossed hammer and lion on his breastplate signified his rank and position.

Merrick struggled to determine which gods he had offended to have his execution overseen by the Crown Prince Rollins himself. He stumbled with the realization, and the hands grasping his forearms tightened to keep him upright.

"Steady yourself, Merrick. Your troops are watching."

The doomed man steeled himself, still trying to see his executioner to no avail. *Oh, gods, what if the prince wants to do the deed himself?* Merrick started to panic a little.

With no fanfare—and much faster than he expected—Merrick was escorted to a spot in front of the smart formation of troops, centered before the damnable prince, himself, who gestured off to Merrick's left. Unable to control himself, Merrick looked in that direction and nearly collapsed. Marching smartly toward him was Wolf Ametta and a half-dozen others, some he recognized and some he didn't. Two were Wolves from other companies, and all were dressed to the nines—spotless armor and new leggings and tabards—all fully armed.

By all that is holy and unholy, Merrick realized, *they are going to have Wolf Ametta do the deed!* His heart sank. His confusion grew as he realized that Wolf Ametta was smiling at him—from ear to ear. *Oh, gods, how can she be looking FORWARD to executing him?* He had thought that they had something approaching a mutual friendship, but he hung his head in shame and embarrassment as he realized that she was a good junior officer and would be following the orders of Lord Ligon or maybe even the prince. *But why would she be HAPPY about this task?*

The High Priest behind him audibly hissed, "Take a knee, Merrick. Face the Prince."

Numbly, he did as he was told, bowing his head to accept the inevitable blow. The High Priest stepped forward to stand beside the Crown Prince. In his confused state, Merrick barely registered that Wolf Ametta and the others had taken a knee beside him, and this was when the High Priest began to loudly intone a general blessing over the entire formation of troops and, more especially, the select individuals kneeling before the dignitaries.

In what seemed like seconds, the High Priest concluded the prayer and blessings, and the Crown Prince began his final speech.

"Recently, the combined forces of Lord Fox's Company, Lord Graham's Company, Lady Gregor's Company, and Lord Ligon's Company—the entirety of my personal Battalion—seized the day and won the field against superior numbers and even a collection of damnable orc sorcerers." The troop formation behind Merrick muttered in acknowledgment with a few sporadic cheers. The Prince continued. "Many lives were lost in this pitched battle. Pikemen, archers, swordsmen, and even almost half of our knights and dames were slain." The prince's voice rose. "They died—every one of them—AS HEROES!" With that, the entire formation cheered. "It pains me to lose a single life, but without their sacrifices, we would not have carried the day. Remember them. Honor them. Celebrate their lives!"

The formation erupted with cheers and carrying on; Merrick could hear the rattling armor and the weapons being beaten against shields and on the ground. He screwed his eyes shut against welling tears as he imagined hearing his own line of pikemen drawing a ragged breath.

A gentle hand on his arm made him snap his eyes open, and he saw Wolf Ametta touching his arm. With a gentle squeeze, she smiled encouragingly. *Even as my executioner, she is bidding me to be strong.*

The Prince continued, "We have witnessed some amazing deeds in the past few days, weeks, and months. Today, on this day of victory, we are gathered to honor some amazing heroes."

Merrick's head shot up. *Oh, by the gods, they're going to knight Wolf Ametta, and* THEN *she's going to behead me!* Merrick screwed his eyes shut and lowered his head again.

The Prince's voice got even louder. "First, we have a trooper who led troops when they didn't have the responsibility and when those troopers didn't have a leader. They took the initiative and, with inspired wisdom, skirted the laws of chivalry by arming their troopers with looted weapons and helped Baron Ligon carry the day."

BARON Ligon... Merrick's mind was reeling. *The poor sod was granted a title and lands!* Then, with a start, realization dawned on him, *which meant that his Company would get a new knight. I hope this one will be a veteran and not some city-bound dolt.*

"This day, by the Crown of King Ronal Rollins, and by the blessings of Talon the All-Father, and of Apsu, Maker of All..." The Prince drew his sword with a loud *schwing* sound. Merrick kept his eyes screwed shut and tried to stretch his neck out to hopefully make the death swing more likely to decapitate him on the first chop. "I, Prince Charles Rollins, hereby elevate Merrick, stand-in Wolf of what was formerly Lord Ligon's Company, to the lofty rank of Sir Knight and hereby place him in charge of what is now Lord Merrick's Company."

The Prince's sword lightly tapped his shoulder, then the other, then the top of his head. Merrick's head reeled with confusion, trying to comprehend what was going on.

"In addition, I hereby elevate Miss Ametta Badia of Medberg to the lofty rank of Lady Dame." The Prince then quickly went down the short line to tap each of the kneeling men and women on the shoulders and heads. "Now, rise, Sir Knights and Lady Dames of Sulon. Rise and greet your peers and troops."

With that, an enormous huzzah went up from the formation of troops. Merrick dimly saw Wolf Ametta stand up, and with little ceremony, she and the High Priest picked him up off his knees. The Prelate took Merrick's hand and offered words of congratulations. In total confusion, he turned to Wolf Ametta—DAME Ametta—who slapped him on the chest.

"What's wrong, LORD Merrick? You look like you expected to be executed or some such silliness!" With a laugh, she quickly hugged him and whispered into his ear, "Thank you for your counsel and support."

The rest of the day was a blur.

MERIAM AND THE SEA

eriam was truly in her element – a beautiful day at sea and nothing between her and the water but her small sailing skiff. Her hair blew wildly as the wind continued to blow strongly and fill her sail. As she steadied her rudder against her hip, her thought went to her missions for today; to catch a huge tuna... and not die.

Not dying was always on her mind, but, being young, Meriam thought she was near immortal. As a skilled mariner, she knew to respect the sea and she knew all the standard mistakes that inexperienced sailors made – with a smile she recalled that she had made most of them herself while she was learning to sail. Fortunately, her training masters were well aware of how young sailors performed, so no permanent harm had come to her. Well, except for that scar on her left hand where she had driven a sail needle through her palm while repairing a sail. She realized that day that she knew more curse words than she had thought possible. Luckily, she was just left with matching scarred circles on the front and back of her hand, so she took it as a learning moment.

Her skiff was well equipped for a long day at sea, and she hoped to get to her fishing spot and back by nightfall. The problem was that she was sailing through the Dragon's Teeth and not entirely sure of her exact destination. She ran down the cryptic description again and again in her head.

During her last few months of apprenticeship she had immersed herself in just being helpful – and ever-present – for the elder sailors and retirees. It was during these boring days that she had overheard a few of the old-folks talking about some of their exploits while at sea. One was talking about a secret fishing spot where he had caught monstrous fish, and the other acted a bit surprised, asking exacting questions about the location and route. With a shared laugh, they both realized that they had both fished the same location over the years, thinking they were the only ones using that particular spot. Meriam made mental notes of every course change and way-point they mentioned and filed them away for after she was granted her master's mark.

With a smile, she looked at the back of her left hand and the newly healed tattoo of half of a compass rose that spanned from the base of her thumb to the knuckle of her pointer finger. Her smile deepened as she looked at the arrowhead that indicated due West – it was truncated so it didn't hide her needle scar. Her sail-master had insisted on that detail to help remind her that she was fallible. If things worked in her favor, in five short years she would get the rest of the tattoo of the compass rose on the back of her right hand. All she had to to is not die!

Letting the wind fill her sail, Meriam let the morning breeze take her at full speed into the Dragon's Teeth. This treacherous area of the Silver Sea got its name from the tall basaltic pillars of stone that extended up to a hundred paces or more above the waterline. Most had tiny patches of dark sand at their base as if each were solitary hairs growing out of moles of some underwater dragon. The Teeth caused the prevailing currents to speed up and swirl about so fast that sailing through their waters was one of the most dangerous trips the mariners of Sulon could make. But the dangers meant little to Meriam because she was confident in her skills as a sailor and she was well aware of how to avoid the most dangerous of the threats she faced as she transited the Teeth.

Sailing southeast for several hours, she had time to drink one of her water-skins and chew on some bread and cheese to slake her hunger and thirst. She skirted whirlpools and unidentifiable, barely submerged creatures that left her breathless, and the whole time she kept an eye to the skies to watch for wayverns

– semi-aquatic, dragon-like creatures that made their lairs high above the water in the Teeth themselves. They were constantly on the hunt for fish and unwary fishermen, with the largest of them able to carry off a full-grown man without much effort. Those carried away were never seen again, so she kept an eye peeled for the aerial threats. Though she saw several during her travels this morning, none seemed to take an interest in her or her small skiff.

Just after the sun reached its zenith, she finally reached the large Tooth referred to by the Elders. The journey wasn't as dangerous as she had heard it was, and she began to think the Elders had talked up the threats to keep less confident fisherfolk away from their rarely-visited spot. With a deft hand, she baited a hook and let it trail behind her skiff as she furled the sail to let her boat drift with the wind. The wind had slacked as it changed direction to blow back to the northwest in the direction of her home port, so her shallow skiff wasn't affected by the current and the prevailing winds kept almost stationary in the water as her baited hook was carried as far as her line would allow it to go. As she drifted, Meriam thought she saw the glint of something reflecting from the base of the large Tooth as she passed slowly past. Straining, she was unable to make out the source of the flashes of light. It was barely a quarter of an hour later when she felt a massive tug on her fishing line, and with a practiced hand, she jerked it to set the hook and prepared for the fight.

She wasn't sure what she had hooked, but the way it dragged her small skiff across the water let her know that it was sizable. Not wanting to lose her catch – or her hook and line – she let the fish tire itself out before she even tried to gather her line and draw the fish closer to her. As she strained to keep her skiff afloat, she lost track of time. By the time she had drew the fish close to her boat to see it, she also lost track of her location in the water.

As she got the fish closer to the skiff, each time it was within a few paces it would run again, allowing her only a glimpse. It was a tuna, and a huge one at that! With a growing panic, Meriam wondered how she would get the mighty fish into her skiff without swamping it. The problem was solved with no action on her part.

The tired fish allowed itself to be pulled close again and this time instead of diving as it had dozens of times before, it breached, flying into the air, letting Meriam get a good look at the size of the gargantuan fish. It was easily as long as she was tall – and nearly half as long as her skiff. The monstrosity arced over Meriam's head and to her horror, crashed into the hull of her small skiff, creating a huge splash that spread out for many paces around her boat.

Her only thought being to keep her skiff from being swamped or tipping over completely, Meriam drew the large utility knife she wore on her hip. Not thinking of the danger, she dove atop the stunned fish and began to hack at the base of its skull to sever its spinal cord to still the flailing fish before it started to struggle in earnest. The grinding of the skiff's hull against sand forced her to stop her grisly actions and take stock of the situation.

The current and wind had driven her small skiff onto the dark sand beach surrounding the large Dragon's Tooth around which she had been drifting. A series of larger waves drove her boat high onto the beach, and Meriam realized that the tide was still going out, so her skiff was high and dry for at least a couple of hours. Leaping out, she pulled on the stern to stabilize it for the wait for the incoming tide. To her relief, the huge tuna was still – her efforts to sever its spine must have been successful.

The trip back was going to be interesting in every sense of the word. A late start back meant that the last couple of hours would be in the dark, and with the massive fish that lay in her boat, she would be drafting much lower in the water than she cared to travel. Any lapse in attention on the way back could mean swamping her boat and losing both her tale-worthy catch and probably her life. Seeing that getting back under way was out of the question for the time being, Meriam decided to take stock of what she might find on the tiny patch of beach.

Walking quickly up the few dozen paces to the base of the Tooth, Meriam decided to travel left around the massive black spire. The Tooth was easily three hundred paces around, and upwards of one hundred paces across, with about thirty paces worth of black-sand beach around the base spreading in all directions. Outside of a few pieces of driftwood and some scattered seaweed, she found nothing until she was nearly two-thirds of the way around, and it was then that she encountered the source of the reflected sparkling she had seen earlier.

In a carved niche about one pace above the base of the Tooth, Meriam found a strange, poorly crafted sculpture. Three crudely carved dolphins made of stone were supporting a small crystal ball that was about the size of her fist. There were no inscriptions or identifying markings on the statue that she could see, and as her hand reached out to touch it, she heard a soft voice in her head saying, "Eridas." As she made contact with the statue, she then heard a noise in the direction of her beached skiff. In a panic, Meriam dashed the rest of the way around the Tooth to see the most horrific sight she had ever seen.

A large wayvern was awkwardly crawling toward her small boat. With rising panic, she realized that the huge tuna was inside, and the wayvern could very easily carry the mighty fish off in its talons. Without thinking, with a warning shriek, she went to draw her utility knife and to her horror realized that she had left it embedded in the fish. Her horror multiplied when the wayvern turned to look in the direction of her angry outburst.

With a roar, the beast turned toward her and began awkwardly waddling toward her. Its movements were jerky and unpracticed on its hind legs and wing claws. At least it wasn't a dragon, with four legs and then wings on top of it. Absently, Meriam recalled a traveling Bard telling stories of land-based wayverns that he called 'wyverns,' and, unprovoked, she wondered if they waddled any better on the ground than their water-based cousins. With a shriek of terror, Meriam realized that the creature had closed most of the distance between them and was nearly upon her. Turning, she ran back around the Tooth in the direction she had come from.

Fortunately for Meriam, the wayvern was slow when aground and she quickly outpaced her. Again unbidden, looking at the brilliant coloring of the fringes around its face, she concluded that the creature was a large female. *Oh, lovely,* she thought. Females were larger and more aggressive than males – or at least that was what she had learned from the Elders. Not tht it really mattered... it was easily three times her size and looked both hungry *and* angry.

If it took to the air, she knew that it would be upon her in an instant, so as she scurried away, she purposefully didn't give the beast the idea that she could easily outrun it, always staying within sight with the hope that it would continue to crawl after her as she avoided becoming wayvern lunch. As she completed the first circuit around the Tooth, she veered out to her skiff and retrieved her previously dropped knife – not that it would provide any real protection against such a beast. As she started another circuit around the Tooth, she passed the crude sculpture again, and again she heard the voice in her head. "Eridas," it said. This time it continued.

"Long have I slumbered. What is it you seek, youngling?"

"SEEK?" Meriam fairly screamed back at the sculpture. "I seek a way off of this gods forsaken beach. I seek a way to get that wayvern to forget I exist and live another day. I seek to get back to port and enjoy the soil of my home again!"

The voice responded, not reacting to her near panic. "The tide will turn within minutes, youngling so your small boat can be refloated. I cannot affect the creature's mind, but I can provide a means for you to defeat or drive it off. Reaching your home again will depend upon your skill as a mariner. You have the heart of a sailor, but you lack self-discipline that will only come with age."

Meriam was astounded. "Who... wha... what are you?"

"Youngling, I was once a respected goddess of the sea and current, but the knowledge of my history and power has been lost over the centuries since the land was sundered." Meriam slowed. "I seek to be known again and regain some of my former glory." The voice hesitated a beat. "Will you allow me to aid you in return for telling others of my powers and interests?"

Meriam didn't hesitate. "If you aid me in my time of need, I will give you whatever help you require – just do something, NOW!" Her voice had become shrill as her panic rose and the wayvern closed on her position near the sculpture.

With no warning, the entire statue flew from its small niche and slammed into Meriam's belly. Gasping in imagined pain from the expected impact, Meriam was surprised that the expected collision of the statue into her torso was, instead, a sense of burning pain that was easily shrugged off. The voice in her head was much clearer, now.

"Get some distance, then stand your ground, young Meriam." Enthusiastically turning to run from the monstrous beast that was nearly upon her, Meriam sprinted away. Just as she was about to disappear from the wayvern's view around the base of the Tooth, she stopped and turned to face it again. Waving her knife at it in what she hoped was a threatening manner, Meriam yelled out a challenge. The creature clumsily redoubled its efforts to catch her.

"Hold out your right hand, young Meriam."

Doing as she was bid, she was shocked as a small ball of blackness appeared in her palm. Her fingers closed about it and she caught her beath as she realized that she could feel a solid ball in her hand. "Throw it at the beast." She again did as she was ordered.

Her fling was off target, but the black sand she hit scattered as if a large stone had landed on the beach beneath the creature. Not knowing what to do, she extended her hand and was pleased to witness another ball of blackness appear in her palm. Taking aim, she threw again.

This time her aim was better, and the black ball struck the draconic beast in the wing. With a screech of pain, a hole appeared to have been burnt in the leathery flap. The beast came on.

Again and again, Meriam conjured the ball of arcane energy and flung them at the approaching creature. Most of her throws were off the mark, but she eventually made more hits – hurting the wayvern with each impact. Each time the beast got too close for comfort, Meriam would again turn to put distance between them again and then continue to fling her arcane blasts at it. The monster got more and more angry with each hit. Meriam took heart in the fact that she could see that she was legitimately hurting the massive creature.

Finally deciding that the threat outweighed the potential meal, the wayvern turned and attempted to take to the air. Meriam dashed closer and as quickly as she could, conjured up her arcane bolts and threw them as accurately as she could. The wayvern's wings had multiple holes in them, and though it made several valliant attempts, was unable to take flight. Furious, the beast turned to face Meriam again.

Being that she had charged the wayvern, when the creature spun around, the pair were quite close together. Knowing that she had one last chance, Meriam conjured forth one final arcane orb. As the wayvern dove in at her with its mouth agape, she fairly shoved the blast down the beast's throat.

The wayvern almost looked like it had a confused look on its horrific face as it gulped. With no fanfare or warning, the arcane blast tore through the back of the beast's neck, carrying a large hunk of meat and a shower of scales with it. Meriam screamed with alarm as the creature crashed to the black sand at her feet.

***

When Meriam got underway again, it was with a renewed sense of purpose and confidence. While she prepped her small sailing skiff, she had taken stock of her supplies and her condition. Tentatively, as if afraid to see what might be there, she had peeled off her blouse.

On her belly, from navel to just beneath her breasts was a very crude tattoo of a pair of dolphins diving into the water, supporting an orb between their upraised tails. The skin around her new acquisition was tender as if it were a fresh tattoo, so she left her blouse open to the elements to keep from aggravating it.

Her journey home was slow and careful, as Meriam didn't have much freeboard to keep the waves at bay. She was satisfied, though, for on the floorboards of her skiff lay a huge tuna that would garner the respect of her Elders, as well as the head of a large, female wayvern, that was sure to earn her the respect of her entire village. Meriam was truly in her element.

Overlord of the Western Marches

The raven-haired giant stood atop the small rise and surveyed the battle-field and the accumulated carnage around him. Hundreds of bodies—no, thousands—surrounded him, and thankfully, most were dead. Not that the cries and moans of the wounded affected him; it was just another sound of a battlefield, much like the buzzing of the death flies that swarmed the entire venue.

He smiled grimly; another successful battle. Sure, the vast majority of his forces had been slain, but his prowess and ingenuity carried the day. The loss of so many troops' lives was inconsequential in that the battle had been won, and the peasantry would repopulate the ranks soon enough. *Hells, they bred like death flies,* he thought as he absently waved his mighty right hand before his face to shoo away the dozens of bloated, black insects for a few seconds of respite until they landed to feed again.

He stood a head and more taller than the locals, and his body was more powerfully muscled than his forces had ever seen before, looking more like a godlike giant than a man. His straight, black hair was shorn just a hand-width in length to keep it out of his eyes no matter what position he found himself. His fine silken shirt had been ripped off early in the battle to completely free up his arms, and when he had worked himself into a sweat by killing the enemy soldiers, he had torn his breeches away from his legs, leaving him dressed in little more than his smallclothes. Well, smallclothes and jewelry; matching golden bands were wrapped around his massive biceps, four large chains hung from his neck, and two matching mithril bracers were worn on his forearms. He wore no rings on his fingers because experience had shown that they tended to affect his grip on his huge sword and slide off when his hands were covered in gore and blood.

His sword was truly a masterpiece. A hand-and-a-half broadsword, nearly as long as he was tall. Presently, it was point-down in the dirt, his mighty left hand balancing on it to let anyone who might look in this direction see it in all its glory.

The blade was as wide as his mighty palm and deeply etched with magical runes along the entire length. Down the middle of the blade was a wide blood groove that was nearly as wide as his thumb. As the battle was over, blood dripped down the entire length and off of the ornate crosspiece, where bits of flesh still hung after taking so many lives.

There was little movement on the battlefield, a few healers doing what they could for the few that clung to life, and several groups of would-be robbers stripping anything valuable they could see from whatever they could reach. Neither captured his attention as their actions were beneath him and warranted no consideration. The dead no longer needed their wealth, and wounded soldiers were of no use to him.

He waved his hand before his face again. *Damnable, death flies!*

The Overlord considered his next moves. There was a town just a league or so west of here that could provide perhaps a thousand troops if the young and old alike were pressed into service. The idiot peasants in this region had little issue with gender, so if women were included, he may be able to get close to two thousand pawns to drive into the next battle. Perhaps it would be enough to put a dent in the defenses of... *what was the name of that town?* His memory lapse momentarily concerned him as he absently waved away the damned death flies yet again.

Bah, it matters naught. King Alaric would pay for insulting his legacy. The way that idiot royal had laughed when the mighty Overlord had suggested that the entire region would soon be under his control! *This affront could not be ignored, even if it took the measly lives of every serf and peasant and townsfolk in the whole damned land!* If necessary, he would leave the entire region bereft of humanity as long as he tore the heart of that lowly king out of his chest!

A dull prick on his stomach brought him out of his reverie enough to register confusion. Death flies didn't bite; they swarmed and spread sickness, but they didn't bite. When they were thick enough, as they were on this glorious day, the biggest concern was accidentally inhaling one of the fat, black insects. *Perhaps a wasp or one of those yellow and black-striped bugs that made honey,* he thought. *A bee,* he concluded with a small grin at his lapse as he waved the death flies away again. His hand seemed to almost move of its own volition, and it almost seemed like the blood-stained bronze skin smeared as his hand moved.

Uncomprehending, he went to wipe whatever stinging insect from his stomach. His fingers brushed against something hard, and he instinctively grabbed at the tiny bug to inspect it. His eyes struggled for a second as he tried to focus on it, and concern remotely registered as to why.

When his vision cleared, he saw a very strangely shaped death fly. Its body was slender with a wide bottom and a long, extended stinger in front, with backswept black hairs sprouting from almost the entire length of it and its stinger poking out from the black mass like a tiny spear. His mind numbly noted that the entire thing was sticky, as if wiped with pitch or honey.

It's a tiny... he struggled to remember the word. *Dart! That's what it is: a tiny dart.* He realized that he chuckled at the recollection. *That was odd.* His mind seemed like it was swimming in molasses. *Why are words not coming? Why would I laugh at a tiny dart?* The confusion mounted.

Suddenly curious, the massive Overlord went to look down and was shocked when his head just flopped down until his chin rested on his chest as if he were a ragdoll. Before he could question his lack of control, the death flies captured his attention. *Why are there so many?* His mind reeled, the query slogging through the miasma that was his thought process. His entire right leg was covered with the bloated, black bodies, and as he absently wiped a swathe away, two things became obvious, even in his haze; his hand felt like it was asleep, almost as if he watched someone else's hand wipe the swarming insects away, and they didn't dislodge as easily as he expected, almost as if they were attached, biting at his skin.

The damned bugs don't bite or sting, why are they sticking to me? The question struggled to gain purchase in his foggy mind. With rising anger, frustration, and concern, he grabbed at one of the fat flies, pulled it out, and raised it toward his eyes. Again, it was difficult to focus on the small pest... and again, it looked like the previous one. *Another spear arrow dart thing. That's it! It was another dart!*

Looking past his fingers, which were quickly becoming numb, he saw that the dozens of death flies that rested on his right leg were all tiny darts, and his swimming vision saw they were all sticky with the sap honey goo.

As he struggled to consider the cause and implications of this, he saw another death fly mini-dart embed itself in his thigh, and as he tried to process this, he heard a forceful exhalation of air off to his right. Dumbly, his head wobbled up so he could look in that direction to see the source of the noise. Scanning near and far, he finally caught a subtle movement just a few paces away.

In a heap of bodies that had once been his flag-bearers, one of the bodies moved slightly. Struggling to focus on the movement, he distantly saw the corpse pull a death fly out of a puddle of goo near its head, place it at the end of a broken length of a standard pole, then put its mouth against that same end and blow hard. The noise was the same, a rush of air, and the raven-haired giant saw yet another dart slowly fly out of the end of the broken pole. And in what seemed like several seconds, it spanned the distance between the corpse and him, then embedded itself in his right calf next to dozens of its cousins.

The standard pennant is still attached to the pole, he numbly thought. Something was seriously wrong, but in his addled state, the thoughts would not follow the proper path for him to decide what was happening.

Angry, he decided that he was angry about what was happening. With a roar of rage, he picked up his massive sword with his left hand and took the few steps that separated him from the moving corpse. Well, at least that was the plan... The massive Overlord watched as his left hand let go of the hilt of his sword and fell numbly to his side.

As his foggy brain struggled to make sense of this lack of control, he watched as his beloved, blood-stained sword slowly and inevitably fell to the ground with a squelch sound as it hit the soft earth. It seemed to take minutes to fall—hours even. He struggled to reason out why this was happening, but even in his groggy state, he knew that it was somehow the fault of the moving corpse.

Slowly, he looked back, fighting to keep his eyes focused.

The corpse of his standard bearer deliberately pushed the bodies of two of his fellow flag-holders off of him, and the Overlord of the Western Marches saw that the guts that had been piled atop the corpse's belly had actually belonged to one of the other bodies. Sitting up and crossing his legs before him, the moving corpse used measured and sure movements to pick up another death fly mini-dart. *It's a dart,* and the massive man heard himself giggle. The corpse placed the dart at the end of the hollow guide-on pole, then placed it against his lips and blew.

It's a blow-pole-tube-gun-thing, the giant thought. As the dart embedded itself in on the side of his torso, the raven-haired Overlord smiled at his epiphany and brilliance at being able to figure out the situation.

"Altidus, Overlord of the Western Marches, today is your day of reckoning." The voice from the corpse sounded youthful, even though his standard-bearers were all old men. The back of a hand wiped away a smear of blood from his forehead and took with it gray coloring and many of the wrinkles that had just been there. "The poison I use is slow acting, but once it has taken effect, it is sure. It paralyzes both the body as well as the mind, as you can see."

"You little would-be assassin..." the giant of a man tried to say, but all he heard come from his mouth was a ghastly "Yaaaaaah" sound. He was barely conscious of spittle dribbling down his chin from his slack mouth.

"It works best in the blood," the youth went on as he pulled a flask from behind him and took a strong pull with a mighty grimace. "It also works when swallowed, but much slower, and you have to have much more in you before you are helpless... unless you drink vinegar," and he patted the flask with a rueful smile. "I should be miles away before the squirts come. Tomorrow will *not* be pleasant."

The Overlord of the Western Marches moved to strangle the youth but was confused when he fell to his knees. *There is no pain,* he thought.

"You shouldn't feel any pain; the poison has a mild numbing effect like a mosquito. And if the wound is small enough," he gestured at the small pile of tiny darts, "you don't even feel the injury."

The raven-haired giant tried again to form words and heard just the guttural groan escape from his lips.

"Lay down, now, Overlord." The boy stood up, revealing that all his horrific wounds were just illusory, smeared on to imitate real wounds.

Fake, pretendal... not realististist. The mighty man's thoughts were becoming twisted even more. As the youth helped him down to the ground, he felt a single tear escape his eye in rage and frustration over some reason he couldn't fathom.

As he lay prone, the boy tilted his head so he could see his beloved sword on the ground next to him.

The boy stood again and, struggling, picked up Man-reaver, the legendary sword of the Overlord of the Western Marches.

"You've used our people as pawns and arrow fodder for too long." The boy almost seemed sad. "Another would slit your throat and watch you bleed out." He shouldered the long blade, which was easy as long as he was tall. "I'm not like that. I'll let you watch me leave until I'm gone or until your heart finally gives out." The boy hesitated, then added, "May the gods treat you as you deserve."

The Overlord of the Western Marches watched as the youth slowly walked away, weaving his way between bodies and slaughtered horses. The raven-haired giant felt a wave of rage and frustration but couldn't figure out who he was angry with or why.

The death flies buzzed.

BIRTH OF A FORESTER

Well, the day started like any other. All the other kids were either playing their stupid games, trying to impress each other with how strong or how witty they all were, or were pretending to help their parents with whatever chores were tasked for the day, trying to spread an hour's worth of work into all-day activities.

Meanwhile, I was one of the "crazy ones" who had jumped up and did my chores for the day and was looking down my nose at the bustle of the village I had to call home before taking off into the forest to find respite. I was in such a rush that I lost track of time, or I would have looked at that big anthill by the corner of the barn to see if they had built it up higher in anticipation of rain for the day. Oh, how things would have been different.

I ran like a deer through the underbrush, leaping over fallen logs and other impediments, the stress of living in that horrid village melting from my back. The exhilaration of being out in the wilderness like this brought yips of excitement and a broad smile. I sped along faster than normal with one goal in mind: today, I was going to visit the magical pool! Okay, as far as I knew, it wasn't really magical, but it felt that way, with the small waterfall churning up the water and the flash of the trout in the pond beneath the falls.

Sitting still in that little nook behind the falling water, I had seen otters playing, several of those huge, long-legged wading birds, and even a white stag. My smile grew as I thought back to that day, and I hoped that I would see it again today. I ran on.

The first problem of the day was slipping on that slimy rock at the pool and twisting my knee as I fell. Fortunately, there wasn't much blood from the scrape, and I was able to limp the last few paces to that special spot behind the falls. Then, I waited.

The birds started first, resuming their beautiful songs as they quickly forgot about me. Before the painful wound had clotted, a pair of squirrels started squabbling in a nearby tree before being run off by a jaybird. A flash in the water caught my eye, and I realized it was some salmon. Was the summer almost gone again? Oh, that meant that harvest season would soon be here, with long hours of having to deal with inane conversations of others while gathering crops before winter set in.

The thought of those unending hours spent having other people try to engage me in conversation soured my mood, and I missed the dark clouds as they gathered.

Well, I missed them until the pond was suddenly illuminated by a flash of lightning and the immediate crash of thunder that left me dazzled. The rain started as I scrambled to get from behind the falls to start the run home. The pain in my knee made me wince; maybe a stop tomorrow at Mother Sufrit's for a healing poultice would help. I gasped as I saw how swollen my knee had become. This was *not* going to be an enjoyable trip home!

The rain came in sheets, and the wind drove them to nearly horizontal, cutting visibility down to almost nothing. I managed a grim smile because I knew the forest better than anyone, so the trip home wouldn't be all that bad. Except for that limp, my aching leg meant no running or jumping to speed the way home.

I felt the temperature drop sharply, and I recalled overlooking the visit to check that big anthill and silently cursed my haste. Just seeing the built-up hill would have let me know that bad weather was on its way.

I thought about the other things I had seen as I left town, recalling those sugar maple leaves turned up, but my haste hadn't let it sink in. Grandfather Emm would be SO disappointed in my inattention! He had taught me so much about the outdoors after Father had died and had witnessed how I had come to find joy in the woods.

Just one more winter, and I would have twelve summers, so I could then petition the Foresters for an apprenticeship. So much time was spent on my dreams of a future with the Foresters that any other fate—any other apprenticeship—drew tears of anticipated frustration and rage.

I shook my head to get the rain out of my eyes and the stray thought from my mind. Normally, I didn't let my mind wander when outdoors, but the slow pace forced my mind far afield.

Finally, I saw the gnarled stump where the black squirrels often fed and realized that I had strayed farther south than intended. With a course change, I limped along. Between nursing my leg, the driving wind and rain, and my thoughts flying more erratically than a chickadee, I didn't see the busted branches of the pit trap until it was too late. I managed a strangled cry as I tumbled in, and as I landed hard, the breath was driven from my lungs.

My first and only thought was to get my lungs working again, but it seemed impossible. Oh, I could exhale just fine, but nothing would come back in. It took what felt like forever before I could refill my lungs, but finally, I was able to resume breathing.

Automatically following advice from Grandfather Emm, I looked about to take stock of my situation. Lying in a deep puddle of water, I could see a circle of light above, and in the lightning flashes, I saw branches sticking from all sides of the opening. I cursed my bad fortune. A pit trap!

The Foresters had warned of wolves and spoke of plans for pit traps on suspected runs to protect livestock. Those pits were supposed to be well to the south of... then it hit me. I had drifted south from my usual route to where they spoke of digging them. Curse the bad fortune!

Still lying there, I kept looking about for anything that may help my situation. My knee throbbed, but the fall hadn't seemed to have further injured it. Nothing else seemed to be off except for the fact that the water level seemed to be rising.

I rolled to get up, and lightning crashed above. Then I saw it—the glowing yellow eyes of a wolf, with teeth that seemed to glow white in the light, and just feet away from me. Fighting panic, I slowly crawled away from the beast, pressing my back against the pit wall, and looked for an escape route.

The wolf was lying on a high spot in the pit, only a few paces away. There were small roots sticking out from the walls, and in the frequent flashes of light from the angry gods above, I saw fresh gouges in the walls—obviously where the wolf had tried to escape in vain. I saw a rock nearly the size of a milker's stool to my side and saw a glimmer of hope. My sigh elicited a wicked snarl from the beast—how I forgot about the wolf still mystifies me. The situation started to feel grim again.

That was when I did it. Against everything Grandfather Emm and my family and the priests and even the Foresters had ever told me about it, I did it anyway. Not caring about the wolf, I looked up to the opening, some three times the height of a man above me, and said it.

"How could this possibly get any worse?" As the whispered words left my lips, I realized what I had done. Unfortunately, at the same time, the Fates heard the challenge... and responded.

I heard a soft rumble from above and noted that even the wolf stopped snarling and looked up. The rumble grew louder, and suddenly, the heavy rain pouring in through the hole above was joined by a torrent of water. Struggling against the gush of water and mud, as well as my bum knee, I fought to keep my footing.

Knowing it was a futile effort, I clambered atop that nearby rock and hung on for dear life to those tiny bits of roots that stuck out from the pit walls. The water level rose so fast! Within what seemed like seconds, the water was at waist level, and something heavy bumped against my exposed backside. It moved suddenly, and a sharp snarl told me that the wolf was swimming, trying to stay above the floodwaters. Right then, I swore an oath to *never* tempt the Fates again!

Soon, the waters were swirling around my chin, and I floated off my perch. The frequent lightning flashes revealed more small roots above, and my cold, wet hands clung to them in desperation. It dawned on me that if the waters continued to rise, I'd be able to just float my way to freedom. The Fates must have realized the same thing because the flood quickly dwindled to a trickle with only half the pit filled with that frigid water.

The storm continued unabated, and in the flashes of lightning, I could still see the wolf swimming, snarling each time it came close.

Another flash came, and I saw a large root sticking off the side, so I grabbed it. Floating there, my feet naturally pushed against the side of the pit, making small indentations in the mud, finally exposing cut-off roots, which provided a precarious perch from which I could prolong the agony of death from exposure or being ripped apart by the near-frantic wolf.

The wolf made a few more passes around as it desperately sought a way out, each time snarling as it neared me. Finally, desperation (and the Fates) forced its hand. I heard it pass behind me again, the throaty snarls filling my ears, and I felt it turn.

Finally, I felt a paw on my shoulder, and my already cold blood froze in my veins. Another paw slapped at my head until it found purchase on my other shoulder, and then the rear paws began to rake my back.

I flattened against the wall in an attempt to escape the claws, and it was only the Fates—*were they appeased?*—that had one of the back paws find my hip, giving it something to stand on. The other paw clawed at me several more times before finding its way to my other hip; the blasted wolf was essentially riding on my back!

The snarls continued unabated.

This desperate standoff continued for what seemed like forever as I lost feeling in my feet and hands in the frigid water. The snarls quieted to low-throated growls, and Grandfather Emm's words prompted me to take stock of the situation again.

The water level was still slowly rising, but not fast enough to lift me out before I'd be totally numb and drown. There were no other large roots sticking out from the wall, and the arched wall didn't allow climbing—even if I could climb with dead hands and that aching knee.

Suddenly, my senses rushed as the wolf gave the tiniest of whimpers. I closed my eyes and felt the beast had begun to tremble, and its tail tapped out a rhythmic tattoo on my bottom. My racing mind searched if I had ever seen or heard of something like this, and I recalled Red when she had given birth to a litter of pupp— *BY THE GODS!* The wolf's body tensed, and I felt the steady pressure of its—*of HER*—tail against my back. Suddenly, I felt something warm roll up my back, between the wolf's belly and my spine.

The wolf was whimpering, but as I turned to see, she snarled and nipped at my face. Only the quickest of reactions kept me from losing my nose or eye. After a moment, a flash of lightning and I saw a tiny form bobbing, still and lifeless in the cold water. The wolf began her rhythmic tail movements again, and I knew what would soon happen again.

Not knowing what to do, I began softly humming that lullaby that Grandmother Bea used to sing when I was young and sleepy or upset. The wolf growled, but the apparent anger quickly gave way to more whimpering. It wasn't long before I felt the tensing again and another feeling of something rolling up my back. I began to cry as I realized just how vindictive the Fates could be.

In desperation, not caring what the she-wolf would do, I reached up and began to dig at the wall with my dead fingers, making a little niche. The wolf growled as I shifted my weight, but I was just too cold and frightened to care. The wolf tensed, and this time, I felt nothing. The she-wolf whimpered again, and I made the hole a little deeper. Just as I was satisfied with the progress, I felt the wolf tense again—right when the Fates played their hand.

A mighty flash of light blinded me as lightning flashed right outside the pit, and the resulting thunderclap nearly knocked me from my precarious perch.

Overwhelmed by terror, the wolf leaped away, and I threw caution to the winds. Feeling around, I frantically swept my hand back and forth, searching for a tiny bit of warmth on the water's surface. I finally found one as I heard a cracking sound. A bolt of lightning provided the illumination needed to see the remnants of a sundered tree from just outside the hole crashing to the ground above the pit. A large branch, still smoldering from the lightning strike, stabbed its way into the water behind me.

I gently placed my precious treasure in the niche I had dug in the wall when I realized that I felt no breathing. Not knowing what to do, I guessed that it must have breathed in water. So, to get rid of it, I gently squeezed the tiny form—squeeze, release, squeeze, release—over and over until the pup suddenly wiggled in my grasp. Another flash of lightning, and I saw that the entire side of its face was white.

Gently, I placed it in the niche. Turning back, I looked for the wolf and saw nothing but the silhouette of the destroyed tree and branch... but a flash of lightning, and I saw the she-wolf's face looking down from outside the hole. The wolf must have scrambled up the branch to freedom, and I turned to do the same, then stopped as I remembered, at the last instant, the tiny treasure I had rescued. Gingerly picking it up with my dead fingers, I clumsily flailed my way to the branch and safety.

It wasn't long before I realized the branch only extended about a hand's width below the water's surface. With dead fingers and my hurt knee, there is no way for me to climb out. What was my salvation now was revealed as a cruel joke. Another flash came, and I saw the wolf watching me—no, she was watching her pup in my hand.

Looking at the branch, then at the pup, then back to the wolf, over and over, I realized that only one of us would make it out of here alive. I tell you the truth, I started to cry. I pushed myself beneath the surface of the water, then pulled myself up as far as I could go. As gently as possible, considering the lack of coordination and feeling in his limbs, I slapped the pup onto the branch as far up as I could reach and fell back into the water.

With one arm over the branch to keep my head out of the water for now, I started to cry in great, wracking sobs, from both knowing that I'd never get to be a Forester and from fear of the unknown of what awaited me after death. I raised my face to the stormy skies above to vent my rage and frustration, and out of the corner of my eye, I saw the wolf with a small thing dangling from her mouth. I honestly tried to scream at the Fates, but my lungs wouldn't even let me do that.

Then darkness took me.

It was the pain that first alerted me. My knee hurt, and I could feel it being bent back and forth. Voices faded in and out, saying that it must be worked like this several times each day to speed the healing. Fighting, I struggled to open my eyes and, with a final great effort, succeeded. The familiar view of the cabin greeted me, as well as Mother Sufrit's smiling face looking down at me—with my own mother's worried face just behind.

"You're stronger than I gave you credit for, child," she said.

I tried to speak, but a spoonful of some magical-tasting blend forced me to swallow. It seemed to warm me from the inside, and I stopped struggling. Mother Sufrit's voice faded into the distance as I lost consciousness again.

"Chicken soup. It works every time."

It took a week or more to piece together the events of that day.

Sometime after the storm hit, a ravening wolf smashed through the shutters of Mistress Blom's cabin, snarled, and snatched the newborn baby right out of its cradle before it leaped out of the window. Mistress and Master Blom's screams alerted their neighbor, the Forester, Master Amon, who quickly gathered some of the other Foresters of the village, and they all gave chase.

They expressed wonder as to why the wolf didn't run straight away with its prize but seemed to hang back almost as if to make sure the Foresters were still following. Finally, it dropped the infant next to a fallen tree, growled at them, and ran off. As the Foresters picked up the baby, a flash of lightning showed my still form, barely floating in the pit below.

Even when pressed, I never told them about the she-wolf, and I let them all go on about being irresponsible by going out into the forest alone and falling into the pit trap because I didn't know what was good for me. Nevertheless, I knew the truth. At least, I hoped it wasn't all just a fever dream.

Though they tried to keep me in the village, I kept sneaking off. Due to this unwillingness and my demonstrated irresponsibility, just before the Choosing where all boys of age were selected by masters for training in their future careers, the Foresters approached me and offered an apprenticeship! Oh, TRULY a dream come true! It was everything I could have wanted! They taught me things in just a few months that Grandfather Emm never even dreamed of.

Then, one day, it happened. I was off checking a line of rabbit snares, and I felt the eyes. Continuing to move slowly as if still unaware, I scanned the underbrush. It took some time, but I finally saw it—THEM! Two wolves peering at me from a dense thicket of alder brush. One larger, one smaller, but not that much smaller.

The larger one was a standard timber wolf, a bit small in size but otherwise not noteworthy. The smaller one, though... the smaller one was familiar. Its face had a wide swath of white on its right side. The memories came flooding back. Stopping where I was, I immediately skinned the three rabbits on my brace and left their carcasses hanging from a low branch. Smiling at the two faces in the distance, I turned and walked away.

They came back many times over the course of the next couple of years, and as my training progressed, I saw them more often. Honestly, I wondered if they sought me out more often now or if I was becoming more skilled and was better at noticing them. One day, the she-wolf wasn't there, and I was saddened by this. Every time I saw the wolves—and then, wolf—I always left tribute. On the rare occasions that other Foresters passed by soon after, none seemed to have found any of the carcasses near the piles of fur or feathers I had left.

Finally, after nearly seven years of training, the Druid, Arac, came to the village for the Foresters' ceremony. After seven years of hard training and spending so much time in the wilderness, I felt much more at home there than even in my own home.

As anticipated as it was, I was disappointed at the ceremony, though Mother was in tears the entire time. All it consisted of was a simple proclamation that I was now a Forester, a Ranger in good standing of the Silver Maple Grove.

Everything was wrapping up, with many smiles and slaps to my back, when the Druid, Arac, suddenly commanded all to stop. As everyone froze, the Druid's voice seemed to take on an ominous, otherworldly tone, and he demanded to know what had happened with the wolf. Several voices told him the story as they knew it, but he continued to look directly at or *through* me.

My words came haltingly at first, but the entire story flooded out. As each part came out, the Druid seemed more and more thoughtful. I pointed out the lump on my knee that had never gone away. Then I showed the Druid, and for the first time, the entire village, the scars on my back from where the she-wolf had tried to climb. Then I told them all about the pup, how they both watched me ever since and my sadness at the loss of the she-wolf.

The entire village just stood there in stunned silence, not knowing if it was true and if the Druid would strike me down where I stood for telling lies. Arac spread his arms wide like a bird taking wing, and everyone spread out behind me as if the Druid had plowed a furrow through the field of people. He pursed his lips, and a strange whistle came from him that seemed both totally natural and alien at the same time as if it should never come from the lips of a mortal.

Within a moment or two of stunned silence, there were gasps from behind me. With no look of alarm on Arac's face, I slowly turned to see what had elicited the alarm and saw a small pack of wolves slowly trot up through the main path of the village without any concern that they may not belong there. At their head was a familiar, half-white face.

Arac stepped around me and dropped to a knee, looking for the entire world as if he were in the presence of royalty, and he spoke to the wolves. The sounds that came from his mouth were those of animals, and I saw several villagers recoil in horror. The half-white wolf looked over Arac's shoulder at me several times as if I were the topic of conversation.

Finally, apparently satisfied, Arac just rolled over from his knee onto his butt to sit down as the half-white wolf approached me. She circled several times and sat before me as if expecting something.

Not knowing what to do, I slowly dropped to one knee as Arac had done, and I heard movement behind me as the rest of the pack surrounded me. Feeling no fear, I waited. The half-white she-wolf began to gnash her teeth and growl as if she had tasted something bad, and I realized at the last second that she was working herself into... the howl broke from her throat like the lightning that split that night so long ago.

The wolves all around me became agitated, and they quickly joined in the chorus.

Oh, the feeling of joy they felt just washed over me. They had a perfect sense of community and belonging, and they knew each other's value to the pack. The emotions just swept over me, and before I knew what was going on, my tear-streaked face looked to the heavens as on that stormy night so long ago, and I howled with them. I howled my joy, and my rage, and my frustration, and my love. The chorus faded away, and I realized that I was sitting and that many tongues were expressing their allegiance and acceptance.

I opened my eyes to see Whiteface sitting before me, with her near-grown pup sitting next to her. *How did I know that?* She turned to the pup and spoke something—I knew it was a language, and at that moment, I swore that one day I would learn it! The pup looked at its mother quizzically. The words were spoken again, and the pup looked at me gingerly, stepped forward, and sat down at my feet. The wolf pack rose as one and exited the village on the same path they entered, leaving that pup in my lap.

A gentle hand on my shoulder broke my reverie, and the Druid spoke, "This is a great gift. Treat this young one as you would a brother or a child, and they will treat you the same."

"And that, my Forester brethren, is the long story of how Leaping Deer became my companion in life and in nature. Since then, her pup, Socks, and her pup, Bear-Render, have served me as well. I now walk with Bear-Render's pup, One-fang. If someone buys an ale or two, I'll tell you the story of how she lost that fang."

About the Author

Matt Thompson was born and raised in the upper Midwest of the US. He's got several college degrees that he has never used and have nothing to do with reality, and he is more than happily retired from the US military. He's a combat vet, a former preacher (fire and brimstone), and he has worked just about every job and position known to mankind.

He lives near Montgomery, Alabama with his wife and son and two doggos that do their best to run him ragged.

www.ingramcontent.com/pod-product-compliance
Lightning Source LLC
Chambersburg PA
CBHW020408110726

47899CB00006B/1904